Family Chronicle

Family Chronicle

by

Charles Reznikoff

with a new introduction by
Milton Hindus
Brandeis University

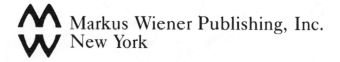 Markus Wiener Publishing, Inc.
New York

*MASTERWORKS OF MODERN JEWISH WRITING SERIES is
issued in conjunction with the Center for the Study of The American
Jewish Experience, Hebrew Union College—Jewish Institute for
Religion, Cincinnati.*

For information write to:
Markus Wiener Publishing, Inc.
2901 Broadway, New York, NY 10025

Cover design: Cheryl Mirkin

Library of Congress Cataloging-in-Publication Data
Reznikoff, Charles, 1894–1976.
    Family chronicle.

    (Masterworks of modern Jewish writing series)
    Reprint. Originally published: London : Norton
Bailey, 1969.
    I. Title. II. Series.
PS3535.E98F3 1988   813'.52   87-40102
ISBN 0-910129-74-6

Printed in the United States of America

Introduction

by Milton Hindus

Many years ago, at a public discussion in The Jewish Museum in New York between Isaac Bashevis Singer and myself on the general subject "Literature and Journalism," I noticed Charles Reznikoff in the audience and invited him to share with us, if he would, his thoughts on the difference between the two concepts, which are so often confused with each other. He suggested that the principal distinction might be said to hinge on what it was that constituted "news" in the world. There is a familiar story about the newspaper editor who tries to explain to the cub reporter what is worth reporting.

"When a dog bites a man," he tells him, "*that* is no news. But when a man bites a dog, that's news!" In other words, news to the newspaperman is whatever is out of the ordinary course of things, unusual, sensational and attention-getting. Now literature, went on Reznikoff, is another matter altogether. Precisely that which is rejected by the editor out of hand as not newsworthy, the run-of-the-mill occurrences of everyday life, challenge the true literary artist to bring out their latent interest. A walk around the park in which "nothing" happened may become the subject of his most compelling pages.

The more I reflected upon this observation, the more cogent it seemed to me and the more helpful in comprehending not only some of Reznikoff's own work but much of the movement of modern literature. It explains, doesn't it, why it was the dream of Flaubert's life to write a great book "about nothing at all." It elucidates Ezra Pound's definition of literature as "news that stays news." It tells us why James Joyce in *Ulysses* found it worthwhile to spend more than 700 pages detailing the way Leopold Bloom spent an insignificant day in June, 1904, walking around the city of Dublin in search of a humble livelihood. And it helps us to understand why there is nothing so stale as yesterday's newspaper, while the pages of Homer, as André Chénier pointed out, after thousands of years continue to be as fresh as the day they were written.

Reznikoff's observation emphasizes the fact that literature is primarily a *process*. In the words of John Dos Passos, art is an adjective, not a noun. About a literary work, the crucial question is not: "What is it about?" but "What is being done with whatever it is about?" The obvious objection may be made, of course, that some of the classics, too, are concerned with subjects as sensational as any covered in the daily newspaper. Think, for example, of *Oedipus* by Sophocles—the story of a man fated to murder his father and marry his mother! Or the plot of Hamlet. What could be more melodramatic? In *Filial Sentiments of a Par-*

ricide, Proust develops a brilliant series of parallels between a gruesome item he once came across in his daily newspaper and the plots of the greatest Greek tragedies.

This objection may be granted, but the question still remains as to why the newspaper item will be forgotten while the tragedies that resembled it will not. "Sufficient unto the day is the newspaper thereof!" observes Joyce in *Ulysses,* but literature aims to be "sufficient" for the ages. Which element in its composition is calculated to make it more than ephemeral? The most important "news" in *Ulysses* is Joyce's style, the adequacy of his expressive devices, his experimental techniques and linguistic novelties, which an unguided journalistic public would find meaningless, or at least immensely difficult, boring and repetitious. The first editor who turned down the manuscript of Proust's *Du coté de chez Swann* did so with the dry comment that though he felt that he might be condemned for insensitivity he could not for the life of him see how a writer expected to interest a reader by describing in sixty pages the way in which a gentleman turned over in bed from one side to the other.

Even a fervent admirer (as I have long been) of Charles Reznikoff's other work (notably the collection of poems for which he has used his favorite title, *By The Waters of Manhattan*) must admit that *Family Chronicle* is not easy reading. But I have now read it completely through twice (the first time, some years ago, when it was issued by the author in a limited private edition, and more recently when it has been reprinted by publishers in England and in the United States). It is hard going, I should add, not in the way that *Finnegan's Wake* is, not because it is filled with neologisms, puzzles, language games, and impenetrable complexities, but because of its seemingly absolute and artless and primitive simplicity.

Reznikoff is uncompromising in his adherence to his own ideas of what makes for literature, and there are no concessions at all to the spirit of journalism in his book. He is not anecdotal; he stubbornly tones down everything that even remotely suggests the melodramatic and the sensational. He narrates every incident in the same restrained, muffled tone, and he avoids every temptation to be *pointed* in his telling of his little tales. He studiedly and purposefully *flattens* them almost completely out.

Ironically, the most pointed anecdote in the book is to be found in Harry Golden's brief introduction to it. Nothing is calculated to create a greater impression of contrast than the one revealed here between the manner of a good and successful journalist, on the one hand, and the maker of a pure literary artifact on the other. The journalist is always aware of his audience, of the limitations upon its attention span, of the consequent necessity of being continually amusing or instructive or at least interesting. The pure literary artificer is oblivious of his reader. He is not concerned with the reader's comfort. He is too busily engaged with the problems of construction and expression which he has set for himself. That may be the real meaning behind the observation that "even Homer nods." It is, of course, not the poet who "nods" but his reader who threatens to go to sleep. Literature may be entertaining, but it is under no obligation to be so; it does not even have to be "readable" (to use a reviewer's familiar epithes of praise). I am not referring here merely to the fact that much of the greatest literature of the world is literally "unreadable" because it is written in "dead language" inaccessible, in its pure untranslated state, to all except those assiduous scholars prepared to devote years to the labor of deciphering it. Literature may be boring; it may be dull; it may be afflicted with all the faults that would be fatal to more ephemeral productions and yet survive them. What is its secret? Is it not, as Reznikoff suggested, that there is a difference between literature and journalism that is not one of *degree* but of *kind*? In *Democratic Vistas*, Whitman proposes to his readers at least one profoundly aristocratic (or, to use the current lingo, *élitist*) thought. Nations, he tells us, may possess "rivers and oceans of very readable print" and yet be deprived of a *literature*, in the proper sense of the word, completely. The corollary of this observation would appear to be that literature is not necessarily to be found in the province of "very readable print" where we had assumed that it was all along, but in a sphere entirely removed and apart from it.

Family Chronicle is primarily a narrative of immigrant Jewish life in America around the turn of the century, but, like Mary Antin's *The Promised Land*, it is almost evenly divided between descriptions of the background in "the old country" of eastern Europe and the early struggles (both economic and spiritual, but economic even more than spiritual) to take root in the United States. It consists of three equal parts: an autobiography of the mother, Sarah Reznikoff, entitled "Early History of a Seamstress," an autobiography of the father, Nathan Reznikoff, entitled "Early History of a Sewing-Machine Operator," and finally, an autobiography of the son, Charles, entitled "Needle Trade." The Epigraph to this "family chronicle" is a perfect one chosen from Ecclesiastes: "Two are better than one. . . . For if they fall, the one will lift up his fellow; but woe to him that is alone when he falleth . . . and a threefold cord is not quickly broken." Here is the reason, in few words, for the survival of the family as the basic building-block of society.

The book seems designed to be something of an archeological "dig" in which the quest is for facts about the lives of American Jewish immigrants which, in less than a century, have become nearly as elusive to their descendants as facts about prehistoric civilizations existing millennia ago. This "dig" preserves all sorts of odd and arresting items, expected and unexpected. There is the saintly grandfather, who simply could not bring himself to return evil for evil but turned his other cheek, as Christians are instructed to do yet so rarely manage to do. There is the expense of buying water from the water-carrier in the shtetl (remembered without lachrymose sentimentality and nostalgia). There is the floor of the living room in the old country made of hardened mud. There are pogroms, naturally; but in the length and breadth of all that has been written on this familiar subject, there are no pogroms more *flattened out* and understated than in the pages of Reznikoff. There are thatched roofs, peasants rolling cigarettes, political prisoners being transported to Siberia, unwilling draftees in the army of the Czar, a boy learning to fast the whole day of Yom Kippur and finding it very painful indeed. In the new world, there are endless details about petty business transactions upon which whole lives depended, encounters with radicals, the pride of a boy in "his father, the foreman of the shop." There are ghost stories in the old country, visitations from "the other world," a girl who chooses a suitor she does not really prefer, because he has a thousand rubles, and a legacy which consists of a pair of phylacteries. In America, there are the wonders of "running water," the long (fifteen hour) working days, the struggle to learn English when one is too tired to do so and tempted to lock oneself in completely to his Yiddish newspaper, the pathos of a servant girl's ambition to rise "from the drudgery of housework to the drudgery of the shop." Reznikoff lovingly preserves not only old facts but old words: the word "tuck," for example, as it was once used in the clothing industry, now described by the unabridged Webster dictionary as "rare"; the word "facer" in the sense of a blow in the face, as in boxing, hence any severe or stunning check or defeat, a word once common but now relegated by the dictionary to "colloquial" usage.

In treating these things, Reznikoff consistently subdues all the highlights in his picture and produces a monochromatic effect which demands the utmost effort and attention from the reader. It is as if he is saying, like so many other modernists, to the latter: "If you want to read me, you must do so on my terms, not yours; you must not expect me to come halfway to meet you." He does this consciously, confidently, because he is convinced of the intrinsic importance of his prosaic materials. It is as if he has taken up the challenge of a sentence of praise of the painter Corot (who was hardly known or appreciated adequately when it was written) by the poet Baudelaire: "He knows how to be a colorist within a narrow range of colors."

Nothing is harder than such a task for the writer or, one may add, for the unprepared reader. It is the sort of thing that Gertrude Stein did superbly well in her initial masterpiece, *Three Lives*—a study of three servant-girls, two German-Americans and one Black girl, Melanctha, which, according to Ralph Ellison, marked the beginning of a new epoch in the serious treatment of his race in American literature when it was published in the early years of the twentieth century. But even Gertrude Stein, gifted and great as she undoubtedly was, was tempted to strain her artistic method (of pitching her narrative on the same low level of verbalization as the ordinary life she was describing instead of striving to stimulate and heighten its interest through such artifice as the journalist is continually tempted to use) to the point of diminishing returns. For some readers, she seems to have reached this point in her next book, *The Making of Americans*, which was about the German-Jewish families of Baltimore (her family and its friends) and which Edmund Wilson described in *Axel's Castle:* "I confess that I have not read this book through, and I do not know whether it is possible to do so. *The Making of Americans* runs to almost a thousand large pages of closely-printed type."

No, literature is not always easy to take! Reznikoff has limited his own variation on the theme of "the making of Americans" (a title which Gertrude Stein may have owed to the autobiography of Jacob Riis, *The Making of an American*) to three hundred medium-sized pages of ordinary type.

Charles Reznikoff belongs to the history of modern American experimentalism in literature, as has long been recognized by men as diverse as Louis Zukofsky, Kenneth Burke, and Allen Ginsberg, and as has been more formally acknowledged by The National Institute of Arts and Letters which, in 1971 (marking the 77th year of Reznikoff's life) presented him with its Morton Dauwen Zabel award for poetry in a public ceremony. But Reznikoff's work may also be legitimately appreciated in the context of Jewish letters, particularly of narratives written in Yiddish by immigrants, only a small fraction of which has been or ever will be translated into English.

"All these old things have a moral value," as young Baudelaire wrote to his mother to explain why he wanted to buy back a picture painted by his father (who had been an amateur of rather commonplace endowments) which he had stumbled upon in the collection of an art-dealer to whom it had been sold after his father's death. In the same vein, it has recently been suggested by some critics that, whatever the limitations upon Solzhenitsyn's purely artistic talents, his works possess an undeniable dimension of moral significance. I am breaking no new ground, therefore, in suggesting that such books as *Family Chronicle*, in addition to their aesthetic merits, make an ethical claim to attention (now being honored apparently) on the part of Jewish readers whose origins are similar to Reznikoff's in both England and America.

The response to the first British edition of *Family Chronicle* could hardly have been more enthusiastic. Martin Seymour-Smith wrote in the *Oxford Mail:* "Those who enjoy Isaac Bashevis Singer (in his realist mood) and writers like him will need no recommendation from me to read this book, which is a classic telling of a noble story—one that must have been re-enacted time and time again among first-generation American Jewry in the early years of this century. It is heart-warming (in the right sense—it is never sentimental) and truly observed."

Chaim Bermant, writing in the London *Jewish Chronicle*, noted that "the Russian chapters, especially those written by Sarah, are worthy of Mendele Mocher Seforim." The *Times Literary Supplement* said: "It compresses a dense social history . . . The documentary approach of *Family Chronicle* foreshortens and condenses: in thus fictionalizing, it silently imbues its materials with a humanity, the force of which derives from its tender and eloquent compactness."

On the vexed question of the *genre* to which the book belongs (fiction or non-fiction), Kenneth Graham, in the B.B.C. *Listener,* had perhaps the most insightful things to say: "Here are three narratives, told by mother, father and son, concerning the life in Russia, and subsequently as emigrants in America, of the Reznikoff family itself, their complex Jewish duties and responsibilities and pressures, the endless necessity of adding copeck to copeck, then dollar to dollar, and the facts of being a garment worker in America before the First World War. Clearly, its merits of clearly arranged narrative, vivid scene, sympathy without strain or commentary, and remembered personalities brought lovingly close to us in their webs of relationships, aspirations and defeats, are enough to make questions of genre unimportant."

The accuracy of these critical responses may be checked by every sensitive and responsive reader of Reznikoff. *Family Chronicle* never had the heightened color of journalistic narrative, but what color it does have does not fade with time.

Milton Hindus
Brandeis University
March, 1987

AUTHOR'S NOTE

My mother's story was published as the first part of *By the Waters of Manhattan* (1930), a novel. (I had published it myself as an autobiography the year before in *By the Waters of Manhattan: An Annual.*) I published my father's story as *Early History of a Sewing-Machine Operator* in 1936. I am indebted to the editors of *Commentary* for permission to reprint in *Needle Trade* whatever was used in the November, 1951, issue as "The Beginnings of the Family Fortune" (the copyright holder is the American Jewish Committee).

C. R.

CONTENTS

*"Two are better than one . . . For
if they fall, the one will lift up his
fellow: but woe to him that is alone
when he falleth . . . and a threefold
cord is not quickly broken."*

ECCLESIASTES IV, 9-12

Early History
of a
Seamstress

by SARAH REZNIKOFF

W E LIVED IN BARON CHICHIRO-
shan's courtyard in the city of Elizavetgrad, Russia—in a
bedroom and living-room, with the kitchen in an outhouse.
Near us flowed the Ingul. We children had a large garden
to play in, and here the Baron's children, Manya and Peter,
often played with us. The Baron liked Israel, my younger
brother. He called him "The Little Rabbi" and gave him a
fur hat and some of Peter's old clothes.

That summer was a happy one for Michael—our elder
brother—Israel, and me. We spent the days looking for berries

and flowers in the garden. I made friends with Elkah and Hannah. How I wanted to go to school like my friends, books under my arm. I asked Father again and again, "When am I going to go to school?"

In winter Father took sick. The rest of us walked about on tiptoe. The house was cold and the windows covered with ice. It was a long time before Father was well. And then one evening he told Mother and Grandfather that his employer would keep him only if he worked Saturdays. (Father was a bookkeeper.) The employer's nephew had just come from Switzerland—and he was put in Father's place.

Hyam Berdichevsky came to our house at the feast of Purim, and Father listened to him with great interest. Next day Father and Mother packed up everything. Late in the afternoon two sleds came to our door. On one the furniture was put, on the other cushions and quilts for us to sit on. We left the courtyard and the garden where we had been so happy. Everybody was saying good-by. I cried, but Father smiled and told me we were going to a wonderful country.

We were going to a village called Znaminka. The horses were good and we went swiftly. It wasn't long before I was dizzy and so were Mother and the other children. Soon not a house was to be seen, only white snow and blue sky.

When I awoke I was in a large room. Mother's bed stood in a corner; on it were piled our featherbeds and pillows. Near this was our trunk. Between the two windows toward the street were our big table and our benches. On the other side of the room was the chest in which Mother kept her trousseau. Near the brick oven was the kitchen table on which Mother prepared our meals.

My head hurt. Mother tied a wet handkerchief about it and I dressed and went to a window. The houses were not close together; they were only one story high and had straw roofs. From the chimneys heavy smoke was rising. The women that passed had colored handkerchiefs about their heads. I ran to Mother and cried, "Everybody has a headache in this awful country!" Mother kissed me and explained that it was the head-dress of the women in Znaminka.

I went back to the window and watched the wide street. Many cows and horses passed and the people looked healthy and strong.

After supper Father gave us our first lesson. Israel and I took to the lessons cheerfully, but Michael was dull. In the city he had been sent to the school of a teacher who struck him on the head and made him deaf. This teacher became known as Berele "Knock-'em-down." At last he killed a boy and was sent to Siberia. Father would explain and explain the lessons to Michael, until Father would sink back in his chair and say, "It is worse than if he were killed."

One day Father came home with Hyam Berdichevsky and a young landowner. They sat up until late at night. When they were gone, Father looked sad. Long afterwards, I understood why we had moved to Znaminka and why Father was so discouraged. Seven years before, the first railway had been built through Znaminka and the contractors of supplies soon became rich. A second railway was planned, but it turned out to be just a few miles long and there was no chance for Father to make money as a contractor.

He had to make a living, somehow, and he was advised to become a glazier: many windows would be needed for the railway cars. Father had a friend in Elizavetgrad who sold glaziers' supplies, and he went there to learn the trade. We were left in Znaminka. Mother used to cheer us up by telling us stories and playing with us, but I often found her crying at her work.

One night I could not sleep and lay watching Mother. She was doing some patching by candlelight and as I saw the tears falling from her eyes, I turned to the pillow and cried, too. When I woke, it was still night. Father sat at the table with Mother. He had brought his father to Znaminka. Grandfather walked about saying his prayers. When he had finished, he asked Mother how she was. She answered that she would be well, if business were better. Grandfather looked at her sternly and said, "A good Jewess does not complain, but is thankful and satisfied no matter how business is."

"That is all very well for a man to say when his children are provided for, but what shall I do here in a wilderness with my boys and no schools? How can I be satisfied?"

"If they are to be great, they will be great even if they are brought up in a wilderness," Grandfather answered. "I have two sons. I wanted them to be rabbis and I hired the best teachers in the city for them. I also had two nephews of mine, orphans, brought up in my house. I made one of them a tailor and the other a capmaker. One of them is now rich. He has horses and carriages, and your Ezekiel hasn't a penny to his name."

Father spoke for the first time. "That is your fault."

Grandfather turned on him. "What do you mean?"

Father smiled. "Oh, you took such care of your store and house that you made me a beggar."

Grandfather answered, "God wanted it so."

"God had no more to do with it than I had. He has more to do than to watch over you and see that you don't sign a blank deed and let Mandel the Usurer take your house away."

Grandfather took a few sips of tea and said, "You always were an unbeliever."

"Unbeliever!" Father cried, "How can I believe in such things? A man takes away your property in broad daylight

10

and because he prays three times a day you don't try to get it back!"

"How can I get it back? How can I profane the name of God by bringing my claim to Gentiles? Do you think I'll send a Jew to Siberia in my old age?"

"What are you afraid of? Why isn't he afraid of Siberia?" But Mother begged Father to say no more.

In the morning our grandfather, Fivel Wolvovsky, looked carefully at my brothers and then at me. "Ai, ai, ai, what is the matter with Sarah Yetta's eyes?" he asked.

"When Ezekiel was so sick last winter," Mother said, "the children had the measles. They had it lightly. I didn't bother much with them; I had my hands full with Ezekiel. While she was sick, Sarah Yetta went off to a neighbor's house; of course, they brought her right back, but it was too late. She was almost blind for a year. She is better now."

"You'll have to see to her eyes: this is very bad for a girl."

At twelve o'clock the white cloth was taken off the table and Grandfather began to teach us. We found the beginning of the Bible very interesting. The house now became lively. Three other boys and a little girl, my age, came to be taught by Grandfather.

Father had brought from Elizavetgrad a case of glass and a glass-cutter with a diamond point. Grandfather was to teach us so that Father could give all of his time to his work. But the new cars came with windows set and glaziers were sent from Great Russia to do what work there was.

Father did a little business in the village as an agent for dealers in wheat. He also worked at winnowing. He was not paid in money, but with chickens, eggs, flour, flaxseed, and other things. The work did not please him. He saw no future for his boys in the village. He would argue with Grandfather again and again about the house and store that had been

Grandfather's, and they would both lose their tempers. Mother would say to Father, "You ought not to speak that way before the children. It cannot be helped. Why aggravate yourself and him?"

Father would answer, "I cannot keep still. He has beggared me."

Afterwards, I learned the story of Grandfather's house and store. My great-grandfather, Israel Wolvovsky, was rich. He had an inn in Zezonova and a dress-goods store in Elizavetgrad. On the boulevard in Elizavetgrad he had a double house with an iron roof. My grandfather was his only son. Grandfather prayed and studied holy books all day, and his father was happy to have so pious a son.

But when my great-grandfather died, Grandfather had to take care of the business. I do not know what became of the inn, but to run a store like Fivel Wolvovsky became a proverb in Elizavetgrad. A man would come to him and say, "I have four grown daughters and you have a store full of goods. I don't know what to do: I have no money and they have nothing to wear." Grandfather would write an order on the store that the man be given what his daughters needed. Grandmother would complain, but Grandfather Fivel would say, "I am only God's cashier. When people are going about barefoot and hungry, am I to hide His money?"

Then a fire broke out and all the stores were burned down. (In those days nobody in Elizavetgrad was insured.) The other merchants failed and did not pay their notes; Grandfather paid everybody and was left without money.

However, he still had his house. He rented half of it to Moses Mandel. Mandel's younger son was a law student. One day gypsies and peasants had a fight in the street. Mandel and his son asked Grandfather if he had seen the fight. He had. "The police are asking us for the names of those who have seen it. Will you sign this?" and they gave him a blank to sign. Grandfather did not think that Mandel who seemed so pious was a swindler.

Uncle had married into a family of another town and lived there. Father was in hiding until someone was hired to be a soldier in his place. He married then, and came to Elizavetgrad to live in the part of the house Mandel had; but Mandel told him that the house had not been Grandfather's for five years.

When Grandfather heard that Mandel would be sent to Siberia for forging the deed, he would not bring the charge against him. "I cannot send a Jew in a gaberdine to prison," he said to Father. "You can live without this house. The world is big and God is great. He will take care of you."

Father was not so easily content to be penniless. "I am not supposed to provide you with riches," Grandfather said. "I was to provide you with learning and to teach you to be upright. That I did." Mandel did not stay in the house long. He sold it to a priest and moved to another part of the town.

Father had no money to move from Znaminka. We moved to a house near the railway. The tracks were on a high embankment and whenever a train went by, we children ran to look up at it. In a hollow in front of the house was a brook and our well. We had a big yard and our door was big and heavy. To the left of the hall was a large store-room, and to the right, another large room: this had four windows, two toward the yard, two toward the street, and in this room we cooked, ate, slept, worked, and studied.

Grandfather would sit at the head of the long table, wearing a black skullcap, a black quilted jacket, black sateen knickerbockers, white woolen stockings and black slippers. At his right sat Jacob, the son of the richest Jew in our village, and

13

three other boys; on the other bench were my brothers, Michael and Israel, and the blacksmith's son.

"Israel, why aren't you studying?" Grandfather said.

"I am hungry."

"You just ate. Everyone ate when you did and no one is hungry but you."

"What did I have? Just a piece of stale rye bread."

"You ought to thank God for that," Grandfather said angrily. Then he turned to Jacob, "What did you have?"

Jacob pulled a long face and to please Grandfather answered, "Soup with just one noodle"—we children burst out laughing —"and roast goose and—."

"He stuffed himself," Grandfather said. "Today is Thursday and he doesn't know his lesson yet. Is it good to eat so much?"

Mother and I were sitting with our backs to the oven. I was making lace and had finished my sixth piece. Mother was patching underwear. "I can see right through them," she said. "There's no place for more patches; it's all holes."

Her eyes were red. "Why are you crying, Mamma?" I asked.

"I was thinking of a song about a woman who has no money to buy anything for her children and whose brothers have forgotten her."

"If parents would educate their daughters, sisters could write to their brothers. Mamma, if you wrote to your brothers, they would surely help you."

Mother looked up from her sewing and said, "My child, no one can help us but God."

"Yes," I said, "I remember that in the story of Noah's ark the bird brings an olive leaf to show that a bitter leaf from God is better than a sweet one from man."

"Man helps a great deal, but it comes to little." Then turning

14

to Grandfather, Mother said, "Did you hear what Sarah Yetta said about the dove and the bitter leaf?"

Grandfather came over to us. "She has her father's brains. But he did not want to study the Torah—only languages." Grandfather put on his coat. "It is going to be very cold."

"Why shouldn't one study languages?" I said. "King Solomon knew a great many."

Grandfather looked at me. "She compares herself to King Solomon. I wanted her father to be a rabbi, but he studied languages instead. What good did they do him?"

I had finished all the lace. "Bring it to Katrina," Mother said, "and ask her for flour and potatoes. The children didn't have enough for dinner, and there is nothing for supper." Katrina was marrying off her daughter and the lace was for the bride's towels. "Look at the frost on the window and Papa isn't home. It is so cold I don't see how he will ride through the fields."

Grandfather sent Michael to fetch water. The other children ran out gleefully to slide on the ice. Wrapped in my mother's striped shawl, I went to Katrina and came back with potatoes, flour, and a dozen eggs.

Mother looked at the potatoes. "My, my, they are as small as hazel nuts. What am I to do with them? And I cannot make noodles out of the flour: it is rye. Grandpa must have something warm and filling tonight. He is fasting today."

We peeled the potatoes to make soup. Grandfather was saying the afternoon prayers. The children ran in and shouted, "A train full of soldiers with beards went by: the people say they are taking men over thirty to the army." (The Russians were at war with the Turks.)

Grandfather said, "Keep quiet now. Go back to your

15

studies." They went to their seats and took up their pencils.

We heard Father in the yard. He and another man came in, their faces covered with snow. They carried sacks of flour and potatoes.

Mother and Father whispered together. I could see that they were worried and asked what the trouble was. Father said with a smile, "A little girl should not know everything."

Mother went to the chest and took out her silk coat. Father put it under his arm and he and the man left the house. Grandfather told Michael to put up the samovar and the others to go home. "Come a little later tomorrow," he said.

Father came back with a middle-aged woman, Dobrosh. She took off her big fur coat and the goloshes over her felt shoes. She had on a blue and red checked dress and had a red handkerchief about her ruddy, good-natured face. Dobrosh told Mother to lie down and rest and began to work about the house. Mother drew the curtains of her bed. The table was set and we had tea. Father had supper with us and then said, "All the children will have to go to bed now. We will not study tonight. Mamma does not feel well and the house must be quiet."

The others went to sleep above the oven, but my head would ache when I slept in a warm place. So I pushed the benches together and put a featherbed on them. When I woke, Father and Grandfather were saying the morning prayers. Dobrosh was kneading dough. I was wondering at a chicken—ready for the pot—on our table, and thinking of Mother's pawned coat, when I heard a strange cry. I looked about. Father and Grandfather saw me and both said, "*Mazel tov* [good luck], you have a little sister." Dobrosh went to the bed and brought out the baby on a pillow.

"Oo, what a dark little thing she is."

Grandpa smiled. "Don't worry. She'll be a better-looking girl than you."

Papa said, "Now go back to bed. It's too early for you to be up."

"But I must study my lesson," I said.

Grandfather said, "I wish the boys were as anxious to study. And she with her blind eyes needs it badly."

Father was helping me with my lesson, when in came our landlord's son—a Gentile. His hat and coat were of Persian lamb. Now he had long icicles in his mustache and beard. "Where are you coming from so early, Antushka?" Father asked.

Antushka took off his hat, untied the belt of his coat, and shook off the snow. He wore a red blouse with a beaded girdle and had on black leather boots. He sat down and began to cry. "What is it, Antushka?" Father asked.

He wiped his eyes on the leather cuffs of his coat. "I just brought my younger brother to the army. I cannot go back to the house because of his wife. How can I face her? Their baby is only two weeks old. Ah, brothers, brothers," and he began to sob.

We all had tea. The sun rose. Antushka and Father went away. Dobrosh waited on Mother. At two o'clock the children were sent home and the table set for the Sabbath. Dobrosh asked Grandfather how her grandson Jacob was getting on. Grandfather said, "I don't know what to do with him. He is like my grandson Michael. A teacher hit Michael on one ear so that blood came out of the other. Since then he can't hear well. God knows what he'll grow up to be. But Jacob was born stupid." New straw was brought in for the floor. Dobrosh put two loaves of white bread on the table and the candles were lit.

In the morning, when it was still dark, we heard a tapping at a window. It was Simon Reznikoff, Grandfather's nephew. He had just moved to Znaminka to go into business with his wife's uncle.

Father, Grandfather and Simon had much to talk about and then Simon said to Grandfather, "Uncle, you will have to teach Nathan."

"How old is he?" Grandfather asked.

"Six. I'd like to have Nathan stay here. I'll take him home Saturdays."

Grandfather told him he could bring his son in two weeks. Mother would be out of bed then.

A few weeks later Mother went for her first walk. Grandfather watched the children writing and I took care of the baby. I began a lullaby. Grandfather turned to me and said, "You sing well, but you ought to know that a woman ought not to sing before men." He pointed to the children and smiled.

"A little while ago we were taught that Miriam sang and danced before the Israelites."

"That was different. They had just crossed the Red Sea. Besides, now we are in exile."

Mother came in, followed by a boy with a bag of flour. Grandfather looked at her, surprised. Mother sat down and sighed.

"What are you going to do?" he asked.

"I am going to bake rolls. I have two customers already."

"What do you mean? You have six children and the house

to take care of." (I had two brothers, Hyam and **Abram,**
younger than Israel.)

"Father," Mother said, "I haven't much to do and I must
help Ezekiel. He is not strong and has eight to support.
How can he do that, especially when he is just learning a
trade? Besides, maybe I'll be able to help him educate the
children."

"God will help."

Mother shook her head. "My father believes that when you
work, God helps you. He does not believe in miracles."

Nathan Reznikoff had been with us two weeks when his
mother asked, "How is my big boy?"

Mother said, "He's a nice boy and has a good head on his
shoulders, but you ought to dress him properly. Make him
a coat and trousers like those of my boys. His shirt sticks out
of his rompers and the children can't help pulling it."

Nathan's mother went on to complain about how much she
had to do. She was annoyed at what Mother had said and
after that called us "The Beggarly Aristocrats" and "The Proud
Beggars."

One day a train crowded with soldiers stopped at the village.
Soldiers were billeted in each house, in some as many as
twelve. In our house the soldiers asked us to put up the
samovar and were happy at seeing the fresh rolls. A soldier
with a big blond beard lifted me in his arms. The tears rolled
down his cheeks and he said, "I left a little girl like you at
home."

The soldiers gathered about the table and were very jolly.
But one, a Jew, stood facing the wall and prayed. Mother
found out from the others that he was fasting: his gun was

lost.   The soldiers said he would be shot for losing his gun in time of war.

Grandfather and Mother waited impatiently for Father.   In the morning I found Father still in bed and Grandfather walking about, very happy.   I asked him about the soldier who had lost his gun.   "The Jews of the village each gave some money and Father went to Elizavetgrad and bought a gun.   He came back at three o'clock and the soldiers left at five."

There were Jews in Znaminka poorer than we. A landowner gave one three roubles to kiss a red-hot poker. His family was without food and the Passover holidays near: so he did.

Some of the landowners were friendly to us.   Father played chess with them and they sent us presents of food.   Once a rich peasant came to our house for a lesson in manners. When the serfs were freed, Marko Prokopenko's father bought the estate of a spendthrift nobleman.   Marko no longer wore the peasant dress; good-natured and intelligent, he gave his children a good education.   Afterwards, he built a power-mill in Elizavetgrad and, though his flour was of poor quality, it was the cheapest.   On the day he came to us Father left word that none of the children should be at home.   He was afraid we would laugh at Marko.   Father taught him how to hold his saucer and how to drink tea from it without too much noise.   For this Marko sent us six fat hens and a rooster. The rooster was so big he could eat off the table.   We had to keep the chickens in the house away from the dogs. Grandfather sneered at Father: he took his hat off when he ate with Marko.   But Mother said her father had said it was only a custom for Jews to eat with their hats on, not a law.

20

Next spring Father bought a horse and wagon and drove about the countryside as a glazier. He came back from a trip to tell us of a man who wanted Mother to run one of his taverns. It was in a small village; but a learned man was there to teach the boys, our living quarters would be free, and what we could make on the fish, rolls and dumplings sold would be ours.

Mother was anxious to leave Znaminka. Our neighbor, Homa Ivanovitch, had married his only daughter to his servant. Homa Ivanovitch's granddaughter, Danilka, was my age and we played together. I was once in his house playing with Danilka, when her father urged me to become a Christian.

"Why?" I asked.

"To have a better god."

"What god?'"

He pointed to the ikon covered with cobwebs and dead flies. "Why, that god," I said, "can't even chase a dead fly away."

He threw me out of the house and would have followed to beat me, if his father-in-law had not stopped him. "Why do you argue with children?" I heard Homa Ivanovitch say.

One midnight Danilka's father brought us a bag of wheat. "If you'll bring it in the daytime, I'll buy it," Father said.

Danilka's father became angry. "Do you think it isn't mine?"

"Well, then," said Father, "there's no reason why you can't bring it in the daytime," and would not buy it.

Since then Danilka's father had a grudge against us. Whenever Father was not home, he would throw stones at our door. One night he threw a stone and we were waiting for more to follow, but none did. We looked through the shutters and saw the sky bright above us. We thought he had set fire to the house and ran out. Then we saw that the town was burning, and the church bells began to ring.

The fire burned for three days, first on the west side and then on the east. After it was over Danilka's father came quietly into our house and sat down. Grandfather said to him, "You were the first to see the fire."

"How do you know?" he asked. Since then Mother was afraid of him.

A wagon came for us, we packed our things, and left Znaminka gladly. Grandfather stayed behind until a new teacher would come.

Mother made the tavern neat and clean. So good was her food that the neighboring villages soon heard of us. In a few weeks Father went away and left Mother happy: she worked hard, but the business was going nicely.

Business became so good Mother had to hire a woman to help her. And then, one day, in came the owner's wife with a constable and served us with a notice to vacate: we were taking trade away from the tavern she ran. We had to leave that day. She was afraid that if the peasants found out why we were going they would make trouble for her, and she had a wagon ready. What could Mother do? She packed up our belongings and we went to Elizavetgrad.

Mother's father, Benjamin Hirsh Venitsky, was not at home. He had gone to tutor a young man to be a rabbi and was to stay away a year. Mother's stepmother and Mother's little sister were living in one room. (Mother's stepmother was childless. Father was her cousin and she loved him like a son.) Before Grandfather left home, he bought her a stall in the market-place and there she sold beans, dried peas, and cereals. She welcomed us with open arms and her landlady made room for us.

In the five years we had been away, Elizavetgrad had grown greatly. But instead of spreading out, the people huddled together and even lived in cellars; and the rent even for these was high and none to be had. Mother did not want to stay in Elizavetgrad. There was no place for us to play, the air in the crowded rooms and streets was bad, and she was afraid we would become sickly. Besides, she would be unable to help Father. All the business was done at the market-place. That was far off, and she could not leave us alone just yet. But her stepmother urged her to stay for the sake of my brothers' education.

In three weeks Father came and Mother and he decided to move to a small town, Dimitrefka. Father knew the town well: he had worked for landowners in the neighborhood. Dimitrefka had a free Hebrew school. Grandfather Fivel would not have to teach the boys. He was now living with my uncle, Abram Loeb; there he had more comforts than we could give him.

Meanwhile, I found out that life with my grandmother would be unbearable. I loved to read, but she thought a girl should only do housework and sew: at ten she was a young lady and at fifteen she was to be married off. One day Grandmother found me reading—a Russian book at that. How she carried on! Books were men's affairs and if I would stop meddling with what did not concern me, I should have pretty dresses and whatever I wished. I told her that what I wished for most was paper and books and at least one lesson a week. Grandmother told Mother how spoiled I was. I asked Mother why women should be against educating girls. She answered that all elderly people thought that if women would read they would not do their household duties.

"Do you remember when Grandfather Fivel gave me *The Tree of Life* to read and memorize? In that it said, 'He who does not know how to read is blind.'"

"A man is meant," Mother answered.

"I don't believe intelligent people think a woman is not as good as a man." And I made up my mind not to listen to Mother or Grandmother and learn as much as I could.

In the autumn we moved to Dimitrefka. There we lived opposite a park. The houses of Dimitrefka were built far apart and each had a garden and many trees. Mother gave birth to a boy. My brothers—those old enough—went to school and Father managed to make a living.

Grandfather Fivel came to see us in the spring. He complained about the way Abram Loeb was bringing up his children. His wife was a bad stepmother: she did not care if the children were taught or not. I told Grandfather how I missed him. He said that he missed us, too, but it was his duty to stay with my motherless cousins and see that they were brought up decently. Then he quoted an old saying, When the mother is dead, the father is blind. Grandfather enjoyed his stay with us. He called my sister "a little Greek girl": she was dark and beautiful. Though she was only two years old, she danced and sang.

At the end of spring Father went to Nikolaiev. Two weeks went by and we did not hear from him. We had only a bag of flour. "Will you be able to sell rolls in the market?" Mother asked me, and baked a hundred rolls.

I had a neat dress and wore shoes and stockings. When I found a place in the bakers' row, they made fun of me and chased me away. "What kind of an aristocrat is this?" they said. I wandered about with my rolls, wondering what to do.

I went to a store where we had bought flour and told the owner how I had been chased from the bakers' row. I asked him to let me stand near his steps. Here I spread my tablecloth and put out the rolls. A crowd gathered: the sight of a white tablecloth under the rolls was unusual and in a little while they were sold. People asked me who my parents were, and Abram Sinkovsky, the owner of the store, said he would send us a two-hundred pound sack of flour. I told him Father was not at home and that we could not pay for it just then; but he answered that I was not to worry about that.

Mother baked rolls three times a day. Israel was taken from school and sent in my place to the market: I had to help Mother at home. Though he was not quite ten years old, Israel was an old hand at selling. He had been selling matches and salt since he was seven.

All we had from Father were hopeful letters, but no money. We wrote him that we were getting along nicely. One afternoon a carriage rolled up to the door and a short, stout, well-dressed man came into the house. He had just come from Nikolaiev. He gave Mother twenty-five roubles Father had sent and told us how Father had struggled until he found work. "It's hard without money to find something to do in a strange place," he said. He lived near us, just around the corner, and made Mother promise to come to tea and meet his wife.

Mother found time to go. He had three sons and three daughters. They would come to see us, Mother said. Eva was my age and I asked at once, "Does Eva go to school?" School was all I thought about. Many and many a time when no one would see me, I would cry because I could not go to school.

"She is given lessons at home," Mother answered.

Three of the children did come next day, among them Eva. They told us their mother was dead. Their stepmother had refurnished the house and had hired a teacher for them. She also wanted the youngest boy to take lessons on the violin. She thought it dreadful to go about barefoot. Mother told them she must be a fine woman: there were stepmothers who did not think their stepchildren should be educated. They said they appreciated what she was doing, but it was hard for them.

Eva asked me to one of the lessons. They did not seem to care for it and fooled about with their teacher. Their stepmother came in and told Eva she need not study any more that day, but could play with me. Eva laughed and said, "She does not play. All her time is taken up with reading and sewing."

"Little girls should have some fun, too," her stepmother said.

In a few weeks Father came home. He brought us all presents. Israel was given a pair of boots with red tops. He hung them on a tree in the woods and then could not find the tree. Father asked him why he had not brought the boots home and then gone back to play.

"We were playing soldiers. I was the general. If I went away," he said earnestly, "my men would be captured."

We went on with our baking: times were bad. Next spring the landlord made us move. He said we baked so much the house would catch on fire.

Mother had an abscess in her throat. She was afraid to

trust herself to the doctors in Dimitrefka and went to Elizavetgrad. I was to take care of the house and do the cooking.

In a few days we ran out of bread. I set about to bake
a sort of biscuit we ate. I made the dough and then tried
to heat the oven. We used dried manure for fuel and I put
in as much as I had seen Mother use. Then I placed two
pots of water inside to keep the flames from the chimney.
When I set a match to the manure, it burst into a great blaze.
I had not realized that because of the long season of dry
weather, the manure was so dry. I ran outside and watched
the sparks flying out of the chimney over the straw roof. After
a while they became less, and I went into the house to find
the fire in the oven dying down. I put the dough in, my hands
trembling for excitement. Then I began to worry that the
chimney was on fire. I took two pails of water and some
sacks and climbed to the attic. I soaked the sacks and put
them on the chimney. They became dry almost at once. I
was sure now that there was danger of a fire. I wet the
sacks again and again until they no longer dried on the chimney. I was looking about for a place to lean against and rest,
when I saw what seemed a man hanging from the ceiling.
Our landlord's grandfather had hanged himself in this attic.
That was why we were able to rent the house: no one else
would live here, I thought, and slid down the ladder. When
I opened my eyes, my brothers were about me. I remembered
the biscuits; they must be burnt black, I thought, and ran to
the oven door. Ugh! inside I found white, cold lumps of
dough.

Later, I saw our landlord and told him that I had seen his
grandfather hanging in the attic. He called me all kinds of
ugly names, but quickly went up with me. What I had seen
was a sack of dried apples and I felt such a fool.

Next day I was sick. Israel woke me chanting the Psalms.

It seemed to me that he said them even better than Father and I cried as I listened. When he had finished, I said, "Israel, I'll not be able to make anything today. I cannot start a fire. We'll just have to buy bread and milk and live on that until Mamma comes back."

He answered cheerfully, "Don't worry. I'm going to market now to sell my matches and then I'll bring some bread."

Mother came back, pale and sick. I hugged her and kissed her and told her all that had happened. She wrung her hands and cried, "The child might have been burned to death!"

Soon our life went on as before. It disgusted me. My mind was starving. I loved to read, but how could I when I had so much to do? I was too miserable to eat and wished to die.

One night I woke and saw that Father had come. I would have risen from bed and gone to him—he had not been home a long time—but I heard my name. Father sat at the head of the table. The light shone full on his face, on his high white forehead and long black beard. In Znaminka they had nicknamed him "Ezekiel-with-the-long-beard." I could not see my mother but I heard her telling him about me. When he heard that I was so unhappy and wished to die, he repeated after her, "She is unhappy," and hid his face in his handkerchief; I was shocked to see him cry.

Then I heard Mother say, "What can we do? We cannot send her to school. I need her at home: I have no other help."

In the morning we all greeted Father and hurried to our work. I said nothing about the night before and neither did Mother or Father. In the evening, Father told us how he had worked in the house of Judge Kormazine, a great and good man. He had spoken to Father about the Jews. Their life was going to be hard, he said. In some places the priests had been ordered to preach against them. The Judge thought that the Jews ought to change their way of living: they ought to learn trades and professions and give up being merchants and middlemen. But, of course, as long as the government would allow only a few Jews in the colleges, only the rich could become professional men.

"In a home where there are stepchildren," Father said, "every one is treated alike as long as all goes well. But when things go wrong and food is scarce, who is treated badly?"

"The stepchildren," we answered.

"That is what is happening in Russia now. The Jews are considered the stepchildren of the country. When things run smoothly, they are let alone; but as soon as there is trouble, they are oppressed. The stepchildren must be much better than the others not to be blamed.

"To show how falsehoods about the Jews spread, Judge Kormazine told me of a case he had. A peasant woman came to the fair with two bulls. A Jew gave her sixty roubles for them and then the woman cried out she had not been paid. A crowd gathered and the Jew and the peasant woman were taken to Judge Kormazine. The Jew said he had brought eighty roubles to the fair, he had paid sixty for the bulls, and had twenty left. These he showed to the Judge. The woman kept saying that the Jew had not paid her. He had seen the money she had and that was what he said he had paid for the bulls. The Judge looked at the Jew's money and said it was counterfeit. Then he asked for the peasant woman's money and said that was counterfeit, too. She fell on her knees and confessed she had it from the Jew. The Judge asked her why she had accused the Jew falsely. She answered that times were bad and she had taxes to pay; she thought it would not matter if she took money from a Jew: the Jews had plenty. There were riots in a number of taverns in the town before the truth was known. And by that time most of the peasants had left for home with the story of how a Jew had tried to cheat a peasant woman out of her bulls.

" 'Each Jew,' the Judge concluded, 'must try to overcome the feeling against Jews by his own work and life.' "

I was thinking of what the Judge had said about Jews learning trades and said, "Father, would you apprentice Israel to a shoemaker or a tailor?"

Father answered, "I should not like a child of mine to be a shoemaker or a tailor. The ignorant people of the town have done this work for generations. When a family has a stupid or a bad child, they apprentice him to one of these trades; and so they have become the trades of the stupid. In the cities, they are in somewhat better hands, but, still, a tailor's apprentice must wait four or five years before he is allowed to use the needle. In the meantime, he has to bring water for his employer and mind the children."

Then Father turned to me and said, "Little girl, you were born into the wrong family with your ideas." I became red. "You were born the eldest girl and this family needs your help badly. We are lucky to have you here to help your mother; otherwise, she could not go on as she does. You can read and write. Many Jewish girls of well-to-do families cannot do that. You are also handy with the needle. Now you must make plans to suit your circumstances. Learn as much as you can, but we could not send you to school, even if we were better off, because you are needed at home."

In the winter Mother gave birth to another boy. The day after Easter, 1881, Mother went to market with her rolls and Father went out on business. They soon came back: there had been a pogrom in Elizavetgrad and everybody was saying there would be others throughout Russia. Mother was crying because her parents were in Elizavetgrad. In our town the Gentiles called a meeting and resolved to defend the Jews against rioters. They sent word to the Jews not to be afraid; however, should soldiers come, they added, they could do nothing. In a few days Father went to Elizavetgrad and found my grandparents robbed, but safe.

The summer was a hard one, especially for Jews. They had no spirit to do anything. In the autumn diphtheria broke out and in Dimitrefka about three hundred children died every week. Luckily, none of us had it. In the winter there was smallpox in town. Our baby, Fishel, caught it and was sick for eighteen weeks. He was so covered with pus we could not touch him. We used to roll him from sheet to sheet, and we soaked the sheets in vinegar, afterwards, to disinfect them. His face became deeply pock-marked and for a long time he could not walk.

Father planned to go to America. Many Jews were going, but Mother would not hear of it. Her father said it might be better for us to move back to Elizavetgrad, and we did. I was twelve and a half years old then. In a little while I began to sew for several families. As for my brothers— Michael worked in a lumber-yard and Israel in a leather store; Hyam, Abram, and Rachmiel went to school; Fishel was still sick and the doctors could do little for him. Whenever Father would say, "America," Mother would answer, "With a cripple?"

We lived in the suburbs behind the blacksmiths' street, near the fair grounds. Our house was one of a row built almost underground: the roofs were only two feet above the street. The light came through four little windows. We had three rooms; one we used for a store-room and to work in. Mother helped her stepmother at the stand in the market-place. Father did a little glazing; he tried many things.

One day Father came with a wagon. The driver carried chalk and cans of oil into the house. Father paid him fifteen copecks. "Only fifteen copecks for all that load?" I asked.

"It is almost three o'clock," Father said, "and that is all he has earned today. How hard it is to make a living!"

"What new trade have you now?" I asked.

Father sighed. "A store wants me to make putty. They pay fifteen copecks for forty pounds."

Father mixed the chalk and oil and beat the mixture with a mallet. He began to sweat and often stopped to catch his breath. "I know an easier way than that," I said, and took off my shoes and stockings. I danced on the putty until it was soft.

Now I had not only dough to knead for Mother but putty to make for Father. I became strong and wiry. But I used to wonder what would become of me. It seemed to me that I was just wasting my life in a hole in the ground. And when Saturday came, I could not read because Grandmother would nag me: I was making my bad eyes worse and would soon be blind.

One day they caught a rat in a trap at the store of the merchant to whom Israel was apprenticed, and Israel's master told him to kill it; but Israel could not bring himself to do it. His master stamped on Israel's foot to make him kill the rat until his foot was so swollen he could hardly walk. For some time he had to go about in a shoe cut open at the top. That Saturday when he came home to dinner, his face had grown worn and dark. After he had gone, Mother cried and said, "Such young children with such old faces."

But Father said, "It is better so: they will grow strong and hard."

32

Three years like this went by. And then one day Father told us that a man who had been a chum of his at school had hired him to buy grain for his mill. Father was to be paid thirty roubles a month. By this time, too, Israel's apprenticeship in the leather store was up. He had worked only for board and clothes; now he was to have sixty roubles a year and his board. Israel gave thirty roubles to Father and the rest he kept for clothes.

Father bought a stout cloth, called "devil's cloth," and Mother and I made suits for the children. I made myself a skirt and blouse of a dark blue goods. The blouse had a little red collar. And we moved to the city. Father bought half a dozen chairs with cane seats. In the middle of our new living-room we had a big round table and in the corner a divan covered with cretonne; the windows had white curtains.

The well was two blocks away. Of course, no *mademoiselle* could carry water through the street. Father told Hyam it was his duty to fill the water-barrel. But if I made him go, he would drop pail and line into the well and fishing them out was a lot of trouble. We could not afford to buy water: we used eight pails a day and they cost a copeck and a half a pail. Israel was now a salesman; he no longer had chores to do for his master's wife and had his evenings off. He would come home and help me bring all the water we needed. But when he could not come, I carried in the water myself after dark.

Father used to go away on buying trips. He would come home for Saturday and Sunday. On Saturday he would go to synagogue with my brothers. Weekdays, Mother would leave early in the morning to help Grandmother. At four o'clock she would be back. I used to be up at dawn, send the children off to school, do the housework, and then I had time enough to do my sewing. Altogether, we had rather a pleasant time of it.

To the right of us lived a Gentile, Anastasia Vladimirovna. Her husband had been killed in the Turkish War. One of her sons was studying to be a priest, another was in a government bureau, and her daughter was a schoolteacher. Across the way lived another widow. She had two daughters. The unmarried daughter was bright and knew Hebrew, but was homely. She and I became great friends and found much to talk about. Near us was a family, the Olanovs, who seemed to have nothing to do with their neighbors.

I made friends with Anastasia Vladimirovna. She was a good woman, anxious to help everyone. Though her son was studying to be a priest, she liked Jews. She taught me how to sew dresses.

Once she said, "Mrs. Olanov's niece, Rebecca, was here a little while ago. I don't believe she has eaten anything today: her lips were dry and her body shivered. Neither she nor her aunt will do anything for themselves: they cannot sew on a button. Rebecca wants to meet you and will be back in a few minutes."

When she came in, I went with her to her aunt. Mrs. Olanov was a young woman with two small children. I could see they were all hungry. I brought seventy-five copecks of my savings to Anastasia for the Olanovs. After that I became friendly with them. Mr. Olanov was a tutor. He had been unable to find work in Elizavetgrad and had gone to a place in the country. It was hard to send money from there, and that was why his wife and children and her niece were starving when I first met them.

Mr. Olanov came home for a few days and one night they gave a party. I danced in the quadrilles, but when the boys and girls began a kissing game, I went off to have tea with the Olanovs. He looked at me so pityingly that I could not help laughing and said, "What are you thinking of?"

"I have heard that you do not enjoy life. You take life too seriously."

"Isn't life serious?"

"A young girl should enjoy it as other young people do."

"I certainly do not enjoy life, but I do not mean by enjoyment what you mean. I am sorry not to have an education, but as for the work I do, that is necessary. I do not mind it. I must carry my share of the burdens of the family. If I had an education, I should not mind the work I do. Anastasia Vladimirovna is of a noble family and highly educated, yet when she has rough work to do, she does it. Some people carry their education about as if on a plate and are afraid to stoop."

Mr. Olanov said, "I suppose you have been reading *Der Yiddishe Moujik.*" (That was a book urging the Jews to give up trading and to work like the peasants.)

"No," I said, "but I'd like to. Do you mean to say," I went on, "that if the water-carrier does not come until eleven o'clock because his horse fell on the way, a woman should keep her children in bed, unwashed and without breakfast, and not bring water from the well because she is a lady?"

The others came over to listen. "Well," said one, "let's take a walk. Good-night," he said, and put out his left hand to shake hands with me.

"Why the left?" I asked.

"It's nearer my heart."

"I'd rather have the right," I said.

They were all embarrassed. When the guests had gone, I asked Mr. Olanov if I had been wrong in saying what I did.

"He did not mean anything by that," Mr. Olanov said, "but you insulted him. Some day he may insult you."

"I am not afraid of his insults and I do not like him. He thinks all the girls are in love with him."

"Do you know him?"

"Yes. He is an empty-headed fellow. His mother sells hot water and his sister sews jackets for peasants. A few weeks ago I was at a Zionist meeting: *there* were young fellows to look at and to listen to."

One day, Mrs. Olanov told me her father had come and would like to see me. "You know my grandchild Rebecca—" he said, "her father left her mother about three years ago, and nothing has been heard of him since. I am not rich, but I thought I would give Rebecca five hundred roubles as a dowry and marry her off. What do you think?"

"Would she be provided for? You may only have another burden on your hands."

"That is why I spoke to you," he answered, "can she do the sewing you do?"

"I have tried to teach her, but she hasn't the knack for it. I think she would do better as a midwife. They do very well. She has gone to the *gymnasium*. Give her the money to take the course. Then, maybe, she'll find somebody fit for her. She's only seventeen and very bright."

In a few months the Olanovs moved away. Later, I had a letter from Rebecca: she was studying to be a midwife.

Before Passover, Father asked me to leave my sewing: a man who sold milk planned to bake matzoth, but the man to take charge had left him. We went to Velvel's that evening. He was tall and blond. His wife, Tilly, was beautiful and kind; she had a lovely complexion and black hair and eyes.

The street they lived on was muddy and so was the floor

of their living-room. Some bread was on the table and many glasses. In the room where the matzoth were to be baked were three large boards on which to roll the dough and a stone on which to knead it. I swept and cleaned the room, and then the flour was brought in.

In the living-room were Velvel's sons. Nahum looked like his mother: he had black hair and shining black eyes and a handsome face. He was clever, too. For supper each had a slice of bread and a glass of milk. Nahum was talking to Father as the others ate, and when he went to pour himself a glass of milk, the pitcher was empty. He took down another from the shelf. This was brimful and some of the milk spilled on his head. "God blesses others with oil," he said, "but us with milk."

Next morning I came early. About twenty-five girls and women worked for us. The fellow kneading the dough kept talking away, making fun of the girls. An old woman, jerking her head at me, asked him, "What is the matter with her? You left her out."

" 'Don't touch me!' " he answered, "is written on her face." I blushed and made believe I didn't hear.

Sometimes he made fun of a girl until she cried. At last I went up to him and said, "You know that these girls are not happy at having to work here. They are ready to cry at an unkind word. You are an intelligent man, why make a fool of yourself?" He was as quiet after that as if he were dumb. I was glad to have found a remedy for him.

I had been afraid that I would be unable to manage so many. But I tried to be natural and not flustered. And everything went smoothly. Father and I had time for long talks. Every evening Nahum helped us with the bookkeeping. He hardly ever spoke to me, but once he lent me a book.

After the holidays we went back to our own work. Father

went away on his buying trips and I did my sewing at home. My
eldest brother, Michael—he sold wood to Velvel—said with a
grin, "Nahum will give you more books, if you want them."
And then he whispered to Mother and laughed. She told him
not to be a fool. I sent his book back to Nahum and he
lent me another. I wondered why he did not come to see me,
if he was thinking of me.

One evening as Israel and I were going to the well, he told
me he was worth more than he was getting. "But in this
city," he said, "there are only small merchants. They cannot
afford to hire me. I'm going to the fair at Poltava. There
I'll meet many in my line."

I thought that great. Israel was only sixteen and he spoke
like a merchant. When we came back, we told Mother and
Grandmother of his plan. But they did not like it at all. "Why
didn't you tell Papa?" Mother said.

And Grandmother said, "In one place even a stone grows.
You must stay in one place."

Israel answered, "Change your place, change your luck. I
have no luck here, I must change my place."

So he left for Poltava. A week went by and we had not
heard from him. Mother said it was all my fault. He would
never have thought of going away, if not for me. Another
week went by and at last a letter came. In it was a little picture
of Israel in new clothes. He was going to work in Kremenchuk
for a hundred and twenty roubles a year, board and lodging,
and was to have half his wages in advance to send to us.
We were very happy that evening. And in a few weeks he
sent us sixty roubles' worth of buckwheat.

I had much to do and wanted a sewing-machine to do it

quickly and better. But Grandmother said, "What are you going to become? A manufacturer? Get married."

Mother, too, said I was going to be an old maid and a rope about her neck. And Father said, "The idea is good, but you can't do anything now with everybody against you."

I wrote Israel about it. By return mail he sent me ten roubles and wrote Mother to let me buy the sewing-machine. Soon I had some girls working for me. Anastasia Vladimirovna was of great help, but she was going to move away. She urged me to learn cutting from the books of the Glazhdinsky system of dressmaking; but I did not have the money for it.

Grandmother became sick and the doctor said she had not long to live. We wrote to Grandfather. But when she became better, he went away again. And then she died. Father, too, was not at home for the funeral.

Later, Grandfather wrote us he was coming to stay. I was afraid of him, because he was so pious and whatever he said went. But I got along with him as well as with Father. Though he was of the same generation as Grandfather Fivel, Grandfather Benjamin Hirsh did not believe that Jews should study only their own books.

One day he told Mother and me about a nephew of his in Rumania. "One of my sisters —a widow—died," he said, "and left a son in my care. He was bright and a good student. When he was about eighteen, the police went from door to door in our town and asked us all to sign our names. When they came to the house where my nephew was, he jumped out of a window. Late at night, he came to my bed and said, 'Uncle, you must help me. I wrote a letter to the Czar. That is why they are asking everybody to sign their names.' I asked him what he wrote and how he came to do it. 'I cannot tell you,' he said, 'but I wrote what should not have been written.' I used to send sugar to other towns and had many barrels in my yard. I made holes in one, put him inside, and got him over the border with a shipment. It took him three days to get to Rumania. Now he owns a leather factory, and I want Israel to go there. It is just the place for him."

Once when he was watching me at my work, Grandfather said, "My sisters could sew very well, and yet when we became poor, they could do nothing with their sewing."

"How did you become poor?" I asked.

"My father was the richest man in the town. He owned most of it. We built a home for old people and kept up a kitchen for the poor. I was the only son and neither I nor Father's five sons-in-law had to work. We studied the Talmud. I was married when I was eighteen and when I was in the thirties and had four children, I was still at my books. There was much to study and I liked it. One of my school friends had become a doctor. Another had married a Brodsky and gone into their sugar business. But I stayed at my books. And then one fine morning Czar Nicholas sent an order that all should leave the town within twenty-four hours, Jews and Gentiles: the houses and grounds were given to soldiers. We took what money we had and went to the nearest town; all had to do something for a living. I wrote to my friend who had married a Brodsky, and he asked me to come to Kiev. There I went into the business of shipping sugar. I did well until the railways were built. My wife died and I married again. I didn't like my second wife. We had no children. My children were all married, and I went back to my books and ended up a teacher. That is all there is to it."

A woman of our acquaintance, Malka Cohen, sent for me. Her son was to be married, and would I make his underwear? She was very friendly, but when we talked price, she would pay five copecks less a piece than anyone else and no more. No matter how much I spoke, and though I showed her how long the work would take me and what it would cost me, she would not pay more and said, "Do you want to be a Fanny Huebsch all at once?" (Fanny Huebsch had more sewing to do than any other seamstress in town.)

I needed the work and took it at her price. And she promised to tell her son's fiancée about me. It took me until four o'clock to cut the goods. I carried the bundle and came home, flushed and tired. Grandfather met me at the door. "I thought you were a sensible girl," he said. "You could have hired a carriage for fifteen copecks and not have carried that heavy bundle. That isn't sensible." I saw two strangers at the table. I put the bundle away and went to see what the girls who worked for me had done.

I suspected that the elder of the two men was a match-maker. The younger was about eighteen, but he wore clothes as old-fashioned as my Grandfather Fivel. After they left, the match-maker—for so he was—came back and had a brief talk with Grandfather. Then Grandfather went into the kitchen.

"Whom do you expect her to marry?" I could hear Mother say.

"Do you want her to marry an ignorant fellow," said Grandfather, "a man a century behind the times? I had a talk with him: he knows nothing of the Talmud. He is just a religious fanatic, an empty-headed fellow who dresses up like his grandfather. I want her to marry a man of today who understands the world."

Next morning, Grandfather sat near me and at last said, "I want to have a talk with you about your way of working. Yesterday you carried home a bundle too heavy for you, you

worked until late at night, and this morning you are up so
early at work again."

"You see, Grandfather, the people here won't pay what
they ought to. One must work hard to make anything at all.
Yesterday, I brought four dozen men's linen underwear to sew
for Malka Cohen. She pays only twenty copecks a piece.
The thread alone costs me six copecks, and I must pay my
installments on the sewing-machine, and my girls must get
something. I spent four hours yesterday cutting up the goods,
and now I must bring it back. And some won't pay you
right away, but you must go again and again. The people
of this town think they will become rich by squeezing what
they can out of those who work for them."

"But if you work so hard," Grandfather said, "in the end
you will be sick and that won't pay at all."

Father was hurrying through his prayers and I could see
by his face he had something to tell me. He put aside his
prayer-shawl and phylacteries, washed himself again, said
grace, and began his breakfast. "My daughter," he said, "I
am not pleased at the way you talk. You should not go about
as if the world were doing you harm. You will not change
the world that way and will only harm yourself.

"Last week you had much to say against Isaac: he ran
away and left his family without means! Now it turns
out that he didn't desert them at all. As soon as he was
over the border, he sent his parents a telegram to care for
his family until he establishes himself. He isn't as bad as you
thought, is he? Now, Malka Cohen is not rich. Her husband
makes a good living, that is all. Malka does her own marketing. Why should you be better than anybody else she
buys from? Thrifty women do not care whether you make
money or lose: what they buy they want as cheap as possible."

"Then they are wrong," I said. "They should care for

others besides themselves. All of us work hard. Mamma, you, Israel and I, even Frieda works, and we haven't five roubles to our name."

"I am worried about Michael," said Father, thoughtfully. "His employer complained to me about him. I am sure he will not keep him much longer. And why should he? There are plenty of better men without work. Can you blame his employer? Even you wouldn't keep the girl who couldn't make buttonholes. You told me how poor her family is, that they haven't enough to eat, and yet you couldn't keep her, because she couldn't do her work. Even you," Father repeated with a smile.

Father finished his breakfast and said, "Bad times, my daughter. You must be satisfied with things as they are. Work and be content."

Bad times! I thought of all the carriages on the boulevard and the ladies and gentlemen riding about in them, but I was afraid to say anything: I should be thought a Nihilist.

That day I was called to another kind of family than Malka's. Mr. Klarfeld dealt in sheep. His eldest son was studying medicine. I was met by the eldest daughter and she was very friendly. In a little while Mrs. Klarfeld came in. I showed my samples. "So young," she said, "and you do this work?"

"I have done it since I was twelve," I answered.

She gave me two rolls of linen and the pattern of her son's underwear. I was to have it ready in two weeks. "Buy the buttons yourself and add it to the bill," she said. For the first time I was in a house where every inch of goods was not measured and the price not haggled over. I was overjoyed at their friendliness and trust in me.

So, little by little, I built up a trade until I had four sewing-machines and eight girls working for me.

Among these, for a while, was our landlady's daughter. Our landlady was a widow and could not make a living. She asked me to teach her daughter to sew. The daughter worked hard, but could do nothing that called for intelligence: she could only run off straight seams on the machine. I taught her to sew peasant blouses—these came ready-cut from the store—and took her to Hyamovsky. She made a sample and he said he would give her blouses to sew. She and I then went to the Singer Sewing Machine Company and I bought a machine for her. She paid them ten roubles and was to pay the rest, a rouble a week. In about three months the company sent me twenty-five roubles. I asked my parents if I should give her the commission. Father said, "Anastasia Vladimirovna made twenty-five roubles on your first machine. You have earned the money. Now you can buy the books from which to learn dressmaking—or a wardrobe in which to lock the goods at night. Then you needn't worry so about thieves." We decided that I ought to buy the wardrobe first, and I bought one for eighteen roubles.

Michael was out of work and became a glazier. Hyam worked in a clothing store on the main street. He came home every night for supper and afterwards went for a walk along the boulevard. One day Mother received a letter in Russian; she could not read Russian, and took the letter to have Hyam read it: he was not in the store and had not been for three weeks. She almost fainted. We waited for him to come to supper. He came at the usual time, singing and jigging, jolly as always. Whenever he was home the house was full of laughter. After supper, he took his cane to go out. Mother stopped him. At her grave face, he smiled and said, "Now it is coming."

"What do you mean?" Mother said. "What do you do?"

"I did something just as an experiment. If it turned out

well, I was going to tell you about it. I want to learn how to make clothes instead of selling them. I don't like to sell. It's no crime to be a workingman."

"I don't understand you," said Mother. "What are you doing?"

"I've apprenticed myself to a tailor."

"Why didn't you ask us first? Perhaps we don't want you to be a tailor."

"I know you don't. That's why I didn't ask."

"I don't mind the kind of work but the people with whom you'll have to work."

"I'm working for a fine man," and he told us his name. Mother agreed that he had a good reputation. "And," Hyam added, "he is a military tailor. I am learning how to make clothes for officers."

"The rakes! The good-for-nothings!" Mother said. "It will not be much to your credit to mix with such people."

"Well," said Hyam, "if you want to be good, you can be, no matter with whom you are." At this, Grandfather came in and Mother said no more, to spare him the news. But he saw that Mother and I were troubled. Hyam went for his walk, and Grandfather asked Mother what worried her.

"We kept Hyam at home until he was fourteen," she said, "and gave him an education we did not give Michael or Israel, only to have him disgrace us by apprenticing himself to a tailor."

But Grandfather took the news calmly. "You can't choose for your children," he said. "They have their own likes and dislikes. It is better for them to be free from their mother's apron-strings. He is old enough to know what he is doing."

"We thought him the cleverest of all," said Mother, "and he turns out to be so unambitious—so low."

"A trade is not low," said Grandfather angrily. "What

happened to your brother Solomon should have taught you not to make children do what they don't want to. Be content to let them go their own way as long as it is honorable." And Grandfather turned to me, "I brought up my three sons to be rabbis. Solomon was only seventeen when he finished his studies. The next year he married the daughter of a rabbi, and became a rabbi in a small town. He had also to kill the animals used for food. This upset him and he wanted to give up his position. He was making a good living and his wife and I made him stay at it. And what happened? One day, without a word to either of us, he gave it up and from that time on spoke to no one. Well, his wife and children had to go to her family and he wandered about from town to town. At last he settled down in a village as a teacher of little children."

Mother sighed, "O what luck I have!"

When Father came home in a few weeks, he had a talk with Hyam. Father wanted to see his employer. But Hyam said, "I'm working for this man just on trial. He's a master craftsman. You know boys are apprenticed to tailors for three years before they learn anything worth while. But I can sew now parts of a coat as well as anybody. And I don't have to do any work about the house. That was made up between us. I won't mind the children or bring water. As soon as I finish work in the shop and have my supper, I am free. If you interfere and make me leave, you'll be blamed, just as you were blamed when I left the store. I am fifteen now and can fight my own battles."

"Have it your way," said Father, "but I hope you'll be an honest fellow."

Saturdays Hyam visited us. He was happy and looked well, so we were satisfied. One evening it was chilly and we had the door closed. A woman banged it open, her eyes blazing.

Mother recognized her. She sold chickens in the market. Without greeting us, "Where's Hyam?" she shouted.

Mother trembled. "What do you want with Hyam?"

Our visitor said sarcastically, "Look at the woman! Just see how she knows of nothing!"

Mother said quietly, "But what do you want?"

The woman began to scream at the top of her voice. When she quieted down, Mother insisted that she tell her what had happened. "I set the table," she said, "and while I made supper for him, I sent Hyam for water to make him tea. I waited and waited and no Hyam. At last I went outside to look for him, and there was the kettle thrown into a corner. Where's Hyam?"

"Shout and scream as much as you like and have all the neighbors in," Mother said, "but I can't tell you where he is, because he didn't come home."

Saturday Hyam came as usual and Mother said, "It wouldn't have hurt you any to have gone for water for your own tea."

Hyam smiled. "I'm fifteen," he said. "I'm a man and I won't bring water if it's only from across the street. She won't work me as she does the other apprentices. And I was not supposed to help her. This was made up between my master and me. He doesn't keep his word. He promised me ten roubles for a pair of shoes two weeks ago. I was going about barefoot and still he didn't give me the money. So I found another place, and am working there now."

"I wish you could eat and sleep at home," Mother said, "no matter how little you'll be paid. What a family you worked for! Even if this is a better one, it could not be much better."

"I don't like to eat where I work," said Hyam, "and the first chance I get, I'll eat and sleep at home."

"But you must keep your word, my son, or you'll have a bad name."

Hyam smiled. "Oh, I am reasonable."

It was not long before he had his meals at home. Our little sister Frieda had to have pot roast ready for him every evening. Sometimes, when the wood was damp and the potatoes would not brown just right, her black eyes would fill with tears at the thought that Hyam might not like his supper. And then he would not eat at home and Mother wanted him to. But Hyam never asked what we had to eat.

When Grandfather Benjamin Hirsh was seventy-three years old, he went to visit all his children. He left in the spring and came back late in autumn. Then he told Mother how poor some of her brothers and sisters were and the children of those better off were not as he wished. He spoke much of his nephew in Rumania. He wanted Israel to go there and escape service in the army. But Father would say, "Why go from one bad country to another? It is better to go to America."

And Mother said, "Israel's time to serve is still many years off. Who knows what will happen until then?"

"Yes, yes," said Grandfather, "but you don't know how quickly that time will come."

One very hot day in July, Grandfather was too sick to go to synagogue and prayed at home. He became worse and I called the doctor. After he was gone, Grandfather smiled and said, "What did the doctor prescribe?"

"A physic."

"I thought so."

"Why, Grandfather, don't you believe in doctors?"

"Not when they can't help you. I know that I am old and my strength is going." I was sick at heart. I kept thinking:

A man like that dies and there is no one in the family to take his place.

Grandfather wrote letters to his friends and had us call the head of the burial committee. He told him where he wished to be buried and they agreed upon the cost of the funeral. Then he called my father to his bedside and said, "The day I close my eyes you must take my fur hat, my new clothes, and what is left of my money and send it to Moses, my youngest son. He is worse off than the rest of you." The next day he died.

That winter was a hard one. It was hard enough to make a living and, on top of that, we were afraid of a pogrom. In the spring, somehow, we became hopeful of better times, though for no better reason, perhaps, than the sunny weather.

One dawn, as Father was saying his prayers and the children were dressing, the man who sold Father lottery tickets came in. "At last I have good news for you," he said, "your number won, Mr. Wolvovsky."

Father asked to see the bulletin to make sure and saw that Number Thirty-one won. He had Thirty. Father sighed and said, "How the money would have helped us."

The man looked through his notes. "Gedaliah, Velvel the Milkman's son, won," he said. At this Father looked at me. I was blushing. Velvel's son, Nahum, wished to marry me. He had said so to Father. But Nahum was soon to go away for his army service, and so Father did not think the match advisable. Though I kept telling myself nothing would come of it, whenever I thought of Nahum, I said to myself, maybe. But now I was sure he would not have me. His brother would give him some of the money, and he would not have to marry a penniless girl.

In the autumn Nahum was taken to the army. He said

good-by to my father and brothers, but did not come to see me. That evening I heard Father say to Mother, "His going away is worse than that of a son. A son will come back some time. Nahum has five years to serve and it will be hard to get another man like that for our daughter."

Next year my eldest brother Michael went to serve his term in the army, but he was let off because he was the eldest son. Father had to go to army headquarters with some papers for Michael. A newly drafted soldier, still drunk, hit Father in the side. He was not strong and the blow weakened him greatly. It pained him all year.

One day, I happened to go to a house near the market for some work, but the woman was out. It was late in the afternoon. Mother always had a good many parcels to carry home, and I thought I would help her. But as I came near her stand, I saw her coming along with a young man.

"Do you recognize him?" she asked. "This is Nathan Reznikoff, Simon's son."

"How could I recognize him? I haven't seen him since we moved from Znaminka."

Nathan Reznikoff had come to stay a while in Elizavetgrad. I was two years older than he and considered myself an elder sister. We spoke of many things, agreed and disagreed and quarrelled. I introduced him to my friends. "What homely girls you go with," he said.

"I am not better-looking."

"O yes, you are. Your forehead and eyebrows are beautiful and your figure is better than theirs." I thought, Nahum liked my long hair, he likes my forehead and eyebrows and figure; perhaps, I am not so bad-looking. My little sister Frieda came over and I said, "Here is what I call a good-looking girl." Frieda had beautiful lips and eyes and an olive complexion.

"But you are cleverer," Nathan said. "I remember you at her age. You were a holy terror. You bossed the whole house."

"I still boss my brothers. But there's one I can't do anything with. That's Hyam."

"He's too smart for you."

"But," I answered, "everyone ought to do his share of the work. He isn't smart, but unfair. And Hyam just did a most unpleasant thing. He apprenticed himself to a tailor."

"Why is that so unpleasant? It's an honest trade."

"Yes, tailoring is honest, but tailors are not. If Hyam wants to be a tailor, don't let him say he became one because it's an honest trade. " Then we spoke of Israel. The more I praised him, the angrier Nathan became. At last he called me a liar. He was our guest and so I said nothing. When his visit was over, we agreed that he was clever, but rather outspoken.

A few weeks later his mother came to our house. She had a bad headache, but in the morning she was better and called to my father in the tone of a rich lady, "I want a few words with you, Ezekiel." Father was in a hurry to go to business, but, of course, he had to listen. "Last night my head hurt so I could not talk to you." And I heard no more of what she said.

But at last Father answered, "Your son is bright, but he is too young and still has his term in the army to serve. You can't be as old-fashioned as your father! He married you off at fifteen without asking you for your consent, and you know how you suffered. And now you want to do the same to your son. And my daughter is two years older than Nathan. It would be ridiculous for them to marry. I know it is written that at eighteen a man should marry; but it is also written, Build a house and plant a vineyard, then marry."

We became very friendly with the Reznikoffs. Elizavetgrad was the nearest city to their village, and Nathan, his father and mother, his brothers and sisters, would often come to town. When Nathan's father, Simon, came, Father and Simon Reznikoff sat up until late at night in talk.

In September, Father told us that he was going away on a trip that would take a long time. He was to be paid thirty roubles a month besides his expenses. "Now," he said to me, "you will be able to keep most of your money for yourself, and I hope you'll have enough for the course you want to buy." He planned to see Israel, too.

It wasn't long before I sent for Glazhdinsky's *System of Cutting for Dressmakers and Tailors.* The books and an instructor's lessons cost fifty roubles. But I was soon able to make dresses that fit. I also copied the patterns in any size for tailors and was paid fifty copecks each. This was easy money and cost me nothing but time, for the tailors furnished the paper. Here, it seemed to me, was a good business for Father and I was eager to have him home: he was quick and would have no trouble making the patterns. I now made house-dresses, too. This was much better than sewing linen. I was paid a rouble and a half for the cheapest dress and all it cost me was two copecks for thread. (I was paid twenty copecks for a shirt and the thread cost me six.) Things were beginning to look brighter.

Father had been away two months. Now the weather became bad—heavy rains and deep slush in the streets. Some days people could not leave their homes. And there were many sudden deaths. Soon we knew there was an epidemic in the country—influenza. Father sent us many letters and at last one that made us uneasy. As we read it, we all felt that he was unwell, but we did not speak of our fear.

One night I went to sleep late, tired and worried. I dreamt that I was in our yard. There was a fiery cloud in the sky, and as I looked at it, it seemed like a lion. I went into the house, and there I found a woman who had lived near us in Dimitrefka. I know I am dreaming, I said, but I just saw a burning-red lion in the sky. That is a sign that your father is dead, she answered. I screamed and woke, relieved to find it was all a dream.

For a long time I could not fall asleep, and then I dreamt again. I was cutting black goods into a dress and someone asked me what I was doing that for. Why, I have to wear it, I answered. I woke up and found Mother beside me. "What is the matter with you?" she asked. My cheeks were wet with tears and I shook for cold.

I dressed myself and tried to forget my dreams. Mother said, "I suppose you were reading a silly novel before you went to bed." I told her nothing and went for a long walk. It was Saturday. When I came back, I prayed with all my might, chanted psalms, and wept bitterly, taking care that Mother should not see me. I felt a little better after that. We all had dinner; the younger children were joking, and Hyam danced about and played with them: it was very lively.

In three weeks we had a letter from Father that he was on his way home. This was on a Monday. Wednesday we had another letter that he was sick, and he wrote that as soon as he reached his stopping-place he would send us his address. On the very next day we had a telegram from a hospital in Ekaterinoslav: Father had been taken there. Michael left on the next train.

When the telegram came, I didn't talk, I couldn't cry or pray. I just waited. I thought, How can Michael bring Father home when he is sick? And in this ,weather? And then I was afraid to think. I began to watch the door Friday morning, though I knew Michael could not possibly come before six at night. I waited until it was dark. The table was set, the five candles lit, and we had our supper. Someone said, "Religious people ought not to cry on Saturday," and I began to cry. I could not stop. I sat at the window and watched the yard. At nine o'clock a messenger came in. I sprang to the door and tore open the telegram. It was from Michael; the message had only two words: *he died*.

When I came to, my arm hurt me: I must have fallen on it. Hyam had just come in, for he still had his coat on. He was saying, "What are you screaming for, you crazy girl?"

"Father's dead!"

"Well, he's dead and buried and you can't help him now."

"Oh, how can you be so cold?"

"I found Rachmiel outside in his shirt screaming away like you."

"But how did you find out?"

"The messenger met me, so I hurried home."

I saw nothing and thought of nothing, I only wailed. Late at night, Mother came to quiet me and took me in her arms. We wept together a long time. When I opened my eyes Saturday morning Mother was reading the prayers. Somebody told me that on Saturday mourners must not cry, because the day is a festival. But how could I help it? In the evening about ten men came and made the prescribed cuts in our clothing; and my brothers said the prayer for the dead.

The first three days of mourning, the neighbors prepared our meals. Mother, Hyam, Abram, and I sat on the floor, as the custom is; but Frieda was only eleven and did not have to, nor Rachmiel, who was nine. Fishel was not quite seven.

Since Mother was in business, she was told she might go to her stand even on the third day, but she felt that she could not.

On Wednesday I found Rachmiel sick. He had a headache and a pain in his side. I took towels, wet them in cold water, and put them to his head and body.

We hardly knew what we were doing. But on Friday, Mother stood up from the floor, and told us all to stand up. She was always so quiet that I was not prepared to hear her say, "We must all be heroes now and not cry or complain. We must carry the burden Father carried, until the younger children can help themselves."

Monday, Mother went to business. I was about to begin my work, but I saw that Rachmiel was weak and pale. I carried him to the doctor. When I came in, the doctor asked, "What happened to you? Were you sick?"

"No," I said, "but my father died."

Dr. Rosenstein shook his head. "A young man, a young man. When I came to Elizavetgrad to study, he was eighteen years old. He used to bring sweet biscuits to those of us too poor to go home holidays. He was well-off—then. . . . How time flies."

"Yes," I said, "he was eighteen then and I am twenty now."

"What did he die of?"

"Pneumonia."

He examined my brother. "What did you do for him?" I told him. "Well, he had pneumonia, too, but he is getting better now."

On the way home Rachmiel fell asleep. I thought that he was dying. I had ten more blocks to go and reached home in a sweat. But a neighbor reassured me. "He is only asleep," she said. "Don't wake him. Sleep is better than medicine."

Michael had written us that it had taken him more than twenty-four hours from Elizavetgrad to Ekaterinoslav, and when he same there, he found Father buried. On his way back, he was going to stop at a number of towns to try to earn his fare.

He brought Father's baggage. Mother opened it, and on top she found a bundle of long sheets of paper, carefully wrapped. They were covered with verse in Hebrew, and Abram was the only one of us who could read it at all. Father had been somewhat free in his speech, and Mother was afraid there might be something Nihilistic in his writing that would get us all into trouble. She was afraid to ask an outsider what the writing was about. In those days it was enough to say of a family, "They are Nihilists," to have them arrested at once; the police investigated at their leisure. There was too much to burn at one time, so Mother burnt a few sheets every morning until all were gone. As she put the first into the fire she said, "Here's a man's life."

We had to give up one of our three rooms to make ends meet. Mother brought a woman to look at the room, and as I saw them coming into the yard, dressed in black and in heavy boots, I said to myself, The same uniform: they are from the same club. Malka liked the room, and she said to me, "I have a little daughter, Duba, eleven years old. You'll take her among your girls and teach her to sew, won't you?" Malka's husband had been a capmaker. He was taken sick with influenza at a fair and died there. She had two children: her elder daughter was engaged to a capmaker, and only Duba was on her hands.

One of Father's acquaintances called on Mother. He would put Israel in business for himself, if Israel would go into partnership with his son, Benjamin. When Nathan Reznikoff's mother came to town, we told her what was being planned for Israel. She said she would furnish the money if Israel and Nathan became partners. We knew Benjamin to be a wild fellow. It seemed to us that Nathan would make a better partner, though the Reznikoffs were not as rich as Benjamin's father. I wrote Israel of both offers. He answered that on his way home he would stop at Znaminka and see the Reznikoffs; but that was nine months off: he would not be free until then.

The president of the city school was another acquaintance of Father's. (They had been at school together.) He had no children. He asked Mother to come to his house, and when she did, offered to adopt Rachmiel. Mother thought this excellent for Rachmiel, but he asked, "What will I have to do?"

"You'll be his son. You'll have a good education, go to the *gymnasium* and the university. You'll have the best of everything, but you'll have to call him father and have his name."

Rachmiel—he was only nine—said, "I certainly should like to be a learned man, but I won't take his name and call him father instead of my father. I'll go to work as Israel and Abram did, and be a self-made man." In the spring, Abram told us that Tsali Kaminski wanted an errand boy, and Rachmiel would do. We were supposed to clothe and feed him. But in a week, dressed in a new white suit, he brought his other clothes home, and told us Mrs. Kaminski would give him clothes and food and had even promised him some education.

When Father had been dead for a year, the eldest son of Moses Mandel—the man who had swindled Grandfather Fivel out of his house—came to ask Grandfather's forgiveness. Moses

Mandel was dead and his son, the lawyer, had died of consumption when still young. Mandel's eldest son had just lost his own son. Though he was not rich he wanted to pay Grandfather something for the house. Grandfather would not take it. "Not now, not now," he said. "God will judge between us."

A brother-in-law of one of our neighbors and his son, Isaac, came to the fair in our city. They were from a village near Poland and spoke a Yiddish unlike ours. When the fair was over, our neighbor asked me if I liked her nephew. "Oh," I said, not thinking of anything, "he's nice enough for a country boy."

She said, "He's young, he's only twenty-one, but he's the eldest and doesn't have to serve in the army. He likes you, and if you want me to, I'll write him and he'll be back in a few weeks and you'll be engaged."

I was surprised and told her I would let her know. I wanted to think it over. I was sure I could not have Nahum. He had still three years to serve and his family had become rich and we were poorer than ever. Rebecca's nephew was not bad-looking and not a fool. If he would live in the city and be among merchants instead of peasants, he would be no worse than my brothers.

When he came, I told him that if we were to marry, we must live in the city. I did not want any jewelry or fine clothes, I was willing to keep on as I had been doing—I had four machines now—I would help him all I could, but I would not go into the country to live, even if I should have only a piece of bread every other day in the city. "It's so stupid in the country. I had a taste of it for several years. If your family will say yes to your living in the city, we may become engaged."

58

During the summer we wrote to each other. In the autumn, Isaac and his father came again to the fair. They brought me two rings and a pair of earrings, and wanted to have the formal engagement at Christmas.

Israel was coming home. With him came Simon Reznikoff and his son Nathan. They had agreed upon a partnership and were to open a leather store; Nathan was to stay with us.

Nathan Reznikoff was always finding fault with me. He would call me proud. I would say that I could not be proud, because I knew so little and was not as beautiful or as wise as I should like to be.

Malka, the widow who lived with us, stood in the doorway of her room and said, "He is right: you are proud."

"But why do you think so?"

"You never go out with the other girls. You think yourself better than they."

I explained that the girls wanted to walk on the boulevard Saturday afternoon, but that I walked about all week and wanted to rest Saturday. "And I don't get a chance to read all week, but Saturday is my day for reading."

"What you say shows that you think yourself better than they!" cried Malka.

Nathan found out that I was to be engaged. His mother came to see us and objected. At Christmas time, Isaac's mother came and tried to persuade me to live in the country. "You'll get married," she said, "and you'll open a little store and you'll live there. You can do better there than here with your sewing-machines."

There were other guests and we talked about life in a village. "Isaac ought to live in the city among merchants," I said. "And, besides, once you are settled in the country, it is very hard to bring up children properly, because there are no schools."

Isaac's mother said, "She is already thinking about educating her children." I blushed and everybody laughed.

When I picked up courage to speak again, I said, "The door is wide open, when you go in; but it is very narrow when you want to come out. I'll go to any city or even to America, but I'll never go into the country."

The guests became angry at me. One said, "What is she dreaming of?" And another, "She wants to fly high."

I answered, "I cannot help it, I was born that way."

Next morning Isaac came to talk to me. We were alone. "You ought to give in to my mother now," he said, "and when we are married, we'll have our own way."

"I don't want to fool anybody, Isaac. And I won't break your mother's heart. I won't even visit you there. I hate the country."

"You didn't have to say you want to go to America."

"But I do want to go."

"Well, Mother said that she didn't want us to become engaged, because it would not be right for us to break it off afterwards, since you have no father."

As he was saying this, I took off their rings and earrings. I went to my chest of drawers and took out the little box lined with red velvet in which they came. I put them neatly inside. He was still talking and did not notice what I was doing.

"Here are your presents, Isaac," I said. "I am the one to break our engagement. Good luck to both of us and you go your way and I'll go mine."

He turned pale. I thought he was going to faint. He didn't touch the box, but stood up and went out. I sent my little sister with the presents to his aunt's house.

What a lot of talk about it followed! My family, too, were against me. "Why am I wrong?" I asked. "If he will live

in the city, I will not break the engagement. I told him all
that before we became engaged."

Mother and my brothers said, "It doesn't matter where you
live: you can be happy anywhere." Finally, my brother Israel
and Nathan Reznikoff went to see the place where Isaac lived.
When they came back, Israel did not say a word, but Nathan
had a great deal to say. He said I would not be able to stand
it one day. "Why, Znaminka," he said, "is a place of refinement
compared to that village. The peasantry there is worse than
ours and there is only one other Jewish family."

Mother shook her head. "I hope you won't feel sorry."

"Mamma," I said, "let me go to America."

"You inherited that idea from your father."

"I don't see why we are staying here. Many people have
gone to America and they are better off."

"Maybe if they were here, they'd be better off too, and if
we were there, we'd be badly off. God is everywhere."

"But doesn't the Talmud say, 'Change your place, change
your luck'?"

"You're too smart, my daughter," she said and went out
of the room.

Many matchmakers came to us and I had other suitors.
Father had said, "If you want to make a good match, marry
somebody twenty per cent beneath you;" but these were one
hundred per cent beneath me.

So a year and a half went by. Israel had to serve his term
in the army. We never thought he would have to go, because
he was short-winded; but he was the first of the Jewish quota
to be taken. Now we could not see how we should keep up
the family. In a few weeks his business would have to be
sold: Nathan did not want to stay. Though he was the eldest
son, in another year he would have to serve, too.

"Israel," I said, "let us both go to America. We'll do well

there and then we can bring the others over. We have enough money just now to go."

He became angry and looked at me with his large black eyes: "I am ashamed of you when I hear you talk that way. Why should you want to go to America? Who goes there but bankrupts, embezzlers, and those who have wrecked their lives here?"

"Every intelligent person who can see farther than he can see from his window goes there now."

"Well," he answered, "then I am not intelligent enough."

I showed him how bad things would be with us if he had to serve four years. "But I expect to be out in nine months," he said.

"I hope so, too," I said, "but I had also hoped that you would not have to serve at all."

Israel went away at Christmas. Before he left, I asked him to take a trip to our Uncle Abram Loeb to see Grandfather Fivel.

"I hope I don't have to go to him soon," said Israel.

"Why not?"

"He is dead."

"Why didn't you tell me?"

"We had the other grandchildren there, but you were so upset over Father's death, we were afraid to tell you." Grandfather Fivel was ninety-six when he died.

That winter was a hard one. The slush in the streets was so deep we could hardly go from house to house.

One Saturday night, we had just lit the lamp and I was arranging my work for the next day, when in came Arele, the cantor. He said, "Good evening," and then looked at me. He made a wry face. "So this is your daughter," he said to Mother. "Pst, what a beauty! And all the money she has!"

He took a pinch of snuff. "Why does she make such a fuss? Much nicer girls than she haven't a chance now."

"Why do you insult me?" I said. "That's a nice way to begin the week."

"I have a right to insult you. I was your father's friend."

"Oh, my father had a lot of good friends."

"But," said Arele, "be reasonable. There's a young man who wants you. His mother is willing to give away her house and everything she has. He's good-looking, too." And he told us his name.

"Oh, yes," I said, "he's very good-looking, prettier than any girl I know. I have nothing against him, but I don't like him."

"What do you mean *like him?* You'll learn to like him when you're married."

Mother said bitterly, "Really, they are honest, decent people."

"Well," said Arele, "I'm going to make an appointment for tomorrow at three o'clock. You'll see him again and you'll like him." I said nothing. "He'll be here with his mother. Good night."

When he was gone, Mother said, "What objection have you to this young man?"

"He stutters so. He makes me sick when he talks."

The next day at three o'clock they came. We had tea. Mother and his mother talked. I said little. His mother had heavy, old-fashioned jewelry on and she said, "I'll give you all, all, if you'll be a good daughter to me."

"I don't wear any jewelry," I said.

"Oh, everybody wears jewelry. You must wear it too." And they went away. The engagement was to take place next day at four o'clock. They had not asked me; Mother had said yes and I did not know what to say. I did not want to hurt Mother, she was so set on marrying me off.

Next day, as always, Mother went away at dawn. I rose a little later: I used to go to bed late. At seven o'clock the girls who worked for me came. I did not know what to do. I did not want to become engaged to this fellow, because I did not want to marry him. Everybody knew that I had broken one engagement and to break another would be dreadful. At two o'clock I went off to see my customers and did not come back until ten at night. Mother was waiting for me. "What have you done?" she said. "Why didn't you tell me last night you didn't want the match?" We argued and argued and in the end both of us cried.

The day after Easter I heard shouts and cheers outside. I ran into the yard and met our landlady and her daughter at the gate. Many men were running along the street. I had never seen any of them before.

"What is it?" I asked our landlady. "A fire?"

"No," she said, "they are going to kill the *sheenies*."

"Oh," I said, "and you whose daughter I taught how to sew say this, you who are always telling me how much I did for you!"

"I can't help it," she said, "but they are going to beat them up."

It was an hour and a half before all of us were home. My brothers locked the shutters and windows and barred the doors. "Wouldn't it have been better to have gone to America when Father wanted us to?" I said. "Now we have nowhere to hide."

"God is everywhere," Mother said.

The riot was over in another hour, but the depression

lasted. Many Jews were going to America as soon as they could. Nobody felt like doing business.

In about a week, Uncle Abram Loeb, Father's brother, came to Elizavetgrad. "You did a dreadful thing," he said to me. "Arele told me about it. How can you face anyone? It is true that you are not ugly, but if you've outrun the homely girls, you've not overtaken the pretty ones. And, besides, you're so poor."

"Uncle, why should I marry someone I don't care for? That would not be honest."

"I know you," he said, "you'll make a good wife. Do you expect to be in love?"

"No, but I want to respect the man I marry. I could not respect that fellow. . . . Uncle, I want to go to America, but I have no money now. I have only fifty roubles in the bank and less every day."

Uncle thought a while. "I'll give you fifty roubles to help you to America," he said, "but you must keep it a secret. Even when you are in America, you must tell nobody. I have many relatives and I can't help everyone."

The thought of America was balm to me. I felt stronger than ever.

Michael, my eldest brother, could find no work. Mother had a sister in a small town near a brewery. Her son met Michael at the fair in Elizavetgrad and told Michael he would try to have him hired as a glazier in the brewery. In a few weeks he wrote Michael that he had work for him. I lent him money for the fare. In a week Michael was back and told us he was engaged to my aunt's eldest daughter.

"But how can you get married," I said, "if you can't even make a living for yourself? And why didn't you stay there?"

"Ah, sister," he said, "it's worse there than here."

"Then how are you going to get married?"

"They promised her a little store and I'll do what I am doing now."

"But you are not doing anything now."

"I didn't want to be engaged to her. They wanted me to be engaged. They told me there was going to be an engagement that day and when I came, I found that I was the one to be engaged. And I couldn't say no before all the guests and put her to shame. I don't know what is going to come of it," and the tears rolled down his cheeks.

In a few weeks the girl came to see us. I didn't like her at all, but Mother told me not to say a word.

My brother was married and worse off than ever. He could not live with his wife's people: they had nine children and were glad to be rid of one. So Michael and his wife lived with us.

Israel had served nine months in the army, but he was not let off and still had three years and three months to serve. He became sick. In the hospital he tore out the fly-leaf of a book and wrote me, "My dear sister, go to America. It is God's will." Mother, too, at last consented. "You want to go and you'll have to go, I suppose."

"I don't want to go, if you don't want me to. You must want it with all your heart, or I won't go."

"How can I want it?" she said. "You know how I'll miss you."

"What would you do if I were married and had to go to some village where you would not see me for years? You would want that, but you do not want me to go where it will be good for us."

"How do you know it will be?"

Elka Budnichenkoff, who lived across the street, was going to America in three weeks. Her husband had been there nine months and had sent her steamship tickets and money for herself and the children. I was eager to go with her.

On the fast of the ninth of Ab I fasted too, and went to the cemetery. On the way I met Nathan Reznikoff coming to the city in a wagon. He jumped down. "What are you doing here?" he asked. I had not seen him since Israel went away. I told him that I was going to pray at the graves of my family before I went to America. I told him, too, how sorry I was not to be able to go to my father's grave, but I could not afford the fare.

"So you are going to America," he said.

"Yes, that is the only way to better ourselves."

"Well," he said, "I'll tell you a secret: I'm going to America too. I'm now on my way to Elizavetgrad to arrange to go with the Budnichenkoffs."

"And your parents let you go?"

"Oh, my mother has changed a good deal since your brother had to serve."

Three weeks went by. Mrs. Budnichenkoff left for America. And then one day Mother came home at one o'clock instead of four. She put her basket down and wiped the sweat from her face.

"What have you there, Mamma?" I asked. "Are you going to make me an engagement party?"

"I suppose I am not worthy of that. I met Nahum Zlinkoff. They are going to America in two weeks and will take you along. I'm going to make you zwieback for the trip. Finish your work and sell out whatever you have—and God take care of you."

I was worried about my sister Frieda and my youngest brother Fishel. Frieda was almost fourteen. Where could she find work when I was gone? Fishel was weak and not bright and had not learned anything.

Mother had spells of crying. "You are not worse off," I tried to comfort her, "than so and so"—and I named women in our town whose daughters had committed suicide—"or those whose daughters have consumption. You ought to be much more hopeful than if I threw myself away on some worthless fellow."

"I trust in God and also in you that it will be right in the end, but now it has a bitter taste."

"A hard beginning, a good end," I said to cheer myself up as well as Mother.

I went to Uncle Abram Loeb for the fifty roubles he had promised me. He lived in Hubovka, a village about fifteen miles from Elizavetgrad.

Abram Loeb's first wife had died of consumption. His second wife was always praying and lifting up her eyes to Heaven. Though my uncle was well-to-do, she would not let him educate her stepchildren; all they knew was what our grandfather Fivel had managed to teach them.

When Uncle's eldest son was nineteen, she insisted that he marry a niece of hers. This niece was twenty-five and so ugly no one would have her. Abram Loeb forced his son to become engaged to her, but before the marriage my cousin became consumptive and died.

Uncle's eldest daughter lost her husband six months after their marriage. When her son was born, she made up a lullaby that began,

"I forget he is dead and I think that he lives,
But when you cry, I remember our sorrow."

Dvoira, the younger daughter, made up a song when she became engaged; the younger son also made up a song about his stepmother.

Dvoira had been engaged a long time. Her stepmother

told Uncle that Dvoira had all the clothes she needed, but all she had was a blouse and an old green skirt someone had pawned at her stepmother's for thirty-five kopecks. The neighbors reproached Uncle. At last he bought some cloth and had a tailor over from Elizavetgrad to make Dvoira a coat and a dress. His wife came from her room as the dress was tried on. A number of the neighbors had come in to gossip with the tailor. She went up to Dvoira and stooping took the hem of the skirt in her hand.

"This is expensive cloth, isn't it?" she said sweetly.

"The best I could buy," said Uncle.

She flushed and screamed before them all, "May you take it off her dead body!"

Uncle stood up and struck the table so that the glasses jumped. "I have lived with you twenty years," he said, "and did not know until now that my children have a stepmother."

When I came to Hubovka, Dvoira had become consumptive. Uncle told me that the doctors said that if she would go to Yalta, she might be cured. That would cost five hundred roubles and her husband did not have the money. Uncle had, but his wife wanted him to spend it in having a scroll of the Torah written and placed in a synagogue in her name.

"But Uncle," I said, "the life of a human being is more than another scroll of the Torah."

"You see," Uncle said, "your aunt has no children. All she would have after her death is this scroll of the Torah. That is just as if she had a son."

"But isn't there time for that? Dvoira's sickness won't wait."

There were tears in Uncle's eyes and he looked wrinkled and old. "Don't tell anybody about this," he said. He promised to bring me the fifty roubles and I went off to see some acquaintances.

They told me of a strange thing that had happened: the

son of a neighbor stole the eggs from the stork's nest on his father's barn and put goose eggs there instead for a joke; after the goslings were hatched, hundreds of storks flew over the barn, making a great racket; suddenly, they crowded down upon the nest and with their long bills tore the mother bird, goslings and nest to bits. When I came to Hubovka, the barn had just burned to the ground, and no one knew how the fire had started.

Uncle brought me the money, and in a few days I was off to America. The station was crowded: thirty families of our town were leaving for the New World. Mother introduced me to the Zlinkoffs, and they promised her I should be with them all the way to America.

In the train, Mrs. Zlinkoff told me that her eldest son, Isaac, a friend of my brother Hyam, had been in America a little over a year. He had sent them all—there were six of them—steamship tickets. Isaac was a tailor and I thought he must be doing well to be able to do that. Mrs. Zlinkoff's brother had given them money for their expenses to the steamer, but she was afraid they would not have enough. I thought, Hyam went to Odessa; why didn't he go to America with Isaac? My brothers are all cowards.

I had only ninety-three roubles. I was told that I ought to have at least a hundred, but the Zlinkoffs promised to help me, if they would receive money in Hamburg—Isaac had written that he would try to send them some. They put my baggage with theirs and I did not have to bother with it.

I was so sick in the train they all thought I would turn back at Kremenchuck, because the worst was yet to come. It took us weeks to cross the border. It would have been no trouble for me to get a passport to leave the country, but the Zlinkoffs had two sons who would soon have had to serve in the army. Most of our party were young men like that. From Kremenchuk we went down the Dnieper to Homel on a large raft. There we met the agent of the men in the business of helping emigrants across the border. He sent us to Wilna and from Wilna we went to Kovno. At Kovno we were bundled into a covered wagon and taken to a village. Here we rested a few days. We left in the wagon and travelled all night and most of the next day through fields and woods, up and down hill. In the middle of a field, a man stopped us and gave us each a passport. Mine was that of a man seventy years old and a young man with us was given the passport of an old woman. It didn't matter, though. In broad daylight we rode into a German city, our baggage was examined, and we were free of Russia.

Here we had to pay our fares. Shestokovsky, who knew my brother Israel, asked me for twenty-five roubles until he could change a hundred rouble bill. "I'll give you the twenty-five roubles tomorrow," he said.

"I cannot do it," I answered. "I have just enough—and perhaps not enough—for the trip. I will not let any of it out of my hand."

"Well," he said, "hold the hundred rouble bill until we can change it, and let me have twenty-five roubles."

"That I can do," I said.

When I went for my steamship ticket in Hamburg, I found I was five roubles short. And no money had come for the Zlinkoffs. The boat for Glasgow was leaving the next day. They advised me to ask Shestokovsky to lend me five roubles —he had plenty—but I felt I could not. "I'll sell my two pillows," I said. I had a good deal of trouble finding my baggage. As I began to unpack it, fifty roubles came for the Zlinkoffs by telegraph. They lent me five and I bought my ticket. I had just one copeck left, but I was on board the boat to Glasgow, and would not need any money until I came to America.

The sea was so rough and so much water poured into the boat, we thought we should all be drowned. At Glasgow, we met the first people friendly to us on the journey. They gave us cider to refresh us after the boat trip, then a good supper and beds with clean sheets.

We were on the Atlantic for three weeks. Our ship was old and slow and this was its last trip, we were told. Sometimes, there was a flood below deck. I was very sick. I said all my psalms and prayers. Some of the people made fun of me, but I didn't care: when I said the psalms I felt better. As we came into the harbor of New York, the cabin passengers gathered on the upper deck and sang *Home, Sweet Home*. I understood the two words—like the Yiddish—and I and some of the others who knew it sang the Russian song beginning:

"I have forsaken my father's house;
The path to it is lost in the weeds."

At Castle Garden a doctor examined us. One of the Zlinkoff children was sickly and they were all taken away. An official asked me to whom I was going. A second cousin of Father's had given me the address of someone in New Haven. "Have you any money?" the official asked.

"Nothing."

He showed me where to get food and drink. He spoke a simple German I could understand. "After Yom Kippur" [the Day of Atonement]—that was the next day—"we will see what we can do with you." He spoke gently and I thought him very kind.

Many of the women were waiting for their husbands. They promised to take me with them. We stood, looking about, like birds in a cage. At four o'clock my name was called. I saw a gentleman outside. He doesn't know me, I thought. It must be somebody else with the same name.

The woman in charge came over to me. *"Mademoiselle,* this is your name, isn't it?"

"I thought it was somebody else with the same name," I said, and walked up to the stranger.

"I am Doctor Zolotaroff," he said. "I don't know you and you don't know me, but my father and your father were good friends. He wants me to bring you to his house."

"How does he know I am here?" I asked. I hesitated, and then made up my mind not to go. "But how can I go with you if I don't know you?" I said.

"Do you know the Zlinkoffs?" he asked. "I am taking them along with you."

The Zolotaroffs were distant relatives of the Zlinkoffs. When the Zlinkoffs were held at Castle Garden, Isaac Zlinkoff went to Doctor Zolotaroff to ask his help. Isaac happened to say that a girl had come with his parents, a Wolvovsky, without relatives or friends in America. The doctor's father knew mine and asked the doctor to take me along.

The Zolotaroffs lived on East Broadway. When we came there, the doctor's father was not at home. After our meal we went into the parlor; it was crowded with people to see the newcomers. I didn't know anybody, though some had just come from Elizavetgrad. I envied the Zlinkoffs because they had so many friends.

The doctor's father came in. Mr. Zolotaroff had a long white beard and a good-natured, intelligent face. He shook hands with everybody and kissed the Zlinkoffs. Then he sat down next to me.

"Whose daughter are you, Abram Loeb's or Ezekiel's?"

"Ezekiel's."

"And how is your father?"

"My father has been dead for almost three years."

His eyes filled with tears. When he could speak, he told me that my father had been one of his best friends. Mr. Zolotaroff's father and mother had died when he was so young he could not remember them; at nine he was apprenticed to a tailor; and it was not until he was sixteen that he could begin to study the Bible and Talmud. Father used to help him in his studies. "Therefore," he said, "you are not to feel like a stranger in my house. Come to me for advice and help and whatever I can do for you, I will do. You are to think of me as your friend—as Ezekiel Wolvovsky was mine."

He asked me if I had any relative or friend in America. I could not remember any. I gave him the letter I had to the man in New Haven. Mr. Zolotaroff knew him: he was a tailor. So was Mr. Zolotaroff. I told him that I had never worked at tailoring.

"The first thing to learn in America," he said "is that you can do everything. You will learn how. The first thing to do is to *try.*"

"What does *try* mean?"

"This is what it means: when you are asked if you can do a certain kind of work, say yes; sit down and do it as well as you can. If the boss or foreman doesn't like the way you do it, he sends you away and you go to another place. By this time you know a little about it and you try again. If you like to work, you are sure to learn."

It became late and I wondered where they would put all the people. The doctor's mother came over to me and said, "Well, daughter, you are tired. Take a hot bath, here is a nightgown, and you'll sleep with me." It seemed to me that I had come to the home of two angels, a beautiful old man and woman who cared for the troubled of all the world.

I had a bath and was in Mrs. Zolotaroff's soft warm bed when Mr. Zolotaroff called to me. "I remember now that you have somebody here, a second cousin of yours, Simon Reznikoff's son. I saw him last week."

"Yes, he's here! I know him well. He was my brother's partner."

"You'll find him at the Bershadskys. Tomorrow is Yom Kippur and he'll be at home."

When I awoke, Mrs. Zolotaroff had gone to synagogue. I asked for Nathan Reznikoff's address. "You have had a good sleep," Mr. Zolotaroff said. "It is almost eleven. Eat something before you go."

"I have fasted Yom Kippur since I was twelve," I said, "and I am twenty-three now. I have always thought it a sin to eat on Yom Kippur."

"But it's foolish to fast. You understand that, don't you?"

"I do not trouble myself about religious questions. I believe in what I was brought up to believe: I like it."

"Your father wasn't such a fool as you," said Mr. Zolotaroff good-naturedly.

"But Father was religious."

"It's cold outside and you're lightly dressed."

"I didn't bring any warm clothes. I was told that it was warm in America."

He gave me his shawl. Mrs. Zlinkoff said to Isaac, "Take her there, so she won't lose her way."

When we were in the street, Isaac said, "Aren't you ashamed to walk with a tailor?" I blushed. "Here you'll find that we are all tailors."

The Bershadskys lived on the fifth floor. I asked for Nathan Reznikoff and told them I was his cousin. Mr. Bershadsky said, "Nathan went to synagogue. He's staying at my sister's now."

"Who is your sister?" I asked.

"Elka Budnichenkoff."

"She lived across the street from me! I made her children's clothes before she left." He gave me her address. I wrote it on a slip of paper and asked Isaac for the address of the Zolotaroffs. I thanked him and told him I did not want to make him come along. I asked my way of the passers-by and came to the home of the Budnichenkoffs by myself.

When I opened the door, their four little daughters ran up to me, hugged me and kissed me. The Budnichenkoffs lived at Ninety-nine Willett Street; they shared a flat with another family. The men would buy men's old trousers, and in one of their rooms they cut and sewed them into trousers for boys. Mrs. Budnichenkoff and the other woman pressed the trousers and sewed the buttons on. They taught Nathan how to use a sewing-machine and he was working with them. All this the eldest Budnichenkoff girl—she was about eleven—told me happily. Now everybody was in synagogue.

Mr. Budnichenkoff came late in the afternoon. He went back to synagogue and it wasn't long before Nathan came. Mrs. Budnichenkoff said, "Stay with us. We are crowded anyway and what is one more? There are enough at the Zolotaroffs. You'll soon find work. I wish I knew as much as you." After we broke our fast, Nathan and I went to the Zolotaroffs. I thanked them for all they had done for me.

"Don't worry about how you are going to get on here," Mr. Zolotaroff said to us. "America is a mother: she feeds you and clothes you and helps you in everything. I wrote a letter to New Haven," he said to me, "but you mustn't sit around and wait for an answer. Look for work."

Next day I did. I was told where to go, but instead of turning to the right, I went to the left. I walked on and on, looking at the crowds. I had never seen so many people. At

76

Brooklyn Bridge, I watched them pouring out of the street-cars and the railway station. All strangers, I thought, and felt very lonely.

I walked on to William Street. At last I asked my way of an old man. He had just stepped out of a carriage. I spoke Yiddish and showed him the slip of paper on which I had my addresses. He walked with me all the way to Broadway and showed me how to go to Walker and Lispenard Streets. When I came there, it was late and in all the shops I went to I was told, "No work."

I went to the Zolotaroffs. They were as friendly as ever. Mr. Zolotaroff worked quickly, a thousand stitches for a penny. Times were bad, he said, there was a financial panic in the country, but better times were coming. I heard a man in the yard calling, "Line, line." What a sad voice, I thought, and went to the window: the man was in rags.

"What does he want?" I asked.

"What we all do," said Mr. Zolotaroff. "Bread."

"Bread?"

"He is asking for clothes-lines to hang. . . . America is a blessed land, a land of great plenty. But it isn't regulated yet. The people have poured into this country from Europe, and some have too much and some not enough. Do you see this coat that I am making? I used to be paid eight dollars for it. Now I am paid only five. The Zlinkoffs will make money, but I am an old man. I can make only one coat a week. That's five dollars. I must try to get better work, but it's hard to get any at all."

Some girls came in. Mrs. Zolotaroff told them that I had already been looking for work. They smiled and one said, "I have been looking for work for three months and can't find any." This frightened me—somewhat.

I went back to the Budnichenkoffs. They were busy. I

threaded a needle and sewed on buttons. I helped set the table and wash the dishes and felt at home.

The next day was Saturday. I did not want to look for work that day: I wanted to keep it as a day of rest. I went to the Zolotaroffs.

"It's lucky you came," Mr. Zolotaroff said. "I have a letter from New Haven. They want you to go there. They have a son of fourteen or fifteen and he is coming here to take you. Go home now and be ready."

The boy of fourteen or fifteen was tall and quite a young gentleman. I was sorry for him—dragging me along in my European clothes, a grey coat and a white hat. I found his father and mother plain and simple and his sisters kind. They had been in America eight years and were doing well. I was to work for them for six dollars a week. They would keep two and a half dollars of this for my board and lodging and I was to have the rest in cash.

I had promised the Zlinkoffs to begin to repay the five roubles they had lent me, and I owed Elka Budnichenkoff for board and lodging; but I first bought myself a pair of shoes—mine were worn out—and a hat for forty-nine cents. And the next week I sent my mother three dollars.

I began to feel that my work did not please the people I was with. I had never worked for a tailor, and at this time they had only coats and furs to fix. In a few weeks, too, the work slackened. I thought it would be better for me to work in a factory. I could do best at waists, shirts, or wrappers. But in New Haven there were only corset factories.

On a Monday, after I had been in New Haven five weeks, we had little to do in the shop. The younger daughter said to me, "Let's go home and work at home." They told me there was a lot of washing to do. I did not mind washing the clothes of my own family, but I did not like to do it for others. I had helped with the dishes and about the house, but this was hard for me to stomach. But I thought I ought not to feel that way about it—I was one of the family—and I washed their clothes.

In another week they had no work in the shop, not even for themselves. They advised me to stay with them until after Christmas, then they would try to find work for me in a corset factory. Beginners were paid five dollars a week. I thought I could do much better at work I knew. Besides, I liked New York better than New Haven. New Haven reminded me of Elizavetgrad. I had to do what everybody else did—buy a new coat on payments to be dressed like the others.

I told the old man that I should be sorry to leave New Haven for one thing—I did not have to work Saturdays. I did not know what I should have to do in New York. "But my children are going to work Saturdays," he said. "They want to build up the business."

In New York I found that the small shops in which I looked for a job were working long hours, from seven in the morning until ten at night; and at that I could not find work. Business in the factories was at its dullest before Christmas.

I lived at the Budnichenkoffs. I had saved some money in New Haven and I paid the Zlinkoffs what I owed. I had my pillows there, and they wanted me to take them away, but I had no place to put them.

One day at the Zlinkoffs, I met an old man who knew all my people. "You have a rich relative here named Shlikerman," he said.

"Yes," I said, "now I remember that my father once wrote a letter to a Mrs. Shlikerman."

"I'll give you her address and you go there."

"I want to find a job first."

I found work sewing flannels. Even experienced help did not do well at that work. After a bad day I came home to find them all excited. Mrs. Shlikerman had been to see me. She left word that I was not to go to work next day, and a friend of hers would bring me to her house. "I can't go there now," I said. "I'll lose my job."

I received a letter from home. They wrote that they were doing well. I knew it was not true, but I could not help them.

One day I was told there was no more work, and I came home in the morning. I went to Mrs. Shlikerman's friend, and she took me to Brooklyn. Mrs. Shlikerman looked like a sister of hers whom I had known in Russia. She was very friendly and said that I must stay with her for a rest. She told me I could not find work until after Christmas, and then she would find work for me. "I have many acquaintances," she said. "In the meantime you will not have to be idle." She gave me slip-covers to make. I also had a chance to fix my coat: it was not very warm, but it did not look so bad.

The slip-covers took me about a week to cut and sew. I found Mr. Shlikerman—a clever, learned, and good man—as interesting as Mr. Zolotaroff. Nathan Reznikoff came to see us, and he and Mr. Shlikerman became friends.

Mrs. Shlikerman found work for me in Brooklyn: one of her friends took me to Siegel-Cooper's factory. Its sewing-machines were run by electricity, and the forewoman had to show me how to use my machine. I understood a little English, but could not speak any. She spoke at the top of her voice. I smiled and by gestures made her understand that I was dumb but not deaf; she laughed and became friendlier.

In about ten minutes I could run the machine, and she gave me part of a nightgown to sew. We did not make all of the gown—some of us sewed one part, some another: this was called "section work." There were five dozen of the part I had to sew in my bundle and when I was through, the forewoman marked it in a little book.

A tall, noble-looking woman sat at the machine next to mine. When the forewoman was gone, she asked to see my book. She showed me by signs that I should have been given twenty cents more for each dozen and that I should speak to the forewoman about it. I did not know what to do. If I complained, I might get my neighbor into trouble. In the morning I brought her a note. In this I had written for me that I did not wish to say anything about the price I was paid, because I did not want to lose the job.

The girl to my left, across the aisle, made fun of me. There was only one other Jewish girl in the place, and she would not talk to me. She was afraid the girls would make fun of her. But the woman next to me brought me a cup and gave me some of her tea at lunch. She tried to teach me the names of what we made and used: sleeves, collars, bands, needle, thread, and the like. I wanted to find out how long she was in America. I learned the words of the question and asked it. She told me that her grandparents were born here. Then I asked her what the other girls were. She said they were foreigners: Irish, Italians, and Bohemians. One day she took my book to the forewoman and demanded that I be paid in full. She came back and told me to look for work elsewhere: now there was work everywhere. And I did not see her again.

Saturday afternoon I went to Mrs. Shlikerman—she had given me a place to board at as soon as I had begun to work at Siegel-Cooper's—and told her what the woman next to me had said. Mrs. Shlikerman took me to a Mr. Kass, who had a large store in New York and knew many manufacturers.

Monday morning Mr. Kass went with me to a factory on Walker Street. They had no machine for me, but would have one in about a week. Nathan Bershadsky advised me to work where he was a cutter. There they made shirts of the best silks and flannels. But I did not want to be a worker always. It seemed to me that at waists or wrappers I should have a chance to be in business for myself. However, I worked with Nathan Bershadsky a few days, until I received a postcard from the place on Walker Street.

The foreman there was a tall, pale, nervous man. He gave me a waist to sew, and when I brought it to his table, looked it over and without a word gave me a bundle of waists to make. The other girls were much faster than I. I was not used to sewing without basting. It seemed to me that European ways were a century behind those here.

One day, a new waist came into style. It was gathered in front and at the collar. The foreman had the goods gathered and then cut it; but when the waists were made, the gathering was out of place. He blamed the girls. The designer was sent for and showed some of the girls how to place the gathering. Only the best hands could do it, and it was such bother they would not.

I finished my bundle of work and the foreman gave me the new waist to sew. I told him I used to make waists like that in Russia without any trouble, but he would have to cut them differently. I cut one waist and it was good. He asked me what I knew of cutting. I told him that I had studied Glazhdinsky's system and had brought the books with me. "You will have to find another place," he said to me the next day. "I cannot have you around: everybody saw you showing me how to make that waist." He gave me an address on Lispenard Street; a Mr. Platt was in need of a designer and I should do well there. I was sorry I had not held my tongue.

82

Mr. Platt set me to work at wrappers. I was paid six dollars a week.

I was living again with the Budnichenkoffs. In about nine months they moved to Forsyth Street. Their rooms were on the top floor. I found it hard to climb the stairs and the smell in the hall was sickening. Nathan Reznikoff was still working for them. His bed was in the same room as the sewing-machines.

That summer was hot; hotter than usual, people said. One day at half-past five Mr. Platt sent us all home. In other shops girls had fainted from the heat. That day I counted the steps I had to climb: there were seventy-two. When I came in, to my surprise Nathan and Mr. Budnichenkoff stopped work. They washed themselves and praised the water. "This is a blessed land," said Mr. Budnichenkoff at the sink, "the water flows from the walls, all the water you want."

After supper, when no one else was about, Nathan asked me to walk with him to Brooklyn Bridge. "I cannot work any more today," he said. "That is the only place to get a little fresh air." As we walked to the bridge, he said, "Do you think I ought to become engaged?" I knew that a relative of his was anxious to have Nathan marry his daughter. I thought it a good thing for Nathan. The girl was good-looking and her family well off. She had a dowry of five hundred dollars and was fond of him. A week before she had come with tickets to a theatre party. Nathan said he would take two. "Why two?" she asked. "I have one." "I'll take my cousin, too," he said, and turned to me. She did not like that, but I thought it nice of him. Her father was with her and asked me jokingly, "How does a girl happen to come to America all by herself?" I had been afraid of that question. Mother had said I should meet it everywhere. "If I had been

83

asked that at Castle Garden, where no one knew me," I answered earnestly, "I might have jumped into the water; but in this house I am well known. Mrs. Budnichenkoff left Elizavetgrad only three weeks before I did." I thought Nathan had this man's daughter in mind, and I said, "It's a good idea. They'll put you on your feet, and you won't have to work so hard."

He gave me an angry look. "I'll get on my feet myself. I want nobody's help. My father and mother wanted to send me money, but I would not take it. But can I become engaged when I am making only seven-fifty a week?"

"If you like each other, it won't matter. She won't want anything of you."

In the meantime we reached the bridge. We found a bench and rested. The air was cool and refreshing. Nathan went on to say he would not marry until he had saved some money and could go into business for himself. I said he was right and he would do well, for he had a good head on his shoulders. "Well, then," he said, "good luck to us!" and took my hand.

"What are you talking about?" I managed to say.

"Have you anything against me?"

"Nothing, but this is no match for you. You know how poor I am, and I must help my family too; and I am not doing as well in America as I thought I should. I am not strong, and I do not want you to be burdened with me."

At last we agreed to say nothing to anyone until Nathan had the consent of his father and mother. "In the meantime," I said, "you will have enough time to make up your mind. Nobody need know, and if you change your mind, nobody will be hurt." We came home late. The night was so hot no one could sleep, and in the morning each of us went to our work.

That night Mrs. Budnichenkoff did not answer me when

I said, "Good evening." I thought she was troubled about something and had not heard me. But when I spoke to her afterwards and she did not answer, I said, "Elka, are you angry at me?"

"Yes," she said. "I never thought you were so false."

"In what way?"

"You are engaged to Nathan and you never told me a word."

Nathan heard us, and came out of the room where he worked. "I told Elka," he said.

She did not believe that we had become engaged only the night before—if we did become engaged. "You are hiding things from me," she said. "I thought you were my friend."

From then on I found her quarrelsome. In the autumn the Budnichenkoffs were to move from four rooms to three. This means, I thought, that they do not want me. Next door to us were the Fertels, and I arranged to sleep with their daughter. It was not comfortable.

Then Nathan quarrelled with the Budnichenkoffs. He and Shestokovsky became partners and they went to New Haven. I was still working at Platt's for six dollars a week. I was good at samples, but other girls made two dozen wrappers in the time I could only make three-quarters of a dozen. One day I said to the girl next to me, "I'm only making six dollars a week."

"What!" she screamed, "I'm doing three times as much as you and I make five and a half!" And what a hullabaloo she raised! Mr. Platt called me into his office and scolded me. I was to have no more than five dollars a week from then on, he said. But I could not get along on that.

Mr. Fertel suggested that I work for a contractor he knew, a Mr. Meyerson. Meyerson had a place on Sheriff Street in a cellar. He said that if I made the trimmings and set in the yokes, I could work there, and took me into a side room to his wife. She had given birth to a child the week before. She had been making the pleating, but now she could only baste it and her husband finished it. I showed them how to make pleatings without basting and ironing. The Meyersons were intelligent. But how poor they were! And they looked consumptive.

When their workers came—there were six of them—each looked as if she would smash everything about her. The girl opposite me had the boldest face of all. She told me she was a Socialist and a "union lady." Mr. Meyerson was afraid of her, gave her work first, and what she said went. She told me what she would like to do to "bosses."

"This one, too?" I asked.

"A boss is a boss. He'll work himself up and be like the rest."

Meyerson went away to the warehouse. At four o'clock several bundles of work were delivered. Next morning I came early. On every machine Meyerson had prepared work for the day. The girl opposite me made the collars. These happened to be of silk with a stiffening of buckram. She put the buckram on top; as she sewed, the silk came together underneath and each collar had buckram—almost two inches of it—over. This she cut off. I thought it best not to say anything, but at last I could not keep still. "Excuse me, Miss," I said, "you are spoiling the collars. They won't fit."

"Do you know what *mind your own business* means?" she said.

"Yes."

"Well, then, do it."

There were ten dozen wrappers in all. The next operator sewed the collars on and gathered in the two inches. And the work went out this way. Meyerson was called to the warehouse. When he came back, he told us he would not be given more work until this was made right. But the girls would not help him.

"What are you all angry about?" I said to them. "Put a wrapper on." A girl did and of course she could not button the collar. "Would you buy a wrapper like this?" I asked.

Meyerson went to the machine of the girl who made the collars, opened the drawer, and took out the pieces of buckram she had cut off. "Here is my trouble," he said. He begged the girls to stay and help him with the wrappers, but they would not.

I helped him, but I said, "I won't be able to be here any longer: the girls will kill me." I should work for the manufacturer instead of a contractor, I thought. I asked Meyerson for the manufacturer's address, went there, and was given work to do at home.

The Fertels had moved into the Budnichenkoffs' old flat. The extra room was Nathan's. He had come from New Haven, sick, and without money. A relative of his lent him twenty-five dollars. He bought a stock of old trousers and made them into trousers for boys. I had a sewing-machine in my room, and there I made my wrappers, but was poorly paid. A girl who lived on the floor below also worked at wrappers, and she told me of Nevins and Ettelson on Lispenard Street. "It would be better for you to work for them," she said. "They pay well. You are careful and they want that kind."

But one morning Mr. Platt sent for me and offered me my old job at seven dollars a week. Nathan advised me to take it: I would not have to carry bundles home and to the factory. By this time I could make any wrapper.

I had a letter from home. They were not doing well. And

Nathan was not doing well. He could not sell his stock of boys' trousers and had no money to buy old trousers.

One Saturday, as I was working at Platt's, I watched the men cutting up thick layers of cloth and the expressmen hauling the bundles away. These are going to contractors like Meyerson, I thought, and people who do not know how to sew a seam, and here am I working for seven dollars a week. I made up my mind to go to Nevins and Ettelson that day and try to get work for Sunday. Mr. Platt wanted me to work overtime or to take work home, but I told him I had something to do.

Nevins and Ettelson had a nice, sunny place on the first floor. A red-bearded man came up to me. "I want to see the boss," I said.

"I am the boss."

"I want work."

"I have no work for you. That's all!" and he walked away.

A boy was sweeping the floor. I asked him who that was.

"Nevins," he said.

"I want to see Mr. Ettelson."

Mr. Ettelson cocked his head and looked at me; he was cross-eyed. "I made up my mind not to give any more work to Jews," he said.

"How do you know my work is as bad as that of others? I know it is said one Jew is answerable for another; but if that is so, you are answerable for your partner who almost chased me out of the place, because I asked for work. Try me," I said.

"For whom do you work?"

"I am making samples for Mr. Platt. I am paid seven dollars a week, but that is not enough for me. I must help my family in Russia. I did this work in Russia and had eight girls working for me."

He said in a gentler voice, "I'll show you why we refused you work," and led me into the show-room. "This is the kind of work they do," and he brought me up to a wrapper on a figure.

I told him what was wrong: the wrapper was of a soft goods and the contractor had used a long stitch that pulled the wrapper out of shape. "You must know how to do this work," I said.

"I'll give you half a dozen of these wrappers. Bring them tomorrow. What time will you be here?"

"Early in the afternoon."

"I pay two dollars and sixty-five cents a dozen for this style." My eyes sparkled.

Next day I was up at dawn. I finished my work early. I could hardly wait for the afternoon. Nathan and Fertel made fun of me. They told me not to be so happy. "You think you're going to be a capitalist," said Fertel, "but you don't know the bosses."

"And you don't know the workers," I said.

Only Nevins, Ettelson, a woman, and a packer were in the place. I opened my bundle. Mr. Ettelson called the woman over. "Very good work," she said in English. "Very fine, very fine."

Ettelson turned to me. "I'm going to send you five dozen of these to make. Have you any other work?"

"No."

"How soon will you deliver it?"

"As quickly as I can. I can bring you some before all are finished, if you want me to."

"Are you doing this work yourself?"

"Yes, but I'll have someone to help me later."

"I warn you," he said, "against hiring men."

Tears in my eyes, I thanked him for the work. He shook hands with me and said, "I am sure you will be a success in this country."

I went home and rested. At half-past four my work came. I could not keep from opening a bundle. I made the collars and belts that day, and brought the wrappers back Wednesday morning. They were examined and I was paid fourteen dollars and fifty-eight cents.

When I came home, Nathan was lying on the couch. He had walked about all morning trying to sell the boys' trousers he had made. "How is your work?" I asked.

He shook his head. "I see you're happy," he said.

I gave him the money. "Deposit it. And I'm to receive another bundle of work soon."

"What have you there?"

"Half a dozen samples. He pays me fifty cents a sample. He's an angel!"

I sat down at my machine. Nathan walked about the room. I was afraid that if I asked him to join me at my work, he would be sure not to. I knew how touchy he was, and that he thought me too ready to tell everybody what to do.

In a few days he happened to say that he hated to use my money for buying the old trousers he made into trousers for boys. "It isn't mine," I said. "There is no *mine* and *yours;* it's ours. But please listen to me: here you are at a dirty work—buying old trousers and making them into trousers for children—why that's criminal! Why should you do that when at my work we have such a future? It's not tailoring; it's not work you ought to be ashamed of. I have my cutting books. You can learn the wrapper trade right here, and when you know that, there are plenty of places where they want young men like you. And you are so good at figures! I see you've made up your mind not to do it, because you think it's against your dignity. You ought to see what foolish contractors there are: I heard one of them trying to excuse himself to Ettelson—the buttons had fallen off his wrappers. I am slow at sewing the long seams. With your energy, if you would only run off the seams for me—we could make three times as much. In a few weeks I am sure you will make a wrapper as well as I. Then you can do what you like—work here or get a job. In time you might be a manufacturer: you've been in business."

Nathan was wild with anger. He called me whatever he could think of, walked up and down the room, and talked and talked. "Well, don't do it," I said, "if you don't want to; this is a free country." But when the next bundle of work was brought, he opened it and took everything out carefully. While I was finishing the work I still had to do, he made the collars and belts.

In a few weeks I asked Mr. Ettelson, "How do you like my work?"

"It's very good," he said.

"Well, a man is doing most of it. He's a second cousin of mine. He's an educated man; he was not a workingman in Russia, but here he worked at knee-pants. I want you to make his acquaintance and all our transactions can be through him. I will have more time, then, for your better work and your samples."

When Nathan went to see Mr. Ettelson, it was raining. The street-car would not stop for him, and he came there dripping wet. As he bent down to undo the bundle, the water ran off his derby upon the wrappers. Ettelson noticed this and scolded him. Nathan came home angry: he would never go there again.

I went the next time, and reminded Mr. Ettelson that

Nathan had not been a workingman in Russia, and was not used to being talked to in that way; soaking wet, he could not help a little clumsiness; and, after all, Mr. Ettelson ought to forgive such little things in greenhorns. Nathan went again to Ettelson and this time they had a long talk: Mr. Ettelson said he would give us a quarter more on a dozen, if we would do our work as well as we had been doing. I seldom went to Ettelson's after that.

One Saturday, when we paid Mrs. Fertel our rent, she told us that from then on it would be eleven dollars. Nathan said, "But you pay only twelve for all the rooms."

"You are making money," she answered, "and I want that much."

We used to take Saturday afternoon off to rest up, and Nathan said, "Let's go for a walk." It was late in the fall and the weather was blustery. "I'm going to look for rooms," he said.

"But how can we?"

"You'll stay there until I fix up a place. Must we work in that tiny bedroom without air—and the water-closet five floors down?"

We found three rooms (at Forty-two Allen Street, corner of Hester)—a sink and washtubs in the kitchen, and the water-closet in the hall—at ten dollars a month. And the house was much cleaner than where we lived. As we walked down the stairs, an old woman stopped us and asked, "Would you let one room to a woman with two children whose husband makes little? They can't pay much."

Nathan said he could let the kitchen. That was just what the woman wanted: it was a big, sunny room.

"What do you want for this room?" she asked.

"What can you pay?" Nathan answered.

"What can I pay? I can pay three dollars. But what do you want?"

She could not believe that we were satisfied with three dollars, and promised Nathan to keep the kitchen door closed so that the children would not bother him while he was working. The old woman then introduced us to her daughter. She lived on the floor below. We hired the old woman to cook for us—she wanted to do it for nothing—and her daughter to sew buttons on the wrappers.

That evening Nathan moved our machines and packages to Allen Street. Then we bought two beds. One went into the bedroom—that was mine—and the other, a folding bed, was Nathan's. This went into the room where we were to work. Nathan had insisted that I move there too. "We don't have to pay people to watch over us," he said. "We can watch over ourselves." In our new quarters we could work as long as we liked; we worked, sometimes, from three in the morning until twelve at night.

A little before Passover I received a letter from Mother. She sent me the address of a cousin who lived in Brownsville, Brooklyn. Nathan said that on Passover we would not work for two days: we would make a holiday of it and visit our cousin.

Brownsville had open fields on all sides, except one, and the air was sweet and clean. The elevated trains that ran on Allen Street used soft coal, and the smoke blew into our windows and choked me. We could rent a store and three rooms in Brownsville, our cousin told us, for only eight dollars a month.

But Mr. Ettelson did not want us to move to Brownsville: it would take another day to bring the goods there and back. Nathan showed him how we could hire help—other contractors had shops in Brownsville—and our deliveries would be better.

Nathan did not want to become a "boss" and have others work for him; but he was anxious to please Ettelson, and we could not do all the work ourselves.

So we moved to Brownsville. That summer I had a letter from home that made me cry. I saw no way out of their troubles but for Mother, my sister, and my youngest brother to come here. "Let us marry first," said Nathan, "and then we'll see what both of us can do for your family."

We were married in September. I went to all our friends and asked them to the wedding. I asked Elka Budnichenkoff to be matron-of-honor and her husband to be Nathan's best man. They were still unfriendly to us, but I begged their forgiveness and thanked them for all they had done, and at last they said they would come. The Zlinkoffs, the Bershadskys, the Shlikermans and the Zolotaroffs were at the wedding too: I was sure there had never been as many intelligent people in Brownsville before. Next door to us lived the Levinsons, excellent people! They had come from Moscow, and were in this country about a year and a half. Mrs. Levinson and Mrs. Bosky, my cousin, prepared the food. A Rabbi Levine married us. Some of our friends, who were radicals, made fun of Nathan and me for having a wedding, but I said, "I am not going to be among the first to jump away from the old customs: who knows where I'd land?"

We wrote home our plan for bringing them here; but Mother's answer was unlike her other letter: Hyam had come from Odessa, Abram and Rachmiel were helping her somewhat, Israel would soon be through with his service in the army, and Frieda had a wonderful offer. A young man wanted to marry her without any dowry at all. "A girl like Frieda," Mother wrote, "does not have to go to America: she can marry where she is. And please, my daughter, do not ask the other children to come to you. I do not want to go to America; do not tear my children away from me."

One day Nathan came from New York and said, "Nevins and Ettelson have no more work for anybody: they are giving up their partnership. I went somewhere else. The new work looks hard to me; I do not think we'll do as well." And we did not. We thought it would help us to sell retail too. So we moved to another street: the rent was a dollar less and the neighborhood better for a retail store. But in a few weeks we received a postcard from Ettelson: he had gone into business for himself. Though times were bad, he gave us plenty of work.

I made up my mind to have nothing to do with our new neighbors. The husband, a young man, wore a beard; his wife had her hair bobbed. One Saturday night, in the spring, I was not well, but I did not want Nathan to stay at home because of me. He went to the Bershadskys and I was studying English. Someone knocked at the door. It was our neighbor. "I see that you have plenty of work," she said, "can you let me have something to do? My husband is on strike, and all we made last week was thirty-five cents. We haven't a thing to live on."

"If your husband can operate a sewing-machine—there is no strike in our line—he can work here."

"Thank you," she said, "but I do not think my husband would care for your kind of work."

I asked her to sit down, but she would not. Her manner seemed to say, I will have as little as possible to do with you; I only want work. When Nathan came home, I told him of the visit. He blamed me: I should have been friendly to our neighbors; they might die of hunger and I, with plenty of everything, did not care what they were doing; I should have been to visit them first.

I was up early in the morning and opened the kitchen door a number of times to hear if they were up. Perhaps they are dying of hunger, I thought. At last I heard voices: they were not dead yet. I knocked at the door and was asked in. I apologized for not having come before, and made some excuse or other; then I told our neighbor he could work with us until the strike was over. His wife could not do much: she was about to have another child; but she could sew buttons on the wrappers.

The minute our neighbor moved his machine into our place, he became very friendly and was everywhere. Whenever Nathan and I had something to say to each other, he had something to say too. He claimed to be a Socialist. As soon as he earned a dollar, he would work no more that day, even if it was only two o'clock. "Six dollars a week is enough for me and my family," he would say. "I am not going to make the bosses rich. You are fools to do more." He would put his feet on the machine and read his Yiddish newspaper. "In New York," he would say, "you can get along without English. Why trouble your head to learn it?"

His wife gave birth to another girl. While she was in labor, he went off to a Socialist meeting and did not come back until midnight. We moved near the Levinsons again, but I was not rid of our neighbor. He moved his machine along with ours.

Brownsville was growing: travelling to and from New York was hard, but many chose to live in the sunshine and fresh air of Brownsville, rather than among the tenements of the East Side. Times were good; there was work for everybody.

One evening my old neighbor with the bobbed hair came

to see me. She said that I ought not to help my husband at the wrappers. I explained that what I did was easy for me, but hard for him; and I liked to do it. I was too devoted to my husband, she said, and was a bad example. I must be rid of these people, I thought; so I said, "Your husband is not here now and I can talk freely. He does me harm and himself harm. There was a time when he could not work at his trade; that time is over. He's a tailor; let him go back to his tailoring. It will be much better for you. You don't have to work. He isn't doing enough."

Her husband came to work next morning at ten o'clock. I walked in from the kitchen and said to Nathan, "We did a favor to this gentleman, but now we'll ruin him. A married man of thirty-five who has two children and comes to work at ten o'clock has lost his bearings. Let him go to his tailoring; among his own people he'll be ashamed to act like this." Nathan was surprised at me. But I insisted that the fellow take his machine away. That night he and his wife came to tell us that he had found a job at twelve dollars a week. They were moving to New York. Good riddance! I thought.

Mr. Ettelson asked Nathan to be his foreman. Nathan was uncertain. Ought he to join the forces of Capital? I thought that he should take the position; by refusing it, he would not change the capitalistic system. He would be helpful and fair; in his position he could be of more help to the workers than in any other. Some of his friends thought otherwise: to be a workingman was nobler. But I told him that he had worked with hands and feet from six in the morning until late at night for five years; that was enough. How long would a man last working like that?

So Nathan became Henry Ettelson's foreman. In two weeks he was disheartened. The work was a strain, he had to be on his feet all day, and he was between two millstones, on one side the workers, on the other the "boss": each had to be satisfied. "This is your problem," I said, "and you must solve it. It is a great opportunity and more future to it than sitting in your own house."

Ettelson's business had grown rapidly and Nathan was in charge of eighty-six machines.

He was still reading a Yiddish newspaper. "You will never learn English, if you do that," I said. But he kept on. At last I said, "If you bring a Yiddish newspaper home again, I'll tear it up." Next night he brought his newspaper with him and after supper settled down to read. I snatched it out of his hands and tore it to bits. He was furious, of course. "I'll do it again," I said. But I did not have to. The very next night he had an English newspaper, and soon knew more English than I.

Nathan was doing well. When his pay was raised from twenty to twenty-five dollars a week, I made a dinner for our friends. Some of them were not as happy about it as we, and one said, "Why celebrate? The time will come when his wages will be five dollars less." Next year, Nathan had another increase of five dollars and a bonus.

I had bad news from home. A little while before Nathan and I had sent my elder brother money to come to America— Michael had never been able to get along—and now they wrote us he could not come: he had consumption.

We had ourselves photographed. Nathan addressed the en-velopes and left the photographs for me to mail. I saw that there was none for my elder brother. Nathan had once quar-relled with Michael's wife, and I thought he was not sending Michael a photograph because of that. How silly, I thought, how cruel! and Michael is sick. When Nathan came home that evening, I told him all that. "Michael is dead," he said.

He had died four months before. They had written us, but Nathan had kept the letter from me.

One day, one of our cousins who had just come from Russia, was in our house; and when it was nearly three o'clock, all the children came running out of school—so many of them—and his eyes filled with tears. I remembered how I, too, had longed for an education. "We are a lost generation," I said. "It is for our children to do what they can."

Early History of a Sewing-Machine Operator

by NATHAN REZNIKOFF

I SHOULD HAVE BEEN NAMED after my father's father. He had died, when only thirty, saving a woman and her children from a shanty carried away by a spring flood; swimming among the cakes of ice he had caught his death of a cold. But six months after my mother's wedding, her grandfather died and left her the most precious thing he had—the phylacteries for which Jacob the Scribe had written the passages from the Torah. Jacob had been the most pious of scribes: whenever he had to write the name of the Lord he would immerse himself in a ritual bath, and so his phylacteries cost fifty roubles in days when common phylacteries could be had for a rouble. Her grandfather stipulated that if she had a boy the phylacteries should belong to her son when he was thirteen, but if a girl, they were to be given to her husband. For such an inheritance, left me three months before I was born, all agreed that I should be named Nehemiah, after my mother's grandfather.

However, I was born without hunger. My mother became sick and fell into a fever and I could hardly squeak. The midwife said she did not know what to do for the child, but if they could get a puppy, it would suck the milk and my mother might be saved. So her father hurried through the village to find a puppy. At the same time my father's mother came from the town in which she lived, fifty miles or so away, to see her grandson.

My mother fell into a kind of sleep. They put the puppy at her breast and it began to suck the milk. Then my father's mother said to my mother's mother, "Let us put the child there—perhaps it will suck now." And I did.

My mother awoke. Her mother-in-law kissed her and asked her how she was. She said, "I was so sick, but now I am better," and at that she felt her baby sucking away at her breast. "See!" she said. "Now I hope, God willing, that I shall be well."

"Listen," she went on, "I just dreamed that a stranger, a Jew I have never seen, not an old man but a man about thirty, came to my bed and asked me how I was. I answered, 'Can't you see that I am sick?' 'You'll be well,' he said. 'How can I be well,' I answered, 'if my child will not suck?' 'I'll hand him to you,' the stranger said, 'and the child will suck.' He gave me the child and was gone."

My father's mother asked, "What did he look like?"

"A dark man, rather short, with a black beard, and he looked at me closely as if he were near-sighted."

My father's mother cried out, "That was not a stranger, my child: that was your father-in-law, may he rest in peace! He surely begged the Lord for your life."

My mother began to feel better and so did I. Every one was sure that my father's father had saved us both; and it was agreed that great as was the merit of my great-grandfather, Nehemiah, that of my father's father was greater, and they named me after him—Nathan.

The Czar had promised the Jews of the Jewish farming colonies in the province that he would draft no soldiers from among them for thirty years. But before the time was up those who had no sons to be taken into the army went away to towns or villages, and almost all the others followed as soon as the thirty years were over. Of five hundred families, settled in four colonies, only forty were left; and most of these did not till the land themselves but gave their fields to peasants to work on shares and went about to the fairs and traded.

The first year soldiers were to be drafted, the colonists were ordered to choose eight—the number five hundred families had to send. My grandfather, since he could read and write Russian best, was the head of the colonies. He went to Kiev and petitioned the governor to take no more soldiers than those due from forty families. He knocked at the door of every Jew who had the governor's ear until the quota was lowered from eight to one. With that the colonists were well pleased, but who was to go?

They drew lots and the lot fell on Velvel's son. Then Velvel said, "Lot me no lots! Why should my son be the scapegoat for all? Let the congregation buy a release for the one who has to go"; for at that time it was the law that whoever had to be a soldier might pay the Government eight hundred roubles, and if he brought the receipt to the draft board it was just as if he himself were to serve.

But where were the colonists to get eight hundred roubles? Velvel said that he would give all he had but could scrape together no more than three hundred. However, my grandfather should add the money—paid for taxes—in the treasury of the colonies. When the harvest was in, every family could give twelve or thirteen roubles and the money would be back in the chest.

My grandfather shouted, "How can I do that? I cannot touch the Government's money!"

At this all the colonists began to shout: one, "Because you are stubborn are you going to put a Jew in the hands of Gentiles?"; another, "Who will know that the money isn't in the chest?"; and still another, "We will put the money back!"

But one of the colonists, Hershel, spoke up. They did not each have a son to be a soldier. And even if that were so, they could not buy a release every year. Why then should each have to pay thirteen roubles? This angered the others, even my grandfather. They decided, then and there, that, because of his impudence, for all of one year Hershel should not be called up to the platform to stand beside the reader of the Torah in the synagogue.

When they had given the release to the draft board and it was settled that Velvel's son would not have to go, the colonists celebrated, and the honor of having the celebration in his home was given to my grandfather. It cost him about twenty roubles. Next morning officers came and took an inventory of everything in the house, put the seal of the Government even on the pots and pans, and arrested him. He was sent afoot, in the custody of a Gentile constable, to be questioned by the nearest prosecuting-attorney.

Then there was a great to-do in the four colonies. They sent for my father. He sold his watch and chain, the wedding-present from his father-in-law; my grandmother went to the neighboring villages and my father to a neighboring town to borrow the rest of the money; and they sent a young man on a good horse to catch up with my grandfather and tell him in Yiddish what had been done.

When my grandfather was brought before the prosecuting-attorney, he was asked if he had bought a release for Velvel's son. He answered that he had. Where did he get so much money? He had borrowed it, and he gave the prosecuting-attorney the names of those from whom it had just been taken. "How is it," asked the prosecuting-attorney, "that I am informed in this letter that you used the money of the Government?"

My grandfather looked at the letter. It was not signed, but he recognized Hershel's writing. He said, "I do not know, but send someone to look into the chest; be sure that the money is where it should be." It was—and in a few days he was set free.

One day, while I and the other boys were chanting our lessons in my grandfather's school, swaying backwards and forwards on our seats, my granduncle banged the door open and stamped in.

Now my grandfather and his brother never could get on with each other. When their parents became colonists so that their sons need not serve as soldiers, the elder two worked in the fields, but my grandfather, the youngest, was sent away to study. He came home, quite a learned man, and even knew how to read and write Russian. His elder brothers were just plain people. His wife, too, was brought up as a gentle-woman and could do nothing in the fields, but the other daughters-in-law had to do everything. As soon as their parents were dead, the brothers went each his own way.

My grandfather bought himself a house and a garden, became a teacher, and made a good living; one brother moved to Znamenka, a village twenty miles or so away, and got along well enough; the eldest had the homestead, and was better off than either. But when the Russian-Turkish War began and his youngest son was drafted to be a soldier, my granduncle spent all his money and had his son made deaf that he might not go to war. At the same time he had to marry off his youngest daughter, and since he did not have the dowry he had promised, he gave away his house and garden instead. So he and his wife were without a home and went to live with their eldest daughter.

Now the young man who had married their youngest daughter had an elder brother, a poor man with seven children. His father said to my granduncle's son-in-law, "What do you, the two of you with only one child, want with a house all to yourselves? Your brother with his large family has nowhere to live; and I cannot take him into my house with seven children. Take your wife and child and come to my house; I will give you two rooms which will be enough for you now, and in a hundred years when your mother and I die, my house will be yours. In the meantime, let your brother have your house." And this was done.

When my granduncle heard of it, he went thirty-five miles afoot in the heat of summer to the village where my grandfather was teaching. As soon as my grandfather had greeted him in no friendly voice, my granduncle loudly told of his complaint: that he and his wife had no place of their own in their old age and that he had given away his house and garden to his own daughter and her husband, but to no one else. The children were frightened at his shouting. "Now write me a petition to the district-attorney at once, for I want my house and garden back!"

"You old fool," said my grandfather, "you have given them the house, and by law they can do with it what they want."

My granduncle shouted, "Is there no justice?"

My grandfather went on, "Then, how can I write 'at once'? My time is not my own now. I am paid to teach and must do my work."

"I will chase all your pupils away and break your bones into the bargain! You must write my petition!"

"Sit down. I'll say the afternoon prayers with the children and then I'll write you your petition." We said the afternoon prayers and the others went home. I went up to my granduncle. He kissed me, spoke gently to me and wondered how I had grown. In the meantime, my grandfather got his writing things ready—paper, a new quill pen, and his glazed inkstand with three little pots, one for ink, another for sand, and the middle one for holding pens. The little pots were of the same size and shape and the same yellow color.

"Well, let us begin," said my grandfather, "what do you want me to say? For it will soon be night and I have neither lamp nor candle here."

The writing went on and they talked together quietly. But when my grandfather was through, long after the sun had set and the room was dark, his brother, to be of some help, thinking he had the sand, caught up the inkwell and emptied it upon the petition.

My mother's brother was sixteen years old and engaged to be married. The winter before, my grandfather had his school in a village about seven miles from Shigrin. In the village was a girl of fifteen, dark and clever; she used to help her mother in the house, her father in his store, and my grandfather thought she would be a good match for his son.

He had Moses come to the village for some reason; Moses and Baila saw and did not dislike each other; then my grandfather sent for my grandmother and made the match. Baila's father knew that my grandfather was learned and pious; besides, Moses was an only son and would not have to serve in the army. As for my grandfather, he could do little for his son. Moses had earned no more than sixty roubles the year before, teaching little boys their alphabet, but his father-in-law would give him five hundred roubles as Baila's dowry, and Moses would open a store at the other end of the village. My grandfather borrowed some money and bought the bride a gold pin with earrings to match; and Moses got a gold watch from her father, which he kept taking out of his pocket and putting to his ear.

His father and Baila's father set the wedding for a day before the New Year. When Moses heard of this, he was displeased, and said to his father, "Why hurry—is the world coming to an end?" My grandfather glared, ground his teeth, and muttered something or other. "I became engaged," Moses went on, "because you wanted me to, but I didn't think you would be in such a hurry to have me marry. I left school only a year ago. I have been nowhere and have seen nothing, and now you want to shut me up in a village, where I shall see nobody and have a yoke on my neck—a wife and children."

My grandfather became angrier as his son talked. "Don't you like the girl any more, you good-for-nothing?"

"I have nothing against the girl, but I have this against you—you want to pull a sack over my head before I have seen anything." And for this, although it was the Sabbath, Moses was well slapped, and that ended the conversation.

Besides, a wedding could not be put off. And so, although

108

my younger brother and the youngest of his own children had eaten too many cucumbers and were sick of a fever, my grandfather hired a cart and oxen and we all rode to the wedding. In their delirium, my younger brother said the prayers he had been memorizing in school and my little aunt played jacks. My mother sat beside them with a jar of water and put wet rags to their heads all the way.

Uncle wore a cap of silk at his wedding, a new woolen suit, patent leather shoes, and a stiff white shirt-front. My grandfather was in his long satin coat and my grandmother, in her best clothes, had a yellow kerchief of silk about her head, tucked in behind her ears. My mother was restless—standing on one foot, as the saying goes—because of the sick children. As I stood beside her, I heard her mutter, as she looked at her brother through her tears, "That's the way I was buried before I grew up."

The next day, while we—the relatives of the groom—were waiting to be led in procession to the wedding dinner, someone of the village came to tell us that the musicians would not play: they wanted the bride's father to give them ten roubles more, for there was to be no dancing afterwards; but he would not, and said to them, "Who can think of dancing when children are dying?" The musicians had answered that that had nothing to do with their livelihood, and if there was to be no dancing they wanted ten roubles more for playing at the dinner; and the bride's father told them to go the devil. Now, since they had no musicians, the relatives of the bride could not come—as always—to invite the relatives of the groom to dinner, and so they asked my grandfather and his family to come without a procession.

My grandmother began to weep. "Think of that—our only son—and we are not to have the honors due the bridegroom's parents."

109

My grandfather, because of his wife's tears, or the meanness of the bride's father—spoiling the wedding because of a few roubles (and if he was a man like that he might not give the dowry he had promised), or because of worry at the sickness of his daughter and his grandson and the unhappiness of his son, began to tear at his hair and beat his head against the wall. My mother got a glass of water and made him drink it. He became calmer, and after a few minutes said, "Send for Moses!"

When my uncle came, his father was calm. He said in a loud voice, "Pack your things and come with us—we are going home!"

"Why?"

"They have insulted your mother."

Moses said, "If they did, they did not mean to. But because of that, you want me to insult my wife—and she had nothing to do with it. I will not go."

We were afraid my grandfather would go into another tantrum. He was silent for a minute and then, turning to my grandmother, said, "Let us go to their dinner."

The windows were thick with frost, as if painted white. My mother sat on the brick bench next to the oven, busy with the little ones, lifting them when they had a coughing spell; one would stop and the other begin, and sometimes both would cough at once. My father coughed so that we thought he would never catch his breath. After a few minutes, when he was better, his head bowed, his legs trembling, he went to the sink and washed himself, put on his short fur coat, because he was cold, and began to chant the psalms. It was so cold and dismal in our house, I begged my mother to let me go to the house of my chum. I wrapped my mother's old shawl about me, put on my father's summer boots—I had no boots of my own—and ran down the road.

My chum's father was a tall Jew, about forty years of age, his clothes good and clean, his hair and beard always combed. He was the richest Jew in the village at the time. He had built himself a large house; he had a tavern, a warehouse for grain, and a store that had whatever one might need—dry-goods, notions, groceries, and hardware. People said that if it were not for his wife, he would still be pasturing calves as when he was a young man. She was so tall and stout she was called "steam-engine," and she had a face like a peasant's; she was strong, too—"like a piece of iron;" it was said of her she could twist the head off the Devil and hand it to him. Once, when two peasants were fighting in the tavern, she lifted them both by their belts and threw them into the street. When she had a child, she left her bed on the third day. She had one child riding from the forest in the dead of winter, on a sled she had loaded with wood. She took off her coat, wrapped the child in it, and came home; and neither she nor the child was harmed.

When I came into the house, she said, "Come, sit near the stove and warm yourself." Her husband looked at me side-ways, out of his angry eyes, and went on chanting the psalms —not sorrowfully as my father and others did. When my chum's father came to the verse, "I lift mine eyes to the hills whence comes my help," he lifted his eyes, but saw the barrels of vodka he had for sale.

A little later in came our schoolteacher. My chum's mother asked the teacher into the inner room, and my chum and I stayed near the stove to play, but I could hear what our elders said. She asked, "Did you manage to send some money to your wife and children?"

"Yes, but eight roubles a month for a woman with four children is not enough."

At this my chum's father said angrily, "Why don't you send more?"

"Because I can't."

"You have eighty roubles for the season; you could send more."

"I have only seventy because Simon Reznikoff"—I heard my father's name and listened—"can't pay more than ten. It is hard for him to do even this, and he wanted me to teach only Nathan, the eldest boy. But the younger boy does not take up much time and I told him to send both. I need ten roubles for myself—to have my shoes fixed, my linen washed, and for a little tobacco; and I must have at least ten to send home for Passover, and then it costs something to send the money."

My chum's mother said, "It would only be right that those who can should chip in, and give you the ten roubles you are short."

Her husband shouted, "Should I pay for Simon that beggar? Not a broken copeck!"

She shouted back, "You fool! What are you shouting for? If you don't want to give any money, don't; but don't insult people."

I caught up my mother's shawl and, without saying good-by to anyone, ran home. I was glad it was so dark there they could not see that I was crying.

My mother was tall and, even when old, walked as straight as a grenadier, never looking to the right or left, and planting her foot at each step firmly on the ground. As for my father, he never grew taller than five feet—if that tall, and in our village he was called Simon "the Flea."

Two years after his marriage, his father-in-law gave him his dowry and told him he could keep him no longer, because he did not want to become a rabbi. My father was then nineteen. He did not know the language of the land, nor the ways of business, for he had been brought up a student of the Talmud; but he lent his money to peasants and, on the interest and what he could earn teaching children, he made a living.

One day, my mother's uncle came from Znamenka where he had a slaughterhouse and a tavern. The village was on a railroad and now that war with Turkey had begun, soldiers were passing through like the sands of the sea for number, and at the station itself there were almost five thousand men at work. But my mother's uncle had no money to buy vodka and cattle. He had been doing well, so he said, even before the war, but he had been sick for a few months and everything went to smash. My father became his partner, put six hundred roubles—all he had—into the business, and moved to Znamenka.

My granduncle fell sick again and took to his bed. His sons and his stepsons and his wife helped in the business, but helped themselves mostly—whoever had God in his heart, as the saying is, put money into his pocket. The sales were many, the profits large, but there was no cash in the till. When my father's partner died in eight months, my father got out of the business with no more than forty roubles.

He still spoke no Russian and did not know what to do— he could not even teach, because the children of the peasants of the village did not study the Talmud. The next years were hard, above all the winters, when every stick of wood counted; but he managed to make a poor living as a go-between of those who dealt in cattle and grain.

My father had gone to the fair at Elizavetgrad and had

done well—he had thirty-three roubles profit. Why then, he thought, for a rouble or two commission, should I go about hunting for a buyer when there are cattle to sell? He had at last enough to pay for a steer himself. He could not do the slaughtering—for the twenty-five years he was to be in the business he never learnt how to handle knife or cleaver— but Gershon who had married my mother's sister was a butcher. And so they became partners.

Gershon was hardly able to say the set prayers, and he knew nothing of writing or reading—or even how to figure. Whenever the price of meat changed and all the calculations he had memorized were useless, he was miserable. If sales were poor, but his money in coppers, he used to go home happy because he had a bag full of money. At other times, when he had taken in twice as much, but most of the money was paper and the bag light, he would hang his head, worried, and say, "No money—and no meat."

The first few months their business was not much to speak of, but after that things were better. In a year and a half, they were worth about four thousand roubles—a good deal of money for Znamenka. Most of it was in hides, which they were going to sell in the spring at the fairs.

This stock of hides was in Gershon's house—straw-thatched like the others. One Saturday afternoon someone set fire to it, and it burned to the ground. My father was taking a nap. A peasant ran into the house shouting, "Your brother-in-law's house is afire!" My mother began to scream, and the younger children, too, screamed.

My father started up. "What is it?" he asked. "What are you all screaming for? This is the Sabbath!"

Mother cried out, "Someone set fire to Gershon's house, and all we have is ashes!"

My father took a deep breath. Then he answered calmly,

"Let us hope God will give it back to us." He washed his hands, and began to chant the psalms for the day.

The day before Passover, my mother was worried because Abram "Cholera," whom she could trust, would not cut my hair. He was angry at my father and his wife said to my mother, "You only come here for favors. After all, my husband is not a barber—he is a tailor."

Abram "Cholera" was a tailor of men's clothes. In our village, at the time, was another Abram, a tailor of women's clothes. The Jews of the village could not call either Abram "the tailor" and know who was meant, and to call a tailor by his family name would be too much honor for him. So Abram, the tailor of men's clothes, was nicknamed "Cholera," because—so he himself had told us—when he was a boy and the cholera was about, he was supposed to be dead of it and came to just as he was to be buried. The other Abram had a goat, and his own beard was like that of a goat; he was "Monsieur the Goat," his wife "Madame the Goat," and their youngsters "The Little Goats."

The two Abrams were always quarreling, although neither had done the other any harm. When one was called up to stand next to the reader of the Torah in the synagogue, the other was almost beside himself. One Saturday, "Monsieur the Goat" asked my father to do him a favor: since the Festival of the Torah he had not been called up to stand next to the reader of the Torah and Abram "Cholera" had been called up twice; wouldn't Rabbi Simon talk to the head of the congregation, his friend, about it? The honor of standing beside the reader of the Torah was, then, the very next Saturday, given "Monsieur the Goat;" and since that Saturday was important, leaving the synagogue, "Monsieur the Goat" said to "Cholera," "Who was called up today? Rabbi Simon himself said that

I ought to be called up today." And now Abram "Cholera" would not give me my haircut.

I had to have a haircut, because they did not cut my hair all winter for fear of a cold, and after Passover one may not have one's hair cut for six weeks. But there was so much to do, neither my father nor mother had the time to see that my sidelocks were not shortened—every really orthodox Jew has sidelocks that have never been cut. My mother gave me five copecks and said, "Go to Vasil 'the Soldier', and have your hair cut, but don't let him do it if he is drunk; he may cut off your sidelocks." At this, I saw a good chance to be rid of them, for no other boy had sidelocks, and because of them I was nicknamed "The Little Pious One."

I found Vasil "the Soldier" sober, and told him what I had come for. He said, "Let me have the money."

"No," said I, "I won't give you the money unless you cut off my sidelocks."

"Your mother will scold me."

"I, a boy, am not afraid of her; why should you, a man who has been a soldier, be afraid of a scolding?"

Vasil wanted the money badly for a drink and began to cut my hair. He had no mirror and, after a while, he said, "Touch your temples; did I cut it short enough?"

I felt some hair above my ears. "This won't do!"

"But I can't make it any shorter—your mother will scold me."

"What a soldier you must have been to be so afraid of a woman's words! How you must have run from the Turks!"

"All right, I will cut off as much as you want, you brat; let your mother scold me, but you will get a good licking every time she looks at you," and he caught up his scissors. When Vasil was through, I put on my hat and it fell over my ears. I felt like a chicken under a sieve.

My parents stared, and my mother cried out, wringing her hands, "God of Israel! He looks like that drunken woman who used to shave her head!"

My grandfather—mother's father—was staying at our house for the holy days. The evening before the Day of Atonement he asked if I fasted. My mother answered that since I was not even twelve I fasted only half the day, but my grandfather said, "O no! I began to fast all day when I was ten." It was decided that I should try to fast all day. I was enthusiastic: if I could fast all day I should be a man and no longer a child.

Until three o'clock in the afternoon I got along fairly well. I was hungry and very thirsty, but I was able to stand it; afterwards, I began to feel dizzy. I could not shout the prayers and was glad to be able to whisper them, and my pride that I was a man because I was fasting was gone. At about half-past five I fainted.

When I was brought to, I found myself in the yard; men, women, and boys had left their prayers and were standing about me. They sprinkled cold water on me and rubbed my hands and head. I saw my mother and my grandfather there too, and heard Jacob, the smith, say, "Let him have a drink of water."

My grandfather shouted, "God forbid!"

But someone brought a bucket of cold water and put it to my mouth, and I drank. When my grandfather saw that, he said bitterly, "Half an hour more and you would have fasted all day. Because of half an hour you have spoiled the day!" I too was sorry that because of a little water I was still a boy and not a man.

Next year, I asked my father what I should do to be able to fast the Day of Atonement. My father said, "For a few days before, eat less, and when you pray on the Day of Atonement, don't shout, and you will be able to fast." This time I fasted all day, but by twilight my hands and legs trembled and I was very hungry and thirsty.

When the congregation was through with all the prayers, and the last blast on the ram's horn was blown, everybody else hurried home to break the fast, but my father was in no hurry. He said the evening prayers, and then, as he walked from the synagogue with me and my younger brother, he kept looking at the moon and said the prayer in its praise. We went along slowly, my father holding his sons by the hand, and he said, "What a wonderful day! That such a holy day should pass so quickly!"

This was too much for me and I said angrily, "What a day! I am as hungry as a dog!"

My father slapped me twice and said, "Because of a word you have spoiled the day!"

My mother gave birth to another son. On Wednesday it began to rain or, rather, pour. The mud of the roads became so deep, my father did not wait until Friday to send for the man who circumcised the Jewish children of the neighborhood, but hired a rig the day before and paid five roubles for what in ordinary weather would cost no more than a rouble. The driver left about noon and came back at midnight with the news that the man was dead.

Early Friday morning my father went to see his friend, the head of the congregation. They called a few more Jews into the consultation and at last it was decided that circumcision ought not to be put off. Now a man who circumcises is not born skilled—each must have his first child to circumcise. Why, then, should not Rabbi Isaac, who slaughtered their cattle and fowl, also become one who circumcises? Maybe

118

all this had happened because it was destined that Isaac should circumcise their children. And they came to my mother to tell her of their decision.

She began to weep and said, "How can I let the child's life be put in danger? Why should this child be worse off than all my others? I didn't find it somewhere."

My father said, "Our father Abraham was ready to make a greater sacrifice. God will watch over our child that nothing should harm him, as He watched over Isaac." The others, too, said what was proper until they talked my mother over.

But nobody wanted to hold the child for Rabbi Isaac. My father had to do that himself; he was pale and kept his eyes closed. The child did not cry much, and my mother fainted in bed because she thought the child had died. They brought her to, the midwife gave her the new Jew to suckle, and the other Jews began to drink and feast.

A few days later, when the wound was healed, the midwife gone, and my mother was bathing the baby herself, she called to my father, "I think the circumcision was not as it should be—our child is neither Jew nor gentile."

My father looked and said, "Well, we'll have to ask someone who knows about it." He closed the book of the Talmud he was reading and went to his friend, the head of the congregation. He came, looked, and shrugged his shoulders. Other men, and women too, came to see and question; at last it was decided to bring Rabbi Moses of Dimitrefka—he had been circumcising children for fifty years and would know.

The weather was bad and the old man unable to come. My mother was worried: if they had to circumcise the child again when it was older, it might not be able to stand it. After Passover, they brought Rabbi Moses from Dimitrefka. He was a man of eighty with a long broad beard; he had become

119

nearsighted and his hands and knees trembled with age. All the Jews of the village came to hear his decision.

The old man took off his long coat and put on his eyeglasses; then he beckoned with his hand. My mother placed the child before him on the table and went away to lean against the wall. My father looked as if he were saying his prayers.

Rabbi Moses took the little legs of the baby apart and put his head and beard between them. The baby promptly kicked him several times in the mouth so that he had to ask someone to hold the feet of the little renegade. Rabbi Moses put his face between the baby's legs again, looked and measured with his thumb nail, and at last took his head away slowly, straightened himself, and screamed hoarsely, "May God help him grow; it will be all right!"

The first pogrom was in Elizavetgrad, the city nearest Znamenka. And a law was passed that Jews who had moved in after a certain year could not live in the villages. There was talk that soon all of us would have to leave. This gave the Jews in Znamenka enough to think about. After prayer Friday evenings, and Saturday mornings before prayer, the boys no longer talked among themselves about their games, but listened to what their elders had to say.

A subscriber to a Russian newspaper used to read aloud what was written about the Jews: how an enemy of Israel wrote that they were not a useful people but thought only about their Talmud and, for a living, robbed the Russians, and that was why the peasants were so poor; others, Jews among them, urged the Jews to give up their study of the Talmud and begin useful work. The head of our congregation thought it would do no harm to teach children trades, but to do that they did not have to give up the study of the Talmud.

My father said all this talk was a waste of time—the Jews were in exile and had to suffer. Now and then we heard of new riots in which Jews were robbed and killed, and lessons were less and less important to us boys.

It seemed to me and my new chum, the son of the head of the congregation, that we should be able to make a living to be ready for whatever might happen. What was the use of reading through the prophecies of the Bible again? What was the good of studying the Talmud after all? What did we care whether or not we could eat an egg laid on a holiday? Or who should pay the damage if an ox gored a cow? There were plenty of rabbis—let them worry about it.

Whenever we were to study the Talmud, we hid ourselves in the garret. Our teacher scolded us, but we did not answer him. Finally, he called us aside and said, "Tell me what has gotten into your heads that you are running away from the Talmud?"

My father was walking up and down the room. As I came in, my mother said, "There he is, our student. Didn't I tell you that he'd never stick to Judaism?"

My father said, "Tell me, my philosopher, how you came to think as you do!"

I stood with head down and tried to answer his questions briefly so as not to anger him. When I had nothing more to say, he was angrier than ever and I knew that in another moment I should be slapped. Just then the door opened and in came my chum's father, the head of the congregation.

"Now take it easy, Simon."

"What!" said my father. "When I wasn't able to pay for him, I worried that my children might grow up ignorant; but now that with God's help I am able to pay, he must go to school!"

"You can bring a balky horse to a hill, but you can't make

121

him pull the wagon up," said my chum's father. "We can make our children go to school, but will they study? You didn't want to be a rabbi, even though your father-in-law would have supported you and your family. The boy is almost thirteen; let him see what he can do—he may be glad to go back to school."

When he was gone, my mother said, "He is right—may I have as good a year."

My father looked at her angrily and then said to me, "Well, what do you think to do, smarty?"

"Give me ten roubles and you'll see."

Father took a red ten-rouble bill from his wallet and gave it to me.

Sunday morning I went to the railway station to look for something to do. There I met Ephraim who had been my father's partner for a while in the old days when we were poor. Ephraim had always taken more than his share. He smiled and said, "I hear that you know it all and don't want to go to school any more."

"Well," I said, "I know more than some. If you want to, let's become partners; I have ten roubles."

"What share do you want?"

"Half."

"What do you want so much for? You are still a youngster and have parents to keep you, but I am a man who has seven children."

"I won't take my share of meat, since I'm living with my parents; and you may have as much meat as you need, but I must hold the money we take in. You are not to put any money in your pocket, because you don't invest any; and every week, whatever the profits are, we share alike. If you don't want it that way, I'll find someone else."

Ephraim did not have a copeck of his own; besides, if our business needed more money, I might be able to get it. "Well," he said, "if you are stubborn about it, all right. I hear that a railway watchman on the line to Kharkov has a calf to sell, but it is too far for you to walk. Let me have the money and I'll go."

"That won't do, Mr. Ephraim; we agreed that I must keep the money; and I'm not a little boy, otherwise I'd be in school —I can walk as far as you."

We went to the home of the watchman, about six miles away, but could not find him. We then went on to find another watchman, and bought a heifer from him for nine roubles. We sent for the slaughterer and by midnight had meat for the next day's market.

When I came home my parents had not been able to sleep for worry. "I wasn't playing," I said quietly, and told them all I had done.

"He's beginning with that Ephraim! He'll take every copeck from you."

"Don't worry, Mother; I know with whom I'm dealing."

Next morning we brought our meat to market in a hired rig. Gershon, my father's partner, came to see what we had to sell and offered us three roubles profit; another butcher offered four. Ephraim would have taken this, but I said, "I don't want to sell to other butchers. When you are shown the corner of a rouble bill you get excited; but I want to work up a trade." We sold the meat retail and made a profit of six roubles.

In three weeks we had earned forty-two roubles; but though I watched Ephraim closely, he pocketed six. My mother, too, kept saying she did not want me to be in partnership with Ephraim. She had not forgotten how he used to deal with my father; and it was thought that Ephraim, angry that my father and Gershon were making so much money, had set fire to the hides years before.

Now that I had money of my own, I could get along without the ten roubles Father had given me. My mother had said, "Where would you be if you didn't have your father's money?" and I wanted to show her that I could do without it. Friday afternoon I gave my father his ten roubles. He asked how much I had left. I told him, and told him too about the three roubles Ephraim had taken.

"Neither your mother nor I want you to be in partnership with Ephraim. You come into my business; there you will have much to do and learn, and I'll give you whatever you may need for clothes and a little pocket-money."

I first went to the fair. The fair of Elizavetgrad was as large as all Znamenka: heaps of hides, the merchants tossing them from place to place to decide upon their value, thousands of horses, cows, and other cattle, and all sorts of merchandise under canvas tents, the owners shouting at those who passed to come and buy.

Somewhat dizzy, when the sun set, I went into the city to find my uncle, my father's younger brother, Jacob. Walking down the main street, I was surprised to see houses three stories high, close to one another as if one house, with large windows to show the merchandise of the stores. Many carriages and wagons were going up and down the street, their wheels and the iron shoes of the horses clattering on the cobblestones; and thousands of people, it seemed to me, were crowding the sidewalks.

I found the dry-goods store where my uncle worked. When he was through with the customer he was waiting on, he came up to me and recognized me, for he had visited Znamenka a few years before. He led me to a seat on a bale of flannel, and I sat there looking about.

Uncle went from customer to customer. He merely shook hands with one, with another he talked, sometimes he called a clerk and told him what goods to show; he waited on some customers himself, and when he did, sold no less than three or five pieces of a pattern. At nine o'clock, when the clerks went home, he went into the office of his employer for a long talk.

On the way home, he asked me what I thought of the business. "You must have millions of yards of goods on the shelves," I said.

"We have ten times as much in the cellar and the warehouse; and in this city there are five such wholesalers."

As we came into his house, we were met by a red-headed girl of sixteen or seventeen, who asked somewhat sarcastically, "So early?"

He smiled and said, "Good evening, Sarah. I brought a guest—my nephew, Simon's son," and turning to me he said, "Nathan, this is your aunt."

My aunt raised her right hand slowly and took hold of the lobe of her right ear, and stared into my eyes. I was taken aback, but stared back and wondered what kind of an aunt this was. Her head was uncovered—unlike other Jewesses, she wore neither wig nor kerchief. I remembered that about half a year before, when my father came from Elizavetgrad, my mother had asked if Jacob had a good-looking wife, and my father had answered that she was good-looking, but—and my mother, when she heard what her sister-in-law was like, had said, "Such a year on all my enemies! That Jacob's wife should go about with her hair uncovered!"

After she had looked at me for a minute or two, she smiled

and asked me how I liked Elizavetgrad. "It is wonderful, but too noisy," I said.

She smiled again, and said to her husband, "You will have to share whatever there is to eat," and went to bed. As we ate, my uncle kept putting food in my dish. He talked and talked, so quickly I could hardly understand him. He asked why I had come, and I told him everything—how I had stopped going to school and why.

He said, "I wish I had the chance to study when I was your age—I wouldn't have given it up, but I was an orphan and had to work hard for my bread."

We heard my aunt calling from the bedroom, "You forget that you must be up early tomorrow, Jacob, and that Nathan is tired—and you keep on talking."

"You are right, you are right, darling." He whispered to me, "She is right."

In the morning we were up early, but my aunt was still abed. My uncle made tea; and after breakfast we went out to buy my things. Uncle walked quickly and bought quickly. Wherever we went, all were friendly to him; and it seemed from their talk, he had done them all favors. By ten o'clock I had everything, and went to the fair to look for the rig which was to take me home.

My mother asked, "Does your aunt really go about with her hair uncovered?"

"It's much nicer than wearing a dirty kerchief like your sister."

"O ho!" said my mother, "you are learning fast."

Saturdays, and whenever there was time for it, my father studied the Talmud; and my mother read the Bible in Yiddish and the prayer-book.

One day, when I was almost fourteen, walking through the

126

railway station, I saw a book on a bench. Nobody was about except the watchman. I asked him whose book it was. He said, "Some passenger left it. It has been there for hours. You can take it. I don't know how to read, anyway." I opened the book and saw that it was in Yiddish—a novel; and sat down on a fallen tree in the woods to read.

When I came home, my mother asked me where I had been all day. I told her. Father said, "Wouldn't it be better that I teach you a page of the Talmud?"

"The Talmud writes of things that were fifteen hundred years ago, but here our times are written about—read it yourself." Father looked at me angrily.

Saturday afternoon I saw my mother reading the book. After a few pages, I saw her smile, and at last she called out, "Simon, this is good!"

My father looked at her and said, "What! are you reading it too?"

She began to read aloud. At first, my father would not listen, but when he did, he too smiled. Mother said, "Now listen," and she read some more and still some more until the afternoon was gone.

Then my father groaned, "What good did this do us?"

Hershel of Knazhe came to Znamenka with hindquarters of beef to sell, and sold them to us for only four copecks a pound. In Knazhe, he said, all that the butchers cared about was meat they could sell to Jews, that is *kosher* meat; the meat Jews were forbidden to eat was sold for any price. "But you haven't so many Jews there," said my father.

Hershel smiled and scratched his little yellow beard. "True, in Knashe we haven't many Jews, but we smuggle the meat into Alexandrovka and other towns—as far as Smiela." At that time, the Jews of the towns paid a tax of three or five copecks on each pound of meat. The Government sold the right to this tax at auction and, after keeping a percentage for collecting it, gave the rest for the upkeep of the synagogues, Hebrew schools, and homes for Jewish sick and poor.

Labe, our apprentice, and I went to Knazhe to buy meat. We stopped at the house of a hide dealer. He asked me how I happened to come to Knazhe. I said, "I am on my way to Verestchak to visit my grandmother and we stopped to feed the horse."

I went to the market-place to find out what was doing among the butchers. When I came back, the hide dealer would not let us go before we had dinner. At the table we began to talk about the butchers of Knazhe. He told us they were almost all poor devils, who did not even own a horse and wagon; the only one well-off was his brother. David was strong, worked hard, and was not afraid of those who had bought the right to sell *kosher* meat in town. Let one of them try to look into his wagon! David knew how to bribe the officials so as not to be bothered. And his wife, Elka Perl, although she had four small children to take care of, sold the meat that was not *kosher* in the market-place while David went to town to sell the *kosher* meat.

As we were about to drive out of the yard, a husky young man came up to us, shook our hands, and asked if we would buy two hindquarters of beef. "We haven't any money," I said. "I am only going to my grandmother's."

"That's nothing. I am David. My brother tells me that if you want to buy meat, I can trust you."

"I may stop on the way back. Show me where you live."

It took us half an hour to get to Verestchak and for about an hour we were at my grandmother's. As we stopped at David's house, he came out and said, "Unhitch the horse. My wife won't let you go without supper, if we do business or don't." He introduced us to her, a good-looking woman, always smiling, with shining black eyes.

After supper, David and his wife took us into the slaughter-house to show us the meat, and she sold it to us. I made a deal with her that I was to come to Knazhe Mondays and Thursdays and take five hundred to a thousand pounds of meat in hindquarters at five copecks a pound and any other meat that might not be *kosher* at four copecks.

My father and his partner liked the deal well enough, but they did not think David would stick to it. I said, "His wife will. She would rather spend the time in the house with her children than in the market-place."

But one Thursday, Elka Perl said to me, "I have no meat for you this time at your price. This is just before Christmas and I can do much better in the market-place."

"Why didn't I want the meat for less during Lent?"

She smiled her sweet smile. "That was your carelessness."

I went along the street to get meat, if I could, from the other butchers, and found that Elka Perl had bought up all there was. But one of them told me in secret that seven miles away a steer had been slaughtered and found to be not *kosher*.

I told Labe to hitch up the horse. Elka Perl came out of the house and said, "Are you going away before supper?"

"Let your hindquarters of beef eat your supper. We must hurry home to slaughter our own cattle for tomorrow's market. You will make supper for us in Lent, when we shall buy your beef at four copecks a pound." I whipped the horse and we were off.

It was evening before we came to the house of the candle-maker. As we stepped across the threshold, we saw the steer hanging behind the door. "What is this?" I asked.

The candlemaker answered that it was not *kosher*, and then asked why I had come to the village. The best swindle is the truth; so I answered that David of Knazhe had asked more than we had agreed upon, and since it would take four hours to get to Znamenka, too late to have the slaughterer get meat ready for the market, I had gone out of my way to send a telegram home from the railway station. The candlemaker sent for his partner, the butcher, and they sold me the steer for what I used to pay in Knazhe.

It was eleven at night and very cold and windy before we were ready to start for home. It was too cold to sit on the sled. We would get off and run behind it until I could no longer feel my toes. We stopped at the house of a friend and woke him up. There my feet were rubbed with snow, and Labe and I given quilts to wrap about ourselves; we left at three in the morning and came to the market-place in time.

Sunday afternoon, David of Knazhe brought us his meat. It was all his wife's fault, he said. My father promised to buy from him again at the old prices until after next Christmas, but he was to put up one hundred roubles as security that he would charge no more. On Thursday, when I came to Knazhe, Elka Perl said, "I never thought you were such an angry nobleman."

"I never thought you were such a clever Jewess, but now we know each other," and we laughed.

One Monday Labe and I were on our way to Knazhe. In winter, we would drive over the fields, but in the spring we could not take all of the short cut without spoiling the wheat. When we came to where we were to turn into the road, Labe drove straight ahead. I caught hold of his arm and said, "What are you doing? If anybody sees us we'll get into trouble!"

He whipped the horse and said, "When the reins are in my hands, I am the boss." I tried to take the reins away,

130

but Labe pushed me and we began to wrestle. Neither of us saw three peasants coming out of the woods with an ax and whips.

The peasants stopped the horse. One of them said, "For driving over the wheat we are going to chop up your spokes and maybe your skins too. Whose rig is this?"

I said, "My father's."

"And this is your elder brother?" another asked, pointing at Labe.

"No, he is my father's workingman."

The eldest of the peasants turned to the other two, "Let us be fair. The wagon belongs to the little one's father. We all saw that the youngster didn't want him to drive over the field. We ought not to do anything to the wagon, but we must cut that big fellow's hide." They thrashed Labe with their whips, but touched neither me nor the wagon.

When we had reached the road and Labe had stopped weeping, he said to me, "Wait, I'll get even with you."

"Why?"

"Because you didn't let me drive—we'd never have been caught."

As we left Knazhe, Labe said, "If you had been whipped too, I'd not care so much, but this way I must get even with you."

When we came to the big hill, about seven miles from home, we stopped to water the horse. I jumped from the wagon and sat on the curb about the well. There was no water in the trough, but, instead of going to one of the houses to fetch a pail, Labe went up to me and said angrily, "Go and get a pail."

"I am not *your* servant. If you need a pail, go and get it."

He hit me on the chest and I fell over backwards into the well. I hooked my legs about the curb and hung head down. Some peasants heard my screams and one shouted to Labe,

"Let the hook down! He will catch hold of it and you can pull him up." Labe did so, before the peasants could get to us.

They asked me how it had happened, but I could not talk. I felt sharp pains in my calves. Labe was white and trembled. He said, "As he was sitting on the well-curb, he lost his balance."

Labe brought a pail quickly and watered the horse; and he and I began to walk up the hill, on either side of the wagon, neither saying a word. The sun had set and the woods were dark. Sometimes, I saw a star shining through the branches. This is a dangerous fellow, I thought. I must tell about this when I get home. He must be sent packing.

When we came to the top of the hill, where we would climb upon the wagon and drive on, Labe stopped the horse. "Take the horse and go home and I will go away into the wide world, or maybe I will hang myself upon a tree, and let them bury me in this ditch. I can't go home to face your parents after you will tell them what has happened."

"Suppose I had been drowned?"

"I'd drive up the hill and hang myself. As I hope that my father's soul is in Paradise, I never thought that hitting you would throw you into the well." He came up to me and, pushing his face forward, said, "Hit me but forgive me."

I said sulkily, "Get on the wagon and let's go home—I won't tell."

My father rented a little store for me and put into it whatever might be sold in the village. I was not quite sixteen at the time. This was my mother's plan. The only thing I liked about it was going to Elizavetgrad for merchandise, but my mother always had reasons for wanting to go herself.

I sat about the store all day, and seldom saw a soul except now and then a peasant, who might stop to buy a package of tobacco or some tar to grease his axles. · The sales were usually made in the evening, when the neighbors came from the fields or their work on the railway. The young peasants would then stand about, and I had to watch them to see that they did not steal. Instead of my friends, as before, they became enemies—above all Mekishka, a rich peasant's only son, whom I once caught stealing tobacco and another time drinking the landlord's milk in the cellar.

In winter, when it was cold, I could not stay in the store, for the only way I had of keeping warm was to make a fire in a pot—like the old women in the market-place. That was too undignified; and I used to wait in the house of my landlord for a customer to call me.

Moses, my landlord, would sit near the oven baking potatoes for himself. He told me over and over again the dirty stories he had heard at the horse-fairs, and how he used to fool the peasants and the gypsies when he was a horse-dealer—before he got his backaches. Leah, his near-sighted wife, walked about slowly, her skirt longer in front than in back, stooping as if she were looking for something on the ground.

When the weather became warm, I sat on the high threshold of my store, and looked out upon the world—the clay huts of the village thatched with straw and the cupolas of the church. I would hear, at times, the screeching of a peasant's wagon along the road, or the squeal of a hog coming out of the mud near the well, when someone came for water; at times, I heard the whistle of a locomotive. Sometimes, I read the newspapers of years before that I used to buy by the pound and sell by the sheet to the peasants for rolling their tobacco into cigarettes. Once in a while, a chum would sit next to me for a couple of hours and we would talk, among other things, of going away from the village. But if my mother happened to come to the store just then—she came every day and always found something to complain about—she would say to me, "Why do you sit around all day bragging? Why don't you move the bag of salt here and the flour there?" And turning to my chum she would add, "You'll come some other time when he is not so busy."

Once, the sister of a chum of mine passed. Fanny was sixteen. As she walked she embroidered a tablecloth. I put down my newspaper that was three years old, and asked her to sit beside me on the threshold. She did, still embroidering the tablecloth, and we began to talk of what I had just read— that three years before there had been a big crop, and of other news people in the cities had long forgotten.

I saw my mother coming. As I watched her face, I knew she would say something harsh to me or Fanny. Mother slapped me twice and said, "You'll carry on with girls, will you?" Fanny blushed and hurried away. I too stood up and walked off. My mother screamed after me, "Where are you off to?"

"Wherever I please. And that nice little store you made for me—I give it back to you. Go ahead and watch it."

I went on home. My father saw that my face was flushed and asked, "What does this mean? Are you sick? Is anything the matter?"

"Yes," and I told him what had just happened, and what I had been feeling for more than a year, and asked for money to leave home. My father listened and walked about the room tugging at his beard. I was sorry for him.

My mother burst into the house with the key to the store in her hand. Father went up to her. "Let me have it," he said, and took the key. He held it out to me. "Do me the favor of going back to the store. It is not right to throw away a business because of a misunderstanding."

Once, when I was in Elizavetgrad for merchandise, I thought

I would look up my cousins, the Wolvovskys, whom I had not seen for almost ten years—we had stopped at their house in Dimitrefka, on the way to my grandfather's. Israel and Sarah Yetta were about my age. They had boasted then that, young as they were, they were earning money, and I had been envious. Ezekiel Wolvovsky, a glazier, could not earn enough; so his wife, Hannah, and the three older children had to help him. The eldest traveled about with his father; Hannah and Sarah Yetta baked little white rolls and sold them to taverns. Israel, who was then about eight, had been selling salt from a wagon on market days and the boss of it would give him a rouble a week. Just before we came he had found a better thing to do: he would buy a case of matches and sell it to the peasants in packages; if the fair was good, he earned as much as a rouble and a half.

Late in the afternoon I walked to the market-place, where Hannah, I had heard, kept a stand. I asked for her at the row of those who sold cereals and did not recognize her at first— she had grown old and brown, and, it seemed to me, much shorter; but when I told her who I was, she smiled and her friendly smile was still the same.

When it was dark we left for her home. I tried to carry her basket, but she would not let me have it. We had walked only a little way when a tall, dark, good-looking girl came up to us, said, "Good evening," and took the basket from Hannah's hands.

Hannah said, "Don't you recognize each other? This is Sarah Yetta," and she said to her daughter, "Don't you recognize Nathan?"

At her home Hannah introduced me to her father. He seemed scholarly and wise, kept himself aloof and took no part in the talk, but I could see that he was watching me. Sarah Yetta showed me her sewing-machines and what she was working at. She looked like her father Ezekiel and smiled just as he did, but I wondered if she smiled because she was thinking how foolishly I talked. When I came home I began to tell my parents of her until at last my mother said, "This is the third time I have asked you how Hannah is, and all you talk about is Sarah Yetta."

The next time I had to go to Elizavetgrad for merchandise, my father said, "Nathan, let Mother go this time. She has to be there."

Mother looked displeased when she came home, just as when she used to go to Dimitrefka to buy geese and they were too dear. She gave me the bills for the goods she had bought and said, "Here, check them," but said no more.

A month later I went to Elizavetgrad. I found my aunt not as friendly as always; when my uncle came home, he too kept looking away. After supper he said, "Nathan, why didn't you come to see us when you were last in Elizavetgrad?"

"I hadn't seen Ezekiel Wolvovsky's family for almost ten years. I thought I'd come over to see you before I went home, but the driver would not wait."

"Has Ezekiel Wolvovsky a good-looking daughter? Your mother told us you can't talk enough about her. The last time your mother was in town she talked to Ezekiel about a match between the two of you."

I could feel the veins in my temples throb for anger. I said loudly, "I know nothing about it." Then I thought that I must not show how displeased I was; so I smiled and said, "Now isn't that like a woman?" And I went on to tell my uncle and aunt how Sarah Yetta looked when she was a child—almost blind because of measles—and how she had changed; that was why I had spoken so much of her, but I never thought my mother would think of making a match between us. She had not spoken to me about it when she went to Elizavetgrad nor when she came back, and this was the first I heard of it. "Be sure," I added, "I will not be married before I know that I am not to serve in the army and before I am able to keep a wife without my parents' help."

When I came home I said to my mother, "Don't think that I am like your brother, and that you are going to marry me off with two slaps."

"You really think you are somebody," she answered; "perhaps the Wolvovskys do not want you."

I understood what had happened. "I don't know," I said, "whether it is the bridegroom they don't want or the mother-in-law."

My landlord wanted me to move from the store, although the lease had another year to run; and because I would not, would strike me when no one was about, for Moses was a strong man, much the stronger. He had rented us the store when he had no money to buy merchandise, but now that his wife was making money selling vodka without a license, he wanted the place for himself. My father thought it best to let him have it, rather than go to law, and rented another house to live in with the right to build a little store nearby.

We did better in the new store and I could stay at home in comfort, for whenever anything was needed I was called; but I was always under my mother's eye and she kept ordering me about. Three months after the new store was opened, we quarreled more bitterly than ever and she said, "Don't forget that you are mine and that your money is mine; what I say and what I want must be done."

"I am yours," I answered, "and your money is yours, but my thoughts and feelings are mine. You may have the store and its merchandise; I will have nothing to do with it; from now on I step in there no more." Nor did I.

I was about to go to Kremenchuk to look for work—it would have been a disgrace to my parents for me to work in Elizavetgrad where they were known, when Gershon, my father's partner, burned his back badly. Besides their trade to take care of, they had just made a contract with the Government to furnish meat and bread to the soldiers who were to march through Znamenka for a sham battle and had given much security. Gershon sent for me and said, "You see how things are: we cannot get help now and the doctor has just told me I won't be able to do a thing for months. Come to us until I am well. You will always have time to work for strangers. We'll pay you as much as you ask, and you will not be working for a stranger but for your father."

"I'll do what you wish and pay me what you wish, because I'm not doing it for the pay." And I took to work. When my father came to Gershon's house to talk over what to do, for there was no butcher to be hired, he found cattle slaughtered and enough meat for the next day. After two years without muscular work I had great pleasure in it.

For the three months Gershon could not work, I worked hard, especially during the month we fed the soldiers. One week I had so little sleep, I could not get up Saturday morning to go to the synagogue for prayers. My father was trying to wake me. I heard my mother say, "He is dead tired; let him alone. This time he will say his prayers at home."

They paid me thirty roubles. I bought a pair of boots, a cap of Persian lamb, and a grey coat of German cloth—and my mother never told me what to buy.

When I became eighteen, I felt that I could no longer stay in the village. My father said, "I don't want you to work for a stranger. I hear that Naphtali, who goes from fair to fair with hardware, is looking for a partner. You will be in business for yourself and at the same time see the world."

So, after the feast of Passover, we became partners. Naphtali said that he had goods worth one hundred roubles—which, when I knew something of the business, I found were worth no more than sixty. My father gave me one hundred roubles in cash; and Naphtali and I went to Elizavetgrad to buy more goods, and from there to the fair at Novobuch.

Business was good—we sold almost all we had brought, but it was hot and dusty in Novobuch and the water was bitter. After the fair, Naphtali said to me, "Before we go to Elizavetgrad for more goods, let's go to Romonovka. It is still two weeks until the fair of Shisterni." Romonovka, where Naphtali lived, was out of our way, but I did not blame him for wanting to be with his family. However, when we were in Romonovka a day or two, he said to me, "It will cost too much for both of us to go to Elizavetgrad; I'll go and you wait here." I did not want to, but my partner had all our money.

Naphtali brought his wife a shawl from Elizavetgrad and their children new shoes and other things. I looked through the bills for hardware, and, remembering what we had paid for certain goods, saw that the prices marked were such that whatever Naphtali had bought for his family had been paid for by our partnership. I said nothing, and let him think I did not understand what had been done.

We went to Shisterni, and from there to the fair at Zogradovka, and sold our goods. But Naphtali would not let me hold any of the money. "At fairs," he would say, "you must know how to hide it." I made believe I did not care.

My clothing became shabby and torn. I bought a ready-made suit, the best I could get, but the coat was too large and the trousers so wide I could get into one leg. After the fair at Zogradovka we had to buy more goods. I said that now I would go to Elizavetgrad too. Naphtali made a face and said that he was ashamed to go about with me to the wholesalers the way I was dressed, but I went anyway.

According to what we paid for goods, I saw that Naphtali's trip had cost the firm about twenty-five or thirty roubles, but still I said nothing. Dressed as I was, I was ashamed to see my uncle, but I did visit the Wolvovskys. I had heard that Ezekiel was dead. This time I found their home unhappy—Hannah and Sarah Yetta tearful instead of smiling.

I next went with Naphtali to the fair at Siroka, and from there to the fair at Pitorovka, not far from Znamenka. We did good business at both fairs, but Naphtali saw to it that I should not have a copeck of the firm's money and I lost count of how much we had. At Pitorovka I met a cousin of mine, a clever man, who also went about to the fairs. I told him my troubles and that I should like to end my partnership.

My cousin smiled and said, "I have a plan, but promise that you will tell no one, not even after it is all over, for it will do me harm." Then my cousin said, "When you see me coming to your stand tomorrow, go away. I'll ask your partner for a loan saying that I must pay cash for some goods. I will take every rouble he has. The day after tomorrow come to me and I'll give you the money. Then you will be able to end your partnership and get what is coming to you. You can't deal otherwise with a bird like that. He'll not be able to blame me for giving you the money, because you are his partner; but you must have sense enough not to let it out of your hands."

My cousin got two hundred and seventy roubles from Naphtali. Early next morning I had the money, put it deep in my pocket, and tied it there. Naphtali said to me, "Pack the cases," and went away. I knew where he was going and waited uneasily. In a few minutes he ran up to me, his face flushed, and shouted, "Give me the money!"

"Don't shout," said I, "I can keep it as well as you."

"You'll lose it!"

"I have carried more money about with me than you ever did and never lost any. Besides, before we settle up between us, you'll see this money no more than you can see your own ears."

"What do you mean? We must go to Elizavetgrad for more goods."

"Not I. Now we are going to Znamenka and those who brought us together shall part us."

"I'll tell your father what a thief you are."

"That you can never prove, but when I say that you are a thief, the bills prove it." At this Naphtali said no more. We hired a team to Znamenka, and my father and Naphtali's brother gave us each half the money and half the goods—one hundred and thirty-five roubles and more than fifty roubles worth of goods.

Israel Wolvovsky stopped at Znamenka, on his way home from Kremenchuk, to talk about going into the leather business with me. We liked the businesslike way in which he spoke, and I felt myself the rustic beside him.

My father wanted me to have half the profits because he was to invest three thousand roubles in cash and indorse the firm's notes for as much as twelve thousand—no one would trust Israel and me until we were quit of our service in the army. But Israel said that since he alone understood the business, he ought to have two-thirds of the profits and I only one.

I turned to my father. "Israel is right," I said. "He ought to have more than I because he knows more, but the business ought not to use your money for nothing. You do enough for us when you indorse our notes. I think Israel ought to have sixty per cent and I forty of the profits, but we should pay you interest for your three thousand roubles." And so it was made up between us.

In Elizavetgrad, I stayed with Israel in his mother's home. Luckily, there was an empty store in the row of leather merchants. We rented it at once. And at St. Simon's fair, when the big leather merchants brought their goods for sale, we bought our stock first-hand. Israel was the best of salesmen, but I soon found out that he was not the best of buyers: he paid no more than he should, but he would buy too much—he liked a lordly gesture—and in selling what was left over we often lost what we had made.

One Saturday afternoon, when I came to my uncle's house, I found that my aunt had given birth to a boy. I was to be the godfather at the circumcision and was greatly pleased at the honor. But when I went to say the afternoon prayers, the synagogue was dark; I sat down on a bench that had been painted the day before and was still wet. At home, I saw a broad yellow stain along the back of my overcoat and in the middle of it "69" in black.

Next morning, I went to a cleaner and dyer of clothes. He charged me three roubles but Monday gave me my coat with the same stain and number—showing worse because the coat itself was cleaned; nor would he return the three roubles. I bought cloth for a new coat and promised the tailor more for his work if he would have the coat ready by Friday. This he said he would surely do, but on Friday the coat was far from ready. It was too cold to be seen among my uncle's guests without an overcoat, and I could not be godfather.

When my mother came to town a few days later to buy stylish coats for my sisters, the elder of whom was not yet fourteen and the younger not yet twelve, I told her what had happened. No sooner did she hear that I had ordered a new coat than she began to scold and call me names. Hannah

142

Wolvovsky said to her, "But you are going to spend one hundred roubles for the girls, who are so young and will not need such coats until they are eighteen. Your son is in business and must meet people every day. He cannot walk about with paint on his coat and a number—like a convict—or without a coat in this cold weather."

"My daughters need the coats now. Do you think I'll keep them unmarried as long as you keep her?"—and my mother pointed at Sarah Yetta. "Why she is over twenty! I'll marry my daughters off when they are sixteen; at eighteen they will be long out of the market. But Nathan may have to be a soldier. What then will become of his clothes? Besides, how did he dare spend so much without asking me?"

I was sitting near the room of the widow who lived with the Wolvovskys and heard her say to her daughter, "Nathan has been telling me how clever his mother is; if this is clever, I am beautiful." I felt that I could no longer stay in the house nor face anyone.

My mother said loudly, "Where are you off to? I'll go with you." When we were out of the house, she said, "No wonder you bought yourself a new coat—you want to show off before Sarah Yetta."

"Mother," I said, "if you insult me again before others, you'll have to come to Elizavetgrad to watch the leather business as you are watching the store in Znamenka, for I will go to America to be far away from you. Nor shall my father nor my grandmother nor all the generations before us hold me back!"

After dinner, one day, I saw that Sarah Yetta was about to go to a customer. "I hope you won't mind if I go along on my way to the store." She was silent. "Are you ashamed to go with me?"

"Not with you, but with your boots. You know the saying: according to your clothes the world greets you when it meets you. It is time that you put on shoes and galoshes and did not go about in boots like a villager."

I answered, "People who see well do not look at the shell," and went out.

I saw that Sarah Yetta was smiling but that she was annoyed. I too was angry. I thought, Perhaps because of the way my mother carried on, Sarah Yetta is no longer friendly. Still, in a week or two, though I was used to my boots and hoped for deep snow that I might have to wear them, I bought myself shoes and galoshes.

Sarah Yetta became engaged to a young man for whom nobody in Elizavetgrad cared much, not even she. He was not a fool, but he had been brought up in a village where his family were the only Jews among a thousand peasants. Isaac kept his hands in his pockets, as if he did not know what to do with them, and when he spoke to anybody, looked at the ground. It had been made up between them that after their marriage they were to live in the city—away from the village she thought he might become as good as anybody: but when the young man and his parents came for the formal engagement, his mother wanted Sarah Yetta to make her home in their village. "What are you afraid of, my child?" Isaac's mother said sweetly. "That you won't have enough to eat?"

The formal engagement was put off until her mother could talk Sarah Yetta into it, and the young man's mother left her some cheap jewelry. One evening, when Hannah was telling Sarah Yetta that, after all, many people do live in villages and that she should not think too much of herself, I said to them, "I suppose it is none of my business; still, it would do no harm if Israel visited these people to see just how they do live. Let Sarah Yetta know what she is to look forward to. At Christmas, when the stores are closed for three days, Israel and I can go to Krilov to buy goods and on our way back we'll visit them."

And so we hired a good team and, after a day in Krilov, came to the village. "As if you had dropped from the sky," Isaac's mother said.

Fifteen or more peasants were sitting or standing about in the house, drinking tea, smoking their cheap tobacco and spitting, the snow on their boots melting upon the floor. This was how Isaac's parents made their living—selling tea, tobacco, and sweets. Their four daughters, dressed as peasant girls but with long skirts, waited on the customers. The girls walked about in mud, for the floor had no boards, and the younger peasants joked with them and handled them in the twilight. Their mother sat in a chair watching every corner and did all the talking to us. She explained that when Sarah Yetta came with her sewing-machines she would teach the girls how to sew and all together they would be able to make a nice living—sewing for the peasants instead of having them in the house and selling them tea.

We stayed an hour or so to be polite until the smell and smoke of the place gave me a headache. Outside, neither of us spoke for a while; then I said to Israel, "What do you say to that?"

He shook his head. "It is bad, but, after all, Sarah Yetta is twenty-one; my mother is worried and would like to marry her off."

At home, Israel spoke a good deal, this way and that, but no one could understand from what he said if he thought the place good or bad. I was sitting on pins and needles; when Israel was through, I told them all I had seen. "Let the fellow come to Elizavetgrad to live," I said, "as he said he would.

Let him try to make a living here." His mother would not have this, and Sarah Yetta broke off the engagement.

Olga's father had been a wealthy man; but one year, when it did not rain, he lost his crops, his cattle died, and he became poor. After his death, her mother, Leah, came to Elizavetgrad. Leah's uncle bought her a couple of machines for knitting stockings, her two daughters worked them, and she sold the stockings in the market-place; in this way they got along.

Olga was seventeen, tall and blonde. She had shining blue eyes and her blonde hair curled—when I looked at it I was reminded of waves driven by the wind. She was as graceful as the countess who lived for a while near Znamenka to whom we sold meat.

I told my aunt about Olga. She listened thoughtfully and then said to my uncle, "Leah has been in Elizavetgrad for almost four years and I have not met her. After Passover, look for her in the market-place and ask her to call with her children some Saturday."

The very first Saturday after Passover, my uncle met me in the synagogue and told me Leah and her children were to visit them, and my aunt wanted me to come too. I came long before the others. Leah had been beautiful, I had heard, and in spite of all her hardships she was still good-looking. I liked Olga more than ever. Leah asked us to visit her the following Saturday. When we came to her rooms, we saw at once how poor she was, but her home was clean. After that, I often went for walks along the boulevard with Olga and her sister.

Sarah Yetta and a cousin of hers—a clumsy ugly girl from a village—and I were asked to a wedding. When I asked

Sarah Yetta to dance with me, she said, "Dance with my cousin, will you? I am dancing with Israel."

I said sharply, "If you want to do your cousin a favor, why don't you tell your brother Israel to dance with her? Why do you try to hitch me to that heavy cart? If you don't want to dance with me, tell me it is Israel's dance, but I do not ask you for any advice as to my partners."

I made up my mind then and there to move from her mother's house: I was tired of Sarah Yetta's talking to me as if I were her younger brother. The next day I went to see my aunt and told her I must look for lodgings because it was too crowded at Hannah Wolvovsky's. My aunt said, "Where are you to go? You ought not to live with strangers. You may stay with us if you will sleep on the couch in the living-room."

In the summer, when it was too hot to sleep in the house, my aunt's mother, the children, and I slept in the courtyard. Before we fell asleep, my aunt's mother used to tell me of her brothers and sisters and of all their children—their business and their troubles. The landlord's handsome daughters would sit on the porch with their young men. She and I could see them against the lighted windows. At first they would talk and joke but, afterwards, she would stop her stories and say, "Woe is me! Like the Gentiles! Don't look, Nathan; turn over, say your prayers, and fall asleep."

Sitting in the garden, one Saturday afternoon, my uncle asked me how I was doing. I had been wanting for some time to talk to him about my business.

"Business is good," I said, "but I am worried. If Israel Wolvovsky is to be a soldier, my father's investment is not safe. If Israel will not have to serve, even if I must the year after, we can put my younger brother in my place; for Israel is honest. But if he is to be a soldier, I must hire a good man to do the selling—for good pay, and he'll never be as good as Israel; nor am I sure that he'll be as honest. And then, if I too must serve, I can never leave the business to my brother; I cannot leave him in the business with a stranger. I think that now, little by little, our business should be wound up. If Israel finds that he need not serve, we'll be able to buy fresh stock."

Uncle said, all in a breath as he always spoke, "I think you are right, but don't be restless; say nothing to your parents because they will talk and this will hurt your business. And it is too early to talk to Israel about winding it up, for the season is about to begin and in the next few months you must earn most of the profits for the year—you would only discourage him. You'll have plenty of time to wind up the business before Israel is sent to his regiment, and even if you lose a few hundred roubles then, your profits this season should pay for all that."

In November Israel Wolvovsky was drafted as a soldier. Neither my father nor Israel himself thought it likely he would be taken, because he was always short of breath if he did no more than walk. A day or two after we knew that he had to serve, I had a talk with him, and told him why the business ought to be wound up and that he would be paid for his help. "I'll help you," he said, "because when your father invested his money, he trusted me rather than you; and I ought to see that none of it is lost, even if you were not to pay me."

I told my uncle what Israel had said. "Someone else in his place," said my uncle, "would have wanted to be well paid."

"Not Israel. Someone else, when he went to the fairs of Kharkov and Poltava with seven thousand roubles, might have run away to America."

After my talk with Israel, we bought no .more and began to pay our debts, even those not due. In a few weeks we sold out all we had, some goods at a profit, some at cost, but nothing at a loss. When we had paid everybody, I said to Israel, "Now let us go to one who understands the leather business and let him say what you lost in giving up the business as we did."

It was decided that I owed Israel fifty-three roubles—this was all he had. He had spent the thousand roubles he had made during the fifteen months we were partners, most of it for his mother and brothers. Luckily, the regiment to which he had to go was only eight hours away by train, and this would not cost him much. He kept three roubles for himself and gave the rest to his sister, Sarah Yetta.

I bought some goods that I could sell in Znamenka and hired a peasant to take me home. When I came into the house, covered with snow, my parents were surprised. Father, shaking my hand, asked, "What brings you here?"

My mother said, "Can't you see that it is all up with the leather business, and he comes home like one who loses the horse and brings back only the whip? Here, he has two bundles of goods for your fifteen thousand roubles!"

I took the notes out of my pocket. "Here you have all your notes," I said to my father. Then I took out the money. "Here is all the money you lent us—and the interest too. I bought the goods out of my profits."

The merchandise I had brought was profitable, and I did not have the worries of a large business to make a living in Znamenka, but I could not stand the place. Every two weeks or so, on one excuse or another, I went to Elizavetgrad.

Once, they were playing *Natalka Poltavka* at the theatre. Uncle and I bought a box, seating six, for six roubles, and my aunt invited Leah and her daughters to come with us. The evening we were to go, my aunt's brother and his wife came on a visit. When Jeremiah's wife heard that we were going to the theatre, she said she must go too. Her husband said, "Of course, we can go; eight can get into a box—they are not always strict about that. Besides, Jacob isn't coming before the second act."

I did not know what to say without hurting my aunt. My aunt too was afraid to say anything for fear of hurting her sister-in-law. So we all walked slowly to the theatre, I beside Olga, my aunt beside her sister-in-law, Olga's sister beside her mother, and Jeremiah by himself.

In a little while, he came up to me and said, "I want to know the number of the box. Let me see your ticket." I took it out of my pocket and was about to tell him the number when he took the ticket out of my hand and read the number aloud, put the ticket into his own pocket and said, "You know the number now; go ahead of us." Olga and I looked at each other, but saw no help for it, and went on ahead.

We found the box, took off our coats, and sat in the worst seats. In a few minutes the others were there. Jeremiah said, "When I came in, I happened to hear that tonight they are going to be strict and no more than six may sit in a box. I am afraid, Nathan, you must leave." The others were astonished. My aunt stood up; looking sternly at her brother, she said, "I will not stay." His wife was about to burst into tears.

I called my aunt aside and whispered, "Why hurt your sister-in-law? She is not to blame. Besides, Uncle will not know where to find you. I'll get another ticket."

I said good-night, politely wished that they would be amused, and was about to go, when Olga said, "Wait a minute. If there are to be no more than six in a box, somebody must leave when your uncle comes. I'll go with you now."

I bought two good seats in the orchestra for three roubles. Olga and I were glad to be by ourselves and we liked the play. But in the box above nobody was amused, and, when my uncle came and found out what had happened, he gave his brother-in-law a talking-to that made matters no pleasanter.

I went to Elizavetgrad again for the feast of Purim. Many passengers changed at Znamenka; going to the train—it was four o'clock in the morning—I saw a woman with many bundles. She was poorly dressed and I could see she had no money for a porter. I helped her, put the bundles under a bench and on the shelves, and sat down, facing her. She thanked me again and again in Ukrainian. When the train pulled out and the conductor lit the candles, I saw that she was a Jewess.

She was going to Elizavetgrad, she said. Her husband was there; why then should she stay in Rygorod? I asked her if her husband's name was not Michael Wolvovsky. "How do you know?" she asked, surprised.

"That's easy. I was in partnership with his brother, Israel, and I know that Michael married a girl from Rygorod."

"So you were Israel's partner?"

"I wish he didn't have to be a soldier, I'd be his partner still."

"You like him so much?"

"Yes, I do, and I like all the family."

"I wonder that you can say so, for I do not like my husband's people at all," and she went on and on to tell me why.

I said at last, "I was in their house as one of their own, and knew everything that was going on. Michael was never able to make a living as a glazier, to say nothing of providing for a wife. No one knows better than I that his younger brother, Israel, spent his last rouble for him when he was married. His sister, Sarah Yetta, gave him the money to buy a diamond for his glass-cutter when he lost it, and she has had to give him—often—money to buy glass. You say that you have heard that they buy their bread, but that is not because they are extravagant or lazy, as you say: they have no time to bake bread—Hannah leaves the house for her stand in the market-place when it is dark and comes home in the evening, and Sarah Yetta works until late at night. They do enough if they bake once a week and are able to cook their supper. Your husband is not sending you any money—not, as you say, because he must help them—but because he isn't earning any. But I'll say no more."

"You may talk or keep still; I'll think as I always did," she said.

When we came to Elizavetgrad, she was about to walk with all her bundles to where Hannah lived—almost four miles from the station. After much talk, I got her to let me bring her there in a carriage, but it was too early for me to go into the house and I went on to my uncle's.

Later, in the morning, as I was washing myself, I heard Sarah Yetta's voice. I wondered what she was doing in my aunt's house. I dressed as quickly as I could and came into the room. "Good morning," I said and held out my hand. "I met your guest this morning." Sarah Yetta did not take my hand and looked at me angrily. I did not know what to say or do, for my aunt was staring at us, and I went into another room until Sarah Yetta was gone.

"Why is she angry at you?" my aunt asked.

"I don't know." I smiled. "Maybe because I brought her

sister-in-law," and I told my aunt what Michael's wife had said.

"Who knows what she said you had said. I sent for Sarah Yetta to do some sewing. You ought not to be angry—she may not be to blame."

"Well, let her be angry until she find out what her sister-in-law is like."

Waiting for the train to Znamenka on the platform at Elizavetgrad, I saw a carriage driven up quickly, the blinds drawn, and a gendarme on the step at each side. The carriage stopped, its door was flung open, and out came four more gendarmes and an officer, to whom a man was chained. They hurried the prisoner into the waiting-room for passengers traveling first-class, and a dozen soldiers with loaded rifles saw to it that no one followed. More carriages were driven up; they brought an old man and woman and young men and women—all pale and in tears.

The man chained to the officer had been pale, too, but had looked proud and calm. His family stood about the window of the waiting-room and the prisoner from within spoke to them in a loud voice; he was heard by all on the platform. "My dear ones," he said, "the tyrannical government has caught another sacrifice, and does not even let him kiss for the last time his own flesh and blood. But do not weep, my dear ones. I die for a holy cause—not for the Czar somewhere on a battlefield but for our country and the Russian people!" In the meantime, the train I was waiting for pulled in, and the soldiers ordered those who were taking it to get into the cars and all others to leave the station at once.

The passengers were all talking about the prisoner. I said,

153

"Whatever his crime, I think they should have let him kiss his family good-by."

A man with stern eyes, dressed as a beggar, was at my elbow and said, "Young man, think less—it will be healthier," and sat down near me.

A Jew said in a low voice in Yiddish, "Take a mouthful of water and keep quiet."

During the week of Passover I was in Elizavetgrad again and I stopped on the main street to read the proclamations. In one of them I saw my name among many others—I was to report for military service in November. I had always thought that I should like to be a soldier, but when I saw my name on the list, I did not want to go at all.

That evening I told my uncle of the prisoner I had seen and what he had shouted. Uncle thought a while and then said, "I have never talked politics with you, Nathan, but I can tell you one thing—be careful. You know Brina who lives in Znamenka—she had a younger brother."

"I remember him. He used to visit her when he was a student in the university at Odessa."

"Yes, but now he is no longer of this world, and his sisters are even afraid to talk about him. They hanged him in Odessa three years ago for—those things. Don't talk politics, if you care for your life, and if you don't want to make us all trouble."

The next evening I went to see Olga. She said, "Why should we stay in the house this spring night? Let us go for a walk on the boulevard." Her sister said she did not want to go. As we walked along, Olga took my arm. We spoke of how hard life was in Russia—above all for the Jews: it would be best to go to America. It was suddenly clear to me that I ought to marry Olga and that we should go to America together. She saw that I was lost in thought and

154

said smiling, "You must be in love, Nathan, that you are so silent."

"You have guessed."

"Who is the lucky girl?"

"I can't even tell the girl herself just yet, because I can only marry if I go to America. In Russia I must be a soldier. And I must first talk my parents into letting me go."

"But I only want to know who the girl is."

"I promise you that you shall be the first to know."

When I brought her home and said good-by, she asked me in an anxious voice when I was coming again. "As soon as possible," I said, "but no later than in two weeks."

I began to talk to my parents about leaving for America instead of serving almost four years in the army. My mother seemed to think it wiser for me to go. When I came to Elizavetgrad again, I told Olga how well things were going.

"If so, can't you ask the girl you love to marry you?"

"I want to be sure, first, that my parents are willing that I go to America. They themselves will then want me to marry here to see the girl I marry—that they like the girl I want to marry. And I am sure they will like her."

Two weeks before Pentecost I went to Elizavetgrad. My aunt smiled and told me that Olga had come to ask for me. "Can you tell me what she wants?"

"Oh, I promised to tell her something, but girls are so curious."

Uncle asked me to come into the garden. We sat down on a bench. "Nathan," he said, "you know that your happiness is mine. Tell me, then, that I may know what to say —do you love Olga?"

"Yes."

"Would it hurt you much if she became engaged to another?"

I could say nothing for a few minutes. "I won't take it to heart," I said at last.

"Your aunt and I were afraid you might."

I told him all I had said to Olga. But if she could not wait a little while, it only showed that she cared little for me.

"But she has had nothing to do with what has happened," said my uncle. "Her mother told me that Olga's sister is engaged, and that a cousin of theirs has heard from his brother in America who has become rich: he writes that he will send for any girl who would make him a good wife. Her mother is coming here with this cousin to talk about sending Olga."

"How can she think of sending her child to the end of the world to a man neither has seen? But if Olga wants to go, don't worry about me." Just then I saw them coming into the courtyard. "Here they are now. I will stay here," and I picked up a newspaper and tried to read.

In a few minutes I heard Olga coming towards me. I saw that she was crying. "What is there to cry about?" I asked.

"Didn't your uncle tell you anything?"

"He did."

"Then you know what I am crying about."

"But I don't. Sometimes people cry because of trouble—and sometimes for happiness."

"I am crying because my mother has come to talk such nonsense. Do you think I have no will or understanding of my own? I have my dreams just as you have yours."

I took her hand as she sat beside me. "I wish I could tell you who the girl I love is, but I want to do my parents the honor of asking them to see her before I ask her to be my wife."

"And if your parents should not like her?"

"I am sure they will. But if not, I have the right to marry the girl I love."

156

A day or two before Pentecost my aunt gave birth to a boy, and I was the godfather. Olga was godmother. When I came home my mother asked, "Who was the godmother?" I told her. "Is she a good-looking girl?

"She is beautiful—and clever too. I wish that you and Father might see her, because I think she is the girl for me to marry and take to America."

The next day my mother bought cloth for a new coat and told the tailor to make it as quickly as possible; but, in spite of his promises, it took quite a while before the coat was ready. As for my father, he would not go at all. "What do I know about girls?" he said to my mother. "If you like her and if Nathan likes her, I am satisfied."

When my mother came from Elizavetgrad, I asked her nothing; and she said nothing until my father said, "Well?"

"If he is going to America," she answered, "let him have her—at least we know whom he is marrying. We have to do here with beggared aristocrats."

I laughed cheerfully, and said, "If that's so, I'm going to Elizavetgrad Friday."

Father said, "Don't wait until Friday. A match ought not to be put off—someone else may become engaged to her. Go tomorrow."

When I came into my aunt's house, she said, "God himself brought you! Did you get your uncle's letter?"

"No."

"Then I'll tell you. A matchmaker brought a young man called Vishnivetsky to Olga's mother. He has finished his service in the army and has a thousand roubles. He wants to marry Olga and take her to America!"

"Does she want him?"

"He is a fine man and her mother is urging her to have him."

"Then I think I'll wait to see what will happen."

"It will be too late!"

"Anyway, I can't go there before evening. They are all in the house working now, and I cannot talk to her alone."

I found nobody at home except Olga—just as I wished. I said, "Olga, the only thing that is left for me to say is that you are the girl I spoke of all the time—will you marry me?" She burst into tears and ran from the room.

I sat where I was, miserable and uncertain what to do. In about five minutes Olga came back. She could not look straight at me. "Olga," I said, "we were good friends such a long time; I should like—whatever your answer—that we should still be friends, but I must know where I am before I leave the house."

She said in a low voice, "I am not to blame: you are too late." Just then Vishnivetsky came in. I said good-by as soon as I could and wished them happiness.

I could not go right back to my uncle and aunt, but walked about to think over what had happened, and if I had been to blame. I told myself that Olga did not love me; and Vishnivetsky was the better man, because he had more money and could go at once, but I had to report to the draft board to save my parents a fine of three hundred roubles. It was all for the best.

I found my uncle and aunt waiting for me. Both asked at once, "What's new?"

"Nothing. She said I am too late." My aunt sighed. I added, "Don't worry about me. If I was too slow for her, she is too quick for me. At a fair you are often given a bill that looks like money, but the holder knows it is counterfeit."

"You are not right, you are not right," said my uncle.

And my aunt said, "Stay here a few days. The course of

true love never did run smooth, but in the end all will be well." I stayed until Saturday, and in the evening went home.

I found time heavy on my hands and went to the railroad station. A regiment of cavalry on their way to Elizavetgrad halted to feed their horses. The colonel shouted to his orderly, "Don't keep my horse standing; walk him there and back," pointing to a post; and he and the other officers went into the waiting-room for passengers traveling first-class to drink at the buffet.

The officers came out tipsy. The colonel shouted, "Orderly, my horse!" At the moment the orderly was near the post. He ran up with the horse, but the colonel had become impatient. As the soldier stood at attention before him, he punched the soldier's face until the blood ran from nose and mouth. At each punch the soldier said, "I am guilty, Your Excellency."

The regiment was ordered to mount and they trotted away. Four cabmen were near the station—two Jews and two Gentiles. One of these, Stopka, had been a soldier for eight years. The cabmen began to gather what was left of the hay for their own horses. The officer in the last squad turned and shouted to the two Gentiles, "Christians, take the hay, but give none to the Jews—beat them, hang them, kill them, those cursed ones!"

Stopka, as soldiers did, saluted and answered, "I hear, Your Highness."

The other Gentile, laughing, stood before the Jewish drivers and said, "You get no hay—the officer does not want you to have any."

Stopka came up to him and said, "You fool, do you think that what an officer says is holy? I would as soon listen to that officer as to a dog; and if you grab, you get nothing.

We'll gather all the hay into one place and then share alike, for we four are alike poor."

I went into the waiting-room for passengers traveling third-class and found a newspaper on a bench. I sat down and read the leading article: Mother Russia has enemies in Europe and in Asia, but the enemies without are not as dangerous as those within; while those without are leaving Russia alone, we must as quickly as possible annihilate the enemies within to be ready for those without. I took the newspaper along. Passing the embankment in the middle of Znamenka I saw a freight train coming from Elizavetgrad. As it went slowly through the village my old enemy, Mekishka, jumped off. He slouched up to me and said, "They have begun to beat up the Jews in the city. If it keeps on, we'll beat them up here too; but I'm going to hang you."

I met my father in the synagogue, and we walked home together. He asked me, "Why are you so sad?"

"Because of what I have seen today, and heard, and read." When we had eaten, I said, "Why should I serve so many years under drunken officers and, if there is war, as this newspaper hints, be killed for a country like this? Isn't it better for me to go now to America? If I do not get along there within a year, I'll not have missed much when I come back to serve. But don't keep me here! I'll take one hundred roubles for my expenses and the rest of my money I leave with you to pay the fine."

My father thought a while and then said, "My son, what you say is foolish. We Jews are in exile and must suffer everywhere. Besides, the Talmud says that the laws of the land we live in are our laws. If it is your destiny to live, you will come back even from war unharmed."

But my mother said, "You are right, Simon; but if there

is talk of war, let him go to America—and as quickly as he can, before the borders are closed."

I was walking across the railway platform at Znamenka, when I saw Olga's sister and the young man who had been courting her, and Olga herself with Vishnivetsky. I greeted them and asked what they were doing in Znamenka. Olga's sister said, "We are going to America."

"Then you must be married and I congratulate you."

"You may congratulate them," said Vishnivetsky, "but not us. Olga doesn't want to marry until we are in America." I looked at her.

She asked, "How did you know that we were here?"

"I didn't. I am just coming from Kaminka where I went to say good-by to some relative because I, too, am going to America."

"But didn't you say that you were going to report to the draft board to save your father the fine?"

"I thought then that I should not be going alone; but now that I have no one to take, I have enough for my expenses and to pay the fine."

Olga put her hand on my arm and said, "Let us take a walk. Show me your station," and turning to Vishnivetsky asked him to excuse her.

I said, "Why? The platform is wide enough for three. If Vishnivetsky will walk with us, it will be very pleasant." In this way we walked about for hours. Olga hinted that she had something to tell me and tried to send Vishnivetsky away; now she was thirsty, now she asked him to bring her a handkerchief from her bag. But I did not want to hear what she had to say, and went for the drink and brought her handkerchief.

In a few days I was on my way to Elizavetgrad to say good-by to relatives and friends there, riding all night because the driver stopped to let the horse graze. When we came to the place where the fairs were held, just outside the city, it was morning. Suddenly I saw Sarah Yetta walking over the fields. I wondered what she was doing there so early. I forgot that we were angry at each other and, jumping off the wagon, went to meet her. "Where are you going?" I asked.

"To the cemetery. I am going to pray at my grandfather's grave before I leave for America."

"Well, I am leaving for America, too," and we wished each other a pleasant journey.

On a day in August I left Znamenka for America. Gershon, my father's partner, brought the horse and wagon to drive me to the station. When I began to say good-by, I saw tears in my father's eyes and my mother fainted. My brothers and sisters were crying loudly. I was almost ready to stay at home. When my mother was brought to, I said that if she wished it, I would not go.

"No," she said, "I shall faint again when they take you away to be a soldier—and, maybe, to war, and then you won't be able to stay."

My father, Gershon, and I climbed on the wagon and drove off. Gershon was begging me not to go. "I served as a soldier," he said, "and am I not alive?"

I hurried into the train not to be seen. My father brought me a ticket to Kremenchuk and gave me my money. The bell rang for the third time, we kissed each other, and in another minute or two the train was leaving.

At Kremenchuk I was to change for the train that went to Romny—from there to go to Vilna and meet the agent of those who were to bring me across the border. But I could not reach the window to buy a ticket. So many peasants were going to Tavria, where the steppes are, for work, they were standing in five rows to get to the cashier—and my train was to leave in a little while.

I saw a well-dressed young man, a good-looking young woman at his side, watching me. The young man came up to me and said, "Where are you going?"

"To Romny. But I can't get a ticket and I'm afraid I'll miss the train."

The stranger said, "Give me the money. I'll get you a ticket." I gave him five roubles. The young man went up to the peasants crowding about the cashier's window, and shouted, "You pigs, give a man a chance to buy a ticket! Because of you I'll miss my train!" They made room for him at once, and he brought me the ticket and my change.

"Don't thank me," he said. "The train is waiting; go in at once. Don't ask your way of any gendarme. A young man on his way has to keep clear of them, eh?"

I went into one of the cars and sat in a corner. It was so dark I could not see what the passengers looked like. When it began to dawn, the young man who had bought my ticket was facing me. The good-looking young woman saw me and nudged her companion. He introduced the young woman as his bride, and asked me again where I was going. I answered, "To Vilna—to look for work."

The stranger smiled. Then he said, "We are Jews, although we cannot talk Yiddish. We were born in Moscow, and have just been driven out by the police. Our parents came from Mogilov to Moscow when they were young; now we must go back, all of us, to Mogilov. But we are going on to America, although just now we are visiting relatives. I tell you all this that you may trust us. You do not have to tell me that you are going to Vilna to go on to America, or that you have no passport. You are either a soldier who is deserting or a conscript who is not going to report. You must stay twelve hours in Romny until the train leaves for Vilna. You will wait at the railroad station, of course, and a gendarme will most likely ask you for your passport. If you stay in a hotel, you must register and they will ask you for your passport at once. But if you trust us we will help you."

I told them they were right—I had no passport.

"We are glad that you trust us," said the young woman. "Now you will go with us, but ask no questions—look, listen, and keep quiet."

As soon as the train stopped at Romny, the young man went down the platform to a porter from a hotel and said something in a low voice; and we left the station. When we came to the hotel, the porter carried our baggage into the basement. We followed him. The young man opened one of the bags and took out some old clothing for himself and a calico wrapper for his wife. "Quick!" he said.

They changed their clothes; and he looked like a cab-driver and she like a servant. He put phylacteries on and kept his face towards the wall, but did not pray. His wife held a towel in her hands and, standing near the window, kept watch. I took out my phylacteries too and began to pray aloud. He said sharply, "Pray quietly and stand in a corner so that you are not seen if anybody passes near the house."

After a while, I heard a heavy step and through the window saw a policeman, a note-book under his arm, coming towards the door. The young woman ran upstairs, opened the front door, went down a few steps, wiping her face with the towel, and greeted the policeman. He asked if there were any newcomers and she answered, "Not this train."

"A bad day for you."

"Let the boss worry," she said.

When they no longer heard the policeman's steps, the young

man turned from the wall and his wife tossed the towel away. He threw off his phylacteries, told me to fold them, and he and his wife changed back into their clothes. Then they sent for the landlord, and asked for the best rooms in the house. The porter carried our belongings to the upper floor. They ordered a samovar of tea to be brought up; opening one of the bags, they took out roast chicken and duck, jam, cakes, and brandy. They asked me to the feast, and I did not say no.

After we had a nap, we ate again and told each other stories. I told of life in the small towns and villages and they of the Jews of Moscow—how because of the search for those who had no right to be there, they had learnt all kinds of tricks. At the station, the young man bought me my ticket to Vilna. In taking the change, I saw that I was charged nothing for the stay at the hotel. I wanted to share the cost of that. At last he said, "All right, give three roubles to the poor."

When the train reached Vilna, before I could get out of the car, I was met by several agents of those who smuggled people across the border. I went with one of them. It was late that evening before his chief could talk to me.

He asked one hundred and ten roubles for the trip to New York. But I wanted to be, if possible, on the same steamer as the sister of my aunt in Elizavetgrad, who was on her way to America. So for fifty-five roubles I was to be brought to Hamburg. After he had my money, he told one of his men to take care of me for the night and ordered me not to step into the street until I went to the train.

His man took me and four others to a garret, a place pitch-dark, full of cobwebs and squeaking mice. Here the five of us sat or stood until past nine in the morning, when, neither washed nor combed, we were led to the station. In the train others came up to us until we were twenty. The man in charge had to tell us not to talk so loudly.

"What of it," he said, "if you spend one night in discomfort, when you have to be hidden from the police? If you do not keep your mouths shut, the conductor of the train will hear you. And at the next station he may call in a gendarme and we all go back to our homes under convoy—then you will have pleasant places to sleep in." After that we kept quiet, and if anyone had to talk again, the rest saw to it that he said little.

At Shavli, the agent told us we were to stop there for the Sabbath. He led us to the home of the driver who was to bring us over the border. We did not stir out of the house. That evening we were crowded into a covered wagon. The driver went as fast as he could and we were well shaken and bounced about. Every three hours they changed the horses. In the morning we stopped at a house in Tovrick. The man in charge put some of us in the garret, some in the cellar, the women in the only room, and me and another, perhaps because we had complained least, into the privy in the yard.

In two hours we were ordered back into the wagon and told not to worry—the coast was clear. "Each of you will get a passport and when the soldier asks for it, just give it to him." I read mine: my name was Bassie Baila Hendler, female, sixty-seven years old, grey-haired, and so forth. I could not help laughing at what had become of me.

We came to a little bridge. A soldier shouted, "Halt!" and said to the man sitting beside the driver, "How many have you there?"

"Twenty-one."

"Have all passports?"

"As always."

"Let me have them." The soldier climbed into the wagon

and counted the passengers, took away their passports, counted them, and said, "Right. Twenty-one roubles." The agent gave him the money, the driver whipped the horses, and in two minutes we were in Germany. The passengers began to joke and laugh at what we had been through. At the railway station, I sent this telegram to my parents and uncle: "Merchandise arrived complete and satisfactory."

The train to which we were led had no seats. Those who became too tired to stand sat on the floor. But in two hours we came to Memel. Here we were lodged to wait until a ship, leaving in two days, should take us to Stettin.

In my lodging-house I met a girl from Elizavetgrad. I had never seen her there, but I knew some of her family and she knew mine. I was lucky, she said, to have to wait only two days, for she had been waiting eight. She was glad she had taken plenty of food with her; she still had plenty for two and if I'd help her eat it, she'd have less to carry. I liked neither her face nor her family, but I had not had decent food since Romny, and was hungry.

The ship was loaded with lumber, below and on deck. There was only one cabin, and the passengers, about sixty of us, sat or lay on the boards of the cargo under an awning. When we were out on the Baltic it began to rain, the sea became rough, the wind bitter cold—and I had no overcoat. The girl from Elizavetgrad took out of her baggage a new quilt that her mother had given her as a parting gift, and covered me with it; under this I was warm and slept.

In Stettin we were led to a train, like that to Memel—without seats or water-closet. But that morning we came to Hamburg. Here I left the girl who had been so kind to me; she went with the others, and I was brought to a lodging-house where, I was told, I might find out what steamer my aunt's sister was taking.

They could not understand my Yiddish nor I their German, and I found out nothing. They did make me understand that the very next day a steamer was leaving for New York and that they would sell me a ticket for fifty-five roubles, but, if I did not buy it before evening, I should have to leave the house and look for another place to stay overnight.

The lodging-house was five stories high. The rooms were stuffy; though the sun was shining, inside the house it was dark. The emigrants were sitting about or lying on the beds—springs without mattresses—or on their bags and bundles. They were mostly Jews, almost all going to the United States, a few to the Argentine Republic—Russian, Rumanian, Polish, Galician, and Hungarian Jews, some without money enough to buy their steamship tickets, others whom the line would not take because their eyes were bad and they would only be sent back, and still others who had to stay in Hamburg because their children had fallen sick.

When I came to the top floor, I was happy to find my aunt's sister and her children in one of the corners. They were leaving the next day on the steamer for which the clerk in the office had tried to sell me a ticket. I went down at once and bought one.

Next morning, several wagons were drawn up before the door and loaded with the packs and bags of the emigrants. We followed our baggage through the streets as if at a funeral. Late in the morning the steamer moved; it was warm and sunny, the air was fresh, and on a deck above us a band was playing.

The sixth day out there was a storm. The steamer was tossed about; inside, nothing stayed in one place, things knocked and fell and rolled. None of the passengers were allowed on deck. We were not far from New York, and one morning saw land. That afternoon the steamer anchored in the port of New

York. At Castle Garden, I changed my last bill—five roubles—for American money, and was free to go into the New World.

I did not know that married women were held at Castle Garden until their husbands called for them. I looked about for my aunt's sister in the crowd outside the building, and at last began to shout her name. A policeman came up to me and spoke in an angry voice. It sounded like gibberish, but I understood one word—"address."

I took a slip of paper from my pocket with the address of my aunt's brother on it. The policeman read it and did not give it back to me. He put his hand under my arm and led me to a cab, pushed me inside, slammed the door and, giving the slip of paper to the driver, winked. The driver picked up the reins and we were off. I tried to open the door but could not.

It was not long before the cabman stopped, opened the door, and spoke to me. When he saw that he was not understood, he made circles on his left palm with the forefinger of his right hand. I understood that he wanted money, and tried to show by gestures that he would be paid when we came to the place we were going to. But, without wasting more time, the cabman went through my pockets; and, finding only two dollars and sixty cents, made a face. He gave me ten cents, closed the door, and brought me to a house on Rutgers Street.

He rang the doorbell. A woman opened the door and he asked her something; she nodded. He motioned to me to come out of the cab, put my bag on the sidewalk, and drove off. The woman told me in German to wait. I waited about five minutes. Then she came downstairs and said I was to walk up to the fifth floor and ring the bell of one of the doors.

But I did not have to look for any number; a young woman was standing in an open doorway, smiling pleasantly, and she said, "Come in, I am Nathan Bershadsky's wife. He hasn't come from work, but he will be home soon. But please tell me where my sister-in-law is and her children." I told her how I had come in the cab. She laughed and said, "Oh, that's why the housekeeper said, 'Mrs. Bershadsky, a millionaire has come from Europe to visit you!'"

Nathan came soon and then Pesach Budnichenkoff, his brother-in-law. The next day Pesach brought his family to the flat he had ready. Nathan said to me, "You will stay with us until you find work." Monday evening he took me to see a friend of his who was a foreman in a cigarette factory, but work was slack and he could not take on a beginner. As we were walking home, Nathan said, "In America everybody must find his own work, and you will have to do the same."

The next evening, after supper, I went to see a cousin of mine who lived nearby. The head of the family he stayed with was a man of fifty, with a reddish beard, tall and stern. His wife was a good-looking woman. As she sat in a rocker she did not take her eyes from the mirror. They had two boarders, both my cousins. After some talk, I found out that the man with the beard was a cousin too.

The cousin I had come to see thanked me for news of his mother, but told me that he had just written her that if she would send him the money, he would go back to Russia, for he could find no work. We were all silent for a while, and then the head of the house, who had been looking at me sternly, said, "So you are little Simon's son. Where are you staying?"

"At Nathan Bershadsky's."

He burst out laughing. "I heard that your father was so pious—and you are in with that gang of atheists! They'll put you on the right track!"

His wife, never looking away from the mirror, said, "They

don't have to put him on the right track—he is there." Both said no more and their boarders, too, were silent.

I said good-night and rose to go. Both boarders stood up and went with me. When we were in the street, my cousin who wanted to go back to Russia said, "Don't be surprised at them. They are good people but old-fashioned. That you stay with people they dislike is enough to have them suspect you. But you can come to their house because you come to see us, and their children will like you. Even Aaron will change his mind when you live elsewhere." The other went on to tell me of his work making corncob pipes for three dollars a week. He would be content but for his fear that the machine might cut off his fingers.

When I told Nathan where I had been, he smiled and said, "That Jesuit!"

In the morning I walked about looking for work. I went into every building that looked like a factory. When I saw people working in the street or on a new building, I thought, I mustn't be ashamed to ask for work, but everywhere I was answered, "No." I came home dead tired and downhearted.

Suddenly someone rapped at the door. When Mrs. Bershadsky opened it, I was surprised to see Olga's sister and her husband. She pointed at me and said sadly to her husband, "He is here—you see Vishnivetsky is not crazy."

I did not see that she was angry. Mrs. Bershadsky asked them to sit down. I asked them how Olga and Vishnivetsky were. Olga's sister said to her husband, "Tell him," and her eyes filled with tears.

I looked at them wondering. "What happened?"

My visitor said coldly and slowly, his left eye twitching, "I will tell you if the lady will do us the favor of allowing us to step into another room."

We went into another room and he told me how, when

they left Znamenka, Olga was angry at Vishnivetsky because he had been watching her, and had not left her alone with me for a moment. She kept saying that it was vulgar of him and, besides, she was afraid to marry him, if he was going to be insanely jealous. And so she kept on until they came to Kiev and, afterwards, kept herself aloof until they boarded the steamer. No sooner had the steamer left the pier than she told Vishnivetsky she would have nothing to do with him; as for the money he had spent, when she came to America she would work and pay it all back. Vishnivetsky complained until all the steerage knew of their quarrel. The passengers schemed to marry them, for then, they said, she would make no more fuss. They had a bridal canopy ready, and pushed her under it beside Vishnivetsky, blocking her way until the words that married them were spoken. But Olga said that was no marriage and she would never be Vishnivetsky's wife. She had to go with him to an uncle of his, somewhere in a small town, but he was writing all their friends and relatives in New York that she still said she would never be his wife. And all that heard of this blamed me.

"Me?" said I. "Come into the other room. I want your wife to hear what I have to say. Besides, all may hear it for I have nothing to hide. Now I understand why Aaron and his wife were so cold to me."

I said to her sister, "You may believe it or not, but when Olga told me I was too late, I was through with her. I am not Vishnivetsky. I force myself on nobody. As soon as she was engaged to Vishnivetsky, she was dead for me, and it was I who gave her no chance to talk at Znamenka—not Vishnivetsky. He knows that. I didn't want to hurt her by telling her what I have just told you. Write to Vishnivetsky that you have seen me and what I tell you. Olga will understand that

172

she must forget me. I am sorry for her, but I pity her only as a friend."

They gave me their address and asked me to come to see them Sunday. They lived with a woman called Ida "the Chicken Dealer." When I came there, as soon as she heard my name, she turned to me and said, "Oh, so this is that nice fellow!"

I said, "Mrs. Whatever-you-call-yourself, if you don't like me, don't look at me; I didn't come to visit you."

Olga's sister frowned at Ida "the Chicken Dealer," and said to me, "I have a letter for you from Vishnivetsky." He would be too glad to believe what Olga's sister had written him, but, since he had taken a number of letters to me and to my uncle in Elizavetgrad from Olga, he could only suppose she wrote others he did not find—and he didn't know what to think. Would I not write to him myself and also to Olga to let her know that she was not to waste any hopes?

"Let me have pen and ink and I will write at once," I said. I wrote just what I felt and gave the letters to Olga's sister.

My second and third weeks in New York were no better than the first. I could get no work. If my father had been a tailor or a capmaker and had taught me his trade, I should have been better off. When *Rosh Hashonah*, New Year's Day, came, I did not have the money for a seat in a synagogue, nor could I ask Nathan Bershadsky to lend me some, for he would only make fun of me. I tried to get into several synagogues, but they would not let me in without a ticket. I went to Bowling Green; sitting on a bench in the open, I said— since I had no prayer-book—whatever I knew by heart.

Their brother-in-law, Pesach, hinted that I was staying with the Bershadskys long enough. If I could get no work, I should try peddling. "No," I said, "I came to America to work, not to trade."

"You are talking nonsense. I have been peddling stockings since I came here, and I make a living. In eight months I have made enough to bring my wife and children here and to furnish a flat. All the help I had was that Nathan Bershadsky let me stay in his home and lent me, at the beginning, twenty-five dollars. And then, I don't think of staying in this business: I hope for something better. Let me give you a basket of stockings; stand on Ridge Street and try to make a living until you have enough to pay someone to teach you a trade."

"I'll do it if I get no work by the Day of Atonement. Aaron's son promised to get me a job at the place where he works."

Two days before the Day of Atonement, walking along a street, I stopped to look at the meat in the window of a butcher shop. The butcher came out and said, "What are you looking at? Do you know anything about the business?"

"I do."

"Then, can you help me tomorrow? I'll pay you well."

"How early must I be here?"

"No later than four in the morning."

I came before four but the butcher was at work. He set me to sawing bones until nine o'clock. After that I ran the errands. The first was to the fifth floor of a house; when I had the heavy basket upstairs, I stopped to catch my breath. The customer gave me a nickel. It seemed to me as if she were giving me alms, and I gave the coin back, telling her to give it to one who was in need.

She smiled and said, "Young man, you are really a greenhorn."

At twelve o'clock there were no more customers. I scraped the block and table clean, swept and washed the floor. The butcher went out to buy a large loaf of white bread. Then he chopped up a couple of pounds of steak and, while he fried the meat cakes, sent me for a pint of beer. When we had had our meal, he gave me a silver dollar.

Pesach was praying in a Galician synagogue. I bought a ticket for fifty cents and kept the rest for cigarettes to smoke after the Day of Atonement. When I came into the synagogue, I felt tearful because of my troubles, but I never laughed as much as I did that day: because of the Galician cantor's singing and pronunciation of Hebrew, the way the worshippers shook themselves, jumped, clapped their hands and snapped their fingers; whenever, according to Russian Jews, they were supposed to be sad, they prayed loud and cheerfully, and at the prayers during the offerings to the Lord they wept.

In the afternoon Pesach went home to see how the children were getting along. When he came back to the synagogue, he said, "Sarah Yetta Wolvovsky has come to America and is now at my house." I went at once to see her.

Pesach Budnichenkoff fixed up a basket of stockings for me, which was to cost me three dollars and seventy-five cents, and told me for how much to sell each kind. Friday morning I took my stand on the corner of Stanton and Ridge Streets and became a peddler. I felt like a beggar. I sold, bargained with the women, counted the money they gave me and gave them change, but kept thinking—for this thought was running through the books I was reading and talk I had heard—this was not an honest way to make a living, this was not work. By ten o'clock in the morning my basket was empty.

I found Pesach at home eating his breakfast. When he saw that I had brought back the basket empty, he said gleefully to his wife, "Do you see that, Elka? And he didn't want to peddle!" Turning to me he asked, "How much did you take in?"

175

"I don't know—I didn't count my money yet." I began to count it and found that I had only three dollars and fifty cents. I stood there like a fool.

Pesach asked, "What is it? Have you lost something?"

"No, but I haven't enough money."

"If so, the women knew you for a greenhorn and helped themselves."

"What do you mean—thieves?"

Pesach laughed. "What thieves! This is America! You will have to learn to watch your basket." While we were talking, Aaron came to tell me that next morning his son would take me to the factory, for he had heard the foreman say they needed help.

The foreman was a young German, tall, blond, and jolly. I thought one of his cheeks swollen until I found out it was only chewing-tobacco. The factory made a folding-bed that looked like a bureau with a mirror—no one would think that by turning a knob it became a bed. This sample of American skill looked good to me. The wood used was white oak; to make it look like mahogany the foreman mixed a pailful of red paint and a workman painted the bed. The paint had to be wiped off quickly before it dried or its color would be too dark and, besides, it would spoil the carving. Then the wood had to be rubbed—that was my job.

I rubbed away and now truthfully was earning my bread "in the sweat of my brow." At the end of the day, I was given an envelope with seventy-five cents in it and the foreman said I was to come to work for four dollars and a half a week. Although I was tired and my hands and arms to the elbows were red with paint that soap and water could not wash off, I walked home proudly.

First, I went to see Pesach and Elka Budnichenkoff to tell them of my luck. Elka said that I ought not to live with strangers and eat in restaurants: for two dollars and a half a week I could stay with them. Pesach was giving up his peddling to go into partnership with Boris, his cousin's husband, who had been a cleaner and dyer in Elizavetgrad but now made trousers for boys—"knee pants." All four of them would work in the front room; but I could sleep there, for they would not use it at night. Elka also advised me to buy lemons to take the paint off my hands.

After supper, we went to tell Nathan Bershadsky of my job and the business Pesach was going into. Nathan wished me luck and said to his brother-in-law, "Well, try it; you can always go back to your pushcart." I also told the Bershadskys that I was to stay with Elka and Pesach. Mrs. Bershadsky said that I ought to stay on for a few weeks in her home until I was sure of my job and had saved a little money. I thanked her but answered that she and her husband had done enough for me. When I left and said good-by, I thanked them again.

Nathan said, "Reznikoff, this is no thanks. We hope that you do well and then, if you help others who come here as you have come, that will be our thanks."

My new lodging was not comfortable. Pesach and Boris used to buy men's old trousers in Bayard Street to make into "knee pants" for boys. When the old trousers were ripped, the dust and smell were bad enough; it was worse when they brushed the pieces of cloth. I used to come from work, dead tired, and had no place to lie down until the others were through—about ten or eleven o'clock.

But they were so friendly that I stayed. Boris's wife sewed on buttons for me, washed my handkerchiefs, patched my clothing, and when she used to wash her children's heads, washed mine too. I did not care much for Boris. I could not forget the three roubles he had charged me in Elizavetgrad to take the stain from my overcoat—and which he did not do—but we were friendly.

Pesach and Boris did not make much at the "knee pants" business, although their wives helped them, and even little Anna, Pesach's daughter, who was ten, sewed buttons on when she came from school. Boris was the only one who could use the sewing-machine and he could not sew more than two dozen a day—fourteen dozen a week. The old trousers for this cost seven dollars and the most they could get for "knee pants" was two dollars a dozen. If the lot of old trousers was bad and they could make small sizes only, these had to sell for twenty cents a dozen less.

Pesach used to sell most of the "knee pants" to a Hungarian Jew. Klein had a store of cheap goods at Avenue B and Fifteenth Street. One Thursday, when Pesach brought him the "knee pants," Klein could not pay him. The next day there was no money to buy food for Saturday; but at noon, when they were all worried, Mrs. Klein brought five dollars in part payment. After that, she saw to it that her husband paid them two dollars a dozen even for the small sizes and that he took all they made—what he could not sell himself to turn over to other dealers of his acquaintance. She also made him pay them cash at once, and she went with Elka and Boris's wife to Ridge Street to show them where to buy food cheaply.

At the place I worked it became slack after three weeks. They laid off almost all the new help and some of the old, but the foreman said I could work for the rest of the week. He had nothing for me to do and so told me to wash the windows. I washed them on the inside, but not outside—I was afraid of falling down. The foreman became angry; spitting out his tobacco, he said, "God damn greenhorn, go at once to the office to be paid off."

Now I walked about in Brooklyn to look for work. I worked

two hours in a sugar refinery as a stoker, but could not stand the heat; and for a few days in a yard where they cut and bundled kindling wood, but was sent away. At last I came upon a Jew in an old shack who was cleaning angora skins. The skin was put in a barrel half-filled with bran; I took off my shoes and stockings, rolled my trousers above the knees, and stamped on the skin until it was white. For this I was to get five dollars a week, but after dancing in the barrel for three and a half hours my employer counted the clean skins and told me I did not do enough. As it was, there was no more strength in my legs.

I told him I could do no better. "All right," he said, "then I will try you at beating the bran from the skins." He gave me two sticks and told me to beat quickly. In about half an hour I could hardly move my hands. He came up to me again. "Mister," he said, "you are no good; you may go."

"All right, pay me for the four hours I worked."

"Get out of here, you greenhorn, I pay only when you work all week."

"Listen," I shouted, "you Galician thief, you will pay me for half a day or I will make a pogrom here," and, taking hold of a line on which clean skins were hanging, broke it; they fell on the dirty floor. I was given forty-three cents and went away.

I bought two rolls and a glass of beer. That strengthened me. I walked from Williamsburg to Brooklyn Bridge, among the factories, to try to get work and, finding nothing, went across the bridge. I stopped to rest in City Hall Park. It was six o'clock, and thousands upon thousands were going home. I watched them—clean, well-dressed, so many happy faces, and thought, Each of these surely has a good home—good food to eat and a clean place to sleep; if so, this must be a good country and I must be patient, until I also find what to do.

179

In the evening Pesach told me of a tannery that was advertising for workers. I woke next morning at five o'clock, but until I found the place they had all the help they needed. I went here and there and at last sat down on a bench in Tompkins Square. Many others like myself were sitting there too, out of work, although some spoke English. I could hardly drag myself home.

It was only two o'clock in the afternoon. Elka gave me a glass of milk and a roll and I felt better. Boris's wife told me to lie down in one of the bedrooms and rest. I slept four hours. At seven I got up and watched Pesach cutting out "knee pants." His business did not seem to take much skill. I said, "Pesach, I have been begging Boris for two weeks to teach me how to run a sewing-machine and he won't."

"What can I do?"

Boris said, "I told you I'll teach you if you'll pay me fifteen dollars and work two weeks without pay."

"But you know I have no money."

"Borrow twenty-five dollars from Nathan Bershadsky or Aaron, let me have fifteen, and for the rest you can rent a sewing-machine and pay for your lodging and board until you begin to earn money. I had to pay fifteen dollars to be taught."

"And if I learn how to work will you give me a job?"

"Sure! And we will pay you two dollars and fifty cents a week."

"Well, that will pay for my board; but how will I pay my debts?"

"That is none of my business."

Pesach added, "When you do better, you will pay them."

"Hopes pay no debts," said I. "Listen, Boris, teach me, and when I earn more than two dollars and fifty cents a week, I'll pay you."

"Not I. I must get mine—cash on the table."

180

After a few minutes, during which none of us spoke, Pesach said, "Nathan, Klein bought a lot of sweaters at auction. They are faded and he wants us to dye them. Boris here can dye them and I would press them; if you will bring them to the roof to dry and back to Klein, we'll take the job and pay you a dollar a day."

"Take it," said I. Next morning a truck brought the sweaters. I lugged them to the flat—it was full of sweaters. When a bundle was ready, I carried it to Klein's store. In three days we were through. But when I was bringing the last bundle to the store, a young fellow of that neighborhood threw a stone at me; Klein took me into a drugstore where they stopped the blood and bandaged my head.

Friday evening, because of my bandage, I did not go with Pesach and Elka to visit her brother. Boris and his wife went to bed. I sat near his sewing-machine and read a newspaper. When I had read it all, I thought for the hundredth time that if I could only learn how to sew "knee pants," I should not have to walk about the streets looking for work. But I did not want to give Boris fifteen dollars; besides, I did not think that he knew much more than how to thread the needle and oil the machine—he was always bringing it to a store on Grand Street to be fixed for half a dollar.

Why shouldn't I, I thought, screw the sewing-machine apart and find out how it sews? If I am not able to put it together again, I can have it done for half a dollar. In about two hours, I screwed the machine together after I had cleaned and oiled it. I tried to sew on newspaper and did. I saw that I had to be able to stop sewing whenever I wanted to; after practising for a while, I could do this too. Then I found that to make a straight seam I must not watch the needle but the "press foot." I learnt how to make the stitch smaller and larger and how to manage the machine's tension; and sewed away on rags until I heard Pesach and Elka on the stairs.

Next morning, when they began their work, I said to Boris, "Why should I pay you fifteen dollars to learn how to use a sewing-machine? There is nothing to learn."

He smiled. "If there is nothing to learn, I'd like to see you make a pair of knee pants."

"Let me have the machine for half an hour and you will see me make it."

"When I am having my breakfast—I don't want to lose the time now. And if you make a pair of knee pants in half an hour, you won't have to pay me anything."

When Boris left his machine, I sat down; the others stood about to watch. Twenty minutes later I had a pair of "knee pants" ready—better than his because the seams were straight. Pesach, Elka, and Boris's wife cheered, but he was silent. Pesach said, "You won your fifteen dollars, but you must work two weeks for nothing."

Someone knocked at the door and a young man came in. He was from New Haven, he said, and Sarah Yetta Wolvovsky was working for his father. She had heard that I was without work and the young man brought me a railway ticket she had sent—there was work in New Haven. I could go with him now, for he was on his way home. But I did not want to go. I did not want to be helped by a girl—above all by Sarah Yetta, who was always telling me what to do. But I turned to Pesach and asked for his advice.

"As for going to a small town where you have no relatives— what are you going to do if you work a couple of weeks and then are laid off? You stay here. We'll give you two dollars and fifty cents a week, but you must work at this wage for two months. In the beginning you will be slow; after two months we'll see how you are. You'll work the same hours we do—

from six in the morning till ten at night, Saturdays and Sundays too, but Fridays only until five in the afternoon."

I thanked the young man from New Haven for his trouble and sent Sarah Yetta my thanks, but I was going to work in New York for Pesach and Boris. I borrowed five dollars from Nathan Bershadsky, rented a sewing-machine for two months for three dollars, and kept the rest for cigarettes and newspapers.

After a while, Sarah Yetta came back to New York; there was no work for her in New Haven. She found a job in Brooklyn and roomed there, but used to come to New York Sundays to visit friends. On her way home, I would take her as far as the ferry, and had to work until eleven o'clock that night to make up for it.

At first the work made my back and feet ache, but it was not long before I was used to it. Pesach and Boris rented larger rooms on Houston Street and to pay less rent moved to the top floor. Now I not only had to carry the big bundle of old trousers—one hundred pairs—twenty-two blocks from Bayard Street, but had to lug it to the fourth floor. When I complained that I was not a porter, Pesach said that this way I was getting the fresh air I needed.

When the two months were up, I was able to make three dozen "knee pants" a day, for which others were paid thirty or thirty-five cents a dozen. I thought Pesach and Boris would pay me at least five dollars a week, and I was surprised when they told me they would pay no more than three. After a good deal of talk they were willing to pay me three dollars and fifty cents and I was to work one hour a day less—that was the best I could get from them. I had no warm clothing, what I had was ragged, and my shoes were torn; otherwise, I would have looked for work elsewhere. After four more weeks of work, I managed to save enough to buy a pair of trousers and have my shoes fixed.

One evening Pesach sent me with some "knee pants" to Klein's home. Mrs. Klein asked me to have tea. While we were at the table, Mr. Klein asked, "How's business?"

"Business is not so bad, but I have little out of it," and I told them what I was paid. They were displeased, and Mr. Klein said to me, "How much would you need to begin manufacturing?"

"If I had twenty dollars it would be enough."

"Suppose I gave you a room in the basement of my house and twenty-five dollars, how many dozen would you be able to make a week?"

"If I go to Bayard Street for old trousers and cut the goods myself, I won't be able to make more than ten dozen."

"What would that cost you?"

"I'd have to have someone to finish and press—that would cost me about seventy-five cents a dozen."

"Then I make you this proposition: I'll lend you twenty-five dollars which you must pay back—two or three dollars a week; I'll let you have the basement—three nice rooms (you could live in one); if you make more than ten dollars a week, you'll have to pay me five dollars a month rent; if less, four dollars; and whatever you will make, I'll buy from you at the price I pay your bosses. And you do not have to sell to me; if you can do better, you are free to sell elsewhere. What do you think of it?"

"Take it, take it," said Mrs. Klein, smiling and nodding her head.

If I say yes, I thought, I shall take away their best customer from Pesach and Boris and lose their friendship and that of the Bershadskys, who have been so kind to me, and, perhaps, the friendship of Aaron and his family. I thanked the Kleins and told them that I had promised to stay two weeks more at the wages I was getting; if, afterwards, Pesach and Boris paid me no more, I would say yes to the proposition—gladly.

Next Monday or Tuesday, while we were having dinner, Pesach asked me to go with him to Bayard Street that he might send back thread and buttons. On the way, without naming Klein, I told him of the offer and that I was telling him this that he might get someone in my place.

He said, "I'll be frank with you. If you leave me now I am badly off, because I told Boris yesterday that at the end of the week, when your time is up, we end our partnership. I thought you would stay with me."

"If so, I won't leave you, but you must be fair."

"We'll do this: you work Fridays until five, Saturdays until one, and the other days until eight o'clock, and I'll pay you five dollars a week until I see how I make out. Is that fair?"

"I'll try it for four weeks and then we'll see."

One day, when they were no longer partners, Pesach came home worried and told his wife and me that Boris was going about to their customers selling "knee pants" at one dollar and eighty cents a dozen. Now Pesach had to look for new trade. In the evening I went to Klein and asked him where we might find other stores like his.

"You don't have to look for other stores. Let the auctioneers sell for you. They'll charge you ten per cent, but it will be worth it, for you will not have to lose any time."

Pesach packed up several bundles, and I brought them to an auctioneer on West Broadway. They sold for two dollars and forty cents a dozen. Pesach and Elka made up their minds to move nearer to Bayard Street and the auctioneers. He found a flat on the top floor. I overheard Elka say, "When we are at Forsyth Street, Pesach, you will not carry the sacks of old pants at all. Send Nathan for them after he has finished his work."

When they had moved, Pesach said, thinking to please me greatly, that from then on I was to get six dollars a week. But I answered, "I don't want to work 'week work' at any price. Others pay thirty-two and a half cents a dozen for making the small sizes and thirty-five cents for the larger sizes. I'll work for you for thirty cents a dozen; I'm willing to help you carry goods to the auctions or buy things—without any pay; but I will not carry the sacks of old pants. Nor should you. You'll find plenty of fellows in the saloons who would be willing to carry a bundle for five cents. Why should we tire ourselves so?"

Pesach and Elka did not like to—but they had to—give me what I asked. The first thing I did then was to buy a new stand for my sewing-machine that made my work easier and quicker. I began to earn seven dollars and a half a week and worked only from seven to seven; Saturdays, I did not work at all. In a few weeks I bought myself a new suit of clothes, shoes, a hat, new underwear and shirts. I was ten months in America and felt myself the equal of any man.

Sarah Yetta Wolvovsky now worked in New York and lived with the Budnichenkoffs. We were both lonely and felt more like brother and sister than second cousins. We made no change without talking it over; it was she who had advised me to ask for "piece work."

One evening, Shura, Aaron's daughter, asked me to buy a theatre ticket—her father's lodge was running "a benefit." I said, "I'll take two."

"What do you want two for?" she asked.

"For my cousin here, Sarah Yetta."

Shura stared and said angrily, "All of a sudden! You don't

know what to do with your money, I suppose."

"Two or nothing."

She gave me two tickets for the seats next to hers; but, of course, after that none of us had a good time.

I was still sleeping in the work-room. In the summer, I could sleep on the roof, but when it rained I had to lie on the stairs.

Evenings, I went out with my cousin who boarded at Aaron's, Aaron's son, and his chum, Bennie. Once Bennie had a good day. He had found a good place to peddle his brass jewelry—near the Twenty-third Street Ferry, and had made more than five dollars. He led the way to Goldstein's. This was a kitchen in back of a saloon on Hester Street. Here we could get broiled liver, served on a round board, for three cents, and for three cents more a big mug of beer—which I could never finish.

This time they put whiskey in my beer. When I began to drink it, I knew it was too strong and would not have it, but Aaron's son and Bennie held me and my cousin poured the beer down my throat. I became drunk and sick. My friends brought me home; I knew what was going on about me, but was helpless. I heard Elka say, "What a country! Simon Reznikoff's son gets drunk in the middle of the week."

I crawled to the roof and it felt like the deck of the steamer among the waves. I heard Sarah Yetta asking, "What is the matter with you? How do you feel?"

"I have a bad taste in my mouth," I said, "and a bad headache." She brought me a drink of cold water and put a wet towel about my head. I felt better in the morning but was ashamed to look at anyone. When my friends came in the evening to ask me to go out again, I would not go, and they went away laughing.

The day was hot and that Sarah Yetta came from work an hour earlier surprised no one. I too stopped work before I used to other days and neither Pesach nor Elka said anything. Pesach himself had come from Bayard Street sick and weak.

After supper I asked Sarah Yetta to walk with me on Brooklyn Bridge. When we came to the second bench we sat down. Sarah Yetta was looking at the moon and I at her. At last I said, "I think you feel as I do—it is hard to be a boarder. Don't you think I ought to get married" She did not answer, and I went on. "I have been thinking about it a long time and now I want to hear what you think."

"I believe it will be a good thing for you," she said slowly. "Her family will help you."

"You don't understand me. Whom do you think I mean? I mean you."

"Don't you think you are making a mistake? You had better think it over."

"I am sure that I am not making a mistake, but maybe you are afraid you will make a mistake. If so, it is for you to think it over."

Sarah Yetta saw that I was nettled and said gently, "I never thought you were talking about me. I thought it was of Shura, Aaron's daughter. As far as money goes she is a much better match. But if you want me, I am satisfied. May we be lucky," and we kissed for the first time since we knew each other.

Next morning, as I was having breakfast, Elka said, "Nathan, I want to tell you of a good match—a good-looking girl, five hundred dollars in cash, and they'll fix up a nice home for you."

"I am engaged."

"What! To whom?"

"To Sarah Yetta."

"Since when?"

"Since last night."

188

"I don't believe you. It must have been made up between you long ago, and you hid it from me." She was angry and would neither talk nor listen.

A few days later Elka began to talk to us again, but said little. At the end of the week, she told us it was hard for her to cook for so many; but if we wished to stay on only as lodgers we might. We were glad not to have to wait until we were called to the table. When Sarah Yetta came from work, she made something to eat which we liked and which cost us less. After a while, Elka said that she was not going to live on the top floor any longer. She rented three rooms at four dollars a month more than she had been paying for four. There was no room for Sarah Yetta, and she went to live with a neighboring family.

The loss of Sarah Yetta as a lodger and the higher rent cost the Budnichenkoffs seven dollars a month. Elka now tried to save wherever she could. One day, when Pesach had gone to Bayard Street, she said to me that I was making too much money: I had saved twenty-five dollars, and had sent Sarah Yetta's mother eleven, and now Pesach could get an operator to do for seven and a half dollars the work I was doing for nine. I answered that the money sent to Sarah Yetta's mother was Sarah Yetta's; as for the operator to do my work, if Pesach could get one cheaper, he should. At this Elka became angry and began to call me names. I stood up and would not work.

When Pesach came back, he asked me why I was not working. I said, "Elka is saying that I suck your blood."

"Don't mind it—it's only woman's talk."

"But I have to stay here and listen to it!"

When Pesach saw that he could not smooth things over, he asked Aaron to talk to me. Aaron came into the house smiling. "So, Nathan," he said, "you are no longer a greenhorn: you have learnt how to strike."

"If I did not respect you," I answered, "I'd not answer you, because you talk to me as if I were a child. Please listen to me without making fun of me."

"Very well, I am listening."

"I have been working for the Budnichenkoffs for nine months. I have never been paid the market-price for my work, but I blame no one because I was willing this should be so. I spent one or two hours every day helping Pesach in other ways and never asked payment for it; and for all this Elka tells me today that I suck their blood and that they can get someone else for less. If so, I do not want to work here any longer."

"Are you through?" said Aaron. "Then I tell you to sit down and get to work."

"I came to America because I did not want my own mother to boss me. If you cannot show me I am wrong, I do not work."

Aaron shouted, "You are an anarchist!"

"If this is anarchism, I am an anarchist," and I left the house.

As I walked about the streets, I met a man whom I had known in Elizavetgrad as a leather merchant. His business now was peddling jewelry in New Haven. I told him what I had been doing and that I was thinking of going into business for myself. If I went to New Haven, he said, there were many buyers of old clothes from whom we could get old trousers cheaper than in New York, he would put up as much money as I needed and, since he took care of his jewelry business only in the evening, he would have plenty of time to buy, cut, and press the "knee pants." Even if we made only twenty dozen a week, we should have about fifteen dollars each. So we became partners. I took my sewing-machine stand along, bought a set of patterns for "knee pants" of all sizes, and went to New Haven.

We could not get enough old trousers from the dealers— no more than for ten dozen a week. My partner said that I could cut and press that much myself and spent all his time at his jewelry business. I saw that I would have done much better in New York. I left my partner our stock that he might have no claims and came back. The twenty-five dollars I had saved were gone. Besides, I had caught a cold and my ears hurt.

First, I went to Aaron's to see if I had any mail from my father. I could hardly get to the door I felt so weak. I tapped. Aaron's wife said, "Come in," but when she saw me, she shouted to her daughter, "Shura, the greenhorn is here. Get me the broom and I'll knock him downstairs."

I said, "Don't trouble. I can walk down." I went to where Sarah Yetta was lodging and climbed to the roof to wait until she came from work. I felt shooting pains in my ears; I had not eaten all day, and I had no money. I heard someone walking towards me. It was Aaron's son. "What brought you here?" I asked.

"The way my mother greeted you. I know you are not to blame for leaving the Budnichenkoffs, but old people can't understand that. What do you think of doing now? Have you any money?"

"None."

"Here is twenty-five dollars."

"I don't want that much until I know what I am to do."

Soon after Sarah Yetta came. She boiled some water and syringed my ears. I felt better—and hungry. At the table, I told her that Aaron's son had promised to lend me money; the only thing I needed was a place where to work.

She said, "Let us ask the Fertels"—the people with whom

she lived. "Maybe they will let you have a room." Mrs. Fertel said that if Sarah Yetta and I were to pay the rent for the flat, eleven dollars a month, Sarah Yetta and Mrs. Fertel's daughter could sleep in the front room, and Mrs. Fertel's son with me in the room where I was to work; we were to pay for the coal and gas too, but Mrs. Fertel would do the "finishing" of the "knee pants."

Next morning, before Sarah Yetta went to work, she syringed my ears again. I was all well. I brought my machine-stand from the pier and rented a sewing-machine. I could do no more until I saw Aaron's son to get the money he had promised.

Towards evening Mrs. Shlikerman, a relative of Sarah Yetta's, came to find out how she was. I was sitting on the stoop. She asked me how I was getting along. I told her what had happened and that I was waiting for Aaron's son to bring some money.

"You don't have to wait for him," she said, "I'll let you have twenty-five dollars."

I said that fifteen would be enough just then. I went to Bayard Street and bought a sack of old trousers, two irons and two pairs of scissors, and set to work. The first month I made thirty-six dollars and the second forty-nine. I paid what I owed and bought myself a coat and Sarah Yetta a fur cape. I had only a little money left, but I had fifteen dozen "knee pants" I had made.

However, I could not sell any. I went to all my customers on Grand Street but nobody would buy. I looked for other stores in Brooklyn and in Newark, but everywhere I was told that they had all they needed for Christmas and would not buy until the spring season. Of course, I could make up stock in the meantime, but that would take money for goods and for a living—more than I dared borrow. Besides, I had no place for stock in my little room.

Saturday evening, when I came back from Newark with my heavy bundles of unsold "knee pants," Sarah Yetta told me that the man she worked for was going to pay her less than she had been paid and she had given up the job. Luckily, our rent was paid three weeks ahead. Sarah Yetta thought that instead of taking another job she would do better if she had work to do at home. She went into partnership with another girl who knew where to get such work. Both had always made single wrappers, but now that they had many to make, of patterns and colors almost alike, they made many mistakes. When Sarah Yetta's partner saw the trouble they had let themselves in for, she quit and Sarah Yetta had to rip whatever they had sewn and match every piece to finish the work.

She would try to get work next, she told me, from Henry Ettelson, whose wrappers, her partner had told her, were easier to make and his help better paid. "If you would take my advice," Sarah Yetta said, "you'd forget about your knee pants and learn how to sew wrappers. We could be contractors some day."

I did not want to listen to her: people would say she had helped me, that if it were not for her—. For ten days I went about looking for work at "knee pants," or anything, and found nothing. But Sarah Yetta was doing well. She had made samples for Ettelson and he sent her a bundle of wrappers to sew.

I opened the bundle for her and put each part by itself, the chalk mark on top, and showed her how the work should be handled when the cloth ran in shades. Sarah Yetta said again that I ought to work at wrappers. For about three hours I walked up and down thinking what to do. Sarah Yetta sewed on quietly. If I did not get work soon I should have to live on her earnings; so I said at last, "Very well, I'll learn how to work at wrappers, but only if, when I know the work, I manage our business."

"I'm sure you'll manage it better than I could," she said.

I began to sew the pockets. It was hard for me to handle the calico, for I was used to heavy cloth; in eleven hours I made just four cents—as "piece work" was paid, but my work was clean and good. The next day I began to sew the long seams and by the third day did more sewing than Sarah Yetta. It took us three and a half days to finish the bundle of work; when we brought it back, we were given two bundles more.

It was hard to run two machines in the little room we were in. We asked Mrs. Fertel to find another flat with a larger room for us. She found a place for seventeen dollars a month and wanted us to pay her twenty-one. We were willing. Then she wanted us to work in the kitchen that she might have the best room for a parlor. But we could not let her have her way: while cooking, she might spot the wrappers.

Saturday morning, on my way to Ettelson's, I saw three rooms to be let in Allen Street for ten dollars a month. I told Sarah Yetta that there we should have a large room to work in, a bedroom for me to sleep in, and a kitchen.

"It would be fine," she said, "but people will talk about us."

"I am not going to give Mrs. Fertel whatever she has a mind to ask us that people may not talk."

When Sarah Yetta saw the place she liked it. As we went downstairs an old woman and her daughter were waiting for us on the floor below. The old woman asked if we were going to rent the flat. We said yes. Then she began to ask us about ourselves and our business, but we felt we had nothing to hide and told her that we were only engaged and were taking the rooms to work in, not to live in, that I would sleep there, but that Sarah Yetta would not change her lodging.

I was somewhat surprised that the old woman spoke Yiddish as the Lithuanian Jews do, but that, when her daughter spoke, it was as Sarah Yetta and I did. The old woman explained that she and her husband had gone from Lithuania to Elizavetgrad; they had lived there twenty-five years and there her daughter was born and married. "If so," I said, "we come from the same city," and I told them my name and Sarah Yetta's.

The old woman became friendlier. She went on to tell us that across the street, in a room behind a store, there lived a poor man, his wife and two children; the man had been paying only five dollars a month as rent, but now the storekeeper needed the room for himself, and the family could get no other, for nobody wanted to let a room to them because of the children; perhaps we could let them have the kitchen for three dollars a month.

"All right," I said.

"For that," said the old woman, "I'll help you. I'll do your marketing and cooking so that your young woman will not have to take the time from her work." I promised to give her a dollar a week for this.

When we were in the street I said to Sarah Yetta, "Say nothing to Mrs. Fertel about staying there. You still have five days before the month is up; until then we'll see what these people whom we are letting into the kitchen are like. If they are decent, you can have the bedroom for yourself and I'll sleep in the workroom—then our living will cost still less."

I bought a folding-bed for myself, a quilt, sheets, and an old stove; in all I spent ten dollars. I told Mr. Ettelson to ship the next bundle of work to Allen Street. When it came, I was afraid we might be robbed, for our tenants were not moving in until the next day, and I spent the night alone in the flat. The cold and the noise of the elevated trains kept me awake, but in the morning, when Sarah Yetta came, she made a fire in the stove and the place was soon warm. We had breakfast together. Our tenants came, and Sarah Yetta and I set to work. On the third day Sarah Yetta, for whom Mrs. Fertel was making it unpleasant, moved in too.

A few days later, Mrs. Shlikerman, Sarah Yetta's cousin, visited us. She heard why we had left the Fertels and then said, "But after all you ought to get married so that people wouldn't talk. I know you haven't any money for furniture, but I'll give you a bed and a bureau."

"The woman who lives with us now," I said, "is just as good as Mrs. Fertel or Elka Budnichenkoff with whom we lived. Besides, we are neither afraid of what people may say nor of ourselves—we do not have to pay people to watch us. In a few months we'll have enough money to fix up a home ourselves, and then we'll be married; but until then we want no presents and no one to be able to say that because of his or her help we were married."

Two weeks before the feast of Passover I quarreled with Sarah Yetta. We had saved up fifty dollars. I said that we ought to buy ourselves clothes for the holidays. Sarah Yetta said, "Buy yourself whatever you wish, but whatever you would spend for me send to my mother."

I did not like that. "We must have decent clothes, for you know the saying, According to your clothing people greet you when they meet you. I can't dress up and have my fiancée go about in old clothes. I want you to be better dressed than I; and we haven't enough for both clothes and your mother. First, we must be decently dressed."

Sarah Yetta began to cry and would not talk to me. I was

sorry to see her cry, but I was not going to let her have her way because of that. I made up my mind not to talk until she should. We finished the day's work in silence and the next day sat at our machines, facing each other, like the deaf and dumb. Suddenly Sarah Yetta said, "Why don't you say something?" and smiled. We bought ourselves new clothes; but on Saturday, when I was paid twenty-six dollars by Mr. Ettelson, I sent Sarah Yetta's mother twenty-five roubles.

The second day of Passover we tried to find a cousin of Sarah Yetta's at an address that came in a letter from Elizavet-grad. We crossed on the Grand Street Ferry. I showed the address to every policeman we saw. We did not understand what was said but walked on as the policemen pointed. When we were too tired to walk farther and were ready to turn back, we saw a Jew and I showed him the address. "The place is called Brownsville," he said. "Take a Broadway car and stay on it until it stops; from there it isn't far."

It took us about four hours until we found Sarah Yetta's cousin. He was a tailor but out of work and very poor. After a while, he took me for a walk to show me what Brownsville was like. "Our houses are small and built of wood, but our rooms are comfortable," he said. "We have no paved streets, but we see the sun and moon from the moment they rise until they set. When it rains, the streets are muddy, and, when it isn't raining, dusty; but we do not smell the garbage in the barrels that stand on the sidewalks." Many, he said, had shops there and their work was brought from New York in express wagons that charged only ten cents a bundle.

When the days became hot and our windows on Allen Street had to be kept closed because of the smoke of the steam-engines that pulled the elevated trains, it seemed best to us to move to Brownsville. We hired a store and three rooms on Thatford Avenue for nine dollars. By August we had saved one hundred dollars, enough to furnish the three rooms and to pay for our wedding.

One Saturday evening, we carried the machines out of the store and put in tables and chairs. The wedding took place in the parlor of our neighbor. Those of our guests who were against religious ceremonies were downstairs in the store. Later, when we all sat at the tables, the eldest of the guests scolded Sarah Yetta and me because we were so foolish—to be married by a rabbi. I said, "It would be foolish for your children to be married as we were, but you know how our parents would feel about it if we were married otherwise, or not married at all. It is better for us to be foolish than to hurt them." Most of those there said that I was right and those who thought otherwise said no more.

Needle Trade

by CHARLES REZNIKOFF

I

Brownsville is now well within the city of New York. The subway runs through Brownsville; it has at least a hundred streets and all are paved; almost all the houses are of brick. Then it was only a wooden village with a few muddy streets that, east, west, and south, led to the fields or marshes of Brooklyn. The people of Brownsville were mostly Jews. At that time, in 1895 or so, they were almost all immigrants, just come from Russia.

My father then was young, too; thin, neither tall nor short; with brown hair and mustache and pale face. His nose broadened out between tip and bridge and was neither long nor snub; his brown eyes bulged somewhat but were neither large nor small; in fact, he was rather good-looking. My mother's long brown hair, when she combed it, fell below her waist. She was tall for a woman and strong. Her face was round and her skin somewhat dark, her cheeks ruddy and her cheek bones somewhat high, her nose short; her lips were neither thick nor thin but were not shapely, and her mouth was firm and large. Her forehead was round and high; her eyebrows long and clearly marked; her eyes, like her hair, dark brown. They were bright eyes. But her eyesight was none too good, for she had been earning her living as a seamstress ever since she was little. Her photographs show her rather homely— and this was always a surprise to those who knew her winsome face.

As for me, I was an ugly baby—to judge from the photograph my mother kept as precious—with head too large for my body. A visitor, who saw me crawling about the floor ready to catch at the wheel of my father's sewing-machine, called me, to my mother's vexation, "a spider." (My mother spoke of it with bitterness when the man who had said it was long dead and buried.)

For two or three years my father had been earning his living as a sewing-machine operator, working from six, or earlier, in the morning until eight, or later, at night; every day except Saturday. (For the most part, the immigrants still kept Saturday as the day of rest, even if it was no longer sacred.) My father did not think the hours long. When he began work as an operator, he had to work every day and every night, except Friday night (when the Sabbath begins), until ten. Then he was sewing "knee-pants" for boys, out of cloth that had been used for men's trousers, dusty cloth, still smelling of sweat and the damp cellar in which the bundles

200

of old trousers had been stored. But now he was sewing "ladies" wrappers out of clean new goods. (A "wrapper" was a loose dress for wear indoors.)

My father's sewing-machine with a new kind of treadle that helped him sew faster belonged to him, and he worked at home. My mother's sewing-machine was there, too. If there was more than enough to do, the daughter of a neighbor or, perhaps, a tailor out of work, brought in another sewing-machine and sewed with my parents. They worked for a manufacturer in Manhattan whose prices for sewing were a little better than those paid by others. But Henry Ettelson's wrappers had to be carefully made. The cloth, of many kinds and colors, was cut in his place according to his patterns, and the bundles to be sewn into wrappers sent out to Brownsville by wagon.

One day, when my father brought back the wrappers he had made, he saw Ettelson together with the designer and the forewoman in the showroom. The three were arguing about a wrapper on the figure. (The forewoman was in charge of the contractors including those, like my father, who hardly had the dignity of a contractor.) My father stood in the outer office, waiting for the forewoman to examine the wrappers he had brought, when the designer caught sight of him through the open door. "Come in here!" he called.

My father walked gingerly upon the carpet of the showroom, well aware of his muddy shoes. "Here is a man who understands his work," said the designer. "You will admit that," he added, looking at the forewoman. She nodded stiffly, her face flushed with anger. (Unlike her employer and the designer, she was not Jewish.) "All right," went on the designer, "then let us ask him how he thinks this wrapper should be made."

Ettelson, who had been looking closely at the wrapper on the figure, turned towards my father. "How would *you* go about 'setting in' the yoke with goods like this?" he asked in his shrill voice.

My father was pleased, of course, to hear himself praised and to have his opinion asked but he tried to keep from smiling. He fingered the goods thoughtfully. Then, speaking slowly and in a low voice, he showed them how he would "set in" the yoke. This was just how the designer had been telling the forewoman to have it done by the operators and, when she would not, he had taken their quarrel to Ettelson.

"All right," said Ettelson, after my father had explained why that kind of goods had to be sewn the designer's way, and turning to the forewoman Ettelson said: "Do it like that, please."

But the forewoman answered angrily: "I am through here."

The designer smiled and Ettelson at once put him in charge of the operators and of the contractors also—until Ettelson could hire a forewoman or foreman.

Now my father hoped to have plenty to do. Things could not have turned out better, he thought. But the times became worse and the designer, for all his friendliness, could only send my father one bundle a week; and there was no work at all to be had elsewhere. One bundle a week was not enough for a man, let alone a man with a wife and baby. Besides, my parents had a neighbor who was out of work and they felt that they ought to share the single bundle. The three used to sew it at night and, during the day, my father and his neighbor looked for work. They found some at last in a shop making "sailor suits" for boys, but neither could earn more than three dollars a week. Times were really very bad.

In the spring, business was better and my father had plenty to do sewing wrappers for Henry Ettelson. But his happiness did not last long: he heard that Ettelson was going to have sewing-machines run by electricity. Other manufacturers of wrappers were fixing up such shops for themselves, and Ettelson, if he was to stay in business, had to have one, too. Now, my father thought, Ettelson will probably have no work at all made outside; for a sewing-machine run by electricity could turn out wrappers faster and cheaper than a man working any kind of treadle by foot. At best, Ettelson's shop would make the most profitable work during the season, and all his work in the slack.

My father knew the man who was to become Ettelson's foreman. He was a contractor of wrappers who had as many as twelve operators working for him, and the work of his shop was as good as my father's. The two had often met in Ettelson's place and were friendly. My father was willing to be his helper for as little as ten dollars a week. The man cheerfully promised to hire my father but, when the shop was ready and he became the foreman, he hired his brother-in-law instead.

However, he was not able to run Ettelson's shop. A great deal of goods was spoiled by the help and Ettelson had to let those who worked outside make the better grade of wrappers. My father never earned as much before and that season made about twenty dollars a week. Everybody in the trade was now saying it was the foreman's wife who had run the contracting business so well. When the season was over, Ettelson let the man go and asked my father to be the foreman at fifteen dollars a week.

Now that my father was offered the job of foreman, after he had been willing to be merely a helper, his conscience began to bother him. He asked for time to think it over and went to his friends to hear what they had to say. One said flatly that he should not take the job, for he must become a "slave-driver" and would only do well just ·as long as he could exploit the help for the "boss;" another said that, just as long as there were "slaves" under capitalism, he would not help matters by not taking the job and he had the right to better himself. Still another said that he must take the job for the sake of his family; if he did not, another would; but my father could see to it that those who worked under him made a living: he should merely drive them, not whip them. This seemed sensible, and idealistic enough, and my father became Henry Ettelson's foreman.

He soon found out that Ettelson's other help, who had been friendly when he came looking for work to do at home, were unfriendly now that he had become the foreman. He knew how unfriendly they had been to the man whose place he had taken, but their unfriendliness to himself surprised him, for he wished all men well.

My father, to make the best showing, wanted the most profitable work made right in the shop; in fact, he wanted the shop to make all that he had feared it would when he was one of those who worked outside. But the designer, who was still in charge of those who worked outside and who had been so friendly to my father when he was one of these, was always trying to send them the most profitable work. He would have done so, too, since he was also in charge of the cutters, had not my father kept watch on what was ready for the sewing-machines. It was to the designer's interest, so the man thought, to have the shop not as profitable as it might be, that his own position, in charge of the work outside, would be the stronger. And when he found my father treading on his toes, asking for this bundle and that, he made up his mind to be rid of him as he had rid himself of the other foreman.

At home, my father complained about his troubles: how irritable Ettelson was and how treacherous the designer. My

204

mother listened patiently at times with her round brow
wrinkled, and told him that he must win out because he had
the interest of the business at heart: Ettelson would see that,
soon enough, because he was nobody's fool. At other times,
with a scornful smile that always angered my father, she told
him that it was better for him to be out in the world, struggling
with men as good as he or better, than to sit in a corner of
his own home sewing away at his sewing-machine.

Whenever my father opened a bundle of work as it came
from the cutting-room, before he gave any of it to the operators,
he looked to see if all the parts were there. If he was short,
as he was time and again, he sent word to the designer; in
a little while, whatever was missing would be sent in with
bits of cloth clinging to it, as if it had been thrown on the
floor among the cutters' rags.

This sparring with the designer had been going on for some
time, with my father blocking him, when the designer thought
it time to change his tactics. When my father next sent for
what was missing, the designer came up to him shouting that
it must have been lost among the sewing-machines or at my
father's own table. The designer supposed that Ettelson would
come to see what was wrong and would merely go back to
his office, the designer's charges ringing in his ears.

But Ettelson, impatient though he was, listened to what
both had to say. Instead of going back to his office, he re-
mained beside my father's table and sent for the bundles
still in the cutting-room. "Let's open them," he said. "Maybe
we'll find the missing collars in one of these." The bundles
were opened and Ettelson went through them himself. He
did not find the collars but saw that in one the belts were
missing. He turned to the designer and asked angrily in his
shrill voice: "How is this?"

"I suppose the marker forgot to mark them. I'll talk to

him about it," and the designer went away, supposedly to do so. My father told the young fellow who swept the place to look among the cutters' rags. Sure enough, by the time the designer was back, the missing collars and belts were on the table.

"Who cut this?" asked Ettelson.

"My brother," said the designer. He added lamely: "No matter how careful a cutter is one of the smaller parts sometimes falls on the floor."

Ettelson did not trouble to answer him and sent for the designer's brother. "You can go," he said. "You are through here." Then, turning to the designer, he added: "Be careful or your contract won't help you."

A few days later, when my father went to the cutting-room for work, there was none: the shipping-clerk, on orders from the designer, had sent away all that was cut to the contractors, and it would be several hours before other work was ready for the shop. My father went back and pulled out the switch; the sewing-machines stopped and he told the girls to be back after lunch.

Ettelson hurried in at the sudden quiet. It was only fair, my father explained, in answer to his angry questioning, that all stop rather than that some work and others have nothing to do. Ettelson was doubtful. Still, it was clear that all the work should not have been sent away and operators of his own shop left without any, and he told the clerk not to ship a bundle again before my father had taken what he needed.

The designer at last went too far. He and the cutters used to work on Labor Day without the double wages they had a right to, and Ettelson would pay them for the three Hebrew holidays which come soon after, when they did not work (the two days of Rosh Hashonah, when the New Year is celebrated, and Yom Kippur, the Day of Atonement). Now the designer told his cutters they were not to work on Labor Day unless paid double; if Ettelson would not pay them double, they were to strike; and, if they did strike, they were also to demand that his brother be hired again.

Ettelson, however, paid them double for their work on Labor Day when they asked for it—and said nothing. Then he took two days' wages from their pay for not working the days of Rosh Hashonah.

The designer asked: "What's this? Why don't you pay us for the two days as always?"

"Because you didn't work," said Ettelson calmly. "When you work for me, I pay you. When you serve God, let Him pay you."

"If you don't pay us, the cutters will strike."

"If they strike, they are through here; and you, too."

"O no, I'm not!" shouted the designer. "I have a contract and it has two more years to run."

Ettelson did not answer him but went into the office. In a few minutes, the cutters were out on strike. Ettelson walked into the cutting-room and found the designer there. He told him to leave. The designer did not budge and went about doing whatever he was at. Ettelson then sent the errand-boy for a policeman. The designer blustered but the policeman put his hand under the designer's arm and led him downstairs. Now, as the sagas say, he is out of the story.

Next day, Ettelson had a new designer. He was not a Jew. A personage in the place where he lived (his home was in a small town near the city), mayor of the town and an elder in his church, he was a man of about fifty with grey eyes, long black beard turning grey, neat black clothes, and a heavy gold watch-chain across his vest. He spoke little and, for the most part, calmly without gestures or inflection: a calm man whom God had made out of a cool Northern earth.

In the cutting-room, not a set of patterns was in order; in some styles, all the patterns of a size were missing; in others, the patterns of a part in all sizes; and the patterns used most were all gone. (Months later, they were found hidden under old packing-cases in the stock room.) But my father helped the new designer every night, sometimes until ten o'clock, until he had the patterns in order again. For this, Ettelson raised my father's wages three dollars a week.

The new designer was polite to my father at first but he found him somewhat of a nuisance, perhaps—shouting at the operators, bustling in and out of the cutting-room and shipping-room, yes, even his readiness to help. And my father, warm with gratitude for the three dollars extra he got a week, wanted to help all the more.

Once the new designer made a good-looking style—one of the best Ettelson ever had. But my father saw that it would be hard for an operator to sew. He told this to the designer as politely as he could, and was about to tell him that the pattern would have to be changed and how he thought it might be made, when the new designer interrupted him to say briefly: "Go to hell!"

My father could take a hint and went away to his sewing-machines. When the first lot of the new style was cut up, he took only two bundles and gave only one to his operators. The other four were sent to the contractors. On the third day, when the wrappers should have been brought back, the contractors came with their work unfinished and said they could not make the style for twice what they were paid.

Ettelson called my father into his office and asked him how he had found the style. My father explained why it was hard to make. "That's too bad!" said Ettelson. "We are

208

overloaded with orders on this style: we never had such a seller. Is there no easier way to make it?"

"There is, but the pattern will have to be changed."

"Why didn't you tell that to the designer?"

"I was going to, but he told me to go to hell."

Ettelson sprang up from his chair and was off like a shot to the cutting-room. In a few minutes, the new designer came up to my father, face flushed and set. But he said quietly: "Please show me what you meant."

"With pleasure," said my father, just as dignined. "But I cannot explain it. If you'll let me, I'll make a pattern."

My father went into the cutting-room and found Ettelson standing there. In about ten minutes, my father made a pattern, cut out a yoke, and then he said to the new designer: "Please come with me. I'll show you how this will work so that any operator can make it."

Ettelson followed them. My father seated himself at a sewing-machine. In a few minutes, he made the yoke and sewed it to a "front": it was as good as the sample. The new designer looked away from my father's elated face for a moment. Then he took his hand, shook it warmly, and said he was sorry for what he had said.

My father's wages were raised again, this time two dollars a week. And Ettelson told his new designer that before a new style was cut, he was to bring the pattern to my father for any changes—if needed.

My father had seven "front-makers" working for him. One morning, five did not come to work. In a couple of hours, he knew, there would be no work for the girls sewing other parts; nor could they take the place of the "front-makers" just like that, for these made about a quarter of the wrapper and the work took most skill. For an hour, my father did not know what to do and puttered about.

Suddenly, it was clear to him that one girl need not make all the "front." He opened no more bundles and gave six girls, who had been working at sleeves, collars and belts, the "fronts" to make: two to join the "centers," two to gather and hem ruffles, and two to sew ruffles to the yokes. The two "front-makers" who had come to work had only the "setting on" of the yokes to do. My father went from one to the other of the eight, showed them how he wanted the work made, stood over them, and saw to it that nothing was spoiled. By noon, the shop was running smoothly without the five "front-makers."

Ettelson had heard that most of his "front-makers" had not come to work. He kept peering about but, since all in the shop were kept busy, he said nothing until my father was back from lunch. Then he stopped him and said: "I hear you're in trouble."

My father smiled. "I'll see you before I go home, Mr. Ettelson. I'll know more about what I'm trying to do."

By the end of the day, my father had gotten as much work from thirty-one operators as he had from all of them before. He told Ettelson how he had hit upon what he called "team work" and the saving because of it. "I must tell you," he went on to say boldly, "that the workers have as much right to the added profit as he who hires them—he has no right to it all!" A good socialist might have said that the workers had the right to all the profit but, clearly, it would not have been wise or useful for my father to go that far. It seemed to him that Ettelson's thin lips tightened, as it was. But Ettelson nodded.

A month later, the shop by "team work" instead of "section work" made about half as much more, the operators earned

a quarter as much more, and, at the new year, my father was
to get twenty-five dollars a week.

One Sunday the sliding doors of the parlor were opened, and
I saw the sun shining through the white lace curtains that
were starched so stiffly I did not like to touch them.   I visited
my enemies, the rubber plants near the window, to look again
at the big thick leaves I disliked, but I had no time to stick
a pin into them secretly and see the white sap.   The doorbell
kept ringing, friend after friend came, and the threshold was
noisy with cheerful greetings.

The children of my age or so, old friends and friends brand-
new, led by me, were soon racing up and down the long hall
of the flat until we were wild with joy.   Just then my mother
called out that dinner was ready.   At this, all the children
scrambled into the dining-room to find my mother bringing
a great tureen of steaming beet soup from the kitchen, while
she and the other women cried out: "Be careful!"   My father
was already seated at the head of the table, filling little glasses
of brandy for the men.

One of the guests, the very man who had said when I was
a baby that I looked like a spider, now said in his dry voice,
looking at my mother with a sarcastic smile: "May I ask
what we are celebrating?"

My mother, busy dishing out the beet soup, her round face
flushed, replied: "We were going to tell you after dinner, but
since you ask—Nathan has had his wages raised five dollars!
From now on he will get twenty-five dollars a week, and we
have invited you all to celebrate with us."

The company turned to look at my father and almost all
murmured congratulations.   But the guest, whose question had
been answered, smiled wryly and said: "Why celebrate?   A day
will come when his boss will *take* five dollars from Nathan's

211

wages." And he helped himself to a nice slice of herring before anyone else should get it.

"I hope not," cried my mother cheerfully, hiding her anger. "I hope, rather, that you will all be our guests when Nathan has his wages raised again." And that nobody might be envious, she went on: "In other shops, a learner must work four weeks for nothing and the foreman gets as much as ten dollars from every learner he takes in. His boss gave Nathan the right to such money but he has never taken it. And in a shop as big as Ettelson's he could make a lot of money that way from the learners!"

By this time, every man had his glass of brandy and the women had been offered some and had all refused. My father, to end my mother's praise of him, called out in Hebrew the traditional toast: "To life!" "To life!" the guests answered and were promptly helping themselves to black olives and slices of herring.

There were now new troubles for the Jews of Russia. *The Evening Journal* had pictures of a mob rushing down a street with scythe blades—tied upright to poles—on which were stuck the bodies of babies or the peevish heads of bearded Jews. Immigrants, cousins and second cousins and even strangers, stayed with my parents for a night or for weeks. Sometimes one came unexpectedly, before the letter he had mailed in Germany, walking heavily upstairs to our door in boots into which his trousers were tucked and wearing a round hat of Persian lambskin like a Cossack.

The men slept on chairs or on the carpet in the parlor. I would sleep like them, wrapped in a quilt and proud of my hard bed. They were jolly for the most part, happy to be in America. My mother, bustling about, asked eagerly after her dear ones still in Russia and, for dinner, brought in plates of hot soup, thick and sweet with cabbage and potatoes, beets and lima beans. A platter of pot roast and more potatoes. Then tea in glasses with a dish of mulberry or pineapple jam to make the tea, sweetened by all the sugar one wanted, sweeter still, while my father at the head of the table, the successful man, told his guests cheerfully about the country: this dear land of freedom. But one had to work hard. Yes, there was a good living for everyone but one must be ready to work as hard as he did.

In those days, my father would come home by streetcar—much slower but not as tiring as the crowded elevated trains. I would go to the corner and wait for him, grateful for the excitement. I always went much too early; many men, the evening newspaper in their hands, would come slowly from the station of the elevated railway and many streetcars go clanging up Madison Avenue before I would see my father. I was proud of my father, of course; I knew that he was no ordinary mortal but a foreman, for whom many people worked and whom people came to for advice and for jobs, and whose wages were more than those of anybody else I knew. And my father's worried face would light up at the sight of his son waiting for him.

II

As Henry Ettelson's business grew, sewing-machine after sewing-machine was added to his place until my father had charge of eighty. Vacations—and Saturday as a holiday or half-holiday—were unheard of in the "ladies" wrapper business or, perhaps, any such business in those days at the turn of the century. My father worked six full days a week, in season and slack, early and late, coming before the operators and staying after they were gone, year in and year out until, although still in his thirties, he was thin ánd weak and so nervous his hands trembled. He smoked much to quiet his nerves; and was nervous, the doctor said, because he smoked much. But he was a successful foreman in the wrapper business and was paid forty dollars a week, besides a bonus at the end of the year; he had three thousand dollars in a savings-bank; an able man, a foreman among men, and a just man among foremen.

One day my father met a man who was a designer of dresses but had taken to drink and could not hold a job. He was glad to teach designing for a few dollars. My father knew how to grade patterns and design styles for wrappers: all he had to learn was how to make a pattern for size thirty-six—the standard. Though he now earned more than any designer of wrappers, he thought this a good chance to learn what he could.

Years before, Alter Jacobson had been hired by Henry Ettelson to sweep the floor and help the shipping-clerk. Alter helped the cutters, too, and in time became one of them. Now, the best cutter in Ettelson's place, he was in charge of the others. But he was paid only eighteen dollars a week. He was very pleasant to my father (who had always ranked much above him) and my father liked Alter Jacobson not only for being pleasant but because he worked hard and was ambitious. Alter would, at times, quietly complain about how hard it was for him to make ends meet, for he was married and had children. Now my father advised him to learn designing that he might better himself if he had the chance.

In a few months, Alter knew how to make patterns. But his teacher, who knew only the dress trade, could not show him how to design styles for wrappers. My father spent many an hour after work teaching this to Alter. When my father came home at night, dead tired but warmed by his own kindness, my mother greeted him coolly. "Alter Jacobson has a hard mouth," she would say, "and will not be thankful—whatever he says. You are just showing off." Needless to say, my father found this unpleasant.

Ettelson's designer left suddenly and a woman was hired in his place. After all, Ettelson thought, a woman ought to know what women wanted better than a man. However, the new designer did not do much. When the season was over, Ettelson sent her away. He stopped my father on his way home one evening to show him a list of designers and asked him who might be best. Then my father told Ettelson that Alter had been studying designing at night: "Give him a chance," said my father. "If you pay him twenty-five dollars a week and hire a boy to help take care of the stock for eight dollars, the house will save twenty dollars a week. You would have to pay a good designer thirty-five. And you can always hire a designer if this won't work."

So Alter Jacobson became Ettelson's designer as well as head of the cutters. He now had the place the designer held many years before when my father first went to work for Ettelson as a foreman. Strong and ambitious, Alter did the work of three. No one who saw his tall, broad-shouldered body leaning over the cutting-table, the light-brown hair falling over the square forehead, the grey eyes intent upon his work, the square jaw and large firm mouth, and heard his calm pleasant voice, could doubt that Alter's star would rise.

When Alter was sure of his job, he had the old rule that gave my father the choice of work changed. Now my father had to quarrel with him every day about what was to be made in the shop and what was to go to the contractors and could no longer show that the shop was very profitable. It was not my mother's way to say much about a matter when it was too late. She listened sympathetically to my father's complaints about Alter; if it was my father's turn to see himself a fool, it was hers to see him as a generous man betrayed.

Ettelson's business was better than ever. Now he spent no more at it than two or three hours a day but he grudged it even that. One morning, he called my father, Alter Jacobson, and the bookkeeper into his office and told them he was thinking of incorporating the business, giving shares to the three of them, and letting them run it: he would then be able to spend all of his time in Wall Street at the stock market. That very noon, when my father went out for lunch, he heard the talk in the trade that Ettelson was going out of business.

My father promptly received a letter at Ettelson's from another manufacturer of wrappers—an Irishman. When my father went up to see him, he met my father warmly, took him into his private office, gave him a good cigar and, as my father smoked and savored the tobacco, said that if my father would come to work for him, he would give him as much in wages as he was getting from Ettelson and a share in the profits of the shop besides. My father saw that he might make as much as a hundred dollars a week with the hundred sewing-machines the place had, if he ran the shop as well as he did Ettelson's. And in a year, the manufacturer added, when his lease was up, he would move uptown and have twice as many machines.

The next day Henry Dix, another manufacturer who had three factories in New Jersey, came to the city just to see my father. He went right up to Ettelson's place of business and Ettelson himself called my father into the office and introduced him. Dix was willing to hire my father for three years at fifty dollars a week and pay him what it would cost to move to New Jersey. Besides, the cost of living in the small town where my father would settle was so much less than in New York City he would really be getting more than a ten-dollar-a-week

216

raise in wages; and life there, said Dix, without a streetcar or train to take to go to work was easier and pleasant. If my father had ever doubted it, he now began to think himself somebody.

A few days later, Ettelson had his own plans ready. He was going to incorporate his business for thirty thousand dollars; my father, Alter Jacobson, and the bookkeeper could buy as much as five thousand dollars' worth of stock each; they would get no bonus, such as they had been getting, for they would share in the profits of the business according to their stock; Ettelson himself would draw only twenty-five dollars a week, as he had been doing, and would lend the business, at six per cent, as much money as it might need. My father had his three thousand dollars, and Alter Jacobson had two thousand, with which to buy the stock. The bookkeeper had five thousand dollars ready and said yes at once; but my father wanted a few days to think it over. And then Alter Jacobson said he wanted a few days, too.

That evening, Alter Jacobson came to see my father. He stood in the little dining-room of the flat, a tall, broad-shouldered man speaking slowly and cheerfully. He saw well enough that neither my father nor mother were friendly but he did not seem to be bothered by that. He seated himself slowly, at my mother's cold invitation, spread his legs, rested his hands on his thighs and, leaning back, said in his deep pleasant voice: "Well, how do you like Ettelson's proposition?"

My father at the other end of the table looked small—a sparrow facing a robin. "I have better ones," he said briefly.

"I understand," went on Alter Jacobson calmly, "that you are not as friendly to me as you were. But I feel no guilt. It was my duty to see that the contractors had a chance to make the better grade of work. I admit that you are not as powerful as you might have been otherwise, but you lost no money because of it. I give you my word of honor that I would rather lose than that you should. But both our interests are now alike. Let us promise each other that one of us doesn't work for Ettelson without the other. In this way, we'll get better terms, for he'll be able to get along without one of us but not without both."

My father had now finished his prunes—he had been eating his dinner at an increasing tempo—and pushed the dish away. "I see no need of making any promise or asking you for any," he said. He hesitated a moment and then, his impulse to be helpful too much for him, added: "If Ettelson will not give me forty-five dollars a week so that I get as much as when I got a bonus and will not give me, also, my five thousand dollars' worth of stock so that I have, right now, a right to any dividends, I will not work for him. I can pay only three thousand dollars for the stock but I want two years' time in which to pay the balance, and I am willing to give Ettelson six per cent for what I owe until I have paid it all. As for you, I think you, too, ought to get as much as you did in wages plus the bonus, and get all your stock now with time in which to pay for it. But do as you like!"

Alter Jacobson mulled over what my father had said and found it good. Then, smiling his friendliest, he bid us good night.

Next day Ettelson called my father into the office. "I did not look for this from you," he began at once angrily—his voice at its shrillest. "You and Alter Jacobson have conspired against me!"

"That isn't true," said my father, becoming just as angry.

"Jacobson told me so!"

"Then he lies!"

"You saw each other last night, didn't you? I want you

to tell me right now what was said—what he said to you and what you said to him!"

"I don't think I have to do that," said my father. Then he added losing his head completely: "As for your proposition, I am out of it no matter how you change your terms."

"Don't be in such a hurry," said Ettelson, as my father went towards the door. "Think it over!" he called after him. But my father ran downstairs and telephoned the Irishman who had offered him a share of the profits that he would work for him.

This manufacturer ran his business on borrowed money. His assistant got him the loans from an elderly relative of hers. She was the very woman who had left Ettelson's shop in a huff, many years before, because she would not tell the operators to "set in" a yoke as the designer—and my father—thought she should. In this shop, the sewing-machines were not on the same floor as the office and cutting-room, and my father knew no more of what was going on than any contractor: he did not know what styles were cut or to be cut and had to work at whatever was sent to him. And the manufacturer's assistant often sent him work for which she had no trimmings ready and trimmings for which no wrappers had been cut; nor was she one—as my father well knew—to take instruction or suggestions kindly.

My father soon had bundles of unfinished wrappers piling up and not enough work for his help. He paid them more at "piece work" than Ettelson did, but at that they could not earn enough to make a living and his best operators left for better jobs elsewhere. In a little while my father was "through." At least he told the manufacturer so. The shop not only did not make any money—it was losing money.

"Be patient," said the manufacturer. "I am willing to take the loss until you get things straight."

But things became worse. My father again asked to be allowed to quit. This time the manufacturer told him that when they moved uptown the shop would be on the same floor as the cutting-room. Besides, he was trying to borrow money from a bank to repay the loans his assistant had gotten him. As soon as he did, he would send her away and put my father in charge of every department.

When Alter Jacobson found out how badly my father was doing, he told him of his own troubles. It seemed to Jacobson that Ettelson no longer trusted him. Certainly, Ettelson was angry at having given him more than he had wanted to. Instead of spending his time away from the place, as he had planned, Ettelson now dogged Jacobson's steps, scolding him all day long in his shrill voice. Jacobson had gotten a clause in his contract that whenever he left the corporation he should be given his share of the profits—whatever they might be at the time— and all he had paid for his stock. They ought to become partners, he now told my father, and go into business for themselves; they knew each other well—neither was lazy and each knew his end of the business; why should they still work for an Ettelson or anyone? And Jacobson assured my father that he had never said a word to Ettelson of any understanding between himself and my father: Ettelson's charge was only a trick of his to find out if what he suspected was so.

And so they became partners. Alter Jacobson left Ettelson's corporation and my father gave up his own job. They went to a boarding-house in the Catskills to rest for two weeks but could stay no longer than one—so eager were they to begin work. Each put three thousand dollars into the business (all they had). They rented a loft on a side street near Broadway, hired a salesman, and went to the wholesale dry-goods houses to buy their goods. They were given the lowest prices and the longest terms: they had only Ettelson to refer to but he gave them the best of references.

Jacobson thought that since he could get along with old cutting-tables, my father should buy second-hand sewing-machines for the shop. They argued the matter for days. When my father went to the showroom of the Singer Sewing Machine Company for a final estimate, Jacobson, to have his own way, signed a contract with a dealer in second-hand machines for another make. He tried to show my father that they had saved six hundred dollars by this deal. However, the old sewing-machines proved troublesome and experienced help would not even try them, for they were used to Singer machines. Before my father and Jacobson could get good contractors, the season was about over.

My father had little to do, since the shop was not running, and Jacobson kept hinting that he was doing all the work. It was not long before my father began to dislike their business thoroughly: if he could only get five hundred dollars out of it, he kept telling my mother, he would let the rest go to the devil and look for a job. While these gloomy thoughts were in my father's mind, Jacobson had been looking about for himself. One Monday morning, he told my father that he was going to work for Ettelson again: their old "boss" had found no one to take Jacobson's place and was not only willing to have him back in the corporation but would pay my father and Jacobson whatever their goods had cost, wrappers as well as goods still in the piece, and would take care of their lease, too.

My father and Jacobson had agreed that the business be given up whenever either wanted to quit it, and now my father saw that if it were not for this he might have made his partner, leaving him for a profitable job, stand all the loss. They had to sell their sewing-machines and fixtures for what they had paid only for the fixtures. Ettelson came up, took over the keys and merchandise, as he had said he would, and gave them his check. They paid whatever they owed and had four thousand four hundred dollars left between them (most of this in accounts and, except for several hundred dollars lost in bad debts, collected by their bank in about three months).

Although my father had been willing to lose much more, he was sad enough at losing in a few months a third of what he had saved in ten years of hard work—doing without much that both he and my mother wanted. Now he was without a business or a job. (As for Ettelson's corporation, with Alter Jacobson in it, there was no place for my father.) Of all this, I, who was then eight or nine, heard little and understood nothing; except that, when the partnership was over, my father brought home his share of the business stationery. I was pleased at getting so much good white paper, although I, too, had little use for it.

My father now wrote a letter to Henry Dix, the manufacturer who had come to see him at Ettelson's, asking for the job out-of-town. Dix was in no hurry to reply. When he did, he wrote that he would be in New York on other business in a few days and my father would find him at his hotel. There Dix explained that now he had foremen in all his factories but, if my father was willing to work for thirty dollars a week instead of the fifty that had been offered, he would be hired as an assistant. My father, who had been unable to get anything to do, said yes at once.

That Saturday he took the train to the little town in New Jersey where he was to work. Dix's superintendent showed him about the factory so that he might know where he was at on Monday. He asked my father home to dinner and led him to the only hotel in town to help choose a room. They spent a pleasant Sunday together—talking of politics and books instead of "ladies" wrappers.

Although my father understood his work well enough, he soon found out that he did not understand the help. The sewing-machine operators in New York had been Jews and Italians mostly, immigrants who needed their jobs badly and who had been screamed at and insulted all their lives—whom my father did not have to handle with kid gloves. Dix's superintendent spent a good deal of time teaching my father how a foreman must behave, if he was to get any work done by Americans, and my father, who liked to teach but not to be taught, found it unpleasant at the age of thirty-three to have to learn how to talk and act. But he tried to do what he was told and make the best of it.

My father did not like the hotel where he lived nor the food, and the owner did not like my father. The owner of the hotel was a scrawny man with a little grey beard and a bald head, who went about in a frock coat, tightly buttoned, as suited the most important man in town, for he owned most of it— many of the houses were mortgaged to him or he had foreclosed the mortgages long before. Now he changed his seat to sit at my father's table and ate no meat but pork, because he thought it bothered my father to see him eat it, and he was always making little jokes about him. My father soon found himself lonely and sick. He sat in his shabby hotel-room evenings, wondering what he had best do for a living. He did not like the town at all: rows of little wooden houses, many unpainted; unpaved streets; the small talk, the drinking, and worse. Although he himself had been brought up in a village, this small factory town was no place to live in after living in New York, he thought; no place to bring up his children.

While he was mulling over these thoughts, perhaps unjustly,

as strangers even in a great and beautiful city may arrive by way of the slums and a factory district, he was told that he had been promoted to be foreman of Dix's shop in a neighboring village. The superintendent drove him over and got him board and lodging—there was no hotel—with a woman whose husband peddled about the countryside and was away from home most of the time. They had a daughter of seventeen or eighteen. Both women were good-looking and friendly—somewhat too friendly my father thought.

One evening, when he was in the store of a young Jew in the village, the storekeeper said jokingly: "Be careful that the husband of the lady you are lodging with doesn't make trouble for you when he gets home."

My father smiled and quoted a Russian proverb: "If you eat no radish, your breath has no smell."

"Oh," said the storekeeper, "he doesn't need a good reason for trying to get money out of you. There has been enough trouble here because of those people. Why do you think the foreman whose place you are taking left?"

Saturday night, my father was back, bag and baggage, to tell Dix he did not want to stay on. Now, he thought, he would surely be sent away and that would save him the trouble of making up his own mind to leave. But, after a short talk with the superintendent, Dix said: "Very well, if you don't like it there, stay here. We'll teach your helper there how to run the factory."

So my father stayed. He went back to his old work and his room in the hotel. The guests he knew greeted him as an old acquaintance and were friendly. Even the owner now spoke to him earnestly—of politics and religion. Still, my father was only waiting for an excuse to leave. He wrote—in Yiddish, of course—to my mother in the small handwriting which was afterwards mine, too: "I know you don't want

224

to move from the city to a place like this. Neither do I. I'll take the first chance I get to leave in a friendly way. But I lost no money by coming here and, after all, it did no harm to try out the job and see what it was like."

III

A historian of the "ladies" wrapper business might note the wide use of the wrapper because it was cheap and not troublesome when women were, generally, poor and too busy to bother much about clothes. He might then show how, as the inhabitants of the country became well-off, generally, and women had more time for themselves, the woman in a wrapper, once the good housewife, became a symbol of the slattern. By this time, women in the cities were no longer buying wrappers as they used to and, sooner or later, neither would women in towns and villages, and on distant farms; yes, the wrapper business was about over. The comfortable kimona, stylish at first, perhaps, because of the Russian-Japanese War and all the sympathy for Japan, would be worn instead; and also dresses of the same goods that wrappers had been made of, cheap and neat, for cheap clothing was still needed.

But the kimona, possibly, and the "house dress" certainly, were then unknown to my mother as she looked anxiously into the future. She wrote my father nothing of what was going through her mind, probably thinking it would do no good until she had something practical to suggest. Besides, her pen was not like that of the psalmist who boasted himself "a ready writer": she wrote with difficulty, even in Yiddish, for she had not been taught much when a girl—teachers and books were dear and what little instruction her father could buy had been for her brothers. And she had since been much too busy to learn. Now she answered my father's letters briefly, and certainly misspelled more than a word or two, at which no doubt he smiled.

Down the street, near the avenue where the railway ran on a viaduct of steel and blackened stone, there was a little sign "millinery," neatly painted in black on white glass, in the corner of one of the windows on the ground floor of a dingy tenement. Here the milliner, a stout middle-aged woman, taught my mother for a fee—perhaps as much as ten dollars—the art of making "ladies" hats. After school, I would find them together in the dark little front-room, which was the "millinery parlor," sewing linings into hats, covering wire-frames with mull, sewing braid to the mull, or trimming straw shapes with flowers and ribbon, while they talked cheerfully to each other.

My mother did not write my father what she was doing. He was so quick at calculating the distance of an ambitious journey the grand sum made the first steps laughable and presumptious. And the news that she had gone back to her needle, by which she had made a living as a seamstress when a girl, would have disheartened him utterly as a sign that she had lost faith in him as he was losing faith in himself.

But there was soon plenty to write about to my father: one of his sisters and her family and one of my mother's brothers and his family were coming to this country from Russia.

Horse-cars were still running on some streets. I liked to ride on them because they bounced up and down, while the harness of the horses jingled. One morning, my mother and I—in a horse-car—went to meet my uncle Israel, my mother's brother. He had just landed and was stopping at his father-in-law's. I saw a tall dark stranger with large black eyes and a small pointed beard, like a Frenchman's in the cartoons, whom my mother rushed at. He seemed to take her embrace and excitement calmly. "Israel! How you have grown! How tall! How handsome!" My uncle Israel said nothing but smiled cheerfully and stroked his little black beard.

As for my father's sister and her family, they stayed with us. My aunt was as busy as she could be, for both her children were down with the measles; but my uncle Joseph sat for hours hunched over the dining-room table, with round ruddy cheeks and pale blue eyes, looking like a well-to-do but morose farmer. He would play with the sugar-tongs or a spoon, bending and straightening it until it broke, or cut paper into threads and then brush the heap to the floor. My mother would have to go down on her knees to pick up the strips of paper, fine as hair, for no broom could get them out of the carpet, and my uncle Joseph would grin at her. Sometimes, seeing his absent-minded look, I would say in my bad Yiddish: "What are you thinking of, Uncle?"

He would put down the scissors or sugar-tongs—whatever he was playing with—to rub his forehead. "What am I thinking of?" he would echo, and for answer smile sourly.

My uncle Joseph was the son of a well-to-do man and he had brought more than a thousand dollars with him from Russia. He had helped in his father's store, where he sold the peasants of the village whatever they might need—tar for their axles as well as tobacco for the cigarettes they rolled out of old newspaper—but here he did not know what to do: he did not have to work in a shop, as my father did and my mother and others who had come to this country penniless, nor, like others, did he have to carry a pack from door to door as a peddler. He had enough money to buy his way into some kind of business as a partner or to open some kind of store; but what business? what store?

My other uncle, Israel, was another sort altogether. He had worked hard for his living, ever since he was a child, and had his own store at last in a large city—a dealer in leather. Before my father came home, on one of his infrequent visits, my uncle Israel had rented a place on Hester Street, in the heart of the East Side, where he did not have to know a word of English, and here he had silk and satin, muslin and woolens: all that a dry-goods store should have for sale.

My uncle Israel's business was going to be good, God willing, so he told my father, but, naturally, he could not trust his clerks. When he went to buy goods with one, the other was alone in the store with no one to watch him; and if he himself stayed in the store and sent a clerk to buy, his man might pay more than he should or buy what he should not, because he knew no better or was bribed. Now then, my uncle Israel wanted someone in the store whom he could trust. Since Joseph, the husband of my father's sister, had found nothing to do and had brought about twenty-five hundred roubles with him from Russia, if Joseph gave my uncle Israel the money and stayed in the store, Israel would pay him fifteen dollars a week—enough for Joseph and his family to live on—and a percentage of the profits when the year was over: Joseph would not only make a living but have a chance to become a real merchant.

My uncle Joseph liked the plan well enough, for though he had broken my mother's silver sugar-tongs and two or three tin ones and had cut up enough paper to make, if it were green, grass for all of Central Park, he had come to no conclusion in spite of all his thinking. "But," said Joseph to my father—not without a peasant's shrewdness, "you will have to be good for Israel: if, at any time, I want to leave the business, he will have to give me all my money back."

My uncle Israel smiled. "Of course," he said.

"I have always found Israel a man of his word," said my

father, eager to help, "and I will be good for your money. Good luck to both of you!"

Not long after this my father was in New York to stay. He had fallen sick and, though every one was kind enough, he told Dix that he wanted to go home and that they should not wait for him: he was not coming back.

My father tried to find work in the city as a foreman at wrappers. There was a job to be had in a small shop, down on the East Side, and the wages only fifteen dollars a week, but he was ready to take it. However a young woman, who used to work for him merely as a "floor girl," was hired instead. Now my father took to "resting" in the afternoon, tossing about and groaning in his sleep, and smoked cigarette after cigarette, the cheapest he could buy. For want of anything better to do, he kept calculating to the penny how much it cost us to live and how long his savings might last.

Just then his brother-in-law, my uncle Joseph, came to tell him that he did not like my uncle Israel's business at all—Joseph did not believe there would be any profits or even a living in it. And he wanted all his money back, right away, as he had been promised. Early next morning, my father went downtown to see my uncle Israel at the store. Israel smiled and stroked his little beard. "I am too busy to talk to you now," he said. "I must leave in a few minutes to buy some goods I need badly," he added, unruffled, "but I'll be at your house tonight."

By the time my father came home he had a bad headache. The towels, soaked in cold water and vinegar, that my mother tied about his head helped little. He walked from his bed to the window and from the window to his bed and could not even remain seated for worry. He did not sleep that afternoon and had little appetite at supper for my mother's pot roast and potatoes. After nine my uncle Israel came, serene as always.

His smiling face cheered my father and mother greatly. They were, of course, willing enough to think that all was well, but my uncle Israel was in no hurry to talk. He took the glass of tea my mother gave him and stirred in a generous helping of her raspberry jam. When he had finished that glass and another steaming glass of tea was again at his elbow, he pushed it aside and said: "Business is not at all as bad as Joseph says. Besides, the holiday buying is just about to begin. You know what a country bumpkin Joseph is," my uncle Israel went on. "Well, the other storekeepers are making fun of him and he wants to run away. Of course, I can let him have his money. But what bothers me is that I'll be alone again with no one to trust." My uncle Israel finished his third glass of tea. By this time his face was brick-red.

"Now you," he said, looking at my father but also speaking to my mother, his sister—she was seated at the other end of the table, plucking at the tablecloth with thumb and fore-finger—"you have not been able to find anything to do and you still have a couple of thousand dollars. How long should a man work for others? If you will put your money into my business, you can have twenty-five dollars a week for your living and be your own boss. We were partners before in Russia. Why not now? We were lucky, and perhaps it is God's will that I should come to America that we might be in partnership again," he concluded piously.

My father never thought he was so important that God would think about him in his troubles and send him a partner all the way from Russia. But he had not forgotten, of course, his brief partnership with my uncle Israel when they were hardly out of their teens—not yet brothers-in-law. (My father's father had put up all the money and Israel had been faithful to the last jot and tittle.) The notion of having a store on Hester Street, in the ghetto, was far from anything my father had ever thought of doing in this country; still, the business was not unlike what he had been doing in Russia.

My mother liked her brother's offer. My father would not have to work as hard as he did when he was a foreman. Besides, he could not even find work at that. And then she was afraid that her brother would be robbed by his clerks and the merchants from whom he bought. "Even if you lose a little of your savings," she said that night to my father when my uncle was gone, "we must help Israel. Suppose we had to spend money on him, as we did for so many other immigrants—some of them only strangers?"

Next morning, my father went to my uncle's store and told him he would become his partner, and they shook hands warmly. Then my father asked when they might take inventory of the stock? "What?" said my uncle Israel, opening his dark eyes wide. "We are too busy now—just before the holidays. How can we take the time to measure every piece of goods? It is more important to wait on customers. You can look at the goods on the shelves and go through the books and see how much business was done since I opened the store; the bills will show how much I bought. I may have made a few bad buys. Well, I put twenty-three hundred dollars into the business and you have twenty-one hundred—we will call it even."

If business will be good, thought my father, what does a few dollars more or less matter; and if, God forbid, bad, what matter how I lost my money? Besides, he was sick of doing nothing—and nothing to look forward to. He gave my uncle Joseph his twelve hundred dollars; with the rest of my father's money my uncle Israel paid a few bills and bought some new stock for the holiday season. And my father became a store-keeper on Hester Street.

For the first few weeks of their partnership the holiday trade kept my uncle Israel and my father busy but, afterwards, there was little to do. My uncle would sit in back of the store, slowly drinking glasses of tea and talking with his clerks or another storekeeper about the cantors in synagogues here and in Russia. (He had a good voice, too, and would gladly have been a cantor.) When little more than a year was over, after the next holiday season, my father and uncle owed about seven thousand dollars for goods and their stock was hardly worth as much at a forced sale—and that was all they had.

"I didn't think it would be that bad," said my uncle Israel thoughtfully. "If we stay on, we must go bankrupt. I am still too young for that and must have credit. I am giving up the store while we can still pay our debts!"

My father had disliked the business of that street—perhaps because he was bad at it. Every sale was haggled over; and customers would buy only after walking away once or twice to be called back from the door or even run after along the sidewalk and plucked by the sleeve. However, when my father saw himself about to lose not only his livelihood but all his savings, it seemed to him that if they could only make a go of the store it would not be half bad, after all.

"Didn't you hint time and again," he said to his partner, "that you had money put aside, that the twenty-three hundred dollars you have in this business is just a beginning—that if the business needs more you have plenty? Why throw away dirty water before we have clean? And why turn me out without a cent? Both of us now know more about this business than we did; we know what will sell and how to buy. Why not put more money into the business as you hinted you would?"

"I have no more."

"But all those hints?"

"In business, nobody must know what you have," said my uncle Israel coldly, as if repeating for a youngster a lesson he should have learnt long before.

My father and uncle had a clever salesman and they told him how things were, for they wanted his help in selling as much as they could. He, however, thought that they ought to buy still more, especially from little fellows, and then settle with the creditors for fifty cents on the dollar. That would be a good deal to pay and more than such creditors could get (when lawyers and court costs were paid) if they threw my father and uncle into bankruptcy; and everybody would think well of them as honest. But my father thought this shameful for the foreman who had left Henry Ettelson proudly and my uncle Israel, new in the country, thought it a bad beginning. No, they made up their minds to stop buying and sell what they had, even at a loss.

In a few weeks they had paid most of their debts. For the sale of what was left of the stock, they began to dicker with an auctioneer—one of those who preyed on merchants about to cheat their creditors. My uncle Israel and his clever salesman with their worried air and whispering, the disordered stock and their insistence on cash, had the manner of absconders so well that, late at night, the auctioneer was hurried into paying more than the stock was worth—to an auctioneer. My father did not have to act a part: misery was written so large on his face that the auctioneer might well have concluded that here was not merely a man about to abscond but about to die.

That night, after the sale, my father and uncle came to our house. My uncle took the money out of his pocket and put it on the table. They set aside what they still owed for mer-

chandise and a hundred dollars for their salesman (promised
if he would be helpful), and divided the rest in half: five
hundred and fifty dollars for each. My uncle took one hundred
dollars from his share and pushed it towards my father.

"What is this for?" he asked.

"Ask no questions," said my uncle Israel, "but take it—
it is yours."

IV

My uncle Israel was soon making a living, so he said, buying
silk and ribbons at auction sales and peddling them to millinery
stores. But my father, who had always hated selling and felt
like a beggar at it, could not bring himself to do that. He
would go from auction-room to auction-room and buy small
lots of merchandise and turn them in to be sold again. He
made a little, sometimes, and sometimes lost a little; in the end
he made nothing and lost his time. He comforted himself
with the thought that he deserved no better: this was merely
gambling—not work.

By this time, my mother made no secret of her millinery.
She was becoming a milliner, she said, neither for her husband's
sake nor her own, but that their children might have the education her parents had neither the money nor the chance to give
her brothers in Russia. She was calm and implacable about it
and my father, if he could say anything against this, no longer
had the heart to say much. Certainly, he was no longer the
successful foreman.

My mother soon thought she knew enough about millinery
to call herself a milliner. If they had a flat on the ground
floor, she now said, she could sell millinery in the front-room,
as the woman was doing from whom she had learnt the trade,
and at the same time do the housework. So my parents
moved to a better neighborhood in Harlem, near a neighbor-

hood better still, from which she hoped to draw her customers. The new rooms cost six dollars a month more and were smaller and dark. Here my mother put her own sign "Millinery," neatly painted on white glass by a signmaker (who charged a dollar for it), in the corner of the single window that opened on the street. And, after some reflection, she bought a cheap bookcase with glass doors to hold her stock.

My father knew a man who had a millinery store on Sixth Avenue, between the department stores on Fourteenth Street and those up the avenue: a prosperous inlet into which the wide stream of shoppers eddied all day. As soon as my mother had half a dozen hats ready, she persuaded my father to take them to his acquaintance and ask for work to be made at home. The storekeeper knew my father only as a foreman at wrappers; and, for reasons he did not trouble to give, he found the hats amusing. "Tell your wife," he said at last brusquely, the busy man whose time had been wasted, "not to make a fool of herself."

My father pushed the hats back into the box and did not care whether he crushed them or not. When he found himself on the sidewalk, it was all he could do to keep from throwing box and hats into the gutter. My mother took the hats out of the box without a word. She tried to straighten the wires of the frames where they had been bent by my father's angry packing. Then she put the hats back on the shelves of the bookcase and, her mouth tightened and round brow wrinkled, thoughtfully closed the doors.

My mother had learnt how to make pleatings when she worked at wrappers and now pleatings were stylish for women's hats. She went to the millinery departments of the large stores and asked for pleatings to make by hand at home. One or two of the stores gave her work to do. She then had my uncle Israel get pleatings for her to make as he went the rounds of the milliners, selling the ribbons and silk he bought at auction. She could not earn much, for the work was slow and difficult, but, of course, that was why she could get any at all. My father helped her cut the goods. With her house to look after (in this she had no help) and her millinery business, such as it was, to take care of, my father would sometimes wake after midnight and see the gas burning in the living-room and my mother still at work. At last he could stand this no longer and made up his mind to get something to do—whatever it was and no matter how humble.

One Sunday he read in his newspaper a large advertisement for sewing-machine operators to work at skirts. He said nothing to my mother and went to the shop early Monday morning. The woman in charge handed him a bundle of six skirts to sew, and he was told what sewing-machine to use. He took off his coat and rolled up his sleeves, oiled the machine and opened the bundle. The girl at the next sewing-machine was watching him.

Suddenly she said: "Excuse me, Mister, but from the way you opened your bundle I can see you are not a skirt operator. What is your line?"

"Wrappers. But I haven't been able to find any work and I'm trying to learn how to make skirts."

"If you'll let me, I'll show you."

With her help, my father made the skirts. He brought them to the forewoman. She examined them but said nothing, and gave him another bundle to sew.

While my father was at the forewoman's desk, he was seen by an operator who knew him. The operator came up to his machine, afterwards, and said: "What are you doing here? Are *you* here as an operator?" My father told him that he had lost his money and had been out of work and asked him not to tell anyone who he was—or, rather, had been. The man, not displeased to see the great brought low, promised.

It was not long before one of the owners came into the shop to look at the work of the new help. He told the fore-woman to send some of them away but he liked my father's work. The manufacturer looked at him longer than at the others, and sent the forewoman for him. "What is your name?" he asked. My father told him. He repeated the name once or twice to himself and then said: "I heard of a man with that name who was a foreman for Henry Ettelson, the wrapper manufacturer. Are you related to him?"

"I am that man."

The manufacturer stared at my father for a moment in silence. "Why do you come here to work as an operator?"

"As you know, wrappers are going out of style and I can't find a job in my trade. I want to learn this line."

The manufacturer smiled. "You don't have to learn. I see that you know how to sew a skirt. Roll down your sleeves— you have the job of assistant foreman. Of course, until you know the line well, I can't pay you what Ettelson did. You will begin at twenty-five dollars a week."

There was a stir and buzz among the help as they talked of my father who had come to work that morning as an operator and, in a few hours, had been made a foreman. My father, as you may well imagine, was eager enough to tell my mother the good news. But my mother was not at all enthusiastic and said with tears in her eyes: "You oughtn't to work any more for a boss—especially as a foreman: you are not strong enough."

Of course, my father did not listen to her. But he was not able to do the work. There were the usual troubles with fellow workers; worse than that, he really did not know the line. In two weeks he quit the job. My father now got a place in the loft of an acquaintance, for which he was not to pay any rent at first, and began to manufacture skirts himself. It took him three weeks to make the first lot; when he sold it to a store, he made no more than twenty dollars. Then he went into partnership with another acquaintance, who knew how to make "sailor suits" for boys. After six weeks of hard work, they were unable to sell their stock and had to turn it over to an auctioneer. The lot brought only fifty dollars.

What on earth was he to do for a living?

My mother told my father, one evening, that when she was downtown she had seen a pleating machine in the window of a sewing-machine company, but it would cost almost one hundred and fifty dollars and would not be ready for a while. It is easy to fall in love with a machine, even if one has no eye for the rhythm of its motion, if it can do swiftly and well what one's own fingers are doing slowly; and my father, urged by my mother, bought the pleating machine out of his by now scanty funds. He then rented a room on Bond Street, near Broadway, in which to make the pleatings. When the machine came, my uncle Israel went about to the manufacturers of women's hats to ask for orders at a cent a yard.

The pleating-machine was not much larger than an ordinary sewing-machine. The room which my father had rented was small, barely large enough for the machine and himself and the little table on which he cut the goods to be pleated; but it was a sunny room and my father worked in it cheerfully at the orders my uncle brought. In four weeks, my father made about fifty thousand yards of pleating (and could have made three times as much if he had the orders). And then pleatings went out of style.

While my father was busy at pleating, a stranger came into

my mother's "millinery parlor"; a burly chap, his troubled face set in a scowl. He had seen her sign as he passed and he told her that he had a wealthy cousin, a jobber of millinery; this cousin would give him straw braid with which to make turbans for women (the small hats stylish then); and he would pay my mother a dollar and a quarter a dozen for the sewing. If she could get a few girls to help her, so much the better— he would give her as much as they could do.

My mother soon had five girls of the neighborhood to sew for her. The jobber's cousin lived in a flat around the corner and I would carry the hats to his house and bring back the bundles of straw and the wire frames. I found it unpleasant to have our home full of strangers and heaps of hats about and pots and pans of water—in which the straw was dipped to be soft enough to sew; but my parents were happy, for they were making a living and even some money. But this work, too, did not last long: the season was over by Easter.

Both pleating and the sewing of straw hats had paid well; and my parents made up their minds to move downtown, near the millinery jobbers and the manufacturers of millinery, to get something to do in that trade. They knew little enough about it; but my father had his training in the wrapper business, and my mother her old skill at sewing, and both their necessity, to help them. So they moved to Fourth Street, half a block east of the Bowery, not quite three blocks from Broadway: a large flat, in which they had plenty of room to work if they found something to do. When they paid the rent for the first month, they had only thirty-nine dollars left, all the money they had in the world and all that was left of my father's great savings—not enough for another month's rent.

As we rode downtown my father sat beside me and spoke to me gravely—sad for no reason that I could see. We had taken the streetcar, just the two of us; my mother had gone ahead, or was coming later, and there was no use going by the elevated railway which was much faster: we should have to wait for the moving-van and its horses, anyway. It was a month or so after Easter and the day was warm. The car was an "open" one—long seats across it and a running board to reach them. My father let me sit next to the bar at the farthest end of the seat, unlike my mother who was always afraid that I might fall off; it was the best place, from which I could see best and catch whatever breeze there was.

"I am sorry we have to move downtown," said my father humbly. His manner was unusual and I found it somewhat upsetting. "I have been out of work for a long time. Maybe I will make a living now. But there are no parks downtown in which to play and you will find the streets dirty. As soon as I can, we will move away. But it may do you good, after all: you will find bright boys in your class. You will not have it as easy as you did in Harlem. You know how smart the boys of the East Side are!"

I nodded uneasily. School had not been "easy" for me. Why did my father think it had been? I remembered, particularly, much difficulty with arithmetic. But the ride was pleasant—I was seldom on a streetcar. It was cool where I sat and there was much to see, in spite of the railway overhead, and soon I felt cheerful as the car rolled steadily down the dark street to our new home.

Clearly, my parents had to do something at once. My father now went to a factory of women's hats for which he had made pleating (the owners were friendly), and asked for work his wife, the milliner, could sew at home. They were making a turban of puffed silk and had more orders than their own help could fill; so they gave him a sample and silk for a dozen hats. If his wife made these to suit, she would be given more to do and paid a dollar and a quarter a dozen.

My father spread the silk on the table at home. The goods had been tucked by a sewing-machine. He could do that easily enough but he could not see how it had been puffed. Of course, he concluded ruefully, they would not trust him with any hat they thought he could copy and sell. (But how did my father, the honest man, do this—ask for work in order to copy the style for himself? If this had been in his mind, as it might very well have been, it must have been only as a seed, the merest mustard seed, hidden in the thought that my mother would only do what she had done, when she was sewing straw turbans for the jobber's cousin, and just what he himself used to do when he had been a contractor at wrappers. Otherwise he might not have been willing to ask for work as he did; certainly, he would not have had the face to.)

My mother studied the silk and said: "They must run rods or sticks through the tucks, press the silk together, and then steam it so that, no matter how you stretch it afterwards, the silk will come together again and stay puffed."

While she made the hats, my father went to my uncle Israel to get a couple of yards of such silk. And, waiting for my uncle to bring it (for he had none in stock), my father whittled a dozen round sticks, thinking that steel rods would rust and spoil the goods. When it had been tucked and run upon the sticks, pressed down and steamed over the kettle in the kitchen, the silk did look as good as the goods of the sample. My father now measured the puffed silk: it would take eight yards to make a dozen hats and the dozen, counting my parents' own work and all, would cost nine dollars. If they were to charge twelve, less the trade discount, they might sell enough to keep themselves busy and have a profit, besides payment for their work.

At this point the impatient reader, particularly if he is sure of dinner and bed this night and for many nights to come, may ask sternly: Was this right? Had they the right to copy the hat they were given to make and to undersell, as they certainly would, the house that had kindly given it?

Probably not. Was a promise not to copy the hat implied? Perhaps. A promise not to copy the goods? Perhaps. Or were they dealing at arm's length, as the law books say, the manufacturers paying as little as they could for work they needed badly enough to have made outside their shop, at the risk that the style might be copied, as it might be if bought in a store or seen in a store-window, buying nothing they did not stipulate for, just as they gave no more than they said they would? Their own folly, as a common-law judge might say, not to ask for a promise not to copy. But sensible people, perhaps, do not ask for a promise that if broken no one would go to law about—where the promisor is too poor to be sued and a style dies too quickly to quarrel over expensively And did it matter so much if, while it rained into the cisterns, another who had merely a pan put it out, too?

Perhaps people who have come to the end of their funds are fools to make fine distinctions between right and wrong, if the law does not forbid the act and even the private wrong in question is questionable. But, then, my parents were apt to be such quibblers, for they had not only the law of the land to think about, which is merely the law of men, but the stricter law given to their fathers amid much thunder and lightning. They undoubtedly told themselves that they had not been entrusted with the knowledge of the way the goods had been made; that they would not make the very same style of hat; that they would not sell to the same customers except

242

by an unlucky and unlikely accident; that ideas, at least in cheap millinery, were common property—in fact, unless the idea was rather common as well as rather new it would not be stylish; that the manufacturers who gave them the hat had themselves found the idea elsewhere and had merely adapted it to their own shop and trade, had kindled their fagot at a common fire which had been lit a season or two before (no doubt in Paris) and which would soon be ashes, whether my parents made the hat or not. That their economic bias determined their judgment is very likely, but this has been said of others and of upright judges, too.

Years afterwards, my uncle Israel and I were talking about a salesman my father and uncle had in another city. They had just found out that the salesman had copied their samples and had tried to make the hats himself, and I spoke harshly of him. But my uncle Israel was not at all angry. He looked at me and smiled: "You are young yet," he said. And that had nothing to do, so it seemed to me, with what we were talking about.

My mother made several hats of the puffed silk, none of which was just like the hat the manufacturer had given my father: perhaps my parents really felt they had no right to copy it. When my mother's samples were ready, she was about to go to the department stores to show them, as she had asked for pleating to make and had gotten it—at least from a store or two; for my father, whose feelings had been badly burnt in the store of his acquaintance, still dreaded the fire of criticism. My uncle Israel, who had brought the silk and watched the whittling of the last of the sticks, the steaming, cutting, and sewing, and had come back the next day to see how my mother's samples were coming on, said he would carry the box of hats for her.

They went to Fourteenth Street because it was near and the hats were cheap and the three large department stores on the street at that time bought many cheap hats. But the busy millinery buyers of two of the stores would look at samples only at certain hours and only on certain days at that; and this was also the rule at the third store. These hours were in the morning and by the time my mother and uncle had reached Fourteenth Street it was well on in the afternoon.

But the buyer of the third store, the least important of the three, was a gentle Jew who held a brusque manner stoutly against all the eager faces pressing against him for orders. My anxious mother and her tall smiling brother beside her, as they came towards the buyer through the crowd of shoppers on the floor of his department (against the rules, too), caught him with his shield down. He did not order them off the floor as he should have done nor did he tell them sharply to come when other salesmen did, but—my mother first as if she were a customer—the buyer showed them the way to the empty sample-rooms. Here he looked at the hats carefully and wrote an order for a single dozen.

My mother and uncle left the store together, sister and brother triumphant. Walking back in the mild sunshine of the late afternoon, my uncle asked: "Why did he have so much to say?"

"He showed me what was the matter with the hats and how to make them better."

"When you have the samples ready," said my uncle, musing, "let me take them to a jobber I know: we'll hear what he has to say."

This jobber, whom my uncle used to look at respectfully at the auction sales, was a shrewd bantering Irishman. He had built up a large business and blazoned the fact on his windows (which now ran the length of a block) in a row of green trees

—from saplings to great oak—painted on each window. Each tree had the address he had moved from into larger quarters, larger and larger quarters, and above all was his slogan, "As I live I grow." A hundred girls and more (during the season) were making hats for him in the basement, sewing away by the light of lamps. He would walk between his tables of goods for sale, in shirt-sleeves and suspenders, wearing an old yachting cap, jolly with those who came to sell as well as those who came to buy.

His "wise cracks" were stenciled on cards and hung about the place. The best was probably: "Come in without knocking; go out the same way." Printers sold the "wise cracks" to other stores to stick in the windows and put on the walls and they became stale, just as the cards themselves, after a while, were covered with dust. (The man himself was to give up his business, one fine day, laugh at it all and put the million dollars he had made into land—real estate. But in no time, it seemed, he lost most of his money. He was back in a store again; a smaller store now without his slogan, of course, or even a glint of Irish green. Unable to make a go of it, he went bankrupt. And, penniless, he walked into one of the lots he had bought and lost to shoot himself through the head —surprising the insects of the place with the rich gift of his blood.)

But when my uncle went to see him, he was still the jolly Irishman, who paid his bills "like a clock" every ten days and whose checks were bright with green trees and his slogan, "As I live I grow," printed in green. Although my dignified uncle, his large eyes alert, could hardly speak any English and understood little more of it than he could speak, he was quite unflustered and as quick to smile at his own blunders as were his listeners. He brought back an order for four dozen hats from this shrewd acquaintance.

"I see," he said to my parents, as he gave them the order and all were flushed with a common happiness, "I'll be able to sell your hats. Now, how shall we make up among ourselves?"

"What do you want?" asked my father.

"There are three of us: let us each have a third of the profits."

My father called my mother aside. "Israel," he said, "doesn't know the millinery trade—nor even how to speak English." (The three always spoke to each other in Yiddish.) "We can get a man who knows both English and the trade for five, say even ten per cent, of the sales as commission, and we have no partner to claim his share of the profits and have his say in our affairs. Now that we are so down ought we to handicap ourselves, right at the start, by having Israel sell for us?"

"He is my brother," said my mother simply.

"Very well," my father replied, "you began this business and you can have you own way." Turning to his brother-in-law, he said again: "Very well."

My uncle caught up the bag of hats and was out of the door in a second. It was only six blocks to where all the jobbing houses were, and he was back in a little while with another order—this one for sixteen dozen. After my parents had expressed their admiration for him, he sat on in silence, lost in thought. "Listen," he said at last, "it isn't fair that the two of you, who are after all only one family, should have twice as much as I."

"What do you want now?" asked my father testily.

"That you and I get forty per cent each of the profits and Sarah Yetta—who is only a woman—twenty."

"I have no right to say anything about her share," said my father. "After all, *she* began this business and took us into it."

"I really don't care," said my mother, "whether I get more

or less—it will remain in the family. Let Israel have his way," she said to my father.

They called their business "Madame Sarah" at first. So many of my father's undertakings had ended badly by this time that he wanted to be sure it was a going business before his own name was in it. My parents borrowed two hundred and fifty dollars on my father's life insurance policy and our home became a shop.

My uncle managed to get small orders from the millinery stores on Grand Street, Sixth Avenue, and other streets. But the firm did not do much until he met a man who owned two department stores in Texas. The man from Texas (not a Jew) used to buy goods at auction sales—buy up everything worth while. (After the sale, he gave the peddlers who stood about some of the goods at cost. "Pick out what you want, boys," he would say. "I was a peddler myself once and remember when I needed a little goods badly.")

I was to see him, many years later, dozing in the showroom while his wife bought as much as she dared. A manager of the stores, it was said, had run off with his money; and husband and wife, now without buyers to help them and follow them, bought timidly, for only a few old acquaintances trusted them—and not much at that. He was still tall and ruddy, the courteous Southerner. But he walked slowly, his hair all white, and no sooner did he sit down than—a strange way for a buyer to act—he would close his eyes: for weariness and age.

When my uncle met him that day on Broadway, fifteen years or so before, he was still brisk and rich; and the eyes of every salesman in the street followed him. "Why don't I see you in the auction-rooms any more?" he asked. My uncle told him what he was doing. The man from Texas thought a moment and then said: "My millinery buyers are now in town. Come to my office with your samples tomorrow morning—before we go out. If your hats are any good, I'll see what I can do for you."

The Texans liked the hats and the prices were cheap enough. The owner of the stores gave my uncle a breath-taking order, almost two hundred and fifty dozen, more than two thousand dollars' worth, and said: "If it is hard for you to ship the order at one time—you may be short of money to buy all the goods you need—make a number of shipments. Send them here to the office and I'll pay for each right away: that may help you." But my father and uncle did not even have enough money to buy goods for a first shipment. Now they went to my uncle Joseph, my father's brother-in-law, with whom my uncle Israel had been in partnership, and he lent them eight hundred dollars of his money.

My parents worked hard, early and late, to ship their orders as soon as possible, not only to have re-orders and their money the sooner but, working where they did, they could get no insurance against fire. The house was full of hats, in boxes and on newspapers in corners, on the beds in the daytime and, at night, on the tables and chairs and the broad old-fashioned mantelpiece. My mother had hired a peasant girl, fresh from Russia, to help with the housework but she was eager to become a sewing-machine operator. It seemed to her that in that house she had a wonderful opportunity to rise from the drudgery of housework to the drudgery of the shop, and she was always hurrying from the stove in the kitchen to the sewing-machine. I did my share, too, and ran errands after school.

The wire-frame makers had their little shops in the old buildings along Bond and Great Jones Streets, where, three or four generations before, the wealthy people of the city had lived—the halls still had empty niches for statues. But the stairs and floors were now sagging, banisters were missing from the railings, and the rooms stank of dead rats. With a constant clicking of their nippers, the wire-frame makers stood over casts of varnished plaster, placing wires along the nails. (That was before machines that could be set to each kind of frame took the place of the plaster casts and wire-frames themselves were replaced by frames of buckram which, in turn, were to go out of style.) Silk and ribbons, chiffon and velvets, were sold in quiet rooms, on quiet streets like Spring and Broome—west of Broadway; but the machinery of the braid manufacturers could be heard in the street, even if six storeys below. The din and scream of turning bars and whirling spindles, without change of pitch, without pause, when I was actually in the loft waiting for my package, would crack my skull, I thought, under its Niagara of unending sound —until I was suddenly used to it and did not mind.

Chiffon was stylish and my parents were using folds of it for hats. My father would run strips of chiffon through a folder which was fastened to a sewing machine; the girls would then slowly sew by hand, row on row, the chiffon folds to the crinoline that was tacked over the wire-frames. But if the folds were sewn on the crinoline by machine, they were flattened and spoiled.

While my father was running off chiffon folds on his sewing-machine one day, the folder broke off. He hurried to the sewing-machine company to have it fixed but was told to leave it—the shop was busy and repairs were being made in turn. He was willing enough to buy another folder but these were in such demand there was none on hand. Well, he could hardly have his own shop shut down for a few days (all they were working at were hats of chiffon folds) until the sewing-machine company received another shipment of folders or was ready to fix his. So he brought it to a machinist, who had his own little shop, to have the folder soldered in place.

The machinist soldered the folder too far to the right. When my father used it, at home, only half of the strip was folded and the stitching ran in the middle. This meant more chiffon for each hat to cover the crinoline properly. That was bad enough but it would take longer and, of course, cost much more to sew a hat of the narrow folds by hand. By then it was evening and the machinist gone from his shop for the day. My father tried to change his way of sewing the folds; when that did no good, his way of cutting them. He bothered about it until midnight and could do nothing, and supposed there was no help for it but to wait until morning and have the machinist resolder the folder.

But his tired mind and fingers would not rest. For want of anything better to do, he tried using a strip of crinoline to push the chiffon to one side as he sewed. So sleepy he could hardly see, he stitched the chiffon right to the crinoline without meaning to—and became wide awake as he saw that it was no longer necessary to sew by hand such folds as the folder was now making. A sewing-machine would do six times as much as a girl sewing by hand and the narrow folds, unflattened and full, made a much better hat: as good as any on the market.

He made a crown and brim of the new folds. At one o'clock in the morning he could hear my mother saying: "What are you up to so late?"

"If you are not too sleepy, I'll show you."

And she, too, opened her eyes wide.

The season was almost over but they sold quite a few hats made the new way. When the slack came, my parents felt sure of their livelihood for the first time since my father had worked for Henry Ettelson at wrappers: they now had a going business, and the time had come to move the shop away from our home.

V

When my parents moved the shop from their home, they gave up the name of "Madame Sarah" and called their business by the dignified, if not quite modest, name of "Artistic Millinery Company."

The fall season was about to begin; but the new hats were almost all of velvet, and the Artistic Millinery Company did not have the money to buy velvet in case lots—cheap enough to sell their hats at a fair profit to jobbers and department stores. There was more money for them in silk or chiffon, bought piece by piece as they needed it. "Let others sell velvet," my uncle Israel said cheerfully, stroking his small black beard, "we'll sell hats of silk."

But there was not much call for hats of silk and, though they did sell a few, they did not even earn enough for their expenses. The partners waited hopefully for the spring season in order to make hats of chiffon folds. In the meantime, my uncle stretched himself on the cutting-room table every afternoon after lunch and took a good nap, for he had nothing to sell, my father sat in the little office, reading a newspaper or a book of short stories, and my mother, with a girl to help her, was in a corner of the quiet workroom sewing away at an order, if there was one, and thinking of samples in chiffon for the coming season. Sometimes, she would begin to sing a Yiddish folk song (she had always been singing when she was younger—and sadder), the girl might join in the song and my father would put his book away and come into the workroom to draw up a chair and smoke and listen (he had no voice at all for singing).

The spring season came at last. Charlie Reed of Cleveland,

251

Ohio, was in town placing orders on his way home from Paris (he could buy more cheap hats than any other jobber in the United States). When he was in New York, he would go about all day to the manufacturers—no shop on an upper floor with too many flights for him to climb or in a street too far for him to go, if he could get his hats cheaper—and, afterwards, he would stay in his office and see the salesmen of other small shops. The line of men would wait along the corridor. All evening they would come, bringing boxes and big bags of hats to show, and Charlie Reed would see them all, if it took until midnight. A glance was enough for him; nine times out of ten, he would call out "Next!" at once; and the next salesman, who had been waiting hours for the chance, would be nervously pulling his best hats out of box or bag. If Charlie Reed bought in his office, he kept the samples and he was as well known for returning goods "not up to sample" as for his large orders and prompt payment.

My uncle Israel took along six styles in chiffon folds—no need to take too many. And Charlie Reed bought all six: two thousand six hundred dollars' worth. Uncle Israel came out of the office, stroking his little black beard, flushed and happy, his black eyes shining. Not a sample left in his hands! Charlie Reed, tall and lean, stuck his head out of the door after him and looked up and down the corridor. It was filled to the very end with salesmen and their boys, waiting with sample trunks, boxes and bags stuffed with hats, and he called out drily: "Anybody else with a beard?"

That was the beginning of a profitable season for the Artistic Millinery Company. Sure of his line and always sure of himself, Uncle Israel sold almost every jobber in the country, going from office to office as they came to town to buy. He was soon known to the trade as "Mr. Artistic"—not without irony, of course; but, wherever he went, in addition to the smiles that

252

used to greet him, he was whispered about and looked at not without respect.

The wholesale millinery trade was then centered on Broadway between Houston and Prince Streets, and the Artistic Millinery Company now moved to a small loft on Bond Street—only three or four short blocks away. The loft was in an old building: one of those houses, still to be seen along Bond and Great Jones Streets, where well-to-do families lived a generation or two, perhaps, before the Civil War. The stone stoops were badly chipped, and the houses all had the same smell of dead rats which made the air of the street, far from any field or tree, fresh and pleasant by contrast.

One Sunday morning, I had to go to the shop on some errand or other, and looked through the basement window as I went up the stoop. The basement had just been rented to a ragman and I saw a heavy lock on the door, for there are thieves even of rags. Inside, a black cat was resting on the floor, in an empty space, its head proudly lifted; beside it, stretched on a new plank as on a butcher's table, was a large dead rat, blood trickling from its throat and making a stain on the white wood.

We had now been living for a couple of years in the two-family house which my father and uncle bought in Brooklyn. It was a small building of yellow brick, sharing a wall with another building just like it; on the other side, a narrow driveway. There was a plot in front in which my father or uncle might have set a hedge and shrubs but never did; and a yard in back which I started digging up each spring but, after a hard Saturday morning or two, I was content to keep it free of the larger weeds. I thought the house and its twin the best on the block and perhaps they were, for the others were smaller, much older, and of wood.

At the end of the street, where it met another street that went obliquely (as it had since the Revolution and before), was a graveyard where Negro slaves were supposed to be buried. There were no graves or markers to be seen but, sometimes, a schoolboy digging there would find an old bone or, if he was lucky, a skull to play with. During the boom days in which our house and its neighbor were built, an enterprising person planned a long row of buildings but he had only put in the stone foundations when he ran out of money and could build no further; and the open cellars were left to fill up with sand and rubbish and weeds. That was the next block, however. The block where we lived we thought pretty enough, especially in the spring, for it had a few trees and in front of some of the houses were bushes and even flowers.

My father and uncle paid eight hundred dollars for their house and had all of three years in which to pay off the second mortgage of twelve hundred. Easy enough, as their business was going.

But good as business was my uncle Israel was finding it hard to spend no more than he made and could never see himself as extravagant: he always had good reasons for spending his money. Besides, it was his business as a salesman—or his business because it was his nature—to be hearty and jolly, quick to tip, to treat, and to spend. "Spend and make!" he would cry.

My father, aghast, would manage to say sternly: "Make and *then* spend!"

"Spend and make!" my uncle would say again, smiling at the heresy and throwing his head back so that his eyes looked narrow and shrewd. "Spend and then you have to make: it drives you to it!"

"But if you don't make?" my father would say gloomily at the thought of being driven and in debt.

And then Uncle Israel would laugh in that hearty way of his and say: "But we do!" Sometimes he would turn to me: "What do you say? You are only a schoolboy and understand nothing but what do *you* say?"

I admired him, his jolly face with ruddy cheeks, large black eyes and shining white teeth, the small black beard which he kept smoothing while he lifted his chin proudly; we all admired him, his little silent wife who walked about like a kitten in his shadow, my mother—his sister, even my father!

Yes, business was good. The slacks might be long and, sometimes, my mother designed hat after hat and none of them would sell but, often enough, her samples were very good (for the women who lived on side streets and in smaller cities and towns, hats new enough to be stylish, six months or a year after they were stylish at the races and on the great streets of Paris and New York, and yet not so new that a woman wearing one of them would feel like an actress or foolish); and then, when the samples sold, my mother would show her girls how to sew the orders quickly and well, and watch them at their work so that each hat might be as good as the sample. And my father knew how much goods each dozen should take and how long it should take to make a dozen hats and how much the dozen would cost, and he cut his silk and velvet so cunningly that a hat might even take less than he had figured and still look as well as it should. My uncle, of course, was the salesman and a good man, too, as no one knew better than he himself.

So, ready to spend in order to earn and still earning, my uncle was always finding something to add to the house he had bought with my father, and both paid for the "improvements": shutters to keep out the summer heat, when the long days were very hot in our neighborhood and its streets that led to the marshes along Jamaica Bay; a porch overlooking the yard, a solid porch that would not shake under my uncle's heavy tread, and this was only fair since my uncle had one room less than we who lived upstairs; and boiler, pipes, and radiators for steam heat, since the kitchen stove could never keep all my uncle's rooms warm enough and gas stoves just made the air bad and helped little, for it was very cold when the days were short and dark in those streets going down to the broad marshes. And then the ceiling of the cellar had to be covered with sheets of asbestos, for the boiler might explode and my uncle and his family burn to death most horribly. My father would protest and my uncle cajole, my father would shout and my uncle mock, until, my father plaintively consenting, Uncle had his own way.

But the millinery business was good and getting better.

There had been great argument between my father and my uncle before they moved their place of business from Eighth Street to Bond Street. The center of the millinery business, at least that part of it that sold to the jobbing trade, was then, as I have said, on Broadway—on the block between Houston and Prince Streets. The manufacturers whose factories were out-of-town had their salesrooms there, too, or on the corner of the very next block. Now Eighth Street was six blocks from Houston and my uncle had explained to my parents, time and again, that no buyer would ever come that far, but, if they were only near the heart of things, he might stand about on Broadway like other salesmen and bring customers upstairs to the showroom. As it was, after he had been to the offices of the out-of-town jobbers who were newly come to town (before they left in the morning to visit the showrooms of the manufacturers on their lists) and after he had been to the city jobbers if he had anything new to show, the best he could do was to stretch himself on the showroom table and take a good nap—which he did almost every after-noon.

The loft on Eighth Street had been large, light, and cheap. My father did not like to leave it, what with the cost of moving and all the trouble, and he had argued that one of the largest manufacturers in the business had his place on that very street. But, as my uncle did not fail to say, that manufacturer sold retailers for the most part and, if anything, it was another reason for moving away: the jobbers might think they were trying to sell retailers, too. Well, they had moved from Eighth Street. And now my uncle wanted to move from Bond Street and he also had good reasons for that. Of course, Bond Street (only two short blocks from Houston) was much nearer the center of the wholesale millinery trade than Eighth Street; still it was too far away. And, although my uncle by using his great skill as a salesman did get a few customers up to the showroom, this was as nothing to what he could do if he was on the block between Houston and Prince Streets, on Broadway itself, in the very thick of things. Besides, small manufacturers had nested in Bond Street—every other little building was thick with them; here the cheapest and shoddiest goods were made; why, buyers sniffed at his card when they read the address.

My father would plunge into his argument with vehemence, shout and gesticulate so, he was soon too tired to keep it up. Certainly not day after day. But my uncle would smile and say just enough to keep his partner in a fury; still calmly talking, now in the morning on the way to work, now in the evening upstairs after supper, any time during the day whatever else they were about; and always in the end, so far, he had gotten leave to have his own way from his utterly exhausted partner. Accordingly, my father now vehemently named a number of good houses that were content to stay on Bond Street. And they themselves had been doing well enough there.

The very reason, my uncle said, for moving, since they had the means to.

But how had they the means to move to Broadway, to so desirable a location—were not the rents high there, beyond all reason, for that very reason. my father cried.

My uncle had his answer for that, too. He had kept it up his sleeve until my father began to weaken. He had, so my uncle said, found the very place—on Broadway between Houston and Prince Streets, among the showrooms of every large manufacturer in the country: every buyer in the country would pass the door, not once but countless times, every day he was in town. And my uncle would stand in front of that door, all day, like the salesmen of the commission men and large manufacturers in front of their doors, too, greeting the buyers in town and telling them what was for sale upstairs. A manufacturer who had a large loft which he had used for a salesroom was willing to sublet the rear of it and the rent was little enough.

How much?

Just a little more than twice what they were paying for this hole in Bond Street.

My father wearily consented to see the place. It was dark; the windows opened on a narrow court; and the air was heavy with the smells of the restaurant underneath. "What do you expect for so little rent?" said my uncle reasonably.

"But it is not little," said my father. "It is more than twice what we are paying!"

"But it is on Broadway," said my uncle.

And so they argued. My father quarreled and my uncle smiled and my mother said she thought her brother was right. My father became angrier than ever and my uncle said quietly that my father, as he had been doing all along, was doing his best to keep their business from growing. And my mother

258

again said that her brother was right. My father almost burst a blood vessel at that. His head began to ache so badly he found it hard to talk because of the pain and pretty soon he said: "The devil take it all! Have it your way!"

And then my uncle would keep on talking for a while, just to show that he still had plenty of ammunition and that my father never had a chance against him.

My uncle was really right, it seemed, about moving to Broadway: he brought up many a buyer and many a buyer came up himself to see what the new (to him) firm was making. Their old landlord had threatened to sue for the rent until the first of May under an old law or custom; but nothing came of it: he found another tenant, most likely, or there was no longer any such law or custom. The air in the shop was close and, on hot days in spring and summer, foul. But no one, at least neither my father nor mother, minded that. Perhaps they thought it could not be helped and, besides, they were busy and happy. As for the help, perhaps they were glad to be working, too. Certainly, they could get plenty of fresh air in the slack.

It was hard, of course, to work all day by lamplight during the bright days of spring and, for that matter, any season. But my father had the best gas-lamps to be bought put in— a bright soft light, much better than the gas jets, just over the long, narrow tables, they used to work by with nothing but a wire screen about the open flame for protection. Few shops were any better and many worse—up many flights to climb or in basements and cellars. (Later, inspectors under the labor laws were to order electric fans put in, but windows on the street, if any, were kept for the offices and showrooms until the great war that began in 1914 made help scarce and workrooms had to have sunshine and fresh air to get any good help at all.)

Charlie Reed of Cleveland came up and bought more than five thousand dollars' worth of hats: two dozen of a style to be sent on at once for his salesmen and the rest in two shipments. The Artistic Millinery Company had to use the stairs that led to Broadway for shipping and getting their goods (there were no back stairs and just one door to the loft). The trade saw the first large shipment as the twenty cases were stacked by the expressman on the pavement, right on Broadway, waiting for the wagon to cart them off. Now Charlie Reed was, perhaps, the shrewdest buyer in the business, and any place he bought heavily at was a good place to know. All the trade was soon buzing with talk about the Artistic Millinery Company: good house, a coming house! And my uncle was showing new buyers into the showroom, good houses he had never been able to sell: his face flushed, black eyes shining and watchful, and smiling, saying little and to the point and that, often as not, comic (in his foreign way) and amusing.

My mother would be bustling about from work-table to work-table, behind the partitions and the door marked "Work Room No Admittance"; showing the new girls how to sew her way and the old help how to sew the new numbers and getting work ready for the girls so that they need lose no time (since they worked piece-work) asking for work and waiting for it, as in other places; or, off in a corner, she would be making a new sample. And my father would do the cutting, using the long knife that fitted into a slot in the table or the short knife, a heavy shears or a light scissors—cutting velvet or plush, silk or satin, for the hats on order; or carefully packing the hats in large paper boxes, wrapping each hat in tissue paper, six or eight to a box, and putting the boxes into wooden cases that still had the smell of the woodyard about

260

them, and then marking each case for shipment—not too much ink or it would run—with the name of the good house to which it was going. (He kept the books, too, and figured the cost of the new hats, and saw that all the frames and the braid and the odds and ends that would be needed were on hand, but my uncle saw to the large buying—velvet by the case or silk by the piece or ribbon in fifty or a hundred boxes at a time.)

A few days after the first of the two large shipments to Reed, when the second was almost ready to be packed and kept for the shipping-date, the Artistic Millinery Company got this telegram: "Hats received returning all cancel balance of order."

Well, this was a facer. Not only the loss of profit and losses on the goods sent back or countermanded. But, just as the trade had seen the shipment and talked about it, now they would see the cases back again on the sidewalk in front of the door, waiting to be carried up the stairs. And how they would talk about that! How they would smile! It would do the Artistic Millinery Company little good, no matter how unfair they might say Charlie Reed had been, no matter if the hats were really just as good as the samples. Besides, Reed had the samples which his salesmen had used; he would have the hats copied to fill his own orders: another manufacturer would then have all their samples to work for Reed and to sell elsewhere.

My father read the telegram to my mother and uncle. Then he walked slowly to a chair and sat down and could not talk or even think. He managed to light a cigarette and puffed away, staring in front of him and seeing nothing.

My uncle looked at his watch. "I have a plan but no time to tell you about it. I have only twenty-five minutes to catch the train to Cleveland! Wire Reed to hold the hats until I get there." And he was out of the door with a wave of his hand and a cheerful good-by.

My uncle was in Cleveland by nine next morning and went at once to Reed's building. Charlie Reed was not yet in. "Show me the hats," my uncle said to an assistant. "I want to see what's wrong." He was taken to the fifth floor where all the hats were stacked on tables. Except for a few, the hats were really not bad.

As my uncle was going from table to table, Charlie Reed came up. "Hello, Artistic," he said. "I see you are looking at your hats. Are they like the samples?"

"They are not good enough for you, Mr. Reed," said my uncle. "I don't want you to keep them. But let me leave them here a while and lend me a bag. After breakfast, I'll take them away."

"What do you want a bag for?"

"I'll take some samples and go over to Hart" (that was Reed's largest competitor in town). "I'll let them have the hats for a dollar and a half a dozen less—what shipping to New York would cost me." This was, of course, an offer to Reed to let him have the shipment for that much less a dozen—or even less if he asked for it: anything to keep the cases off the street in front of the Artistic Millinery Company's door. And it was also a threat, if Reed didn't want the hats, to sell them to his competitors or even to his customers in town. But my uncle spoke simply and pleasantly.

Charlie Reed smiled. (By this time he had cooled down and he, too, saw that the hats, except for a few, were really not bad.) "You don't have to do that. I like the way you came out here to see what was wrong—ready to make it good and not whine about it. I'll take the hats as they are and you make the second shipment better. Come downstairs with me. I'll give you a check for them and go right home." (It was clear he did not want my uncle to call on Hart or any other jobber in the city—with or without samples.) "Have your breakfast and go right home." And Charlie Reed did not even take off the dollar and a half a dozen.

Now my uncle said they ought to move again—the loft was too dark and dirty: customers would wrinkle their noses when they came into the showroom and he could not tell whether it was at the hats or the smell of the place. Time and again, a roach had run out of a sample: true enough, he had been able to laugh the roach off by saying there was no charge for it. But there was a clean loft, a large loft—from Broadway all the way to Mercer Street; large windows at either end; in the next block, right next to the building where many of the jobbers had their offices; and it could be had for twenty-eight hundred dollars a year. "That might sound like a lot," he said smoothly, as he saw my father about to jump from his chair, "but rent is never figured in business."

My father stared at him, his eyes about to pop out of his head. He swallowed once or twice and said: "We have not used all of this small place; we can do twice as much here. If you would only hire a salesman—." Here he touched on another old grievance but kept himself from going off on that tangent. "Who would move from a place at a rental of seven hundred dollars a year to one that will cost four times as much with no certainty of any increase in business?" he cried dramatically. "It will cost us more than we have ever made in a year above our expenses and our living since we are in business! And in so large a place we will need a girl in the office, for I cannot be everywhere as I am here; we will need many more lights—."

My uncle, seeing that my father was about to go into tiresome details, interrupted him. "You don't understand how to run a business," he said, watching my mother out of the corner of his eye, for he had called her out of the workroom to hear about the new loft. "The true business man makes the world believe he has a lot when really he has nothing," he added importantly, as if he were reciting some maxim of a cabala only he and a few chosen souls had read and understood. "But if a business man makes himself look small, he will never have anything," he concluded, smiling broadly.

Before my father could say anything, my mother turned on him and said sharply: "What are you always arguing about? Must you always say no to everything he says? You are just like your mother! He sees how to make the business grow but you won't let him."

This was hardly likely to make my father silent. But though he talked and talked he could do nothing against the two of them; and in the end they moved to the new loft that was a block long.

VI

There used to be a Catholic shelter for orphaned boys near the shop. They were a rough and dirty lot. My mother hired a couple of them for a day to sweep the place clean of the season's litter. One was blond—Gregory's angel for sale in Rome. The other boy teased him and fooled about, poking him in the ribs, tripping him and punching him, but he took it all meekly, never turned his head nor raised his hands, and tried to do the sweeping as well as he could. Later in the day, my mother came upon him alone in a corner, sad and thoughtful: his face was so gentle and beautiful she was surprised at it. He was about fifteen but tall and well-built.

"Why do you do this work?" she said. "Why don't you learn a trade? What will become of you?"

"Who'll hire me like this?" And he looked down at his torn clothes and broken shoes. "Besides, I have no references."

"I'll bring you some clothes tomorrow," my mother said. "Be here early." He had picked up a hat somewhere and, when he put it on, looked comical.

In the morning, my mother brought—in two bundles—an old suit of my father's which was still good and an old pair of his shoes, of which the soles were sound, and a clean shirt, clean underwear and socks, even a necktie, and she had bought him a cap. The boy was waiting at the street door.

My mother thought the makers of wire frames might give him a job: a bundle of frames was worth little and suppose he ran off with it? But they glanced at him as he stood waiting and shrugged their shoulders. It was getting on towards noon and she had found nothing for him, when one of the girls came to tell her the water-closet was stopped up, and she sent for the plumber. He was an honest man and did not charge too much. When he was through, my mother said to him: "Do you see that boy over there? He is homeless but is willing to work. You can save him from becoming a thief or a suicide. Why don't you take him to work for you? Teach him your trade."

The plumber looked at the boy and thought a while, thinking perhaps of tools and lead pipe that might be stolen. "I'll take a chance," he said, and the boy went away with him.

That was in the old place. The plumbing in the new place was good and it was two years before my mother sent for the plumber again. When his helper, who had come instead, was through, she went to see if everything was right and saw the young man about to kneel before her. She was frightened, thinking he had gone crazy, and tried to pull him to his feet. He took her hand and was about to kiss it, but she snatched it away.

"Don't you remember me?" he asked. "I often wanted to come and thank you, but I hadn't the nerve."

Their first season in the new place was not bad but what it cost, rent and all, took all the profits above what they drew for a living. (To placate my father somewhat, my uncle had hired a salesman. But he did not sell anything because my uncle had added the salesman's commission to the prices he was to get; and so in time he left and they merely lost whatever they had paid him by way of advancements.) My uncle was now drawing eighty dollars a week. This was not enough for him and in four months he had taken fifteen hundred dollars more—almost all he had in the business.

One afternoon, when my father went into the office from the workroom to rest a while and smoke a cigarette, the bookkeeper—for they had hired one—told him that my uncle had asked her to make out a check to his order for three hundred dollars. "Wait until tomorrow," my father said. In the evening, my uncle came up from the street where he had been watching for customers and went to the bookkeeper for the check. My father, who had been waiting for him, called him aside and asked: "What do you want so much money for?"

"Why," said my uncle, "the holidays are coming and I must have money."

On the way home—my uncle, as always, had been gone an hour when my parents left the shop together—my father told my mother about the check and how he had put the matter off until the next day because my uncle now had no money in the business to draw.

"As long as he was drawing his own money," said my mother, "you could not stop him, but don't give him ours. He'll have to learn how to get along on his earnings."

That evening my father went downstairs to see his brother-in-law. He found my uncle drinking tea. "Before you take any money from the business more than your salary," said my father, "we must see if there is any money for you to draw."

"There is," my uncle said calmly. "Before I asked the book-keeper to make out the check, I looked through the books. Don't worry: we'll be able to pay all our bills by the tenth."

"That is not what I mean," said my father. "We must see if *you* have any money to draw. You have already drawn fifteen hundred dollars more than your salary—and that is all you had in the business."

My uncle laughed softly. He took a sip of tea slowly, savored the mulberry jam he had used to flavor it, and then said: "Whatever I drew was not enough. I should have more."

"Why?"

"Because. What are you except an operator or, let's say, a foreman? You should get at most thirty dollars a week. And Sarah Yetta is only a forelady—she should get twenty dollars. Both of you are now drawing one hundred and twenty dollars a week. But what am I worth who brought the business to Broadway? If I," and he tapped his breast with his fore-finger, "didn't bring you orders, what would you make?"

My father shouted: "Did you come from Russia to hire me as an operator and your sister as a forelady? We took you into *our* business, you greenhorn! But pay us what we have in the business and you can keep it!"

When my father came upstairs again, breathless and glaring, my mother saw at once how angry he was. "Have you been quarreling again?" she said and drew her mouth askew.

"Yes," said my father, and he told her what my uncle had said and what he had answered.

"You shouldn't have offered to give him the business," said my mother slowly. "I will have something to say about that if he tries to hold you to it."

Next morning, when my uncle came to work—as always an hour later than my parents for there was no buyer to see that early (nor as late as they stayed)—my father said that he would take out the three thousand dollars my parents had in the business. "Then we cannot pay our bills," my uncle answered hotly.

"Then," my father said calmly, for it was his turn to be cool, "each of us will put his hand in his pocket and put into the business enough to pay the bills."

"I have no money."

"What did you do with the fifteen hundred dollars you drew from the business?"

"I paid a debt I owed my father-in-law."

"Then go to your father-in-law again and borrow money to pay your share of the bills. I am not going to keep Sarah Yetta's money and mine in the business while you draw whatever you like and, besides, go about giving yourself such airs."

After lunch, my uncle called my father out of the workroom into the office. "I want to talk to you about your three thousand dollars," he said gently.

"Talk," my father answered gruffly, trying to harden himself against any blandishment.

"I can't get any money from my father-in-law. He told me he is buying a house and will have to use every dollar he has. If you take your money out, we won't be able to pay our bills on time and that will hurt our credit."

"You know that I don't want to hurt the business," said my father, "but you are not to draw your profits before they are made. I'll wait until next month for the three thousand dollars—only if there are no extra drawings. If I see you draw an extra dollar, I draw out every dollar that Sarah Yetta and I have in the business more than what we should have according to what is left of your share."

My uncle smiled his friendliest and held out his hand. "Very well," he said and they shook hands.

A month later, when they had paid their bills and been paid by their largest debtors, my uncle gave my father the check of the firm for three thousand dollars and said angrily as he did so: "Here is your money. But you will be sorry. What a businessman! Keeps his money in a savings-bank instead of using it in the business."

"Well," said my father, calmly pocketing the check, "I don't think much of the businessman who spends his money before he makes it and, if times are not as good as he hoped, his creditors have to pay for it."

When they were about to begin to make samples for the next season, my uncle said: "You will not make any samples until we get things straight between ourselves. Since I am the one who built up this business, I want half the profits."

My mother said sharply: "What are you talking about?"

"Say what you like, I am not getting as much as I ought to and you two are getting more than you should. If you will not give me half the profits, let others judge between us."

"That suits me," said my father promptly, glad to be able to air his troubles. "Let others listen to us and show you how unreasonable you are."

"Whom do you think we should choose?"

"Take whomever you want to and I'll take whom I like. If they can't agree, they take a third man. I'm willing that your father-in-law be the third man." (He had stayed in our home with his family for a while when they came to this country, long before my uncle did, and he had always been friendly. And my father was never one to question a smile and a handshake until he had good reason to.)

As for the other two judges, my father and uncle agreed to take men who were in lines of business other than millinery that the quarrel might be secret in the trade. My uncle chose a friend of his, a manufacturer of muslin underwear, who had done well in his own business in which he was, like my uncle, the salesman, and who was supposed to be as learned in the Hebrew law as in the ways of business. Henry Dix's designer and the head of all his factories, under whom my father had worked at wrappers many years before out in New Jersey, was in town and my father asked him to be the third judge.

They were all to meet at the home of my uncle's friend. As my father was about to go there, my mother said: "I am going, too."

My father, sure of himself when it came to making a speech, turned to my mother and smiled: "What are you afraid of? That I won't be able to argue my side without you?"

"No, but I want to go."

When my uncle saw my mother he, too, was surprised and asked: "What did you come for?"

She smiled. "Do you really think," she said, "that I have no interest in what is going on? Our grandfather would have said, 'God will judge between us,' but I don't want to have any business dealings in Heaven. I will straighten out my affairs right here."

They all sat around the large table in the dining-room. My father and uncle first promised to abide by the decision of their judges. My uncle's friend, the host, then said: "Who should be the first to talk?"

The man from New Jersey answered, moving his hand towards my uncle: "This gentleman, of course, since he is the plaintiff."

The others nodded, and my uncle began by saying that, if he did not sell, his partners would have nothing to do. His selling had built up the business and yet he had only forty per cent of the profits and now he wanted half. And, as the salesman, he had to spend a good deal for clothes.

The man from New Jersey leaned forward and asked: "Since when are you getting forty per cent? Did you ever get any more?"

"No."

"You all agreed as to your shares when you became partners?"

"Yes."

My uncle's friend, the manufacturer of muslin underwear, now turned to my father: "What do you say to his demand?"

My father told them how the business was begun, how it was run, and whose money ran it; besides, his wife and he were two and my uncle only one; and because my uncle would let no other salesman work for the business, it did not grow as it could; he told them everything: how much money they had, how much business they did, what their profits were and their prospects. My uncle stirred once or twice, but the others listened patiently.

When my father was through, the manufacturer of muslin underwear asked my uncle: "Have you anything to say?"

Uncle shook his head and then said: "I have this to say: he said a good deal he should not have told."

The judges smiled and the host, the manufacturer of muslin underwear, turning to the man from New Jersey and to my uncle's father-in-law, said: "Gentlemen, let's go into the next room and talk it over."

At this my mother spoke up. "I also have a share in the

business, and I wish you would listen to me before you go away."

The man from New Jersey said: "She is right: she is also a partner."

"Very well, let us hear what she has to say," said the manufacturer of muslin underwear, resigning himself to a rambling speech and, perhaps, the last argument—tears.

But he did not know my mother. She was much briefer than my father or her brother and her plea did not falter into a lesser grievance. "I began this business," she said. "I lent it to my husband and my brother. For this and for my work in it now, I am getting twenty per cent of the profits. I am satisfied. But if they are quarreling about their shares and can't agree, I want my business back. You can only decide about their share of the profits. The business itself is mine: I didn't sell it to them and I didn't give it to them." My father and uncle listened, wide-eyed with surprise, because my mother had never said a word about any claim of hers.

While their judges were away, my father and uncle sat in the strange room, staring into space so as not to look at each other, unable to say a word. At last the others came back and this was their decision: neither my father nor uncle should have a larger share of the profits; they had merely done what they should, and my uncle's work was no more important than my father's or my mother's.

At this my father could not help smiling and stole a glance at his brother-in-law. My uncle and mother were sitting stiff on their seats, looking at the manufacturer of muslin underwear, who was speaking for all the judges and was not yet through. But because my uncle must spend more for his clothes than he would otherwise, since he was the salesman, the "outside man," the firm should let him have two hundred dollars more a year, just as it paid his railway fare and his hotel bills. At this my uncle wrinkled his brow. Although he himself had complained of the cost, he found it undignified to be furnished with clothing—almost the way a lackey is given a uniform. Certainly, the matter was turning out not at all to his taste. But the judges were still not through; as for my mother's claim, she was right: the business was hers, and neither her brother nor her husband had any right to it.

At this my uncle jumped up and shouted at the judges: "What do you mean by taking away from me the right to the business? I came here for my just share; instead of giving me what I asked for, you take away the business itself from me. I won't stand for your decision!"

The man from New Jersey answered coldly: "Do not get so excited and listen: you came to us as three partners with your claims; we heard all of you, and you gave us your word of honor to abide by our decision; now don't make yourself foolish and fools of us. Our decision stands even in a court of law."

VII

I had been up to see the shop when it was first on Broadway and had been glad because my parents were glad. But I did not like the gloomy place and its smell and could not share the sense of achievement my parents had in having their small sign among the great names of the business. When they had moved again, I could not help being awed at the great loft a block long, newly whitewashed, and saw visibly, for the first time, that their business was successful. I gave little heed, at that time, to my father's gloomy remarks about the cost of the new place, for my uncle and mother were cheerful enough, and even my father's face lit up at my awe.

But at heart I cared little about it all. I was to have nothing to do with this business or any like it; I was to study and to make my living otherwise: my parents had always spoken of their business and all ways of making money by trade with distaste. And, if it was their doom because they had come to the country penniless and ignorant, if they were to be worms and crawl about, their children should have wings.

When I was in high school and used to go to the city on a Saturday afternoon, I never went to the shop if I could help it (they used to work all day Saturdays then), although my father would reproach me for it, afterwards. I did not want to run any errand; I did not want to meet those to whom my father would introduce me proudly and who would greet me with a friendliness I thought uncalled for by our brief acquaintance; I felt alien and clumsy there. Once, passing the shop with an acquaintance I told him of it, and my companion looked up at the large golden letters of the sign above the windows with what I thought—somewhat surprised—was awe.

Back from my first year at college for the summer vacation, I went up to the shop one day. As I opened the door of the workroom the warm air rushed into my face. The sunlight came faint and watery through a skylight (there was another loft above). I saw a long row of gas-lamps burning—although it was almost the middle of the summer day—above the narrow work-tables at which the milliners sat and sewed and above the cutting-table at which my father was standing. I caught a glimpse of him, a large shears in his hand, his pale face shining with sweat, so bent upon his cutting he never noticed that his son had opened the door. I saw my mother, too, and the fat jolly forewoman—both going about from table to table. There must have been thirty or forty girls at work under the lamps, shut off by the partitions of showroom and office from the light and air of the windows that faced Broadway. And by cases of hats to be shipped, and the rows of paper boxes for packing, from the windows in back (although these, on Mercer Street, were too far away to be of much good, even if that narrow street let in breeze and light).

I closed the door and went back to my book and seat in the cool quiet office. I could have wept, not only for my mother and father but for all those shut in on so bright a day, away from the sunshine and fresh air, spending almost all their bright hours at trifling and monotonous work. I wanted to be among them, to suffer as my father and mother did in the heat and foul air, and I was ashamed of myself out in the airy office. I opened the door again and went up to my father.

"What is it?" he asked, his eyes upon his work. "Don't bother me now!"

VIII

It was an ill wind that was blowing for the Artistic Millinery Company. Would the wind change? Certainly. But the Artistic Millinery Company must last until then. And if they had not moved to so expensive a loft, if they had not hired bookkeeper and shipping clerk, how much easier it would have been to outlast bad season and slack, slack and bad season. This was the burden of my father's speech. He went about the workroom and sat smoking in the office and walked along Broadway, head hanging, face ashen, as if he was to be shot at dawn for someone else's blunder—which he had protested against—and was without hope whatever of any life beyond the grave where it should all be made right.

My uncle, however, as if this gloom gathering about the business was nourishment to his spirit, like a plant whose leaves find in a fog the moisture its roots lack, was never as cheerful; he walked along as if he had plenty of orders at the bookkeeper's desk. And no stranger could tell that the only order might be one already shipped but kept there by my father that he might not have to see the bare board of the file. My mother was not as cheerful as her brother. But neither was she as sad as my father. She went about her business, her brow unwrinkled but her mouth set, making new hats and still other hats in the hope that one might sell; in spite of my father's stare of despair—from which he found it hard to rouse himself to figure again and yet again the cost of goods and labor and the selling price—and in spite of my uncle's smile and the sweep of his arm with which he would wave aside samples he had no use for.

When it was still a month before Easter and department stores were buying as much as they could, the Artistic Millinery Company (with no retail trade to speak of) had not a thing to do. My mother set about making samples for the fall and went through the department stores to see the newest styles—whether brims were becoming smaller or larger, crowns higher or lower, shaped like a ball or dented.

One night, towards the end of March, I heard the door bell ringing and, as I sat up in bed, heard someone kicking at the street door. My father and mother were in the hall before me and my uncle and aunt were there, too, all of them in night clothes and robes, wondering whether or not they ought to open the door. We could see, through the curtain of the door that opened into the little vestibule, two men outside. My father was ahead of us all and I hurried to stand beside him. I could hear my mother calling: "Be careful! They may be thieves."

Whatever they were, the two men were strangers. From the vestibule, my father shouted through the heavy pane of glass in the street door: "What is it? What do you want?"

The two had stopped ringing the bell and kicking the door when they saw my father and the rest of us in the hall and now one of the two shouted: "Open the door! Your place is on fire!"

"What? The house on fire?" said my father. Those of us in the hall looked at each other and lifted our heads to sniff smoke—and could not smell any.

"The children!" cried my uncle's wife and was about to dart into her flat.

"No, no," shouted the stranger, "not the house! Your place of business!"

My father hesitated another moment and then turned the knob. The strangers pushed into the vestibule. "We have an automobile and you can go with us," said the one who had been doing the talking.

"Who are you?" my father asked.

"Adjusters."

"Adjusters?" said my father, wondering what the word meant. Nor did I, for that matter, know just what they claimed to be.

"Of insurance. You're insured, aren't you? Let's handle your claim! Come into our car and we'll take you right to your shop."

"How do you know the place is on fire?" asked my father. "How did you know where I live?"

"You're in the directory, aren't you?" said the man's companion impatiently.

My father and I dressed hurriedly. I could hear my mother saying: "Don't go with them! It may be some kind of trick!"

My father answered angrily: "I am not a fool!"

We found my uncle downstairs, dressed and waiting. As the three of us went out into the sharp night air, we saw an automobile against the curb and the two men inside it. They told us to get in. But we went on towards the station to take the train. The strangers drove along slowly behind us, urging us to get into the car; when my father and uncle no longer answered or turned to listen, the adjusters stopped by the light of a streetlamp, found the name of another firm on their list, and were off.

I wondered sleepily how they could think my father and uncle would turn a claim over to strangers who came in the middle of the night kicking at the door. They had said, in answer to my father's question, that the fire had started in our loft. Perhaps there had been no fire at all and it was just, as my mother had said, some kind of trick. But I was too sleepy to do more than think vaguely about it.

My father, my uncle, and I sat silently together as the almost empty train went quickly through the night. We reached the bridge and a clock I always glanced at: I saw the hands at four and thought for a second it had stopped, until I realized it would really be about that time.

When we came near the shop, we saw the police keeping a crowd of onlookers a block away. The fire-engines were still there and the hose was stretched along the gutters. The police stopped us, too; and we stood among the idlers and those—on the way to work early in the morning—who lingered. The fire was still blazing in a building next to the one in which our loft was. My father and my uncle turned to each other and I said light-heartedly, speaking for the three of us: "The fire was not in our place at all. Not even in the building. The adjusters made a mistake."

We were standing close to a policeman. (I was glad to have him there, because I did not like the looks of many of those about us, come, I supposed, from the lodging-houses along the Bowery to watch the fire.) The policeman turned to me and said good-naturedly: "Where is your place?"

I told him and the policeman chuckled. "That's where it all started: it spread from there. You should have been here an hour ago! The flames were a block high."

My father and my uncle asked him eagerly how the fire had started—in what loft, wondering if the insurance companies would pay them if the loft was theirs (my father thought there might be some such clause in the policies). But the policeman could not answer their questions or thought it wiser not to be seen talking should his sergeant look that way, and became silent.

We waited for daylight, listening to the axes of firemen in the buildings that had been burning, to the tinkle of breaking glass, and then heard the fire-engines leaving slowly, one by one—a tired, unhurried ringing of bells. In the dawn my father, my uncle, and I saw the blackened windows of our loft, the blackened windows of the loft above ours and of those below, and knew for certain that the fire had been in that building, too, even if it had not started in our loft. The street was heaped with burnt rubbish. The crowd about us, in broad daylight, was growing larger as more and more were coming to work.

"There's no use standing here," said my father. He led the way to a restaurant where, nodding for drowsiness, I had coffee and cake.

"What shall we do now?" asked my uncle.

"Why," said my father, "I will call up our insurance agent later. As for you," he said, turning to me, "go home and tell your mother what has happened: she is worried about us. Tell her there's no use coming to work today." I was glad to hear my father speak calmly and see him sure of himself.

When I was on the last of the flight of steps that led from the station of the elevated railway, I stumbled for drowsiness and fell. A woman about to climb the stairs saw me and stared. She thinks I'm drunk, I thought, somewhat pleased to be thought a gay dog; besides, I did not care—so trifling did everything except the fire seem.

In the afternoon I was back on Broadway. The newspapers had large headlines and a long account of the fire. And my father told me what he had heard from insurance men and the firemen left on guard. The loft below ours, used for storage by a firm which ran a chain of hat stores for men, had been stocked for the summer season with straw hats, six to a box and the boxes stacked to the ceiling, from Broadway to Mercer Street and from wall to wall. Except a lane for the shipping clerks. When the first alarm had sounded, smoke was coming out of our windows (that was why it was being said the fire had started in our loft); the firemen broke into our place and went through it but could not find the fire. This was in the walls or in the floor or among the boxes of hats downstairs, because of a faulty flue or defective wiring or, perhaps, because a shipping clerk had been smoking on the sly (working late that night). However that might be, after the firemen had gone, the straw hats burst into flame and the flames, leaping a hundred feet into the air, set other buildings on fire.

Men were greeting my father and my uncle with a knowing smile and one stopped them to say jokingly: "Can't you set fire to your own loft without burning the block down?"

My father and my uncle could hardly blame them, for my uncle himself whenever he heard the fire-engines used to say: "Bad business!" And once, when reproached, had answered drily in Yiddish: "If one doesn't kindle, it doesn't burn." Their consciences were easy, however, and jokes and mock congratulations did not bother them. I did mind the black looks members of the firm downstairs (who were not Jews) gave my father and my uncle: it was said there was not enough

280

insurance to cover the stock of straw hats beneath us and the firm would lose heavily under a clause of their policies that made them co-insurers. But, then, I also heard that the fire-marshal was looking into the cause of the fire and in the end the members of the firm downstairs would know that my father and my uncle were not at all to blame.

The Artistic Millinery Company had enough insurance (although not much because it really never had much to insure); and it did have stock and machinery, and the leavings of past seasons, which the fire had turned into cash. There was no clause in the insurance policies, after all, about any fire starting in the loft (through no fault of the insured) which could be the basis of a refusal to pay; and the fire, luckily, was between seasons and there were no orders for us to lose. The mail, that very morning, brought the Artistic Millinery Company a check for more than four thousand dollars from the last of the doubtful accounts, the largest account on the books, so that these showed the firm fairly well off. "Now," said my father, "if we could only get rid of the lease. I would be happy."

My father and I went to the door of the building, at which a fireman stood watching, and my father asked leave to go to his loft and see the damage. The fireman let us pass into the bitter smell of goods burnt and soaked and we walked up the stairs slowly, leaving footprints on the wet wood, not even trying to, dodge, after a while, the heavy drops black with charcoal that fell everywhere—fell on our clothes and hats and hands.

The staircase was solid enough all the way to the loft. Neither the ground floor nor the loft above it had been touched by the fire. This had burnt a hole in the middle of the Artistic Millinery Company's floor (all the skylights of the loft below had fallen in); fully a quarter of the ceiling of our loft was gone and most of the roof. My father and I looked through the loft above us straight into the sky, just then blue and sunny, the sky of a mild spring day. The Artistic Millinery Company's workroom—machinery and stock—was gone, fallen into the loft below; but the office and its furniture were only wet. And in back of the loft the great box, lined with tin, into which the sweepings were put each night for the ragman to take away in the morning, was still there, the dirt and litter safe and dry.

As my father and I stood looking about, the tenants of the loft above us, fellow Jews, came up the stairs with their lawyer. The tenants greeted my father warmly. (Their stock had been large and was fully covered by insurance.) Now they, too, were wondering if they were bound by their lease. My father asked the lawyer what he thought and was answered but coldly by that stately gentleman: the statutes and cases examined and pondered, when he had an opinion, he would be back to see his clients; and my father, also, if he wished him to. But, offhand, he did not see how the landlord could hold the Artistic Millinery Company to the lease—or his clients.

The Artistic Millinery Company rented a small place by the month in the office building next door, and my mother, with two or three girls to help her, set about making samples. The matter of the insurance was soon settled without any trouble, and the Artistic Millinery Company paid in full.

The lease was another matter. The lawyer of the tenants who had been above us was a relative of one of them— or his wife. Whatever the tie, they were sure that because of this he would be devoted to their cause and, since their cause was ours (for the leases were alike in the general provisions), he would be devoted to us, too. The lawyer came,

282

one day, into our place in the office building, a stately chap, and my father asked him cheerfully if he still thought the fire had ended our obligation to pay rent under the lease. He said, colder than ever: "If you want my opinion, you will have to retain me: two hundred and fifty dollars if we go to trial, one hundred and fifty if we do not, and fifty dollars of this right now. My fee is so low only because I am also handling the case for the tenants who were above you."

Now the old law of England, and American law to the extent that it comes from the English, is chiefly a law by landlords for landlords. Under this law, where property is leased to a tenant and destroyed by fire during the tenancy the tenant must continue to pay rent even if, through no fault of his own, he has nothing to tenant. But most legislatures of the United States, if not all, elected as they are chiefly by tenants, long ago provided by statute that if the property leased is destroyed by fire, then the tenancy should end and with it the obligation to pay rent, unless there is an agreement to the contrary; for in a free country, such as ours, the tenant may be free to contract to pay rent under any circumstances. The lease of the Artistic Millinery Company provided that if the building was totally destroyed by fire the tenancy should end and, if the premises rented were so damaged by fire as to become untenantable, rent should not be paid until the landlord had repaired the premises, provided he chose to do so; but, once the premises were repaired, the obligation to pay rent again was there.

The roof of the building was mostly gone and most of the top loft, including some of the ceiling of the loft rented by the Artistic Millinery Company—about a fourth of the ceiling and some of the flooring; but the walls of the building were standing, the store and the loft above it were just damaged by water and the loft above the first, just below ours, where the straw hats were that had made such a pretty bonfire, had merely part of the ceiling gone. The ordinary passer-by would certainly think the building damaged, badly damaged, but hardly totally destroyed and, even if the premises actually rented to the Artistic Millinery Company were untenantable, as the loft above us certainly was destroyed, the lease, read plainly, did not terminate in either event. Unless, of course, the landlord chose to terminate it.

But a lawyer, who is certainly no ordinary passer-by and no plain reader of leases, even if there were no fee in it for him, might very well find a number of questions breeding in the gutted building. To begin with, is not a building without a roof a building destroyed within the meaning of the lease? But if it is not a building destroyed within the meaning of the lease, did not the parties intend that if the rented premises were destroyed (as distinguished from "untenantable") the lease was to terminate? And was not the provision as to the destruction of the building only in the lease because by mistake—to be corrected, of course—a lease with provisions (already printed) for the rental of a building, not of a loft, had been signed? And other questions, no doubt, in which good lawyers delight and on which they feed.

My father and my uncle—and I, of course—had been thinking about the matter as well as we could before the lawyer stood before us asking for a retainer. The landlord's agent had already notified us that he was going to set about repairing the building as soon as he could. But it would certainly not be ready before July. By that time our season should be in full swing. Besides, what if the repairs would be reasonably delayed as repairs generally were? And so my father, who had always been against the place, anyway, because of the high rent, said: "If we wait that long, we'll lose the fall season. We must rent a loft now in which to work." For the place where we were was just a large office—good enough only for making samples. "But who will rent us a loft for only three months?"

My uncle, too, was anxious by now to get out of the lease. (He had found it hard to get buyers up to the showroom: it is easier to get a buyer, come to see someone else, into a showroom on the same floor, or even on another floor. But we were the only millinery firm in the building.) So my uncle agreed, this time, with my father. Yes, they should rent another loft at once and defend the suit, if any. "But," said my uncle cheerfully, "they will never sue us. Why, this agent has hundreds of lofts to rent and it will give him a bad name among business men if he sued for rent in a case like this! And what jury will bring in a verdict for the landlord?"

However, my father and my uncle did not think the lawyer's fee low or the prospect of an immediate retainer pleasant, and they talked together hurriedly while the lawyer stared and fumed. They knew his opinion of the law in the matter— the tenants who were above us had told them that—and it was what they had all hoped for. The Artistic Millinery Company had their own lawyer, of course, at least someone who had acted in a small matter or two for a fee of five or ten dollars: a poor shabby fellow, who had studied law at night, working in a shop during the day. Bright enough but unsuited, clearly, for an important matter like this. So my uncle walked to the little table serving as a desk, told the bookkeeper to write out a check for fifty dollars and, with a sweep of his arm as if by that gesture to make up for any delay, gave it to the waiting lawyer.

"Now," said that gentleman, somewhat mollified, after he had dictated the terms of his retainer to the girl and had it signed and pocketed, "let me see your lease." He glanced at it and said: "Just as I thought—the same as the other.

Go right ahead and rent another place, if you want to. That building is destroyed. Of course," he added with an air of caution, suitable to a lawyer, "you can never tell what a jury will do. But," and he smiled for the first time, "what jury will bring in a verdict for the landlord in such a case?"

"That is just what I was telling him!" said my uncle, striking my father playfully on the shoulder, all smiling broadly. And the lawyer walked out, a good fellow after all, leaving a feeling of festivity behind in the four of us—my father, my uncle, my mother and I (for you may be sure my mother and I had been listening closely).

My father and my uncle now set about looking for a loft. They did not wish to move from the good block they were on, or away from the better block (next to it) where they had been before this, and a good loft in so narrow a radius was not easy to find: this was too small and dark; this had everything, plenty of space and light and even a supply of "live" steam" for the manufacture of blocked hats, but, of course, was much too dear. One noon, my father came back from lunch and said he had found the very place: across the street, large enough for all our needs, light and cool with windows on three sides, in a building into which every jobber who came to the city would come, because the showrooms of some of the best manufacturers in the country were in the offices below and above. And the signs of our firm when placed, one on the very corner and one along Broadway and another along the side street (it was a corner building), would be seen by everybody who came to the district.

"But what," said my uncle, interrupting my father's string of praises, "is the rent? I was afraid even to go there because I knew it would be dear."

"It is cheaper than you think—even a few hundred dollars a year cheaper than the rent we have been paying."

286

"But how about 'live' steam," asked my mother, "so that we can make blocked hats if we have to?"

"No," said my father, "there is no 'live' steam, but we'll be no worse off than we were." My mother, ever anxious to be better off, was not exactly pleased at being no worse off.

"Just a minute," said my uncle and sat down, holding his head. When he had rubbed it well and collected himself somewhat, he said to my father: "I have always been the one to spend money and you have been the one to say no. Now when I am looking for a cheap place—all this while you have been complaining about what we have to pay for rent —you want to move to a place as dear as the one we are rid of. And we are not at all sure that we are rid of it but we may have to pay the rent for it, too. Now I must say no!"

At this my father began to laugh and said: "I have always thought that you spoke just out of contrariness. This proves it!"

"Not at all!" said my uncle. "Don't you understand? I have been the one to jump ahead, you have been the one to hold back—that made us a good team; but if you are now the one to jump ahead, I must be the one to pull back."

"I am glad you admit my holding back had some value," said my father. "This is the first time you ever said so. I wish that you and Sarah Yetta would remember what you have just said. But, anyway, it is the best place we can get right now." Whether it was the best or not, the role of "holding back" was not my uncle's; he gave it up after that single protest.

Really, the new loft was the best in the city for our show-room. And my uncle was soon standing proudly in the street with other salesmen (for some of the best factories in the country); in front of the silver signs at either side of the door, on which the name of our firm shone brightly, and under the great signs above that could be seen by everyone in the district. Many years before, when my father had been a foreman at wrappers, he had worked in the old building just across the side street. Now, when he thought of it, he, too, was not without pride at being where he was—to have climbed again even higher than when he had been Henry Ettelson's foreman.

But behind the large gilt letters of the Artistic Millinery Company's signs there was soon unhappiness. The fall season for which the partners had cheerfully made ready was worse than the bad season before it. The line was ready in plenty of time, but the jobbers came to town and went home and left us so few orders we could not look forward to enough business to keep the help going the month or two we had been pretty sure of. Even the jobbers whose credit was not of the best would not buy and the only order of any size was from one whom my uncle had not sold for a long time— looking for him to fail. In the showroom of the Artistic Millinery Company he was humble and bought eagerly so that—in my uncle's opinion—his credit was hardly better. But for want of other orders it was shipped.

My parents and my uncle blamed their poor business on the lack of demand for hand-made hats, and indeed the factories making blocked hats of velvet or plush were as busy as could be; they blamed the manufacture of hand-made hats by the jobbers themselves, for by this time the jobbers were all making their own hats, and the best (an old story by this time) were not even buying a few dozen from the Artistic Millinery Company to copy; my uncle blamed my mother's styles, and she went out each noon, after her lunch, to study the windows of the department stores and at night

288

studied the pages of the fashion magazines for new hats. "What's the use?" said my uncle. "The trade has all gone. If they come back this season, they will come only to place re-orders and to buy new styles from the factories whose hats they have been selling." But my mother went ahead making new samples and put them on the shelves of the showroom; my father hardly had the courage to figure the prices they should sell at, and my uncle hardly glanced at them.

My father and mother, soon enough, were wondering how to keep the piece-workers going—only five or six of the help worked by the week and were kept the year round (a girl or two to help my mother in making samples or to work at orders when there were no samples to make, a girl to help my mother on the floor, bringing goods to the milliners and taking hats away, a girl at the sewing-machine, a girl to help my father keep the books, and a boy to help him pack and ship and to run errands). If the piece-workers scattered during the season, it would certainly not be easy, if possible, to get a shop of trained help together again before the slack. When there was only work for a day or two, my parents came one morning to find the piece-workers fled—gone to work elsewhere; they, too, had been anxious not to lose their season and were not blind to how little work was on hand and to the anxious faces of their employers.

In the meantime, the loft that the Artistic Millinery Company had abandoned was ready, newly plastered and whitewashed, elevators running; and a formal demand for the rent was made. It seemed that the Artistic Millinery Company was going to be sued after all, if they didn't pay. My uncle spoke to the landlord's agent and pointed out the harm it would do him among business men if it were known that he brought suit so unjustly. All of which the agent blandly admitted (tongue in cheek, no doubt); however, the agent was only an agent, and the landlord only the trustee for an estate and he had to sue to protect himself. In due time, my father and my uncle as co-partners, for my mother's name had always been kept out of the firm, were served with a summons and a bulky complaint.

I was with them that summer, helping where I could, day by day drinking from the same well of bitterness that they did. But it bothered me much less. True enough, my father and mother had said to me: "Do not worry. We have put aside money for your education—that will not be touched by us whatever happens." But I did not look for anything really bad to happen: my parents were too wise, I thought, and worked too hard; it seemed to me that they were living according to the maxims—and must have the rewards.

The action for rent came to trial in the winter. The defense of the Artistic Millinery Company was still that the building had been destroyed by fire and the lease terminated according to the provisions, but now that the damage had been repaired quickly and the building was as good as new, the defense, somehow, did not look as sound as it did when the building had neither roof nor top storey. However, my father and my uncle comforted themselves with the thought that no jury would bring in a verdict for the landlord.

Their lawyer had also said that a suit should be brought to amend the lease to read that it would terminate if the rented premises were destroyed, and asked for another fee— only fifty dollars. This suit was not, he had gone to the trouble of explaining to my father and my uncle, within the scope of the defense at law for which he had been retained and which would still be necessary (although much easier) if the lease were amended. They did not fully understand but did not want to antagonize him, so late in the life of the action against them, and paid the fee. Thinking about the suit, the lawyer concluded the question might just as well be brought up at the trial of the action for rent, for, according to the code, the judge could sit in equity as well as at law to do justice and carry out the intentions of the parties. However, neither my father nor my uncle had much hope in any such claim; really it had not mattered to them if the clause read "building" or "premises" when they had signed the lease. They had been concerned only about the rent they were to pay. As for the rest, they were ready (as tenants generally are and generally have to be) to trust in God, the protection of the state's laws, the city's ordinances, their own wits, the landlord's common sense, and to luck. But that a jury would favor them against the landlord, just as it would favor one of their workers against them, this my father and my uncle understood and looked for.

The case, however, never went to the jury for its favoritism and its verdict. The judge, after hearing the defense, directed a verdict for the landlord, finding, as the seemingly outraged lawyer of the Artistic Millinery Company explained to the gaping partners, that they had no defense for the jury even to pretend to consider—no evidence at all of the building's total destruction. (For it was the building's total destruction, not that of the loft, the jury were to consider, if anything.) Of course, they should appeal and an appellate court must reverse the judgment. His fee would be modest enough, under the circumstances, and luckily the trial had been so brief printing the minutes would not cost much.

Yes, they would appeal. But not because either my father or my uncle had any faith left in their stately lawyer and his defense. That their plea would never reach the jury at all in a trial by jury was quite new to them and showed them simply (as if they did not know!) that the law had pitfalls—that the best they could do was to get out of its neighborhood as fast as they could. But they had no money with which to pay the rent, past due and to be due, under the judgment. Yes, they had to appeal and hoped that, somehow or other, the tide in their affairs would turn and, by the time the appeal should be decided, there would be enough money to pay, if they had to, judgment and interest, costs and all. Of course, they had to put up a bond for the judgment; and that is what my uncle's father-in-law could do for them, and did.

Next day, the telephone rang again and again after their creditors read of the judgment in the newspapers. My uncle arranged with the landlord's agent for leave to sublet the loft, if he could, even at a reduction in rent (to be paid directly to the landlord by the sublessee). This would cut down the loss, should the judgment be affirmed—or reversed. And, as our hopes were rising, perhaps simply because we were alive, the tenants who had been in the loft above (who, of course, had also lost their case) told us of another lawyer—another relative—just the man to handle the appeal. And he was hopeful, too, of a reversal, all the more so because the verdict had been directed against defendants.

This lawyer, unlike the other, was short, stooped, and near-sighted; he had a shrill impatient voice, quickly sarcastic. His office was in two or three small rooms, crowded with old law-books, at the end of a long corridor in an old building. Clearly, he was a man who had burrowed long in law books and was just the one, in the thinking of our good friends, the other tenants, to find the law for a successful appeal. And, indeed, he had an ingenious theory ready on which to base his brief— in part at least: the building, by analogy to a ship, was at law totally destroyed, even if only partially destroyed in fact, since it could not be used for the purpose for which it was intended; just as a ship with a hole in it would be considered totally

292

destroyed at law, although most of it was undamaged, except by water, and in fact it might be resting on the bottom of the sea. A building without a roof, likewise, could not be used for the purpose for which it was intended; for the purpose of its tenants it might just as well be at the bottom of the sea and, therefore, should likewise be considered—at law—totally destroyed within the meaning of the lease.

I found the theory worthy of that face, which I thought shrewd, of that glance, which I found sharp (in spite of much reading). There were, no doubt, plenty of cases to show that a ship, partially destroyed, was totally so at law; the only difficulty was that there had been no case to hold that a building partially destroyed was totally so, certainly no case in the jurisdiction. As I was to find out, judges are not apt to make rulings without precedent. And apt to insist, in their unimaginative way, that land and water, ship and building, are not alike—as if ships were not raised from the bottom of the sea to be repaired. The trial lawyer smiled at the ingenious theory and assured us, without any breach of professional etiquette, of course, that we were making a mistake in taking the appeal away from him; but this time neither his words nor his bearing impressed my father and my uncle.

The spring season proved to be no better than the fall and when it was over, at least for the Artistic Millinery Company (the factories making blocked hats of straw were just beginning to be busy and still had three or four months of work ahead), the business was worth no more than what the machinery was worth, such as it was, and the fixtures, including the splendid signs—at best a few hundred dollars.

My father drew his savings—and my mother's—from the savings-bank and put it back in the business. As for my uncle's father-in-law, now that he was on the bond for the appeal, he could hardly be expected to do any more. With my father's and mother's cash, the company still had a respectable bank-account, but it was clear to any credit man who read their statement how little business they had been doing in the past year, compared to the years before; and it was clear, too, to anybody looking into their many windows from the office building across the street how few girls were at work.

Partners may quarrel when they are making money together, as my father and my uncle quarreled as to how they were to share their profits. But it is common knowledge that partners are pretty sure to quarrel when they are losing money; all their old wounds then burn afresh and every day adds at least another.

One Sunday afternoon, seated on the porch of my uncle's house, my father and my uncle were talking over their business troubles with my uncle's father-in-law: how the fall season had again begun badly; how (my uncle was saying) of customers who had come to the city to buy he had, by his great skill as a salesman, managed to get a number into the showroom; how they had looked at the line and walked out—the friendliest had made some excuse, just come to town, want to look around before buying, will be back, but the others had glanced at the hats, as my smiling uncle had rolled up shade after shade, and had gone out, angry at having been cajoled into wasting even five minutes of their time. My uncle's father-in-law listened, a sage now that he was rich, smiled and nodded.

It was hard enough to get a customer to come into your showroom! (my uncle was saying). If he only had the hats, how he could sell! My father was only a foreman, and not a business man at all; my mother a forelady who had at times designed a hat that was so so because he had been there to sell it, and now even he, good salesman that he was, could not sell her hats. So my uncle went on talking to his father-in-law on his own cool porch in the quiet of a warm Sunday afternoon, both having dined well on cold stuffed fish in jelly with grated horseradish, red with beets, on chicken broth, good and hot, with plenty of noodles, on plenty of roast chicken, plenty of cakes sprinkled with almonds, well browned, and plenty of hot tea with mulberry jam; talking quietly without bitterness, my uncle smiling at his misfortunes. Unlike my father who, although he had dined just as well in his own home, was listening angrily.

At last he could swallow no more and interrupted my uncle to shout: "Again! So I am only the foreman and your sister a forelady! If we had the money, I would end our partnership this minute! But as soon as we can, we end it and I will have to stand for your insults no longer!"

And my father came home in a rage that he kept fanning in long talks with my mother—that night and every night, next morning and every morning. Until they became so busy they had other matters to talk about. For they did become busy. They had never been so busy: orders came by every mail, by telephone and telegraph; buyers had to wait to get into our showroom; buyers coming in met others going out, urging my uncle to hurry their orders; until at last I, for one, was—incredibly—sick of orders.

For a new hat was on the market, a cap rather than a hat, a soft hat without a frame or much sewing; except for the tacking in of a lining and the tacking on of a band of ribbon or braid, the hat was made by sewing-machine, and was just the thing for girls and young women—who bought most hats, anyway. And my father, cutting the velvet for the new hat, found he could do much better with velvet twenty inches wide (the ordinary width was eighteen). This was his secret. The hat could be copied, of course, and was copied, as the Artistic

Millinery Company had copied it and adapted it to our shop and our trade, but no one could make it as cheap as we did or make as much on it at our price.

Those who took the trouble to look into the Artistic Millinery Company's place from the lofts and offices across the street saw the loft almost empty—and in the middle of the season. For we needed only a few sewing-machines and operators and a few trimmers to turn out the hat, it was so easy to make. And we were working on one hat with two or three different trimmings instead of on twenty or thirty hats, each different, as we usually did when busy. The Artistic Millinery Company's turn had come at last. (It was now clear to my father and mother that any hat they would make from then on must be made, as much as it could be, by sewing-machine; the milliners, working slowly by hand, were to have little to sew, except to stitch the finishing stitches or to tack the trimming on—and the trimming itself would be easy for any beginner; for women's hats had now become simple and mannish— "tailored." And who understood the use of the sewing-machine better than my father and mother?)

The first to buy the hat, which the members of the Artistic Millinery Company were afterwards to call affectionately "the soft hat" (although it had a number like all our hats and one we were not to forget, as we remember the numbers of houses in which we live or work for a long time and our birthday and the birthdays of those dear to us), the very first was a small jobber of no credit whose order was left on the bottom of the quickly growing heap of orders to be shipped—until my uncle tore it from the file and threw it away. But in the eagerness with which the buyer had looked at the hat my uncle saw that here indeed was something to sell. That very day he had four or five orders from the two or three jobbers still in town and from two of the best of the city jobbers.

In October, the appeal from the judgment against the Artistic Millinery Company in the action for rent was heard. I went to court that morning and was somewhat put out to find our lawyer dressed up in morning coat and striped trousers as if this was almost as much an event for him as for the Artistic Millinery Company. And when I looked about at the benches for visitors, empty except for two or three persons, I saw the lawyer's wife (whom I had met in his office). The lawyer who spoke for the landlord was important in the profession—I knew the name well—and he stood before the row of gowned judges in his everyday clothes, his hands in his coat pockets, tall, thin, white-haired, rocking a little on his feet, amused at the thick brief of his "young friend" and the ingenious argument. But it was all really simple. Two or three of the judges smiled pleasantly and nodded; one of them, afterwards, questioned our lawyer sharply and another cut the answer short.

Our lawyer came away, it seemed to me, bedraggled in his immaculate get-up and I thought I heard him—in the corridor—concluding for his wife the argument that the judge would not let him end. None the less, I was cast down when I found out in a month or so that the judgment below was affirmed. Affirmed without opinion, as if there was nothing worth saying about our defense. We could still appeal and this our lawyer was eager to do without any other fee; but now that my father and my uncle had the money to pay the judgment neither wanted to bother about it any longer, for there would be, they were sure, only more to pay in the end.

The season of "the soft hat" lasted well into October. The Artistic Millinery Company had barely started working at it before July was over, but in eight weeks or so the firm cleared about ten or twelve thousand dollars, enough to pay whatever was due on the judgment and enough to let my father and mother draw their savings again out of the business and leave enough for my uncle to have a couple of thousand dollars as his share. Even the trimmers, who were just beginners, were making thirty or forty dollars a week, instead of six or eight.

With the last order shipped, my father turned again to what had been festering in him all those busy months—the end of the partnership. And he was so set upon it neither my mother nor I said a word. She had, indeed, grown as tired of her husband's complaints about her brother as of her brother's overbearing manner (although ready enough to forgive it with respect to herself) and was willing to let the matter take its course. As for me, optimistic as Thoreau's manufacturer of mousetraps in a woods, I was certain the success of any business, and certainly of a business in which style, workmanship, and quick shipments were important, was dependent upon those in charge of the factory; that selling, even selling as good as my uncle's, mattered less and that, given the goods, selling would in time almost take care of itself.

My uncle in fact was worried in spite of all his scorn for foreman and forelady. The date set for the end of the partnership near, he would come to the shop early in the morning when he would find only my father there and ask what the devil he meant by wanting to force him out of the business. Did he want to ruin him? And he would rail at my father—overbearing as ever.

The firm name of the Artistic Millinery Company and its good will belonged to my mother, as the arbitrators had decided long before, and my uncle had to move away. He went next door, on Broadway of course, hired a foreman supposed to be one of the best in the trade for a good salary and a share of the profits, took the firm name of the Artistic Hat Company,

and sent out cards with his picture on them telling all who had
dealt with the Artistic Millinery Company where he had moved
to. So that those who knew him as "The Artistic"—all the
buyers—might very well think the firm itself had moved. I
supposed my father and mother could stop him by an in-
junction but my father would not hear of it nor would he,
afterwards, copy any of my uncle's hats when shrewd buyers
tried to profit by a supposed rivalry.

Before my uncle walked out of the Artistic Millinery
Company's place for the last time, he suddenly turned to me.
(I had been standing silently by, as my father and my uncle
wrangled to the very end.) My uncle smiled at me as he smiled
at his best customers and briskly held out his hand. "There
is no need for us to quarrel," he said.

"Certainly not," I answered, just as warmly, and the tears
came into my eyes, for my uncle had been very dear to me.
And I knew that he would have trouble getting anybody to
manage a shop for him as well as my father and mother had,
just as my parents would have trouble getting anyone to sell
for them the way my uncle could.

My father seemed bewildered: as if he did not know which
way to turn, as if my uncle had gone away suddenly and the
separation was not his own wish and act. As if the grudge
he had nursed so long against my uncle, now that it was
quenched, had left him without spirit or resolution, except
to explain at length to fidgeting buyer or unhappy salesman,
who, perhaps, had spoken lightly of the separation as introduction to matters that concerned themselves, the cause of it
and all his grievances. My father had known, of course, that he
would have to take charge of the selling and I had thought,
in spite of his silence, that he had some plan; for certainly
he had planned the separation long enough. But I found that

my father was quite uncertain what to do and wished (and really did not wish) to hire some salesman or other—but whom he did not know.

My father had a good friend who sold braid and who was always ready, even eager, to copy for him any style of braid my father had bought elsewhere and thought dear. But I doubted his friendship somewhat after my mother found, on measuring braid with which he supplied us cheaply, that it was one or two yards short of the dozen each piece was supposed to have. I was not quite persuaded it was all the fault of the shipping clerk. Now this friend brought up a salesman, a friend whom he puffed heartily, for my father to talk to. But I recognized him as one of the shabby crew who used to wait—like myself—in the outer office of a buyer for a hurried word, the chance of showing samples in a corner and, if lucky, an order for two or four dozen.

Then my father began to confer with a chap who had the air of a policeman directing traffic. I was not taken in by the belly and heavy jaw, nor by the good clothes and the large flower in the salesman's buttonhole, nor even by his choice diction and precise utterance. The man had a good list of references but, after all, there he was—looking for a job. I stood to one side and listened and saw my father ready to hire him. He wanted as much as my uncle had drawn each week. My father was willing to pay that. But, warmed by my father's friendliness or, perhaps, forestalling an accusation, the salesman went on to say that he sometimes drank. One had to, of course, entertaining the buyers (though my uncle never had to); and he wanted to warn my father frankly that my father might then find him quarrelsome and insulting, at least saying what my father might think insulting, but he was not to mind. For, of course, the salesman would not mean it— in spite of the proverb.

300

No sooner did the door close behind this candidate for my father to think it over and let him know in the morning if he was wanted—my father had hesitated at the very last—than I said with a grin: "You didn't want Uncle, no matter how good a salesman he was, because he insulted you; and here you have a salesman who may not be any good at all but who already promises to insult you."

My father looked at me sadly and said: "They are all like that, the devil take them! What shall I do? The trade will be here in a week and we have no one to sell for us! I'll ask about him."

My father by now was ready to forgive insults, but drinking, he found out, sometimes kept the man from business for a day or two. This would be unfortunate if the trade was in town and that would be just when he would do most entertaining: a dilemma—but we did not see why it should become ours.

Later that day an old friend came in—the resident buyer of the Texan who had given the Artistic Millinery Company their first large order. The Texan's firm was now of no importance and the resident buyer, it seemed to me, was just a seedy little fellow. He listened, friendly enough, to my father's long account of the separation from my uncle, perhaps because the troubles of those who seemed successful were pleasant for him to listen to just then, perhaps merely because he was tired of walking about and glad of an excuse to sit down. But he did give my father advice that seemed to us sensible.

"What you need," the resident buyer said, "is a commission man to sell for you: who would not want drawings or salary and will just get a commission for what he sells." And he told my father of one—just across the street—who was doing very well. "If you can get him to take your line you are sure to do well. He carries a number of lines, of course, and will not take yours if it conflicts with one he has, but he may have room for yours, too."

When my father went downstairs to ask the salesmen at the door what they knew of this commission man, they said he was too important to handle a line like my father's and went on to regale him with tales of the man's temper: how once, for example, one of his manufacturers sent him new samples while he was on the road; upon opening the box, he liked them so little he threw the hats out of the window; and a Negro shoe-black at the hotel door, seeing the hats come flying down, thought they had fallen out or been blow away; he chased them up and down the street until he had them all and then, grinning and bowing, brought them back to the commission man's door looking for a handsome tip instead of the cursing he got.

Well, even the timid may become bold.under necessity, and my father went across the street, hoping that he would not come flying out of the window to the hilarity of the salesmen—like the samples in the story. He found himself in a great loft running the length of the block from Broadway to Mercer Street, in which were rows of long tables and showcases of samples, a couple of young men to wait on trade and a pretty girl to try on hats, and, in a far corner, watching the door from a snug office, a keen-eyed man, grown fat. Although neither my father nor I had ever heard of the man before, he had heard of the Artistic Millinery Company; in fact, he could not help seeing its signs and he proved to be, surprisingly enough, interested in its hats and agreed to take the line.

IX

It was now the summer of 1915 and the great nations of Europe had been at war a year. The price of everything was going up, slowly at first, each buyer protesting, uncertain whether or not he could get a better price to cover the extra cost, for, surely, the war would stop any day—some day soon, and he might have all his goods at these high prices on his hands. Buyers were adding the extra cost to their prices and charging an extra profit on this extra cost, as they should, but, for the most part, timidly, afraid to anger customers; they were not as yet buying as much as they could to hold as prices rose, year by year, day by day, pricing their goods at market value— not the cost—to sell and be sorry. Why, even the newsboys, then, had hardly learnt to shout the headlines instead of the scores of baseball games, as the younger ones still did those days in the August of 1914 when Austria and Germany, Russia and France and England went to war.

Everyone caught what he could of the downpour of orders— great reservoirs full, pails full and buckets full, and those who had only a dipper, a dipperful. My parents now had so much to do they were leaving the house at dawn. Their commission man did all the selling and their line was good for months and months (no longer sudden changes of style from Paris). Whatever the Artistic Millinery Company shipped, since everybody was doing well, was paid for. (As for those whom my father and my uncle had been afraid to sell to once, because they had buildings stored with goods and little cash, with their goods gone up in value beyond hope or reason they were better off than those who had always bought carefully and had plenty of cash and little goods.)

The term of the Artistic Millinery Company's lease was about to end and I urged my father to move to a side street where he could get a loft as good as the one he had—with "live" steam, too—for no more than a third of the rent he was paying. The commission man would do the selling and my father had no need of any showroom on Broadway—no buyer ever came to see the Artistic Millinery Company now, anyway; the burden of the rent which had weighed heavily on my father's shoulders would be gone and with it the foolish pretense (of my uncle) that the Artistic Millinery Company was a larger house than it was. My father agreed quickly enough and used the possible need of "live" steam for blocked hats to save his face.

But my mother—her brother's sister in this—did not like moving to a side street. She was to say with some vexation, afterwards, that the two of us, my father and I, had taken the business away from Broadway and that my uncle smiled broadly when he had heard of it; for he, of course, would stay on Broadway with his last breath and dollar.

With the armistice, after a lull, men in business began to make more money than ever and prices went higher than ever. The end of the war, it seemed, had brought no panic after all, as many had feared. And now because many bins long empty had to be filled, much that was uncared for and left undone because of the war had to be rebuilt and built, or simply because after so much misery and death the wish to buy and take delight in all that the living might have and do was common, selling was easy. But a good line to sell was hard to get, for any good manufacturer had enough to do.

My uncle was not one of these, as I saw long before, and could not better whatever was wrong in his shop just by changing foreman or designer. He had lasted because he made money buying recklessly, and during the war it paid. Still, he was always burdened by his expenses and spent his cash, never much, so freely the first slump after the war was enough to sink him. But I was startled at reading in the newspaper one morning the name of my uncle's firm among the small list of those in bankruptcy.

From then on, with little credit, so that he could not make

money on large purchases, my uncle was unable to run his factory at all. He became a salesman for others. As soon as he could, he was a commission man. But before he reached the dignity of this (by then the good times were over), I met him once in the street, his clothes worn and his necktie wrinkled and frayed, when almost all were spruce and prosperous. More white hair than black in his beard, but still sure of himself, although no longer as cheerful; sure, too, that he had never been at fault—and with many grievances.

Soon after the war, a new and very good paste was sold to millinery manufacturers for making goods or feathers stick to frames; but the smell of it was vile and the girls who worked for the Artistic Millinery Company said the paste gave them a headache. My mother disliked the stink as much as anybody, but would not set any of her help to doing what she and they found so unpleasant. And so she did the pasting herself. Sometimes, at night, a blue patch would come out on her leg or arm, paining her sharply; her doctor could not account for it, and no one thought it had anything to do with the paste. (Long afterwards, when my mother no longer made the hats that needed pasting, or any hats, I heard in a talk on industrial diseases of a strange sickness—the symptoms like my mother's —that milliners in Chicago had, and even died of, until it was traced to an excellent paste made of chemicals for ammunition.) But my mother was soon to become sick of another disease. No matter how good the fall season, business for the Artistic Millinery Company always fell off at the end of September. The next two months were more or less slack (until the first orders for the spring season which did not begin to come in until December—if then). Fur hats were good that fall. Our commission man persuaded my father to price a line cheaply— really only to pay expenses during the slack so that the Artistic

Millinery Company should not have, as always, quite a loss. The fur hats my mother designed were good-looking—she was by now an old hand at it—and the orders so large the commission man thought it worth while to send his men on the road with the hats. The Artistic Millinery Company became as busy as if it were the middle of the season. My mother, handling the fur (dyed rabbit skin sewn together by the furriers and cut into strips), measuring it and cutting it for the milliners and taking the fur hats away for shipment, two months and more of this, had the first attack of her asthma that winter. She was to be sick with it for the rest of her life.

In a few years she was never to breathe easily, choking at fur and feathers, at the dust in a room or in the street, before it would rain or when it snowed, after she had eaten this or that, and she was often to wake from her sleep choking. This was for her, perhaps, the real profit of the only time the Artistic Millinery Company worked right through from season to season.

Suddenly there was talk of a "strike." The Artistic Millinery Company's help did not belong to the trade-union which had, as yet, little following, and were as satisfied as people can be who work for others. Most of the workers in the trade were earning as much as they ever had and the hours were never better. But the spokesmen for the union did not talk much of bettering wages or hours (which my father, for example, might have added to the cost of his hats—and shorter hours meant less work in the shop for him, too); they were asking a guarantee that each shop keep its help at no less than a certain wage for at least a certain number of weeks—long enough to give the workers a living the year round: instead of the uncertainty in which the help were overworked at times

306

and without any work at other times and no one, no matter how good, was sure of job or livelihood.

Desirable as this was—to make millinery (at least for the help) as stable a business as others in which the fashionable was not the chief ingredient traded in, my father did not see how he could comply with any such requirement as the guarantee: a bad season or two would not only damage the Artistic Millinery Company—and it had weathered many—but would ruin him. And every manufacturer felt as he did. But the union officials argued that the effect of the demand, if met, would be that the small manufacturers who kept themselves going by cutting prices—and wages— would be out of the business and only the well-managed, stable firms left—who could well give the guarantee demanded. The grievance was real. Whatever was to be said for the remedy, it was certain that a strike would be called throughout the trade in the city.

My father, besides, had (naturally) no wish to give up the right to dismiss any of his help and have union-rules and a shop-chairman to think of. Certainly, he found it hard enough to run the shop as it was. My mother and he thought that if there should be a strike—it would be a long strike since all the help had money—it might be as good a time as any for them to quit the business, rest a while, and find, perhaps, something easier to do for a living. They were then worth about thirty, or thirty-five, thousand dollars; their children grown and—at least my father thought so—educated sufficiently; they themselves were fifty, sick and weak, my mother troubled by her asthma and my father by the diabetes from which his father had died.

The chief of the Artistic Millinery Company's workers— the man who made frames and helped my father with the cutting—told him that as soon as the strike would be called, since it would be general to unionize the trade, all the workers would have to strike. My father agreed that they would have to if they were to escape the stigma and danger of being "scabs"; he himself was not going to run the shop during the strike. However, he was assured, at the time, that he would be told just when the strike would be called and he would not be left with work unfinished. But, either because it was thought good tactics to have my father—as well as other manufacturers—caught with hats in work and so make him come to a settlement the sooner or because his help had no more notice than he, whatever it was, when the strike was called, they promptly marched downstairs. And my father and mother did have work in hand (which the help might easily have finished that day), goods cut up and worthless unless made into hats. My mother now sat down and made the hats herself (for a mail-order house that had orders to fill), and it took her all of three weeks' hard work.

Every morning, as my parents and I came to the shop, we saw some of the help walking up and down as pickets, and greeted them. (My mother was sorry for them and thought it a hardship for the older women to have to walk up and down in the street.) And they greeted us just as pleasantly at first.

Times were still good. A man who had become rich as a baker but who scorned the bakery for his son, and wanted to set him up in the manufacture of men's straw hats (because they had a relative handy who worked at the line), bought the Artistic Millinery Company's plant. A loft was hard to get those days and the buyer could use the fixtures and the electric wiring. The Artistic Millinery Company's help, who had never believed that my father would really go out of business, when they saw him sell the place (he told them what he was doing), saw the place where they had worked sold to a stranger in another line, and my father's smile when

308

he went away for the last time, were disheartened and angry, as if he had cheated them somehow.

My father had no notion what to do next. But there was no urgency. My mother and he could rest and they could go wherever they liked and my father could always, if he had to, go back to the millinery business when the strike was over—so he thought—although he hoped he would find something better to do.

My father lost almost all his money—which he had put into real estate. But if it had still been in the millinery business would have mattered little, perhaps, so fast did values fall. A relative, who was a jobber of sweaters, made room for him, now an old man. An apron tied about his vest, he stood at a table sorting the merchandise, some of it clean, some merely dusty from the bins or shelves where it had been kept, some just rags and dirty. He came early to open the place and stayed late to close it, glad of his small wages because it kept him among those who earned their own living and helped him keep the little flat in which he and my mother now lived. I shared my wages with my father, of course, but he would take only enough to eke out his own earnings.

My mother's asthma was as bad as ever but she went about cheerfully; time and again, my father or I caught her doing the housework herself to save her husband's pennies and her son's. She still had plans for business: now she was thinking of selling a food of wheat and spinach and, indeed, made a quantity of it and was vexed when a stranger, who had heard of it and bought a few pounds, began to make it himself; now she thought the manufacture of bindings, which she had seen for sale in the stores, would take care of my father's troubles; but she herself was too weak to do much more than urge her schemes cheerfully on husband and son.

Now, too, she had time for reading English, which she had never been able to do easily, and for learning how to write it. She would write in pencil, and then look up almost every other word in the dictionary to rub out her mistakes in spelling. Her handwriting was that of a child, a child writing carefully in a large round hand, and my father—mocking a little—and I would often see her, a little wrinkled old woman with iron-grey hair, bent over the copybook with all the eagerness of a willing pupil.

And then my mother caught cold and with her asthma found it doubly hard to breathe. One night when my father came from work, so tired he could hardly stand or keep his eyes open, he found her in bed. He sat up with her until she begged him to lie down on the couch in the living-room. No sooner did he do so than he fell fast asleep. The window of the bedroom was wide open, for the weather had been warm; but at night it turned cold and a cold wind blew into the room. My mother, chilled, called for my father to close the window, afraid to leave the warmth of her bed; but call and bang as she did on bed and wall my father slept too soundly to hear her. In the morning she had pneumonia. She apologized to us for her ill-timed sickness striking her hands in vexation on the quilt.

Well, she got better, in spite of her asthma and her weakness. But no sooner did she begin to walk about than she felt pains in her body worse than any she had ever had, even in giving birth, and the doctors found she had a cancer. Now the round of doctor and nurse began again, other doctors, other nurses, and in the end my father and I knew that she would die: she might live a few weeks or a few months at most but then she would die. She lay in bed in a hospital and greeted us calmly. The doctors gave her a drug to ease the pain and she would close her eyes when her son or husband came because she was sleepy or to make believe she was asleep.

310

I went out-of-town one week-end and came to say good-by for only a day or two. I tried to shake her hand but she held it pressed to the blanket and would not lift it. Perhaps she was afraid that she would never see me again—that this good-by would be the last. That evening I was visiting a friend and was to spend the night in a hotel. Speaking of my mother, I meant to say that she was very sick, and found myself saying calmly: "She is dead." And no sooner had I said this than I felt that I ought to take the train back to New York as soon as I could.

The corridor of the hospital was noisy with the sound of someone breathing heavily. My mother's room was pretty far down and it was not until I was almost there that I realized it was she. The nurse told me that my mother had awakened out of a nightmare and had called for me. When she was told that I had been sent for and was on my way, she did not believe it and said that I must have been killed in the train wreck in which she, too, had been. And when the nurse answered that there had been no wreck and she had been on no train, she pointed to her body where the surgeon had cut her open and said: "Of course, I was in a wreck! Look, how I am hurt!" With that she fell asleep again and from that sleep into a coma. When I came into the room, blood was seeping out of her mouth, for the cancer had ruptured a blood-vessel.

And so she died. In the morning, the woman in the other bed who had never spoken, in despair at the cancer eating at her breast, looked quickly at the empty bed, her eyes wide with terror, and turned away.

A week or so after the funeral, I was taking a walk. When I came to where the Artistic Millinery Company had been, the buildings were gone: torn down to make room for a wider, but no less dingy, street.